The Jagged Scar

Nick Rippington

DEDICATION

To my teenage guitar-playing daughter, Olivia...
Keep on rocking!

Novels by Nick Rippington

Boxer Boys series
Crossing the Whitewash
Spark Out
Dying Seconds
Bare Lies

Standalone Thriller
Rabette Run

'There are ogres, you know.
They're no legend.
They're fact, they are.'
— Anthony Boucher from Zacherley's Vulture Stew.

The Jagged Scar

Prologue

IT WASN'T AN easy story to write. Rape was a tricky subject. The pen moved hesitantly at first but soon it gathered pace. After all, scribbling details on paper was far simpler than confiding in someone face-to-face, whether it be a family member, close friend, police officer, or medical professional.

Finally, the deed was done, the letter signed, and the name of the intended recipient scrawled on the front. The writer stared at the finished article, folded it, and put it in the secret hiding place.

There was a faint noise. The squeak of rubber-soled shoe on ceramic tile. Rising from the chair, the writer went to investigate.

The hallway was dark.

'Are...are you back?'

Nothing.

Perhaps it was the visitors, but they weren't due for half an hour. It would be a real pain if the guests arrived early. The writer's lover had gone to the local shop to stock up on ingredients for the evening meal and hadn't even started cooking. Thankfully, there were no headlights visible through the frosted glass of the front door to indicate a car had pulled up outside.

Before returning to the lounge, the writer felt an urge to check the kitchen. On pushing open the door, it was instantly obvious something was wrong. On the table sat a syringe, a spoon, a lighter, and a plastic pouch. To the untrained eye, the pouch looked to contain a kitchen spice like cinnamon or paprika. The writer knew differently.

It wasn't spice.

It was heroin.

And it had been left for a junkie.

This was no random act. There had been so much soul-searching, arguments, and recriminations in that house. Drugs had been banned completely, and any found hidden away in obscure places had been unceremoniously flushed down the toilet. There had even been a period of self-imposed 'imprisonment', the writer locked away in a room as part of the painful recovery process.

As the temptingly placed works were examined, the squeak returned.

Close this time.

Very close.

Before the writer could react, a hand snaked out, covering their nostrils with a piece of material doused in something strong and overpowering.

After the briefest of struggles, all vision faded, and the lights went out.

The writer took that smell to the grave.

PART ONE

February 1971

One

THE MONSTER HAD an alarming abundance of facial hair and was the size and shape of a fridge. The wooden bench groaned with relief as it rose slowly and started moving towards the fresh meat which had just been deposited in the cage. As the footsteps grew louder, the other inhabitants lowered their heads so as not to make eye contact.

'Oi, you!'

The runaway kept her head fixed on the linoleum, the knot tightening in her stomach as a pair of tattered canvas shoes came into view. 'Hey, I'm talking to you!'

Before the young girl could respond, chunky fingers like iron rods clamped onto the collar of her leather jacket, yanking upwards so that she had to stand or risk damage to her favourite item of clothing. 'I'm s...sorry,' she muttered.

'Fink you're clever, do ya? Ignoring your elders and betters. Well, you ain't better than me, girl, understand?' The Monster pulled back one thick arm, the hairy knuckles bunching, a letter tattooed on each finger. L...O...V...E. The girl shut her eyes, awaiting the impact.

'Hey, meatball, enough of that.'

Time stood still. The atmosphere thick with tension.

'What did you call me?'

'I called you meatball cos you've obviously got mince for brains. Now let the kid go.'

For a moment, nothing happened, then the runaway was forcibly dumped back onto the bench. She opened one eye and looked in the direction of the new voice. Silver-blonde hair was whipped up on top of the woman's head like ice cream in a cone; the eyes large, green orbs with black blobs in the middle which reminded the youngster of those coconut-flavoured Liquorice Allsorts. The fur coat had seen better days and the woman's black stockings had more ladders than the fire brigade. Something about the way her hands constantly played with each other warned the runaway that, like everyone in this madhouse, the interloper was slightly unhinged.

'Don't even think about it,' she told the Monster, who still had her fist drawn back but was now facing in her direction.

'I'll crush you like a walnut.'

'Maybe,' said the blonde, 'but then you'll have Blaize Hathaway to answer to.'

Silence descended and for a moment, everyone seemed frozen in position. The Monster looked confused. 'You're one of Blaize's girls?'

'Better believe it,' said the blonde. 'So why don't you wobble off back to that little hole you crawled out from?'

Slowly, the Monster lowered her fist, grunted, and trundled off back to her corner.

'OK, young 'un, you can open them peepers now,' said the blonde. 'There's always one that tries it on with the new kids. Lucky I was around, eh? Now, why don't you tell me your name?'

Reluctant as she was to give anything away, the runaway felt she owed her rescuer an answer.

'It's Red,' she said.

'Oh yeah?' The blonde wasn't convinced. 'And I'm fackin' Purple. Where you from, Red, if it ain't too rude to ask? Not from the Smoke, judging by the accent. Also, you're a bit quiet...not like the gobby shits around here.' She cast her gaze back in the direction of the Monster, who was now chewing gunk-encased fingernails and avoiding eye contact.

'I'm not...from here, I mean.'

'Where then? Don't tell me...' I won't, she thought. If I tell you, they'll whisk me back there before my feet touch the floor. In her paranoid state of mind, she imagined police officers loitering outside the holding cell, listening for clues. For a second, she wondered if the blonde could be a plant, put in with her to help the desk sergeant piece things together.

'I'm living in Brixton.'

'Are you now?' The blonde raised an eyebrow, and for the first time the youngster noted her long, thick lashes. 'Now, if I was a betting gal, I'd have you down as a runaway. Are you a runaway...Red?

No skin off my nose if you is or if you ain't. I won't be blabbing to the rozzers, will I?'

Red's new acquaintance fell silent, her expression indicating that she was holding a debate inside her head. Eventually she wobbled closer, stiletto heels click-clacking on the floor. She plonked herself down next to Red and the schoolgirl slumped forward as the bench rocked. The concept of personal space hadn't entered her fellow prisoner's head.

'Mates call me Kat,' said the blonde woman, thrusting a hand in Red's direction. For a weird moment, she thought the woman was demanding payment for services rendered until it dawned on her that she was just being friendly. After an uncomfortable pause, she shook the hand. 'Real name's Kathy Rose. What's your family name? You have a family?'

'Oh...'

'Ahh, OK, you haven't thought one up yet,' said the blonde, letting out a rasping cackle that had the same effect on the nerves as chalk on a blackboard. 'I know. I'll give you one. Smith is popular around 'ere. Or maybe we could borrow one from a film star: Hepburn or, I don't know, Redgrave. Red Grave, get it?' The cackle burst forth, then turned into a raking cough. When she finally bought it under control, she asked, 'Got any smokes?'

'I'm sorry I don't...'

'How old are you? Fourteen? Fifteen? Bit young to be in here...what they got you for?'

'I was attacked in the street.'

'Seriously?' said the girl called Kat. 'The last time I checked, being attacked wasn't no crime. That might be part of the story cos you got that bit of plaster on your head and a graze on your cheek, but even the rozzers don't usually arrest people for getting themselves beat up. Domestic, was it? Run away from the fella? Blinkin' 'eck, I can't imagine the state he's in. I'd bet you can handle yourself.'

Coming from someone who was obviously accustomed to being locked up, Red wasn't sure she should take it as a compliment. It was probably a natural response to the image she was trying to perfect – heavy boots, leather jacket, and jeans. Her friend Marc had said she might as well have 'Rock Chick' stencilled on her forehead.

'Don't get me wrong,' Kat continued. 'I'm lovin' the look. What's that on your shirt? Status Quo? Right headbanger, ain't you? Like the make-up, too, all a bit random. What do they call that eyeshadow again? Sunburst? That black eyeliner works as well, gives you a sort of witchy, *Addams Family* feel. And that jacket with the studs don't come cheap. Shame you can't do much with the hair – once a ginge always a ginge, I say.'

Red wasn't sure she was enjoying the critique but bit her lip and fought back the desire to respond.

'Anyway, this geezer – it was a geezer, right?' said Kat, not waiting for a reply. 'There's always one in the background when a girl gets into trouble. Never trust a bloke, that's my motto. They take what they want then...woosh, you don't see 'em for dust.'

Red felt compelled to defend her best mate. 'He isn't my boyfriend,' she said. 'Marc's nice, like. I hope he's OK. He was getting beaten up, and I tried to help him. Then someone hit me, and I blacked out. When I came around, the police were there. I don't know where he is now.'

'Had it on his toes if I know blokes, as they always do when trouble comes around,' said Kat. 'Have you two...?'

Kat was switching from one subject to another so rapidly it was becoming confusing. 'Have we what?'

'You know, you dumbo!' Kat jabbed her in the ribs with a bony elbow, making her fall sideways. 'I'm wonderin' if you did the dirty deed before he ran off and left you on your lonesome.'

'We haven't...it's not like that at all. We came up...'

Red clamped her mouth shut instantly, realising she was about to reveal too much. Kat was a stranger, and she had to remind herself there could be an underlying motive for her questions. She'd already given away her best friend's name. When she'd first been interviewed by the copper at the desk, she'd stonewalled him, not giving her real name or any details. Before having her escorted to the 'holding tank', he'd said he would be contacting the authorities in order to get to the bottom of her story. It seemed unlikely this stranger was involved, though, despite her inquisitive nature.

'Let me tell you something, darlin',' said Kat. 'My experience of men is they're all after one thing. If this bloke of yours ain't tried for a bit of 'ow's yer father yet, it won't be long. Mark my words.'

The word "mark" prompted Red to zone out from the incessant babble and wonder about the boy who'd persuaded her to travel to London with him. They'd been close from an early age, but at no stage had he ever as much as laid a hand on her knee. In fact, it was she who once tried to move their relationship on, only to suffer a knock back when she tried to kiss him during the tender part of a film. As she moved in to seal the deal, he turned back to the screen and in an instant, the moment was gone.

'He's not like that,' she said.

'What? Lovely girl like you and he ain't made a move?' Kat shook her head at the scurrilous situation. For the first time, she seemed lost for words, her expression indicating she was grappling with a problem in her head. Just when it seemed the conversation was over, her face lit up again. 'Maybe he bats for the other team.'

Red shook her head to indicate her confusion.

'God, you are young, ain't ya?' said Kat. 'I'm suggesting this Marc prefers munching on a pillow to a boob.' She looked earnestly at the schoolgirl, her animated face inches away. Red shook her head slowly, trying to interpret Kat's strange use of language. 'Oh, for gawd's sake, I'm saying he's probably a bloody queer.'

Red flashed back to that morning. She and Marc woke side-by-side on the floor of a squat in Brixton after a Valentine's party the night before. The invite had come from a roadie called Chancer, who they'd met at a Tyrannosaurus Rex gig in Cardiff. Though this new acquaintance had spent a lot of his time talking to her, she couldn't help noticing the way he flirted with her friend. It had made her a bit jealous.

Marc's whole life was a contradiction. There was an innate shyness about him, yet he overcompensated by being loud and flamboyant. His clothes were straightforward and almost boring, yet on special occasions, like the gig and the party, he'd dressed in outrageous gear, adding glitter, stars, and make-up to the ensemble. She'd told herself it was just 'his way', but she did recall someone shouting homophobic insults at him in the street once. He'd bridled at the remarks, though, and with good reason. For God's sake, his dad was a steelworker who lifted weights and played sport. You couldn't come from more masculine stock than that.

'If you've had to think about the question, then pound to a penny he is,' said Kat. 'I wouldn't worry about him. He's probably away with the fairies now, if you'll pardon the expression.' The cackle erupted again.

Thinking of Marc was making Red feel even more isolated. He was probably back in the Valleys right now, having left her to fend for herself. Which was fine, because she'd never intended going back, anyway. Home was no longer where the heart was and if she was ever to break away from her miserable existence, the time was now. It meant some things, like friendships, would have to be sacrificed.

Though she was still suspicious of Kat, she was starting to realise it wouldn't hurt to have an ally. What was there to lose?

'We went to a café for breakfast this morning,' she said. 'It was me, Marc, and this Chancer guy. I had told them I'd pay because neither of the others had money.' Kat flicked her eyebrows skywards in disgust but said nothing. 'It was OK, though,' said Red. 'I'd been left some money in my nan's will and Chancer had promised to pay me back when he got his roadie wages.'

'I'm sure he did,' said Kat.

'I felt I owed him for inviting us to his party. Anyway, we all had a cooked breakfast and cups of tea in this café, but when it came to paying, I couldn't find my purse. Then this Chancer made a dash for it and dragged Marc along with him.'

'You got caught holding the tab? Typical!'

'I had no option but to run too and just about managed to get away, but when I caught up with the boys, they were in a fight with these skinheads. Marc was on the ground and this big bloke was kicking him, so I tried to stop it.'

'That went well,' said Kat, smiling.

'Not really,' said Red. 'The big bloke punched me, and I must have blacked out. I woke up, and these coppers were there. They were quite nice at first until the café owner turned up and told them what I'd done. Then they tried to arrest me, so I made a dash for it. One of them caught up and started groping me so I kicked him in the you-know-what's. That was when they threw me in the van.'

'I suppose that classifies as assaulting a policeman, but running off without paying for your scran? It's hardly up there with the great train robbery or the Krays.'

Red shook her head, having no idea what Kat was talking about. 'Really? You ain't heard of the Great Train Robbers? You are young. One of the most famous robberies of all time. As for the Krays… well, they're these twins who ran everything north of the river. Naughty boys, they're behind bars now, but I remember them being sweet to me when I was a kid, particularly that Reggie.'

Red interrupted the woman before she got into her flow again. 'Why are you in here?' she asked.

'The usual reason,' Kat replied. 'Men.'

She didn't elaborate and Red didn't feel able to push the issue. They sat in silence for a moment, each with their own thoughts. Then Kat said, 'We both need to get out of here, right? I'm pretty sure you don't want the rozzers digging into your past. You ran away for a reason, I'm sure, and if you stay here, you'll get a one-way ticket home. Not only that, but ugly mug over there is dying to have another go so I wouldn't want to leave you in here alone.'

They both looked over at the corner where the Monster was rubbing a rough hand over her knuckles. A cold chill travelled up Red's back. 'Listen, a lawyer mate of mine will be here soon to get me out,' said Kat. 'He works for my boss Blaize. I'll have a word on your behalf, see if he can spring you, too. There's always a way.' She gave Red a wink. 'We'll find you somewhere to stay and if all else fails, you can crash in my room. It's a bit pokey but clean enough. I'll speak to the boss and, who knows, there could be a job just crying out for your talents.'

Two

'IT'S YOUR LUCKY day, girl,' said the desk sergeant, handing back the silver bracelet, which was the only valuable item she still had. The rest of her stuff was back at the squat.

'Apparently, your "uncle" kindly agreed to take you into his care. The café owner has been paid his outstanding money and, in the circumstances, there's no point in holding you, what with all the paperwork that would entail.'

Red wrestled to keep a straight face while inside her stomach turned somersaults. She was excited, relieved, and a little bit scared. Everything she knew about Kat she'd learnt from their brief conversation in the cell while her new "uncle" was a complete enigma. He might be a kind-hearted person trying to do right by a troubled young girl, but worst-case scenarios swam around her brain. She remembered reading Oliver Twist in which a youngster of similar age had been recruited as a pickpocket by a grubby London crook. Could her new 'uncle' be a modern-day Fagan?

She had no time to dwell on her predicament. The moment she was clear of the desk, Kat slipped an arm through hers and led the way outside to an expensive-looking dark brown car which shone under the gaze of a nearby streetlamp. It was later than she thought, the evening drawing in.

'Blinkin' 'ell, mun, what time is it?'

Too late. With all the excitement, she'd let her guard down again.

'You're a Taffy!' said Kat. 'I've met plenty of Welsh blokes up here for the rugby. They're all right, as it happens. Quite polite, though they won't take no for an answer. Randy buggers. And drink? I ain't never seen the like. Think they're all Dylan bleedin' Thomas, too. Either that or singers.'

'Y...you won't tell?' said Red.

'Your secret's safe with me,' said Kat. 'We're mates, ain't we? Blaize will love ya.'

'Really?'

'I'm sure. Her hair's even brighter than yours! You could be her long-lost sister for all I know...She's a sucker for the sweet look, too, and I reckon you'll scrub up quite nice without the rock gear. Right, here's Woodsy. Have you ever been in a Jag?'

Red shook her head, letting her eyes travel the length of the vehicle. It looked new, the silver bits on the bonnet and the chrome wheels sparkling like sixpences.

'Welcome to the Jaguar XJ6,' said a man in a shiny silver suit. 'Beautiful motor, ain't she?'

'Jack's paying you too much,' said Kat.

'Yeah, well, keeping tarts like you out of nick is a full-time profession.' He turned in the Welsh girl's direction, opening the back door and ushering her inside. 'You're Red then, eh? Scott Woodman at your service. What do you make of the wheels?'

'Smells lovely,' she replied.

'Leather seats,' he said. 'It's also got power-assisted steering and air conditioning, which was an optional extra. You girls are lucky I let you sit in it. I should have put newspapers down.'

'Don't be mean, Woodsy,' said Kat. 'Red's had a rough day and, as usual, blokes are to blame. She went to help this geezer out and got a slap for her trouble. Of course, the man she tried to rescue then ditched her. After putting up with all that, she deserves some hot food and a bed for the night, so get a move on, would ya?'

'Yes, m'ludy,' said Woodsy. Red giggled. He'd altered his voice to sound like Parker, the English chauffeur from the *Thunderbirds* TV puppet series that was so popular. 'Listen, you don't pull my strings and you're no Lady Penelope, right, Kat? I'm a respectable lawyer. If it wasn't for me, you'd be waiting for some snotty magistrate to tell you you're a bad girl and slap you with a big fine – or maybe throw you in the clink.'

'That's why I love you, Woodsy,' said Kat. 'You'd drop everything to help a damsel in distress.' Though the words were issued sarcastically, Red had a feeling her new friend had a soft spot for the well-dressed man in the driver's seat.

'Apology accepted,' said Woodsy. 'Now where did you have in mind to fill your faces?'

'Greek Street, I reckon,' said Kat. 'Make for the Soho Grill – you get a right good nosebag in there.'

The car rumbled to life and soon they were immersed in a neon wonderland, Kat doing her best impression of a London tour guide. Though Woodsy was keen to show what his new car could do, he ended up cursing as they spent most of the journey bumper-to-bumper in traffic. Feeling tired and sensing she was drifting off, Red stared through half-closed eyes as the sights of the capital drifted by, accompanied by an ever-changing soundtrack of wailing sirens, car horns, screeching brakes, and the occasional sweary rant of an irate motorist.

She jerked herself awake as the car approached the entrance to what appeared to be a castle. As a Welsh girl brought up on historic tales of brave knights, fire-breathing dragons, and fortified strongholds, Red was immediately captivated.

'This is Tower Bridge, lovey,' said Kat. 'Pretty, ain't it? And that down there is the River Thames, which cuts through our fair city like, well, a jagged scar, I guess. You don't want to end up in there, darlin', I can tell you. It ain't as cheery as it looks.'

Kat chuckled, but Red thought it was a strange thing to say. She couldn't imagine any circumstance where she would want to jump into such a murky expanse of water. She wasn't a swimmer and without armbands she would sink like a stone.

'They call it Tower Bridge because it sits right next to the Tower of London,' said Kat, pointing at an ancient brick structure surrounded by a wall. 'If you were naughty in the old days and gave the king or queen the 'ump, you'd end up in the Tower with the rats. Mind you, see that green next to it...?' Red nodded.

'That's where Henry VIII had two of his wives beheaded.' The familiar cackle ripped through the car. 'Typical man, eh? Got bored of the wife so it's "Off with her 'ead". There are blokes I know who'd do similar just because a girl didn't give 'em what they wanted, so be warned.'

Though Kat had treated it as a joke there was an underlying message. Red wondered who these men were and in what circumstances she was likely to encounter them. She shut her eyes again to combat the sensory overload, concentrating on the soft thrum of the car's engine. Pretty soon, she drifted into sleep.

'Oww!' A well-directed elbow to the ribs brought her back to the present.

'Get a load of this, doll,' said the blonde, leaning forward and pointing through the windscreen. A panorama of lights stretched out around them, the impact forcing Red's mouth open with wonder. Massive neon advertising hoardings on the side of imposing buildings implored those passing to buy products like Coke, Cinzano, gin, and Wrigley's gum. 'Piccadilly Circus,' said Kat. 'Now this is your real London – the West End. It's where I live, girl. Buzzin', ain't it?'

'Incredible,' agreed Red. 'All these lights. It must cost a fortune in electricity. My, umm, stepdad goes mental if any of us leave the hall light on for more than ten seconds.'

'Tight, is he?'

'We've never had much money.'

'What happened to your real old man? Run off with a bit of skirt, did he?'

Suddenly, Red found herself on the defensive. The question hit home like a thunderbolt to the heart. 'N…no. he's, umm, dead.'

'Oh, love.' Kat pulled her close and gave her a reassuring squeeze. 'I should be more careful about asking questions until my brain is in gear. Ahh, look, we're here.'

THE SOFT DOUGHY pastry and rich, meaty sauce exploded on her tongue. Red couldn't remember enjoying the first mouthful of a meal so much. At home, Mam relied on convenient packet meals like fish fingers or faggots. If she fancied a break from the kitchen, she would send the boys to the chippy. Any natural flavour would have been drowned out by vinegar and eroded with salt before the food arrived home. As for school dinners, everything came lukewarm and covered in congealed gravy, the vegetables so undercooked they would resist the first thrusts of the fork.

'How's the steak and kid?' asked Kat, who was more intent on gauging Red's reaction than tucking into her plate of pork sausages, runny egg, chips, and thick buttered bread.

'Mmmmm,' said Red, swallowing down her first mouthful and cutting into the soft pie to free up the next. 'It's bloody lovely, mun. Tasty, like.'

'I can tell you're enjoying it. Half of it's around your chops,' said Kat. 'Saving it for later?' The cackle erupted again, but Red didn't join in. Something was still bothering her.

'Look,' she said. 'Thanks for paying for this.'

'Well, you had your purse stolen didn't you…and I owe it to you after what I said about your dad.'

'About that… I should explain,' said Red.

'You don't have to if you don't want to,' said Kat. 'I'm all ears, though.' She wiggled them in a way that her companion thought impossible, and, despite the sombre topic, she couldn't resist a smile before composing herself for the story.

'Dad worked down the pit,' she said.

'Like a car mechanic, you mean?' Kat cut into a sausage and lifted a small piece into her mouth before chewing on it disinterestedly.

'No, a coal mine,' said Red. 'Every night I would listen for the front door to open and his heavy boots thudding on the hallway tiles. He would be totally covered in black dust – head-to-toe, you know? All you could see were these two white eyes peering out at you. When I ran downstairs to greet him, his face would crack, and you could see the laughter lines appear. "Don't you go getting coal dust all over that child, Morgan Jeffrey, you hear me?" Mam would warn him, but he would just wipe his hands on a paper towel and pick me up, anyway.'

'Aaah,' said Kat. 'You've painted a proper lovely picture there, girl. I can almost see 'im. Jeffrey, you say?' Although she now went by her mother's maiden name, Red realised she'd given away too much and there was no putting the sauce back in the bottle. 'Don't worry,' said Kat, touching her nose. 'Your secret is safe with me. We all got names around 'ere different from the ones we were born with. Now, don't keep me in suspenders.'

The phrases Kat came out with were funny and refreshing. Red took a bite of pie, washing it down with a sip of Pepsi. 'I don't know exactly what happened, but one day at the pit there was this explosion,' she said. 'Dad didn't survive.'

Kat's hand shot to her mouth. 'That's terrible!' she blurted.

'Yeah, although my mother says he was probably lucky in some ways,' said Red. 'There's a man in our village who did walk away from it and his face was burnt terrible, just a mass of scars and lumps.'

For a moment, they sat in silence, Kat trying to take it all in. Then she wiped breadcrumbs from the tablecloth onto the floor, as if she was symbolically preparing a clean slate. 'Come on then, eat up,' she said, breaking the gloomy silence. 'This is the start of your new adventure, darlin'. Tell me, though...won't your mum miss you?'

Red shrugged. 'Mam will be OK. She's got the boys, and she's got Osean.' She couldn't help the sneer that came out when she delivered his name.

'Osean's your mum's new fella? That can be awkward. It sounds like you ain't a fan.'

The Welsh girl shook her head. 'I hate him, but Mam says she couldn't cope without him. She calls him "her rock" and won't hear a word said against him. He came into our lives when Mam was trying to bring us up on her own. He's strict, though, particularly with me.'

'You had a special relationship with your real dad, so it's no wonder you struggle with someone trying to replace him. Is that why you're here?'

If only you knew the half of it, thought Red.

'There's no escape from him,' she said. 'He didn't just marry Mam and move in. He's also the deputy headmaster at my school. For the boys and me, he's like this constant presence. It's not just me who hates him, neither. Most of the other kids at the school pretty much despise him and avoid me because they think I might be spying on them for him. Do you know he has traffic lights outside his office? When they're red, it means some kid inside is having a tough time.'

'Wow,' said Kat. 'Has he ever given you the cane?'

'No,' said Red. 'He's quick to haul me out of class when he thinks I need sorting out, though, and my brother Elf got lashed for messing around. It wasn't even his fault. Some other boys were throwing paper aeroplanes at the back of the class and when the teacher looked up, he saw Elf with one in his hand. Elf claims to this day that it just landed on his desk, and he was gonna chuck it in the bin. Funny really, though, cos Elf and Osean get on well and he's good with my older brother, too.'

Kat chuckled. 'I've got brothers. They ain't afraid to tell the odd porky pie.'

'What's pork pies got to do with anything?' asked Red. 'You talk funny sometimes.'

'Listen to yourself, would ya?' said Kat, before releasing another cackle. 'Right, your first lesson in Cockney. Pork pies is Cockney slang for lies. It rhymes, see? Like, if we wanted to go up to the second floor, we'd take the apple and pears—'

'Stairs?'

'You'll be speakin' proper Cockney in no time.' Kat reached for a piece of bread and ran it around the side of her plate, scraping up the remaining egg yolk. When she was satisfied, she folded it in half and put the entire thing in her mouth. Then she wiped her hands on a paper napkin. 'That's me done. How about you? Do you want any pud? They do a lovely spotted dick, if you don't mind the expression.' This time, the laughter erupted full force. Red felt relieved, as if she'd survived an interrogation. Pushing her plate away, just a few runner beans remained, floating in congealed gravy.

'To be honest, I'm stuffed,' she said. 'I think my stomach has shrunk after all those hours without food.'

'Lucky you had quite a big breakfast then.' Kat cackled again, then stood and removed the fur coat from a rack behind her seat. 'Right, Mrs,' she said. 'Let's make tracks. Things to do, people to see. You said you were at school. How old are you, exactly?'

'Thirteen,' said Red. 'I'm 14 in a couple of weeks.'

'I guessed something like that,' said Kat. 'You look young, too, so I suggest you keep your head down. You don't want to catch the attention of the rozzers again. Now you're sure you don't want to head home and spare your mam the worry? Woodsy could drop you at Paddington Station or get someone else to do it. I mean, you ain't got any stuff with you, so I suspect soon enough you'll be missing your home comforts.'

Red shook her head vehemently. 'No, I'd like to stay,' she said. 'At least for a bit.'

'All right then,' said Kat. She felt around in the pocket of the coat and pulled out a small piece of card. 'Here,' she said. 'It's Woodsy's number. You should keep it handy in case you get in any more scrapes.'

THREE

'AIN'T YOU A pretty little thing?' The woman with the wavy, fuchsia-coloured hair looked like a glamorous star from a Hollywood movie. 'What's your name, lover?'

Kat jumped in to rescue the tongue-tied Welsh girl. 'This is Red.'

'Of course, it is,' said the woman called Blaize, studying the runaway closely. 'I'm glad you've got a new friend, Kat, truly I am, but I'd like to speak to the organ grinder, not the monkey. So why don't you toddle off? You must have work to do, catching up with whatever you were doing before being rudely interrupted by those dumb rozzers last night. Leave Red to me. I'll give her the grand tour.'

'Sure, Blaize.' Kat put her hand on her new friend's arm. 'You're gonna be all right. Salt of the earth, she is. Took me off the street and gave me a career. Play your cards right, she can do the same for you. Just listen to what she has to say.' Kat leant forward, her rough lips brushing Red's cheek. 'Catch you later, yeah?'

Once Kat had gone, Blaize stood and came around the desk. They were in her office at the Cat and Fiddle club in Dean Street, just around the corner from the Soho Café where the two girls had eaten. Taking a monogrammed handkerchief from her sleeve, Blaize then moved up so close to Red that she detected a steely glint in the woman's eye. 'Now let's have a proper look at you, babe,' she said, grabbing Red's face in her bony fingers and turning it sharply, first one way then the other. The woman had a grip like the metalwork vice Osean kept in his garage. 'Don't struggle,' Blaize said. She spat on the handkerchief and rubbed roughly at the schoolgirl's cheek.

'What are you doing, mun?' Red asked, trying to suppress the quiver in her voice.

Blaize's mesmerising blue eyes stayed fixed on her. 'Just tidying you up, love,' she said. 'Can't have sloppiness, can we? And that Kat, well, she's left a big red mark on you with her lipstick. Silly bint. There.' She stood back to admire her handiwork.

'How old are you, dear?' she asked.

'I...I'm...'

'Tell me the truth,' said Blaize. 'I'll know if you're lying.'

'Fourteen... in a couple of weeks.'

'That's what I thought. Bit of a problem there.'

'Why?'

'Well, we get a lot of important people through these doors, and I wouldn't trust most of them, to be honest. If they suss you, I'd have some rather irritating questions to answer, and you'd probably end up being taken into care. Neither of us wants that, do we? Never mind, I'm sure I'll find a use for you that will keep you below the radar.'

She raised Red's arm and twisted it, checking for something. 'Perfect, perfect,' she said. 'Nice silky skin, a few freckles, which is no surprise given your hair colour, but you're a real treat. Men can be rather partial to a redhead, you know? Obviously, my colour's a bit fierier, but it ain't natural.' She patted the extravagant bouffant that stood high and firm on top of her head. 'I was closer to strawberry blonde than ginger, but didn't really like it...a personal choice, you understand? So, I experimented with dyes during my dancing days and...voila!' She primped her hair. 'Meet Blaize.'

'Your hair's lovely,' said Red.

'Kind of you to say so, dear. Thank you.' Blaize offered up a smile that didn't quite reach her eyes. 'I can tell we're going to get on famously. Now, follow me, and I'll get you some proper clothes.' Red noticed the woman's nose wrinkle as if there was a nasty smell in the room. 'You could do with something a bit more, ummm, ladylike.'

Red loved her rocker gear with a passion, but realised she had no alternative. Any spare clothes she'd brought to London with her, including underwear, had been left in her bag at the squat and she had no idea when she might be able to retrieve them. Anyway, if Blaize could make her look older, it might protect her from inquisitive authority figures. She followed the club owner out of the door and through a maze of corridors, studying the woman as she walked. Blaize wore a low cut, shiny black dress which displayed her prominent cleavage to great effect. Puffing out at the bottom, the dress came up short, displaying slender legs clad in patterned stockings. The red shoes on her feet had a decorative bow on the top and raised her up on six-inch stiletto heels. Red thought it was a skill just to stay upright let alone walk.

At home in Wales, Red had alternated between daps and her favourite boots, which her stepfather told her were more suited to the Hell's Angels than teen girls. As for her cleavage, from the day Red's breasts began to form, Mam had insisted she keep them covered up. She didn't want the neighbours thinking she was like 'All the other little scrubbers around here with their wares on full display'.

After climbing a set of stairs, Blaize stopped outside a door on the right, inserted a key, and twisted. When it opened and Red was invited to enter, she was dazzled by bright white light at first, but as her vision cleared, her mouth dropped open, stunned by the sheer size of the room. What was more astonishing was the fact it was filled wall-to-wall with clothing racks. The amazing range of garments looked as if they'd come straight from the shops. Some still had tags attached.

'Don't worry, babe,' said Blaize. 'I know these aren't really your style. A lot of this stuff is for the dancers, who need different costumes each night. This stuff over here is more up your street.'

Following Blaize down a narrow avenue between two coat rails, Red came to a set of shelves which ran along the back wall. It was like being in a big Cardiff department store like JP Morgan, only much more crammed. There were blouses, skirts, and underwear piled on the top two shelves while a rack of shoes contained every variety and size she could imagine.

'Some of these were mine,' said Blaize. 'I modelled for the top fashion houses and magazine companies who would let me keep stuff. I was a right old clothes horse back in the day. It was almost expected in the 60s that girls of my age should be a bit dressy. Then I met Jack, and he lavished me with stuff regularly to keep me sweet. You'll meet him soon enough. We've been together since the heady days of free love.'

She picked up a colourful silk scarf and draped it around her neck, standing tall and walking slowly between the clothing racks, her nose in the air. When she got to the other end, she spun on her heels and walked back, looking haughtily from side to side. 'Still got it eh?' she said.

Red couldn't hide her confused expression. 'I'm talking about the catwalk stroll, for goodness' sake,' said Blaize. 'My, you're a naïve young thing. I used to parade along a narrow stage wearing the latest designs as the camera bulbs flashed. For those few moments, it felt like the eyes of the world were upon me. Fabulous.'

'Why did you stop?'

'Are you serious? Look at me. I'm no spring chicken, darlin', and I wanted something for myself. It's all right parading your wares every night, but it can get a bit tiring and one day the clothing companies will just push you aside and move on to the next young thing. Anyway, Jack didn't like me doing it. He said the dirty old blokes in the front row were leering at me.'

'Oh.'

'Don't look so worried. Jack's all right. A bit overprotective but a girl needs a strong man to look out for her in life, don't you think?' Red nodded to be polite. She guessed her mother had felt the same way about Osean when she'd brought him home. Briefly, she let her mind wander back to the first time she and her brothers had been introduced to the man who would become their stepfather. Mam had ushered them onto the bus to Cardiff dressed in their Sunday best and when they arrived, they were taken to a posh restaurant in a square called The Hayes. After entering, Mam had directed them to a corner table where Osean sat with his nose in a book. On their approach, he looked up, his face creased into what he obviously thought was an accommodating smile. Red had thought it more like an uncomfortable grimace.

She remembered his black hair being parted at the side and swept across a large forehead where it was held in place by an abundance of gel. The sides and back on his square, solid head had been shaved, and Red had chuckled when her elder brother whispered, 'Good God, mun, her new boyfriend's Hitler!'

She couldn't correct that first impression but was fascinated by the black stubble running down to his ears. It resembled iron filings like the ones she'd collected with a magnet in a lesson at her junior school.

Putting down his book, Osean had then stood and bowed like a butler in an Agatha Christie play. Walking forward, he gathered up one of their mother's hands in a sweeping gesture and planted a kiss on the back of it. In response, the two boys whispered and giggled, earning a filthy look from her. 'This is Osean,' Mam had announced in a loud voice. She introduced them one by one, and Red felt an uncomfortable tingle travel up her spine when the older man gave her hand a kiss, too.

'It's nice here,' Mam said.

'Yes,' said Osean. 'This restaurant chain is nationwide now, but did you know it was established by a couple of Welsh Italians in the valleys? I thought it would be nice to meet at a Berni Inn as a nod to our heritage. It shows just what can be achieved with a little brains and ambition, eh? Hard to believe it all began with a small café in Treorchy. Now, the food is wonderful, and they import the best steaks all the way from Argentina. What would everyone like?'

At that moment he'd smiled at Mam and she smiled back. Red should have spotted the signs then.

'I think I've found the perfect little ensemble for you, darlin'.' The club owner's voice dragged her back to the present. Blaize was holding out a red leather miniskirt and cream fitted jumper with a pair of patterned pink and white tights.

'It will look great on you, mark my words. Now we just need something to replace those ugly boots.'

FOUR

BLAIZE LED THE way downstairs into a bustling hive of activity. Girls in various stages of undress rushing to and fro, getting ready for their performances. Red felt extremely self-conscious and embarrassed in her new clothes, which were just about the exact opposite of what she'd normally wear. No one was taking any notice of her, though, as they readied themselves for the evening's events.

'Lovely, aren't they, my girls?' said Blaize. 'If you lined their admirers up along the street, the queue would stretch from here to Southend. This place will be heavin' before long – and it ain't the only club we've got. Jack and I got into the business right at the beginning. Thanks to the old man who left me some dosh, we bought our first little shoebox six years ago, and it's taken off from there. Place was packed out every night, and we had to expand. Now we have this wonderful establishment, plus The Princess Court, Glamour Puss, and Flambe, which are all a short walk from here.'

Red couldn't imagine how Blaize juggled so many businesses. Mam had two jobs in town, cleaning a public house early in the day, then moving on to a shift at the bakery. She regularly complained about how hard it was to stay on top of things, yet by contrast Blaize seemed like a human tornado, blowing through room after room, exchanging pleasantries, passing on advice, and never forgetting a name. She must have spoken to between 20 and 30 people during their meandering walk through the downstairs area of the club. Eventually, they reached a door guarded by a man in a black suit. 'This is one of Jack's penguins,' Blaize said. 'Ain't that right, Archie?'

If he considered it an insult to be likened to a strange waddling bird, the bouncer didn't show it. He just bowed his head politely, leant forward, and pressed on the exit bar, allowing the door to swing open. 'I know it's early in our, umm, relationship, but I have a little job for you,' said the club owner, stepping out into a cobbled alley. 'I need to assess how best to use your talents. Don't look so worried, though, you won't be alone. Your escort should be here any minute.'

'Escort?' The croak in Red's throat betrayed her nerves. She'd heard the word a couple of times, and from her recollection it had always been used in a derogatory manner, having something to do with the sex trade.

Blaize read her mind. 'Nothing sleazy or out of order – and it ain't against the law, if that's what you're thinking. Out on these streets, there are a lot of girls and boys like you. They arrive in London without two pennies to rub together...and I'm not talking about those new-fangled things they introduced today – you know that decimal money?'

Red felt sparkling green eyes burning into her like lasers. She nodded again. 'Great. I knew you were a bright one. Anyway, I'm sure you have an idea how these kids must be feelin'. They've left home for a good reason – just like you did, no doubt. Maybe their parents beat them or kicked 'em out, and they were forced to live with other relatives who had no time for them.' As she spoke, her eyes never moved from Red, carefully gauging her reaction.

'Anyway, to cut a long story short, these kids turn up here believing London is the land of opportunity,' said Blaize. 'They get off the train or are dumped in the middle of town with no idea where to start looking for those opportunities. There are people out there who'll take advantage of that situation, of course. You understand?'

Red nodded. She wasn't one hundred per cent sure what this knowledgeable, intelligent, and obviously highly respected woman was telling her, but guessed she would work it out, eventually. Just as the woman was about to turn away, she stuttered a question. 'Take advantage?'

'Oh, love, there's so much you have to learn,' said Blaize. 'There are bad people around. When the kids arrive, they could be mugged and have their money stolen, like you did. Then some "kind" soul will turn up and offer them a way to get back their cash, but it's likely to involve some rather, umm, sordid things. We want to offer them a clean slate, on their own terms.'

The conversation was interrupted by a whistle. Red and Blaize turned as one to see a young black man in a tweed flat cap, gold-braided waistcoat, and flared trousers sauntering confidently towards them. As he moved, the trousers rode up his long legs to reveal a pair of white ankle socks over brown shoes with fancy tassels. Red remembered her brothers trying to get Mam to buy them similar ones. They were called loafers.

The new arrival was a skinny boy, a few inches taller than Red. She guessed he was in his late teens. There was a mass of bushy hair springing out from beneath the cap, which seemed too small for his head. 'Greetings, my Queen!' he shouted, giving an elaborate bow to Blaize. 'Is this the little sparrer you were telling me about?' He walked straight up to the Welsh girl with a bright smile on his face, holding his hand out for her to shake. For a moment she hesitated, so he grabbed her arm, raised it and twisted her in the sort of spin she'd seen on that *Come Dancing* TV programme.

'Classy,' he said with an approving nod.

'Yes, she is,' said Blaize, giving him a stern glare. 'So don't get any fancy ideas, Jerry, because she's out of your league. Plus, she's jailbait. Now, come on, I have things to do, people to greet. I can't be hanging around in dark alleys waiting for you to grace us with your presence now, can I?'

'Sorry, Queen. I was just playing around.'

'Plenty of time for that once the work's done,' said Blaize. 'There are young strays out there who need our help. I'd like to see if you can work as a team. I've told Red the brief details, but you're the one with the street smarts, Jerry, so it's your job to bring her up to speed.'

Red looked around to get her bearings. There were tall buildings on either side of them while the unfiltered glare of a single streetlight 100 feet away bounced off the glistening cobblestones beneath their feet, which were slick from an earlier shower. Despite being in the bustling centre of a thriving city, she felt she was getting a false impression of the area. They had to be just a short stroll away from the bright lights and vibrant sounds which attracted entertainment seekers like moths to a flame, but there was an underlying stench of mould and decay, mixed with a cloying aroma that hit her at the back of the throat. It reminded her of the time Elf blocked the toilet and they had to get Mr Moffett, the plumber, to dig a toy soldier out of the U-bend.

'Oh, and Jerry,' said Blaize, turning back from the doorway. 'When you've finished for the evening drop any new recruits with Maisie. She has spare rooms.'

THE YOUNG COUPLE walked in silence for a while, Jerry striding out ahead while Red struggled to keep up. Eventually, she felt herself falling so far behind that she stopped abruptly and shouted, 'Do you have to walk so fast? My little legs can't go as quickly as yours.'

He treated her to another toothy grin. 'Sorry, darlin', people say I's a bit rapid, you know? I used to run the 100 yards in real quick time. If I'd carried on, who knows? I could have gone to the Olympics. Serious.'

'Well, this ain't the Olympics, mun, and I'm no good at running, especially in these shoes.' She looked down at her feet. The beige footwear she'd chosen had a chunky heel and she felt like she was walking on house bricks. Blaize had told her they were called wedges.

'You talk funny,' said Jerry, 'and what's that on your feet? Fancy! I guess Blaize fitted you out with all the clobber, did she?' Then, realising she might take the comment as an insult he added, 'Sorry, no offence.'

'It's fine,' she said. 'And, anyway, you talk funny, too.' They grinned at each other. 'Yes, Blaize let me choose. She's so nice…'

'She's good, sure,' said Jerry, cutting her off abruptly. 'Now, can we get movin', do you think? We're nearly in Leicester Square. It's one of the main tourist areas, so it's a place where runaways tend to gather. Now listen, this is the way it's gonna go…We talk to them, tell them we can hook them up with some work and lodgings, then take 'em to the flop.'

'What's a flop?'

'It does exactly what it says. It's a place for people to flop when they ain't got nowhere to go. Blaize's best friend Maisie owns this place down near Tottenham Court Road. They've known each other for ages. In fact, they first met as strippers in the Windmill Theatre...'

'Blaize was a stripper? I thought she was a top fashion model. She told me...'

Jerry's look of concern told Red he had spoken out of turn. To hide his embarrassment, he let loose a burst of infectious laughter. 'Well, she did do a bit of modelling, too, I guess, but that was just for extra pennies, dig? The way they tell it, she began as a chorus girl in the old Soho music halls. She didn't need to do that really, cos apparently her family was rich, but her old lady was keen for her to have a career on the stage. I don't think what she ended up doing was quite what mother had in mind, though. As a kid she did all sorts, ballet and tap dancing, which got her the big chance. When she met Jack, everything changed.'

'How so?'

'Well, he's the king of porn, ain't he?'

'Porn?'

'Yes porn, girl,' he said. 'It's where the money is. You know, them magazines with girls in the altogether which get us blokes all hot under the collar? Jack used to import these dirty mags from

Holland, then joined forces with the Epsom Salts. Next thing…'

'Epsom what?' Every time Jerry opened his mouth it seemed to raise a follow-up question. He sighed.

'Epsom Salts means Malts, which is short for Maltese?' he explained.

'Oh, that Cockney slang thing.'

'Right. Well, anyway, these gangsters from Malta set up over here after the war. They weren't very friendly types. They got a reputation for walking on the wrong side of the law, if you get my drift, and fought long-running battles with other gangs to make a name for themselves in Soho.'

'Is Jack a gangster, too?'

He laughed out loud again, prompting strange looks from passers-by. 'Jack treads a fine line, but he's managed to stay legit. Pure East London Cockney, he is, with the gift of the gab. He's certainly done a good job keeping the rozzers on side.' He rubbed two fingers together.

'He pays the police, like?'

'Everyone has a price, love.'

They walked on for a bit, Red mulling over what she'd been told. She was struggling to subdue an element of excitement at the new world opening up in front of her. As she looked over at Jerry, she realised his attention was focused straight ahead and he was speeding up again.

'What is it?' she asked.

'Young woman there, sitting on the pavement.' He nudged his head in the direction he was walking. A girl with brown, straggly hair sat beside some railings in front of a sign saying Leicester Square inside a red circle with a white background. Where the railings finished, a set of steps led downwards, and people were hurrying in and out.

'That's the entrance to the Tube,' he explained. 'It's a favourite location for beggars and such. She looks like one for us. I'll do the talking and you watch. Help if you think you can. Remember, we need her to trust us and feel safe. Dig?'

'Dig,' said Red, saluting. He smiled and cuffed her on the shoulder. To her surprise, she found herself smiling, too. She was starting to like this strange boy.

As rapidly as he had sped up though, Jerry suddenly pulled to a halt, his smile morphing into a look of concern. 'Oh, that ain't good.'

'What's wrong?' asked Red.

'That geezer,' he said. 'The one in the raincoat and poncey hat.' Red saw the man immediately. He was tall, but his head was bathed in shadow from the trilby he was wearing low over his eyes. He was walking towards the girl, a large bottle in his hand. When he reached his target, he dropped to his knees and held it out to her. The girl took it from him and drank from it greedily.

'That's kind,' said Red.

'Yeah, and I'm the Queen of bleedin' Sheba,' said Jerry. 'If I know anything, girl, that ain't water. I bet there's somethin' a bit stronger inside.'

'How do you mean?'

'I've seen geezers like him before,' said Jerry. 'They add a little bit extra to the mix just to liven it up. The girl, or boy, drinks it and next minute they've lost control of themselves.'

'It's…poisoned?'

'Not poison exactly, but more than likely, that bottle contains a drug, and I'm not talking about aspirin. Next thing you know he'll take her somewhere and…'

'OK!' She shut him up before he could paint the sordid picture. 'What are we gonna do, mun?'

'Look for someone else,' said Jerry. 'We've missed our chance now.'

'No!' she said, surprised at her own vehemence. 'He could hurt her.'

'Look, Blaize and Jack wouldn't want us to bring unwanted attention to ourselves. We have no idea who that bloke is.'

She gave him her best angry scowl. 'So, your big idea is we leave it, mun? I can't do that,' she said. 'I've a better idea. You distract him and I'll grab the girl.'

'And what then?'

'I don't know, but if you aren't gonna help, I'll have to do it myself,' she said, aware of the glaring weakness in her plan.

'Bloody hell!' he said. 'Right, if we get split up, meet me at the Eros Statue in 20 minutes. Just ask someone. They'll know where it is. Now, come on or it will be too late. Hell, I don't believe you've got me into this.'

THE MAN IN the hat helped the girl to her feet and led her away from the Tube station. Red and Jerry set off in pursuit, concentrating hard as they became immersed in the busy West End crowds. There were distractions everywhere: electronic billboards advertising shows, films, dancing, and drinking. She had to keep focus.

'Come on, keep up, mun,' she said.

'Serious?' he said. 'Just a few minutes ago you were the one complainin'. Now you're acting like you got wings on them heels.'

Red barely registered his protests. She was on a mission and if he'd known her better, he would have realised he was fighting a lost cause. When he tapped her on the shoulder, she swung around angrily.

'Listen,' said Jerry. 'If we're doing this, we have to do it my way. Same plan, but with a slight adjustment. We ain't got any idea where we're heading, right? So we need to tackle it on our terms. You dig what I'm saying?'

She nodded to keep him happy but turned back, her levels of anxiety peaking as she realised their targets had disappeared from sight. 'Fuck!' she said.

'It's OK,' he said, pointing at two figures scrambling across a busy main road.

'Shit!' she said. 'Well, hurry up, Jerry, mun, or we'll lose them! Tell me the plan while we're walking.'

'You swear a lot for a kid,' he said but before she could respond he outlined his idea. It would require some good acting on his part, and she would need to be ready to move quickly, but it could work. They stepped out into the road, paying little attention to the honking of car horns. The two figures were a short way ahead now, having slowed to negotiate the traffic. Where earlier the man in the hat had been walking alongside the girl with his arm linked through hers, now she was tucked under his shoulder, her feet dragging on the asphalt. The drug was taking effect but working to their advantage by slowing the kidnapper down.

'Are you sure you're up to this?' said Jerry. 'That perv might grab you, too.'

'You won't let that happen.'

'Shit girl, you think you know me after one date?' He chuckled at the shocked expression on her face. 'Joke, right? But when you've lived this life for a while you learn that the best way to survive is to avoid getting up in other people's bidness. Dig?'

'Oh, bloody 'ell!'

Jerry turned in response to Red's cry and was just in time to see their quarry disappearing into a dimly lit side street. At one stage, the girl slipped on the wet road surface only for the man to haul her back to her feet. He must be strong, Red thought, because the girl was virtually a dead weight now. She began to worry that Jerry would be no match for a full-grown man.

Quickening her pace, she spotted a large car shrouded in shadow. It hadn't occurred to her their quarry might have a vehicle nearby, though it made perfect sense. How else was he going to magic his victim away? Breaking into a run, she then paused momentarily to hop from foot to foot, removing the wedges as she did so. Freed of her burden, she began closing the distance between her and the target. She could hear Jerry's breath quicken behind her.

'Wait!' he cried.

'There isn't time,' she said. 'He's got a car. If he gets to that, it will be the last we see of her.'

Suddenly, Jerry shot past her into the narrow street. His claim of being fast was no idle boast. He was eating up the ground between himself and the stumbling couple, his hand in his pocket, searching for something as he ran.

'Hey, mister,' he shouted. 'You dropped this!'

The man turned slowly. Red tried to see his face, but the poor lighting made it impossible. Bending down, he sat the drugged girl against the wall and turned to confront Jerry. On tiptoes, Red branched off and hid in a recessed doorway.

'What is it, boy? I'm in a hurry,' said the man, his gravelly voice rising above the noise of traffic on the main road.

'I think this is yours, sir,' said Jerry, waving something above his head. 'You dropped it back there.'

'What?'

'Here...' Jerry walked forward, cutting the distance between them rapidly. The man in the hat looked wary, the even crunch of his heavy boots slowing down. They sounded menacing on the cobbles. There was a cape fluttering around his shoulders, reminding Red of a book she'd borrowed from the school library; it was about Jack the Ripper, a real-life serial killer who preyed on women in east London. Dotted around the pages were various images and drawings of a cloaked figure which were destined to fill her nightmares for weeks to come. She watched, barely able to breathe, as the two men came together in the middle of the road and began a whispered conversation.

Damn! She was supposed to be rescuing the girl but was so fascinated she almost missed her cue. She crept along the wall, shoes in hand, and was practically level with the two men when the character in the hat swivelled and caught sight of her, his mouth opening in surprise. Before he could react, though, he pitched forward onto the cobbles in response to Jerry's push. Moving quickly, Red reached the girl and bent down beside her on the pavement. 'Hey, cariad, stand up. We need to go!' The girl's eyes blinked open, but she had a glazed look and shied away from Red's helping hand.

'You little piccaninni bastard!' The hateful growl came from just up the road and, looking over her shoulder, Red watched the big man stumble to his feet, grabbing his hat from the floor. His head was completely bald and when a light from a passing car flashed across his face, she noticed a long, diagonal scar spreading downwards across one eye. It looked like he had been attacked with an axe. 'I know all about you savages,' he shouted. 'You'll get what's coming to you…' Red saw a flash of silver in the kidnapper's right hand, sparkling in the moonlight.

A knife!

She was in two minds about whether to continue with the mission or help Jerry out of his predicament. Then she heard a groan and turned to see the girl shaking her head and coming to her senses. Stick to the plan, she mumbled to herself. Jerry can easily outrun that brute. Red summoned all her strength to haul the girl into a standing position and lean her against the wall. Behind her, she heard footsteps, but sensed they were heading in the opposite direction. Glimpsing over her shoulder, she saw Jerry hurtling towards the far end of the street, the tall man in pursuit. When her new friend reached the busy main road, he turned to taunt his adversary. Spotting her opportunity, Red wrapped her arms around the girl and dragged her in the opposite direction, towards another busy thoroughfare. If she could just reach the bright lights, they would be safe. The kidnapper would realise it was too crowded to pursue his target.

'Hey, you! Leave that girl alone, she's my…my daughter.'

The voice came from behind her, and she span around, the girl wedged under her left arm. Her heart rate accelerated, adrenaline pumping around her body, as she realised the man had wizened up and was heading back in her direction. Jerry still stood at the other end of the road shouting insults, but the kidnapper wasn't going to fall for the same trick twice. Red had to move quickly, but the odds on her success were narrowing.

'Come on, cariad,' she whispered to the barely conscious girl. 'We're going to find you a nice safe place to spend the night.'

'Wash is…where am I? Feel all…floppy. Weee.'

For a moment, the girl broke away and stumbled off the kerb, twisting and turning as her legs gave way beneath her. Red caught her before she crashed to the ground, but the sound of shoe studs scraping on gravel nearby told her a bigger problem was approaching. She knew that noise well. Her brothers wore the same metal studs on the soles of their shoes. They were called Blakey's.

She looked up to see the man just feet away, his knife pointing in her direction. It wasn't a big weapon, more like one of those Swiss Army things the Boy Scouts revered, which stored all sorts of useful implements like a screwdriver, a can opener, a corkscrew, and a pair of scissors. Leaning forward, he made a grab for her hair with his free hand and Red had to let go of the girl to take evasive action. The man stumbled forwards but recovered quickly, steadying himself for a second attempt.

Wumph!

Suddenly, he was flying backwards, a blurred shape clinging to his torso. The hat rolled in the gutter; the bald head and ugly scar reflecting in a streetlamp as the man's face contorted in fury. He twisted to face his attacker, grabbing for the knife which had fallen into the gutter. Reacting first, Red stepped forward and kicked it into a storm drain just as a training shoe came crashing down on the kidnapper's fingers. Red wanted to applaud Jerry, who looked in her direction and grinned.

'Go on wid you,' he said. 'Bloody hell, you must have a sweet spot for me, hanging around like that.'

Smiling, she hauled the girl into a standing position. At the same time, a shrill whistle sounded at the other end of the street and she turned to see a blue uniformed policeman running towards them. On the ground, the scarred man shouted, 'Help! This black bastard is trying to rob me.'

'I'll deal with the rozzers,' Jerry told Red through gritted teeth. 'Get out of here. You can't afford a second visit to the cop shop. You only got out this morning...and God knows what they would do with the girl. Probably send her back to her family – and I expect that's the last thing she wants.'

Jerry maintained his grip on the kidnapper, who squirmed in a desperate bid to free himself. It must have been like trying to hold on to a live, wet fish.

Two more policemen were advancing towards the disturbance now and she relaxed, feeling the pervert would get what was coming to him. When they got the man back to the police station, she felt sure they would search him, find the drugs in his possession, and commend Jerry for his bravery.

FIVE

RED AND THE drugged girl were soon mingling with the hordes of evening revellers. The Welsh teenager looked around for a statue. *What did Jerry call it?* In all the excitement, the name eluded her. Everyone seemed so busy that her shouts of 'Excuse me?' and 'Please can you help us?' fell on deaf ears. Most of the passing pedestrians refused to even look at them while others focused their eyes on the pavement or tossed their heads with disdain. She wasn't surprised. The girl looked completely off her trolley, and she was no oil painting either. Her red hair was a tangled mess and her shoeless feet filthy from street grime.

It was time for Plan B. Red groped in her pocket and retrieved the card Kat had given her in the diner. She read the neatly printed name on the front: SJ Woodman, solicitor at law. It was accompanied by a number. Securing her hold on the girl's wrist, Red pulled the runaway through the pedestrian tide to a red phone box.

Inside, a woman in an expensive-looking fur coat was just finishing a call. Red noted the pearls around the woman's neck and guessed she was dolled up to see a show in nearby Shaftesbury Avenue. Resting the runaway against the side of the box, she then waited by the door. When the woman exited, Red pushed past her to secure the booth.

'You impudent little madam!' shouted the woman. 'You need a lesson in manners, young lady.'

'Fuck off!' said Red. The words felt liberating for a moment until the image of Mam wagging a finger in her direction flashed into her mind. She could just imagine Osean's reaction when he was informed of her insolent behaviour later that day. The fallout would have been horrendous.

As she began closing the door, she heard the woman exclaim to passers-by, 'I've never been so insulted.'

'I can't think why not,' the Welsh girl muttered, smiling at her own joke.

Attached to the phone box windows were business cards looking very similar to the one in her hand. The difference was that these advertised a range of services provided by girls with exotic names like Luscious Linda and Curvy Colette. Lifting the receiver, she rested it under her chin and dialled in the numbers before rummaging through her coat pocket for the change Blaize had given her that evening. The nightclub owner had described it as 'mad money' and instructed her to use it 'in an emergency'.

Bleep, bleep, bleep...she dropped four old pennies in the slot, cursing the time it took to complete the connection. Finally, the annoying sound stopped, and she asked to speak to Mr Woodman.

'Hey, Woodsy!' The man who had answered raised his voice to make himself heard above a hubbub of background noise. 'One of the floosies I'm guessing...can you take the call?' The man's accent sounded like that funny, bearded Australian named Rolf, who presented a programme on the telly which taught kids how to swim.

'Shut up, Bradley, you woodentop.' The solicitor's voice was instantly recognisable, even though it was slightly muffled. A rustling sound followed before he came through loud and clear. 'To whom do I owe the pleasure?'

'Woodsy? It's me, mun.'

'And who is me?'

'Red. Remember? You picked me up with Kat from the police station.' Silence, and she thought for a moment she'd been cut off.

'Ah yes, now I've got you,' he said just as she was about to hang up. 'You're the ginger-haired ragamuffin who gave our Boys in Blue a headache over the river in Brixton, yes? Please tell me you haven't got yourself in bother again. Bailing someone out twice in one day is even beyond my many skills.'

'It's not about me!' Red's voice betrayed a nervous excitement. 'Blaize sent me to Leicester Square with a boy called Jerry...'

'I know Jerry. Little crook's been working for Blaize ever since she caught him trying to pick her pocket in the West End. Put him on the phone, would you?'

'I can't,' she said. 'We got separated.'

Beep...beep...beep.

Feeling flustered, she looked at the remaining coins in her hand. She could just about scrape enough together to continue the call. She dropped some in the slot and realised Woodsy was still talking.

'Can you hear me?' he said. She told him she could. 'What do you want me to do?'

'We found this girl, see, down by the Underground station. We were supposed to take her to stay with a woman called Maisie, right. Then a bloke came along and gave her a bottle of drink, only it had drugs in according to Jerry.' She knew she was rambling but couldn't stop herself. 'Jerry reckoned he was trying to kidnap her, like, probably, so I said we had to follow...then there was this fight...'

'Where are you, Red?' said Woodsy.

Beep...beep...beep.

Shit!

'Central London,' she said.

'I dunno....Wait...there's a theatre showing something...Oh Calcutta?'

'I know that's...' The line went dead. Red looked helplessly at the earpiece as a continuous high-pitched whine came down the line. She could only hope the message had been clear enough.

Pushing her way out of the box, she was confronted by a crowd of people gathered around the girl on the floor. Putting her head down, she barrelled her way to the front.

'Bloody cheek!' shouted a woman with a strong Cockney accent.

'Young people are animals these days,' said another. 'I'd give 'em the birch,' said an overweight man with oily black hair. 'It's the only way they'll learn. It's the parents to blame.'

Yeah, thought Red, if you only knew the half of it.

She found the runaway slumped against the door, a trickle of vomit escaping the corner of her mouth and spooling on her denim jacket.

'Hey,' she said softly, shaking the girl's arm.

'She needs an ambulance,' said the Cockney woman. 'She's one of them drug addicts. Disgusting it is, littering our—'

'Why don't you mind your own fuckin' business?' said Red, pinning the complainer with an icy glare, her fists bunched at her sides.

'Charmin',' said the woman. A green paisley scarf covered her hair and was knotted under her chin. 'What sort of language is that for a young woman to be using, eh?'

'Anyone got any water?' asked Red. 'She's not well.'

A young man in a suit, tie, and waistcoat emerged from the crowd, handing over a bottle. She thanked him and opened it, giving her sick companion a swig. Then she settled her against the phone box and locked her in an embrace, leaning back and closing her eyes.

She didn't know how long she'd been sitting there when she heard the tinny beep of a car horn. 'Oi!' A man's voice. 'Are you Red? I'm your ride.' She looked up to see a bloke leaning out of the driver's side window of a blue Hillman Super Minx. He was young, his slicked back hair swimming in Brylcreem. The sleeves of his cheesecloth shirt were rolled up and on his visible arm was a small heart-shaped tattoo. Didn't Teddy Boys go out of fashion? she thought.

'Who are you?' she asked.

'I'm Billy, but friends call me The Kid. Woodsy sent me, Treacle. Said you was in a spot of bovver.'

'It's her,' said Red, indicating the runaway. 'She's been drugged. I was supposed to be taking her to this place called the flop...'

'Maisie's gaffe,' said Billy. 'Hold your horses.' He flung open the door and strode over in his brothel creeper shoes, hoisted the drugged girl up and placed her effortlessly over his left shoulder. 'She'd better not be sick in my car, mind. My pride and joy is that.'

He was a big, toned man with thick biceps who looked like he spent time lifting weights. The nosy parkers quickly dispersed, fearing that if the girl was a few bob short of a pound, then the boyfriend was probably equally barmy.

'Jerry reckons this bloke put pills in a bottle of water then gave it to her,' said Red, walking alongside him.

'Sounds about right,' said Billy. 'Bloody pervs. Should have their dicks cut off. Right, get yourself in the motor and don't worry about the tin lids. They're my boys. We've been to a boxing show.'

Tin lids? It was more of the Cockney language she realised. Must have meant kids. 'Me misses will be doing her nut, me keeping them out so late, but a man's got to do what a man's got to do if you ask me,' he said.

Red opened the passenger door and climbed inside. Looking over her shoulder, she saw two boys with short back and sides haircuts gawping at her. When the back door opened, they switched their attention to their father as he placed the unconscious girl next to them.

'Who's she, Dad?' said the eldest boy, a heavyset youngster with more than his fair share of puppy fat. 'She fackin' stinks!'

'Language, Maurice. What have I told yer?' said Billy. 'Mum would have your guts for garters if she heard that comin' out your north 'n south.'

'What are garters?' said the boy.

Billy cuffed him around the head. 'Don't be smart...and give the lady room to breathe. We don't want her thinking we Dolans ain't got manners.'

Once they were settled, Billy turned the key, and the car rumbled to life. 'Love this motor,' he said again, shifting the gear stick on the steering column and edging out into the night-time traffic. 'Next stop Flopsville.'

THEY ARRIVED OUTSIDE a four-storey terrace, neatly ensconced in a street full of identical houses. Stone steps led up to the red front door, and a gate guarded access to a basement entrance. 'You've met Jack and Blaize?' said Billy.

'Only Blaize,' said Red. 'She's really nice.'

'Jack's a good boss. I got a nice little number. You know, a bit of driving and, well, other shit besides. He ain't done too bad for his'self, to be fair. As well as them clubs and the mag shops, he owns properties, too, and rents 'em out to his people. I've learnt a lot from him and one day...well, he knows where I am if he ever needs someone to step up.'

Billy climbed from the car, opened the rear door, and hoisted the girl over his shoulder again. Red heard a gentle groan. 'I think she's coming round,' she said.

'She'd better not chunder,' said Billy. 'These threads cost me a pretty penny down Carnaby Street.'

Red fell into line behind him as he climbed the steps. A shout made them stop for a minute and turn back. The younger boy was leaning out of the window. 'Wh...where are you going, Dad?' he asked in a sleepy voice.

'Won't be long, Arnold, just stay there, eh? That's a good lad.'

'Me youngest,' Billy told Red. 'I call him Arnold after my old man, but his first name is Clive.'

It seemed late for the boys to be out, she thought, but wouldn't dare question Billy's parenting skills. She was a fine one to talk, anyway. When she was home, she was ordered to bed at the stroke of 9 in term time, but over the last two days she'd broken every rule.

'They're good boys,' said Billy, interrupting her thoughts. 'Mo, ummm Maurice, is the oldest, then Clive, and there's a girl at home, Cilla. We've been to see my mate's boy fight. He's pretty good. Name's Frank and he and our Mo are thick as thieves. The boys love it down the gym. The atmosphere, the ring, the canvas, the smell of chemicals and leather, nothin' beats it. I want them to learn so they can look after themselves and no one gives 'em grief. It's a tough world.'

'Sure,' said Red. She was about to mention how her eldest brother played rugby, then realised she would be giving too much away again. She still didn't feel ready to reveal her identity, particularly to strange men she'd just met.

Billy's hand was poised above the ornamental knocker when the door swung open. A woman in a brightly coloured mini dress stood there, a cigarette burning away in a long holder. Her blonde hair was in a bob style and Red detected a hint of amusement playing across her lips. 'Well, look what the cat's dragged in,' the woman said. 'Hello, Kid. Ain't seen you in a while. You been up to no good again? Ain't been banged up, have you?'

'Not me, Maisie. Slippery as an eel, ain't I?'

'Hmmm,' she said. 'Either that or Jack's paid them to look the other way. What you got for us then? I don't remember ordering a sack of veg. And who's the little doll? I hope you ain't playing away. She's young enough to be your...'

'Don't be daft,' said Billy. 'It's Blaize's new girl, innit? Woodsy asked me to pick up her and her, umm, mate here.' He angled his head to indicate the girl on his shoulder. 'Apparently, your tender loving care is required, Mais.'

Red felt vulnerable, the woman's dark-brown eyes piercing into her. 'Yeah, well, I'm all out of that soppy shit, but I can give them a bed for the night, sure. Let's get them washed and in the morning, I'll see what they're all about.' She jerked her head in the direction of the drugged girl.

'This one's been on the mother's ruin, right? Or does she stick needles in her arm? You know I've no truck with heroin users, Bill.'

Red couldn't hold back any longer. 'Some bloke drugged her, and it knocked her out,' she said.

'Ahhh, this one talks,' said Maisie, addressing Billy. 'Always a bonus. Pretty, too, for a ginger. Got a lot to say for yourself 'ave you, girl? You'll have to be careful about that. The men don't like it.' She tossed her head back and laughed. 'What's your name?'

'Red.'

'And you must think I'm green.' She laughed again. 'I'm afraid you two will have to share a bed until we can sort something more permanent.'

'I can't stay,' said Red. 'I need to get back to Blaize and make sure Jerry's OK.'

'Boyfriend is it?' said Maisie. 'You're better off here, love. Now, what about the other one?'

'Up to you,' said Billy.

She blew out smoke and looked to the sky. 'Shit, OK,' she said. 'Bring her in then…hey, is that your boys in the car? Go get 'em and one of the girls can make them an Ovaltine. They'll freeze to death out there.'

'They're fine, Mais. They got their coats, and it's character building, right? Anyway, I ain't sure this is the ideal place for young 'uns.' He winked.

'As if you're the guardian of all morals,' said Maisie. 'You've seen inside a few of these rooms yerself, as I recall.'

'Whatever you say, Mais. Now give us a hand, will ya? Where do you want the veg?'

HAVING BEEN FORCE-FED strong tea with copious amounts of sugar, followed by a bowl of tomato soup, the drugged girl started coming to her senses.

'You gonna tell us your name, hun?' asked Maisie.

'Barbara.' Her voice came out in a whisper. 'People call me Babs.'

'You're a tender little kitten, ain't ya, Babs? Now, how old are you and how did you end up in this state?'

'I'm 14…15 in a few months,' said Babs. 'I'm from Tamworth. It's in the Midlands. I've been trying to find work, but it's hard.'

'When did you arrive?'

'Three weeks ago,' said Babs.

'And where you been staying?'

'I had a room in a hostel for a couple of nights until my money ran out. Since then, I've been begging on the streets and sleeping in doorways.'

'Isn't going home the easiest option?'

'No!' said Babs. 'I don't get on wi' my parents.'

'I guess you're old enough to make your own decisions,' said Maisie. 'Here's the deal. You can stay here, in this room, for a very reasonable rent. You can work for me, and we'll see if you got what it takes. I'll show you what to do in good time, but now you need rest.'

Above them there was a thump, as if someone was banging on the floor, followed by the rhythmic squeaking of springs.

'It can be a bit noisy, I'm afraid. Some of the girls have, umm, male company. Still, it's better than getting your head down in a shop doorway, ain't it?'

SIX

BILLY DROVE RED back to the Cat and Fiddle while the boys slept in the back seat. 'Our missus is gonna kill me,' he said, fixing his eyes on the dashboard clock. It was 11.15. 'I have to see Jack yet.'

He parked in the alley where Red and Jerry's adventure had begun a few hours earlier, then led the way to the back entrance of the club. 'Wouldn't get in through the front dressed like this,' he explained. 'That's reserved for the hoi poloi, get my drift? Mind you, the air around here can make a pristine white suit resemble a coal miner's uniform in just a few hours.'

The mention of miners made Red think of home again and a sense of shame washed over her. Everyone would be worried sick. Don't be stupid, she told herself. You know why you're here. No regrets.

The door opened and with a cursory nod to the bouncer, Billy walked through. Following him down the narrow corridor, she was stunned to see girls in various stages of undress lounging against the walls smoking, chatting, or passing in and out of the numerous doorways along the passage.

'This is where it all happens,' said Billy. 'There's some real fackin' artists down here, great dancers...Is that what you wanna be, darlin' – a dancer?'

'Blaize says I'm too young,' said Red. 'Anyway, me mam says I've two left feet and no rhythm.' At least that had been the excuse she gave for cancelling junior ballet lessons.

'Well, I'm sure a good-lookin' piece like you won't struggle for work,' he said, his eyes scrutinising her from beneath thick, black eyebrows. Something invisible crawled inside her skin, making the pale hairs on her arms rise.

'You leave my new girl alone, d'you hear, Kid?' Blaize's voice boomed from one of the doorways. Red turned to see her attaching a pair of wings to the glittery costume of a dancer. The Welsh girl reckoned she put on more clothes at bedtime than the girl was wearing now. 'Red doesn't need you ogling her. You know she ain't even 14 yet, don'tcha? I'm pretty sure the thoughts you're having are illegal. Now push off, Kid, or I'll get Jack to bar you from my clubs.'

Billy gave Red a wink. 'See you when you're a bit older, girl,' he whispered, swaggering off into the distance with his cocky walk.

'Come here, Red, darlin',' said Blaize. 'It's time you met my other half.'

Red was grateful for the invitation. There was something sinister about Billy she hadn't noticed before and she had a horrible sense of déjà vu — hands pushing down on her, a voice growling that she was a naughty girl. Shaking her head, she grasped for reality and drove away the demon.

JACK HATHAWAY SAT at a small bar in a back room, puffing on a cigar and looking pleased with himself. If there was an award for king of cool, he would win it hands down. Red could tell by the way Blaize acted around him that she was besotted, transformed from hard-nosed businesswoman to giggly schoolgirl in the blink of an eye.

'Here's my boy,' she said, giving him a big hug. 'Don't he look splendid, eh, Red?'

The Welsh girl felt her voice catch in her throat, not sure how to respond.

'Sorry, darlin'? Can't hear you,' said Jack. 'I think you'll find the answer is yes.'

'Give her a break, honey,' said Blaize. 'She's just a kid.'

'Yeah, well, you know what they say don't—'

'You dare! I know what you mean, and it's an obscene expression. People have been locked up for less.'

'Don't be prudish about it, some of our clients would pay top dollar—'

'Not another word,' said Blaize. 'The girl's been through enough and she did well tonight...I think we've found a new spotter.'

'OK.' The good-looking man lifted a chunky glass containing some dark liquid and waved it in her direction. 'I drink to your better judgement, Blaize.'

'I met this naughty fella back in the early 60s,' Blaize confided, even though Jack was within hearing distance. 'He was one of my favourite customers. He stood out from the dirty mac and top hat brigade, that's for sure.'

So Blaize really had been a stripper. As if sensing the new girl's surprise, the club owner expanded on her story. 'Truth is, we all start somewhere, and I was a dancer at The Windmill, a famous ballroom around here. One of my pals told me you could get more money by taking your kit off. I was a bit like you, I guess, and was dead against it until I saw her act. I was flabbergasted. She would just stand on stage in the altogether, placing her hands strategically in certain places to cover her bits. It was nothing like the strippers nowadays who twist around poles and perform like contortionists.'

'That sounds weird,' said Red.

'Totally,' said Blaize. 'The money was good, though, I tell you, while the dirty old perverts were something to behold. They would sit in their chairs with something strategically covering their, umm, whatsits. Some of 'em brought bowler hats and you could see them bobbin' up and down from the stage. Disgusting!' She screwed up her face, but Red could tell she was trying to hold back laughter.

Jack felt no such compulsion. He chuckled, then embellished the story. 'You ain't mentioned the pervs who cut holes in their coat pockets,' he said.

Blaize ignored him, fixing her attention on Red. 'It took all my willpower to stop myself from laughing my tits off,' she said. 'I'm glad I didn't have to clean up the theatre afterwards.'

'Yuck!' said Red, but she was giggling too. 'Why weren't you allowed to move while you were on stage, then?'

'It was the law, girl, passed down by the Attorney General himself. He said if you weren't moving it couldn't be classified as musical theatre and therefore didn't qualify to be banned under the lewd behaviour act. Crazy.'

'This woman has one hell of a body,' said Jack. 'I couldn't take my eyes off her. I bought some flowers from Covent Garden market then talked to the theatre manager, who knew me cos he was a regular in one of my magazine shops. He let me wait outside her dressing room until she came out. When she did, I gave them to her and invited her for a drink. The rest is history.'

'But how did you afford all these clubs?' asked Red.

'We were both earning pretty well,' said Jack. 'I had the shops and Blaize's family were well off. She had this idea there was room for more than just sordid strip shows. She'd heard stories about the scene in Paris, so flew out there and got work in the Moulin Rouge and places like that. What's the Paris equivalent of Soho again, babe?'

'Le Pigalle,' said Blaize, sweeping her arm around as she put on her best French accent. 'They were way ahead of us with the whole erotic dancing thing. When I came back, I gave lessons to some of the girls over here and choreographed some dances. They loved it, and so did the punters. When the law relaxed a bit, we started packing places out. When the old man died—'

'He was bloody loaded,' interrupted Jack. 'A master builder who earned his dosh when the country was rebuilding after the war. I'd like to think we put the inheritance to good use.'

'Didn't like my old man much, though, did you, Jack?' said Blaize.

'He always looked down his nose at me. Thought I was a wrong 'un.'

'But you were, darlin'.' She laughed. 'And speaking of wrong 'uns, I almost forgot. That mate of yours, Billy, is loitering around somewhere. He said he needs to see you.'

Jack jumped down from the stool and marched over to where Blaize was standing. Without warning, he lifted her up, twirled her around, and then dropped her back to the floor before giving her a long kiss on the lips. Red didn't know where to look.

'Stupid man,' said Blaize, finally breaking free. 'Now go and do some work.'

Jack tapped her backside then winked at Red. 'She loves me really,' he said. 'She just likes playing hard to get.'

Then he was gone.

'Sorry about that,' said Blaize. 'He's a right fruit cake. Don't know why I married him. Well, I do. It was the money.' She winked at Red, but the Welsh girl knew she was lying. It would be obvious to anyone they had a relationship forged in steel. Red was looking forward to the next part of the Blaize story when one of the tall men in penguin suits burst in.

'Boss, boss, there's something you should see!' he said.

'What's happened, Chaz?' said Blaize.

'It's that black kid who works for you, boss,' he said. 'He's in a bit of a state.'

'Jerry? Where is he?'

'The office upstairs.'

Blaize turned to Red. 'Wait here for me, love,' she said.

'No!' Red couldn't keep the pleading out of her voice. 'Please! I need to see him.'

Blaize examined her closely. 'Well, OK then. If it's as bad as Chaz says, though, please don't chuck up in my office.'

Seven

A HUM OF excited conversation filtered down the stairs. Red and Blaize ascended swiftly and found people gathered outside the office doorway. On seeing Blaize, they stood aside immediately. Red followed the club owner through the door and when she saw Jerry her first instinct was to put her hand to her mouth.

The cocky kid who'd spent just over an hour with her earlier that evening was sprawled in a plastic chair, a man with a needle and thread fussing around his left eye, attempting to stitch up an ugly 4-inch gash above the brow. The other eye was completely closed, the lid a montage of dark colours, while his jaw looked lopsided, a front tooth noticeably absent. His clothes, which had been pristine earlier that evening, were damaged beyond repair. All the buttons were missing from his shirt while his trousers were ripped in several places. There was so much dried blood it looked like he'd been set upon by a pack of wild animals.

Blaize dropped to her haunches and put a hand on the injured boy's shoulder, but he pulled away, wincing.

'You'll be OK, Jerry darlin',' the club owner muttered. 'Doctor Robert will fix you up and you'll be your normal handsome self in no time.'

The doctor continued to pull stitches through the damaged eyebrow as Jerry's lips twitched, the pain written across his face. He looked in Red's direction.

'Hey,' he said, attempting a smile which came out as a grimace.

'I told you not to move,' said the doctor.

'What happened, mun?' said Red. 'Did the police get the fella? They were just behind you...'A grunt escaped his lips and the Welsh girl realised with alarm he was attempting his trademark laugh. It sounded like it was being amplified through a broken gramophone speaker. Leaning forward, he coughed blood onto the floor.

'Watch the carpet, it was only put down last week,' Blaize said to lighten the mood. 'Sorry, Jerry. On the bright side, you'll be pleased to know the girl you rescued got to Maisie's safe and sound.'

There was a whistle as he took a deep breath through broken teeth. It was followed closely by a coughing fit. The doctor stepped back.

'Nothing more I can do,' he said. 'He needs rest and possibly a trip to the hospital to get his ribs checked out. He's taken a right pounding.'

Red felt close to tears. Despite what Blaize had said, she couldn't imagine how long it would take Jerry to fully recover.

'Why did you laugh when I mentioned the police?' she asked.

He looked at her out of his one good eye then winced as another jolt of pain shot through his battered body.

'They...did this...to me.'

'Wait!' Blaize was furious. 'The rozzers did that? Fuckin' bastards. Remember, Jerry, we know people...I'll have 'em thrown out of the Met on their ear. If you don't have their police numbers, then give us descriptions cos no one treats a member of our little family like this.'

The boy winced again, and it took Red a short while to realise he was attempting a smile. She felt her heart skip a beat. Jerry had been kind and friendly to her, perhaps one of the first people closer to her age that she really felt could become a good mate. The sight of him now produced a dull ache in her insides. It was her fault. She'd insisted they rescue the girl.

SLEEP DIDN'T COME easily that night. Red offered to stay with Jerry, so Blaize organised two cot beds to be placed in one of the empty rooms upstairs. The bed was comfortable enough, but the visions prevented her mind from switching off. She kept seeing the kidnapper's hat falling off during the struggle and the nightmarish scar down his face. Fortunately, Jerry slept well enough. She could hear the faint whistles as his breath weaved a path through broken teeth and swollen lips.

When the sun seeped through the small skylight window above them, she stared at him for a while, grateful that he was getting some respite after the carnage. She almost fell out of bed when his better eye opened and his eyebrow rose, the ugly stitching visible in the morning light. 'You wanna picture, girl?'

'S...sorry,' she stuttered.

'Hey, I know. I look hideous.'

'I'm worried about you. The doctor said you could have broken ribs and your breathing sounds a bit...off.'

'I'm not surprised,' he said.

'Yeah...sorry.'

'Don't keep apologising,' he said. 'Look, Red. I am black, dig? This ain't...my first beating from the fuzz and it won't be my last.'

He attempted to pull himself into a sitting position on the cot.

'I'm not sure you should get up,' she said. 'Blaize wants you to rest.'

'Fuck it. You need to know...what happened?'

She nodded. Despite her pleas for him to take it easy, she was desperate to hear the full story.

'Those fuzz,' he said. 'They assume people like me are troublemakers because of the colour of our skin, dig? When they turned up, they separated us and that perv got talking to them. I couldn't hear what was being said, but it seemed all nice and cosy like. Moments later, they let him walk away, just like that. I protested, of course, and told them exactly what had happened. I saw the look on one of their faces, though, and that was when I knew I was in trouble.'

'They did this, though?' To Red it was unthinkable those responsible for upholding the law could inflict such injuries on an innocent person.

'They took me to the station and tol' the officer behind the counter I'd been robbing people in the street,' he said. 'I never reached the cells, though. Something smashed me in the back on the way there, then three of them jumped me, hitting me with dem sticks, beating me good. After they'd done their worst, they just dragged me to the back door and threw me out. I wasn't even charged.'

'The man who grabbed Babs went free, though?' Red was horrified. 'That means he can do it again and again...and next time we won't be there to stop him.'

'Serious,' said Jerry.

EIGHT

BILLY SUCKED ON his woodbine, then rapped on Jack's door. He could hear two people talking. He recognised the voice of his boss but not that of the other man, which boomed out in a loud and confident manner.

'Who is it?' shouted Jack.

'Billy.'

'Come in, Kid.'

As he pushed open the door, Billy's eyes were drawn to an overweight man in a beige suit and monogrammed tie with a symbol on it he didn't recognise. The stranger was perched on the end of Jack's desk, which creaked with alarm at the weight being applied. He was leaning over, leafing through a magazine with a bikini-clad girl on the front.

'Oh, I fancy a bit of this,' boomed the stranger. 'Majorca looks fab.'

'It is,' said Jack. 'We went a couple of years ago. Stayed in a place called Palma. Lovely little fishing harbour and food to die for. I'll look into it.'

'Your Blaize and my Delilah will get on swimmingly,' said the big man. 'While they're shopping and having a good old gossip, we'll be enjoying the local hospitality...says here the swordfish steaks are thick as your arm. I fancy myself a bit of that, provided the buggers cut off the sword bit. Wouldn't want to get me gnashers around that or it'll be a trip to that thieving dentist of mine. He's always off to sunnier climes with my money, so it'll be nice to see the boot on the other foot.' The man was suddenly aware they'd been joined by a third party. 'Who's this young fella, then? The face isn't familiar, and I know a lot of faces.'

'Meet Billy Dolan,' said Jack. 'We call him the Kid.'

'Billy the Kid.' He nodded slowly. 'I like it.' The big man got to his feet, and the desk creaked with relief.

'It's always a pleasure to meet one of Jack's boys.' He thrust out a hand. Billy hesitated before taking it, feeling alarmed when the man gripped him strongly and applied pressure to the first knuckle. Before he knew it, the hand had been withdrawn.

'I dare say our paths will cross in the future. What's your line of work, son?'

'He's my driver,' said Jack.

'Ooh that's posh, Jack...Your own driver. Any good?'

'He used to race stock cars down Romford. He ain't bad, as it happens.'

'Interesting. Well, much as I'd like to shoot the breeze with you geezers, I got places to be, people to meet.' The big man headed for the door, then turned. 'Silly me,' he said. 'I didn't introduce myself. I'm Gordon Fogarty, but you can call me Detective Chief Superintendent Fogarty. Got it? Now, what about that drink, Jack?'

Billy noticed Jack roll his eyes behind the copper's back. It seemed strange. He was normally quite generous with the alcohol. Many a night he would give the barman a shout and order a free round for his group. It would be delivered on a silver tray. That wasn't the only thing that surprised him about this liaison, though. He thought Jack hated rozzers because they regularly raided the magazine shops, accusing him of breaking the 1959 Obscene Publications Act. Now, here was Jack, considering going on holiday with a representative of the Old Bill.

Billy watched a brown envelope change hands. The police officer clutched it in his meaty fist, then transferred it to an inside pocket. At the last moment, he had a change of heart, pulled it out again, lifted the flap and flicked his thumb through a thick wad of banknotes. A drink? You could buy a soddin' brewery with that, thought Billy.

The man called Fogarty looked disappointed, though.

'Bit light this month, Jack old son,' he said. 'You know my boss is terribly thirsty and I've got to wet the whistle of the higher ups with the city force. It's peanuts compared to what you pull in. You don't get something for nothing.'

'Sure...' said Jack, holding his hand out. The copper returned the envelope, and Billy watched as his boss slipped another bunch of notes into it until it was too thick to seal. He passed it back. 'I meant to ask, did that rowing machine turn up?'

'Yeah, you cheeky wanker! Implying I might need to lose a bit of this were you?' The copper jiggled his belly up and down, chuckling as he did so. Oh great, the fucking laughing policeman, thought Billy. Mind you, he wished all rozzers were shaped like Jack's guest. When he and his mates were on a job, it would be a piece of piss to outrun a wheezy fat fucker of his proportions. The armed robbery business was becoming tougher these days, with everyone watching TV dramas like *Dixon of Dock Green* and *Z Cars*, then thinking they were bloody heroes. If that wasn't bad enough, the robbery squad was now being issued with firearms. It was a darn sight more perilous than five years ago when Billy first crossed the pavement.

Jack came from behind his desk and patted the fat man on the pocket containing the envelope. 'Take it easy, Foggy, eh?' he said. 'You know I got you that gym stuff for your own benefit...I swear it wasn't meant as a joke, scouts honour. It would be a bloody expensive joke, wouldn't it? Exercise equipment doesn't come cheap.'

'If you say so, Jack,' said the copper. 'I'll let you off but upset me for real and all this goes away. You hear me?'

'Don't be like that, Foggy. Mates, aren't we? I'll sort that holiday, right? My treat. But you'll want to be in peak condition for all the birds out there, won't ya? So, use the machine. No one wants you conkin' out before your time. If you won't do it for me, do it for Delilah.'

Billy studied the copper closely. He'd gone red in the face and his knuckles had turned white where he clenched them tightly at his side. He looked like he might explode, and Billy imagined a scenario in which the walls and ceiling were dripping in pig blubber.

Not nice.

The tension evaporated when Foggy began to laugh. 'I guess you're right,' he said. 'Too many three-course dinners at those police charity events. Not to mention those lunches your missus puts on for us down at your gaffe in Kent. It's hard to resist all these temptations when they're put in your way. When I was on the beat, I was a trim fucker. Now I get ferried around everywhere. I'll give the rowing a go, I promise. By the time we're relaxing on that golden sand on the Med, I'll be a bronzed Adonis.' He slapped Jack so hard on the back that the club owner almost collapsed across his desk. Then he aimed a punch at Billy's stomach, which the younger man twisted quickly to avoid.

'Driver, eh?' he said. 'Useful to know. See you again sometime.'

Not if I see you first, copper, thought Billy.

'SORRY ABOUT THAT, Kid...now what can I do you for?' Jack sank back into his chair and leant forward; his fingers entwined in front of him.

'Mind if I take next Monday off, boss?'

'What's happening? If it's a school play again that'll be the third this month.' Billy bit his lip but didn't respond, so Jack continued. 'Better I don't know, I guess. A bit of work on the side? Well, I can't stop you. I suspect you need the cash, what with the kids to bring up and what your poor Jean is going through. Just don't get caught. I know you think you're too clever for that but you ain't, OK? I used to think like you. Then I spent time in stir and learnt the error of my ways.'

'Why were the filth here, Jack?'

'Oh, Billy, what have I been telling you? You must see the bigger picture. From where you're standing, I guess it might look like the bloke's shafting me. Have you heard the phrase "keep your friends close and your enemies closer"?'

Billy shook his head.

'That fat fuck ain't stopping the raids though, is he?'

'Maybe not in the way you'd think.'

'Oh, come on, Jack! Your shops are always getting turned over,' said Billy. 'It happened just last Wednesday in Greek Street. Or have you forgotten already?'

'No, but tell me, how long did we shut down for, eh?'

Billy shrugged. 'They took loads of your stock away, I know that much,' he said. 'I saw 'em. Must have cut into your profits, that.'

'OK, and did you see where they went afterwards?' asked Jack.

'The mags?' Billy suspected it was a trick question. 'Must have been taken away and burnt, or something, maybe transported to the local cop shop or wherever the vice boys hang out.'

'Think closer to home, Kid,' said Jack. 'Bateman Street, to be accurate.'

'What? Round the corner?'

'Exactly. The cops entered premises there, dumped the stuff in the cellar, and drove away.'

Billy thought about it, but it didn't make sense. There was no police building in Bateman Street as far as he was aware. There certainly wasn't a blue light there – a few red ones, perhaps.

'I can see you're confused, Billy,' said Jack. 'Let me explain...That underground storage facility has wooden doors at the back of it, right? And when you open those doors, there's a passageway. And when you walk through that passageway guess where it comes out?'

Billy shook his head. 'Incinerator?'

'Simpler than that,' said Jack. 'It's a bit of a magic trick...abracadabra, you end up downstairs at the World of Fun.'

'But that's...?'

'Correct! The very establishment they raided in the first place! Magic, eh? The building with the cellar belongs to me, too. So instead of being incinerated on a big bonfire of porn, my goods have just been taken for a ride around the block. I send my boys through the passage, they load up the trollies and transport the confiscated mags back into the shop from which they were taken! We're open again in 45 minutes, an hour tops, and the world keeps turning.'

'Why bother? It's...'

'A minor inconvenience,' said Jack. 'All it costs is a few spondooliks in a brown paper envelope to keep Foggy and his pals sweet and they, in turn, can make a big song and dance in front of their bosses about how they raided a major porn supplier. They can film it all as evidence and claim the goods were later destroyed and that fools the top brass into thinking they're ahead of the game.'

'Fackin' crooks.' Billy tried to process the sheer audacity of it all. He'd always thought cops were beyond reproach. His dad and mum had held them in high esteem, believing that if any trouble knocked on the door of their house on the estate, the bobbies would sort it out. It seemed the idea of black hats and white hats you saw in the cowboy films was simply a myth. There was obviously a whole heap of grey in between.

'You need to learn fast, kid,' said Jack. 'The cops call this area the jungle, right? Well, if this is the jungle, then Detective Chief Superintendent Gordon Fogarty is the lion king and we're just the monkeys, swinging around the trees to keep him in peanuts.'

Nine

'LOVE THIS ONE...turn it up, Kid, would ya?'

Arthur Lee reached forward between the front seats of the transit van, making a grab for the transistor radio. In the passenger seat, Billy couldn't avoid the whiff of stale beer and something even less pleasant on the big man's breath. Geoff, the younger of the Lee brothers, smacked the hand away and twisted the volume button himself.

The music was like the background soundtrack to a western, the sort of gentle beat that accompanied cowboys clip-clopping across a prairie on horseback. The song was a new one on Billy, who wasn't too impressed. He preferred the rough and ready, no-frills rock of the Rolling Stones and would have appreciated a bit of 'Midnight Rambler' to get the blood pumping faster. His opinion wasn't altered when the singer gently purred lyrics which could have been written by his youngest son.

Behind him, Arthur was fully committed, his tone-deaf screech informing the others rather too loudly there was a woman who 'ain't no witch' but he liked the way she twitched. She gave him 'Hot Love', apparently. What the hell did that mean?

'T. Rex are gonna be big,' mumbled Arthur as he pulled a ladies' stocking over his head. The effect did little for his looks. He had the sort of pock-marked, squashed-up face only a mother could love.

'Bit early for putting on the gear, ain't it?' said Billy. 'What if some passing bobby notices you? He ain't gonna need any clues to work out what you're intending to do.'

'Fuck off, Dolan,' said Arthur. 'Who died and made you king?'

Arthur Lee might have been a few inches taller than Billy, but he was clumsy, slow and, most of all, thick. The Kid had no doubt he could handle the big lug in a scrap. His only problem would be if the quiet brother joined in, but he reckoned Geoff wouldn't want the hassle. He only came along for the ride and, boy, did he love a ride. He and Billy had become acquainted on the East London and Essex stock car circuit. Though Billy had been one of the top drivers, he'd rarely managed to get the better of his closest rival from up the road in Harlesden, north London. It was as if Geoff had been born in a car, moulded to the seats like some half-man, half-machine. He was always first choice as getaway driver.

'Hold up, there it is!' shouted Geoff. The shout shook Billy from his thoughts. He swivelled just in time to see a white Security Express van pass by. Right on schedule. A little while earlier, a red Mini had overtaken as they parked up in the layby, a signal that the action was about to start. That Mini did the same recce around the Waltham Forest branch of Sperlings Bank every Monday morning to make sure no dangerous criminals were lurking in the vicinity. Billy knew this because the driver, a bloke called Oz, drank in his local and had carelessly revealed his secret during a game of darts.

Geoff manoeuvred the Ford Transit onto the main road. They'd 'borrowed' it from a rental yard in Enfield, switched the plates and planned to dump it as soon as the job was done. Now all Geoff had to do was find somewhere to park close to the bank so that Arthur and Billy could carry out the raid. By Billy's estimation, the whole job should take no more than three minutes, meaning they could be clear of the scene by the time the fuzz showed up. Billy had planned it meticulously, which meant despite Arthur's protests, he was in charge.

Ch...ching.

Alerted by the noise, Billy turned to see what Arthur was doing. In his hands he had a Winchester 1200 pump-action shotgun which he'd dragged out of the happy bag at his feet.

'No crazy stuff, right?' said Billy. 'We don't want to hurt anyone, Arthur. Got it?'

He looked at the eyes peering out through the stocking, hoping for an indication his words had sunk in. Instead, the vacant look didn't change, his accomplice just opening his mouth slightly before issuing forth another rendition of the T. Rex song's closing medley, 'La la la la la la la'.

Mad fucker.

Billy knew it was dangerous going on jobs with Arthur, but there were few people with the balls to take on such a high-risk caper. The older Lee brother was bonkers, but at least he wouldn't suffer an attack of last-minute nerves. Leaning forward, Billy then pulled a stocking from his bag and put it on before picking up his own shotgun, part of a job lot he'd bought from a mate with contacts in the military. He placed it in his lap, smoothing the wooden stock, before hefting the weapon in his hand, a jolt of adrenaline passing through his body. He felt confident...unbeatable.

'He's pulling in,' said Geoff.

'Don't go straight behind him,' said Billy. 'Park over the road.' He pointed to a spot and Geoff reversed perfectly into the space indicated.

'Good work, Reginald Molehusband,' said Arthur from the back. Billy chortled. No matter how often Arthur made the joke about the character invented for a 60s public information film on reverse parking, it always made him laugh. Geoff flicked his brother a V sign. Billy became aware of an old lady taking a keen interest in them from the pavement and averted his eyes instantly. When he looked again, she was 60 yards further on, wheeling her shopping trolley across the road at a crossing. He opened the door and slid down onto the pavement, then walked around to the back and let Arthur out. 'Let's do this!' he said.

Dressed in blue boiler suits and heavy boots, they raced across the road and fell into step behind the two security men pushing through the bank's glass doors. Billy's calculating brain took stock of the surroundings. There was a smattering of customers, including the old lady, and three people seated behind a long counter. 'Now!' he shouted, and Arthur smashed the butt of his shotgun into the back of one of the security guards while Billy administered a sharp elbow to the other target's collarbone. As the two men lurched forward onto the floor, Billy raised his gun and fired into the ceiling.

Blam!

Plaster rained down, coating those below in dust.

Blam!

Arthur let fly at the glass sections of the door, which shattered instantly, creating a wall of noise.

'Right, everyone on the ground!' shouted Billy to make himself heard as he approached the counter. 'Do as I say and we'll be out of your hair in a minute and no one will get hurt.'

At the same time, Arthur grabbed the suitcase attached to the wrist of a guard.

'Not gonna be a fuckin' hero are you, son?' he asked. 'Otherwise, I'll just have to chop off your fuckin' hand.'

'Keys...in my pocket,' the guard stuttered. Billy had gambled on the fact those entrusted with delivering the money weren't paid enough to risk tackling dangerous armed robbers. He watched

Arthur reach into the young man's trousers, his hand emerging with a bunch of keys. He undid the cuffs, then moved across to the other guard and went through the same process.

At the counter, Billy waved his shotgun in the direction of a teller and indicated for her to stand. 'Empty the tills into here,' he said, passing over three cloth bags. The woman, who was about his age, nodded. She had permed blonde hair, blue eyeshadow, and wore bright red lipstick. Not bad looking, but he couldn't afford to get distracted. She opened the till and started removing notes.

'Give your mates the other bags,' he said, nodding in the direction of an older man and woman cowering on their knees.

'Aaaaargh eeeeeeh…!'Christ.

The noise made him jump. He turned to see Arthur raise his gun and aim it at the far side of the bank. The old lady they'd seen outside was slumped beneath a side window, her hands over her ears and an awful sound emanating from her mouth. 'Wait!' he shouted.

Blam!

Too late. The woman fell as if poleaxed, ending up sprawled across the floor. The other customers were frozen with their mouths open, numb from shock.

'Fuckin' 'ell mate, what the fuck?'

'See what fuckin' 'appens if you move?' shouted Arthur, ignoring his partner. 'Now get in that corner and stay there, all of ya!' He nudged the guards with his feet and they both crawled over to the place he'd indicated. There were now six people gathered on a small section of the floor. Billy could tell from looking into their eyes that they were consumed with fear.

'Are we done?' he said to the blonde woman behind the counter. 'No funny tricks.'

The woman nodded, passing the bags back over the counter. He pushed them inside his boiler suit. 'Thanks for your cooperation, ladies and gentlemen.'

Then he turned and headed for the exit, Arthur following him out of the door with the two cases. Once across the road, they clambered into the van. 'Yes, you fucker! Clockwork. Let's go!' shouted Billy, the adrenaline coursing through his veins. Geoff gunned the engine of the transit.

As they slalomed through the streets, Billy looked over his shoulder. 'That old dear better be OK, Arthur,' he said.

'She'll be fine,' said Arthur. 'I would give anything to see the old bill's faces when they try to work out what's going on.'

'OVER HERE...I think she's been shot. Apparently, the big fucker unloaded on her when she started screaming.' PC Cliffy Simpson was kneeling beside the victim, checking her pulse. He'd been patrolling his beat just around the corner in Walthamstow High Street when the message came through on the radio. He and WPC Irene Brookman responded as quickly as they could, but by the time they reached the premises the crooks had long gone, leaving behind scenes of carnage.

All the glass had been blown out of the double doors inside the entrance and there was a hole in the ceiling. The floor was covered in white plaster and masonry and a few customers plus two security men were huddled together in one corner, too shocked to move.

The old lady was the biggest worry. She lay in a crumpled heap by the far window and wasn't moving. Cliffy feared the worst.

Bastards.

Armed robberies were an everyday occurrence in London, and criminals seemed to be getting more brazen as they perfected their art. Despite the fact the Metropolitan Police and their City of London colleagues were being armed to combat the threat, the number of villains being brought to book was irritatingly small. To the general public, the boys in blue seemed to be fighting a losing battle, and it didn't put them in a good light.

Cliffy's response to the challenge was to work harder, putting in more hours and wearing out more shoe leather on the streets of his neighbourhood. By building a rapport with the locals, he hoped he could pick up snippets of information which, with luck, would lead to an arrest or two. Unfortunately, he'd heard stories of fellow officers using more questionable tactics to get results. One of the questions that regularly cropped up at job selection boards was, 'How many suspected persons have you arrested this year'. To improve their chances, some of the more dubious CID types were known to "fit people up" by planting evidence on innocent suspects.

When the ambulance people arrived, Cliffy left the old woman to them. 'Will she be OK?' asked young Irene, falling in step beside him. He shook his head, unable to answer the question.

'What do we know?' he asked.

She took out her notebook. 'Two men wearing stockinged masks burst in just as the Security Express guards entered the premises to deliver the float for this week's business. They were pushed to the floor and their cases taken, then the gunmen kicked off, firing into the ceiling and at the doors. That was when the old lady started screaming and the bigger bloke fired shots in her direction.'

'I couldn't see a wound, though, and there was no blood.'

Behind them, two ambulance staff rushed by with a gurney. Someone shouted, 'Hurry up, we're losing her!'

Cliffy and Irene turned to watch the unfolding drama. One of the crew was leaning over the woman, pressing on her chest then blowing air into her mouth. After several attempts, he finally rose, looked at his colleagues, and shook his head.

TEN

'THIS IS GLADYS Matthews, of Uppings Road, Walthamstow,' said Detective Chief Inspector Marcus Braddings. He was directing his pointing stick at a picture of a smiling elderly woman with grey hair surrounded by youngsters – her grandchildren. There was a cake with lighted candles on the table next to her, the dancing flames reflected in her glasses.

'Gladys had just celebrated her seventy-eighth birthday with her three children and eight grandchildren.' His eyes looked across a sea of faces, some in uniform and others wearing the suit and tie combination favoured by the CID. Many of the audience were visibly shaken, one particularly tough-looking DC wiping something from his cheek, his eyes glistening below an overhead strip light.

'Mrs Matthews was waiting to make a deposit when the two gunmen burst in,' said DCI Braddings. 'She screamed and one of them fired in her direction, causing her to fall. She died from a massive heart attack, which doctors believe was brought on by shock.'

'Fuckin' cowards,' said one of the uniformed coppers, his words greeted with mumbles of agreement.

'I know what you're thinking,' said Braddings. 'You want to get straight out onto the streets and hunt down these callous thugs. Unfortunately, the legal boffins will see it a different way.' He paused and waited for the hubbub to subside. The DCI was known as a bit of a showman when it came to his briefings. He would wait until he could hear a pin drop before speaking. When silence was restored, he continued. 'Our guys at the scene were shocked to discover a vast quantity of rice on the counters, the windowsills, the furniture and the floor.'

'Do you mean household rice, sir?' asked a young DC in the front row.

'Well, I don't know of any rice with explosive qualities,' Braddings replied. 'Mind you, it would explain the vigorous reaction I got from that Vesta curry last night.'

Some light laughter elevated the mood, but died virtually as soon as it began.

'What these criminals did was hollow out the shells, remove the shot and replace it with rice,' explained DCI Braddings. 'Thus, if you were hit by one of these projectiles, it would hurt like holy hell, no doubt leaving a nasty bruise, but it wouldn't kill you. Consequently, any charge that results from this savage incident is likely to be one of manslaughter.'

There was a collective groan, angry voices filling the room.

'Wait,' said DCI Braddings, his hands making calming motions. 'That doesn't mean these scum have get-out-of-jail-free passes. If we do our jobs properly, they'll be put away for a long time. We mustn't forget these heartless blaggers took firearms into a bank and put the fear of God into everyone there. Consequently, a family lost a loved one. I can't see any judge in the land going easy on them.'

'NO RESPECT, THESE young 'uns,' said Flo Mansfield. 'Not like the old days. Whatever you say about them boys, they always respected their elders.' The barmaid was onto her favourite subject, the Kray twins. It didn't seem to matter that the pair of sadistic psychos were responsible for at least ten murders Cliffy knew about, they were treated as royalty in these parts.

PC Cliff Simpson had heard all the stories. He'd grown up on a poverty-ravaged east end tower block estate, the son of a London bus driver, and had been used to hardship. Rather than turn to crime to gain a leg up, though, he'd adhered to the strict moral compass handed down by his parents. That wasn't to say there wasn't temptation. As a promising teen boxer, he'd come into direct contact with a variety of dodgy geezers and had, at one time, climbed into the ring at the local gym with Reggie Kray, fighting out an honourable draw. The bout had ended prematurely when Cliffy tagged the gangster on the jaw and his twin threatened to join them in the ring. When things calmed down, a Kray associate offered him the chance to become muscle for the gang. He rejected the invite as gently as he could.

'Who's disrespecting the twins then, Flo?' he asked, the stool squeaking as he adjusted his 16 and a half stone frame into a more comfortable position.

'I couldn't believe the cheek of it,' said the barmaid at the Bullfinch, eyes darting left and right. 'This big lout came in, boasting his family ruled the roost in north London and saying he had big plans.'

'Cocky upstart.'

'That's what I thought,' she said. 'He was coming on strong, mind, and I knew what he wanted. He thought a bit of boasting would get him inside me drawers. Anyhow, I told him Ron and Reg were mates and he ought to watch what he was saying. Guess what he replied? He said, "You think I'm worried about Gert and Daisy? Those two ladies have had their time and are now knitting booties in stir". I nearly fainted – talk about disrespect!'

'Sounds a bit full of himself, all right,' said Cliffy.

'I told him he was taking a risk talking like that on their manor,' said Flo. 'He came back with, "I'm Arthur Lee and I'll take on all comers, including them old queers". I said, "You got Ronnie's permission to say that 'ave ya"?'

Cliffy laughed. 'I'll give you something, Flo, you got plenty of front.'

'Glad you noticed,' she said, leaning forward to give him a bird's-eye view of her ample cleavage.

'Put them away girl, I'm a married man as well you know,' said Cliffy, smiling.

'Shame, I like a man with a bit of meat on his bones.' She patted his forearm. 'Fancy another?' Flo lifted the tankard and waved it in his direction. But Cliffy had heard enough.

'I'll pop in for a catch up another time, doll,' he said. 'I've had a busy day. You heard what happened this morning, did you?'

'Some bank was done over, up Walthamstow,' she said.

'That's right. I was first on the scene.'

'Gruesome!' She screwed up her face but shifted closer. 'That old dear...Did she die in agony?'

'You know I can't tell you anything, Flo. It's an ongoing operation, but you could help bring them to justice...'

He saw the glow of pride and self-importance cross her face. In her mind's eye, she was probably imagining the flashbulbs of the press photographers going off as they gathered around to hear how she broke the case. 'What can I do, officer?'

'Keep your ear to the ground like you always do,' he said. 'You've already got me wondering about this Lee fella.'

'Funnily enough, he told me to "Watch the news" but I think it was just an idle boast. You're barking up the wrong tree, there, darlin'. All mouth no trousers, him. Any road, he wasn't from around here, only popped in to see a mate.'

'Which mate?'

'Oh,' said Flo. 'Billy.'

'Doesn't ring a bell.'

'He's in here often enough. You must have seen him. He ain't the loud type though, not like that Arthur. Plays his cards close to his chest. Good-looking lad, I'll give him that. Another that's been snapped up, unfortunately. Got dustbin lids an' all.'

'Kids?'

'Three of them. Doesn't look old enough, which I guess is why he got the nickname.'

'Oh?'

'They call him Billy the Kid,' said Flo. 'Funny story, really. Reggie himself gave him the name when Billy did a bit of work for the firm back in the day – running errands and that. Reg used to say, "Let the Kid handle this" or "The Kid can do that". The nickname stuck.'

'Where does he hang out, this Billy?'

'I'm not sure I—'

'Listen, Flo,' Cliffy moved closer to the bar, keeping his voice down. 'It was a bit more than your run-of-the-mill robbery. Someone's mum, someone's grandma...you hear what I'm saying?'

Flo's hand shot to her mouth. 'Oh, my giddy aunt, you're right. What am I thinkin'?'

'Don't worry yourself.' He lowered his voice to a whisper. 'Not your fault, is it? I just want justice for her. This was the work of a heartless thug who doesn't deserve protection. You've got a heart of gold, Flo, I know that. If you can do anything to help, it's best you tell me now.'

There was an awkward silence between them, and he was about to leave when she spoke again. 'Listen,' she said. 'I don't know nothing about this Arthur geezer, right, but he did give me this.' She fumbled in her apron. 'He scribbled it on the back of this paper bag.'

She handed it over. The bag had the name of a bakery on it, somewhere in Harlesden, north London. Arthur Lee had scribbled his number on the back. Bingo!

'As for Billy, he's from your old stamping ground in Barking. I hear that he and his girl have a council house up on the Greenways Estate.'

'You're a star, Flo,' he said with a wink.

11

RED SAT IN the bar of Glamour Puss, one of Blaize and Jack's smaller clubs, sipping at a Coca Cola and watching Jerry make his way across the empty dance floor from the toilets, his stylish high-heeled boots clicking on the polished wood. He sat down opposite her and smiled. The bruises were fading, but there was still a nasty gash on his chin and an ugly scab across his eyebrow.

'You OK?' she asked.

'Cool,' he said. 'It was kind of Blaize to give me time off.'

'She's a good person,' said Red. 'She's letting me stay above the Cat until I get myself sorted, like.'

'You have your own room?' said Jerry.

'Well, I think it's an old store cupboard, but it does the trick.'

'Why are we here?'

'I'm supposed to be meeting Kat,' said Red. 'Do you know her?'

'I'm not sure.' Jerry shot her a cheeky grin. 'There are lots of girls.'

'I'll introduce you,' she said.

'Cool.'

'I thought she'd be here by now, to be honest. The barman's been giving me strange looks. I'm sure he knows I'm underage.'

'Nah, probably fancies you,' said Jerry. 'The way you're dressed and your make-up...you blend in nice. Truth. I can't tell the age of most of the girls around here once they've fancied they'selves up with make-up. It's Soho, dig? Everyone wants to fit in.'

'What if he calls the police, though? If I get in trouble again, they'll send me home.'

'You really don't want that, do you?' said Jerry. 'Why? You don't look neglected or badly treated, and you're not trippin' on drugs like most runaways. Looks to me like you've been brought up right.'

Red shrugged. 'It haven't been the same since my father died,' she said.

'Don't tell me...there's a wicked stepdad?' He laughed. 'I'll have to call you *Cinderella*.'

'Well, they don't keep me in rags and give me all the housework, like,' said Red. 'But, yes, I do have a stepfather and Mam worships the ground he walks on. She always takes his side when...'

She let the words hang in the air, feeling she'd already revealed too much. She trusted Jerry but didn't want to test their relationship by telling him what he didn't need to know.

'What about you?' she said in a badly disguised attempt to change the subject. Fortunately, Jerry didn't seem to notice.

'I ain't got a clue who my dad is,' he said. 'He did a runner before I was born, and Ma tried her best to bring us up. Then she fell ill and died, so the do-gooders shipped us off to a home.'

'That's terrible. How many of you were there?'

'Four. My three sisters and me. I wasn't going to live in no home though, so had it on my toes.'

'You ran away?'

'I know it sounds bad, leaving them girls, but they had each other, right? One day when I've made my fortune, I'll go get them.'

'It's hard leaving your family, isn't it?' she said. 'I feel the same guilt when it comes to my brothers, particularly the younger one. I used to bounce into his room every morning. I hate to think of him waking up and finding I'm not there.'

'Why not write him and explain?' said Jerry.

'Are you mad?' said Red. 'Mam and Osean would be all over it before the ink was dry.'

'Send it to someone you trust then, who can give it to him without your parents finding out,' said Jerry.

She thought about it. It wasn't a bad idea. Maybe once her feet were firmly under the table, she would do that.

'How did you end up working for Blaize, then?' she asked.

'I was livin' rough on the streets,' he said. 'One day I stole some sweets from this corner shop and the fat fool of an owner chased me. As I turned a corner...blam! I bumped into this woman. She called me every name under the sun and accused me of stealing her purse. Truth. I looked about and there it was, lying on the floor, so I gave it back to her, hoping for some kind of reward. She just turned and walked off, dragging this heavy bag. I caught up with her and offered to carry it.'

'I'm guessing that was Blaize.'

'Yeah.' He laughed. 'First impressions, right? She wasn't the big boss like she is now – far from it. I followed her to this club and as soon as we were through the doors, she took her bag and disappeared. I went for a wander and ended up in the bar with a bunch of old men, most of them sitting on their own. Suddenly there's music and lights, and this blonde bird strides out on stage in just her underwear. My eyes are poppin', man, as she starts weaving about, shaking her bits.'

Red was trying hard to contain her amusement.

'Next thing she's taking off her kit, swingin' her bra around a finger and throwing it off the stage, followed by her panties,' said Jerry. 'Well, being from a poor family I hate the thought of people throwing stuff away, so I scrabbled around on the floor picking 'em up and stuffing them in my pockets. There's fishnet stockings and suspenders and all sorts...'

'Pervert!' she teased. He slapped her on the arm and continued with his story. 'Suddenly I'm joined on the floor by two old boys who fancy some souvenirs. The three of us are havin' a right old tug-of-war, if you get my drift. Then security arrives and they're throwing us out until someone shouts, "Not him! He's my floor manager". It was Blaize. She was the blonde girl in a wig. After the show, she asked me to pack her things in her bag and gave me a pound. Riches!'

'Tidy.'

'She had six or seven other shows that night and offered me the job full-time. You could say I got in at the first floor in the Blaize/Jack empire.'

Their conversation was interrupted abruptly by a commotion at the bar. Red turned to see a shambolic figure brush past a chair and knock it to the floor. He then weaved his way to the counter. 'Billy the Kid,' she whispered.

'I know him,' said Jerry. 'At least, I seen him about. He's one of Jack's boys.'

They watched Billy make three unsuccessful attempts to mount a bar stool. The lone barman approached him and there was a whispered conversation before Billy's arm shot out and grabbed his inquisitor by the tie. Drunk as he was, his reflexes were impressive. As the altercation heated up, the thunderous opening chords of a rock song burst from the speakers.

'Oh shit,' said Jerry, clambering to his feet.

'What you doing, mun?' said Red. 'You're supposed to be resting up.'

'I can't just leave it.' Before Red could intervene, her friend was on the way to the bar, still managing to walk with his customary flourish and swagger despite his recent horrific injuries.

BILLY NEEDED JUST one more drink to take the

demons away. He'd be back to normal in the morning, but tonight he intended to get totally wasted. The only thing stopping him was the moron behind the bar. 'You got a death wish, ya piece of shit?' he demanded, his fingers tightening on the barman's throat. They were nose to nose now, and Billy was contemplating dropping the nut on the prick.

'Hey, Billy, stop, man.' A hand grabbed his right shoulder, but despite the intrusion he was determined to hang on to his original target. The barman was halfway across the counter, his expression a mixture of shock and distress. Shitting himself. Unfortunately, the nagging voice wouldn't cease. Finally, Billy twisted to look at the newcomer, wondering whether it was best to punch him out first then return to his unfinished business with the barman.

'The bouncers will be here any time, brother. Dig?' the annoying voice buzzed in his ear. 'Release the man and have a drink with us.'

A drink. That was all he wanted, wasn't it? The piece of shit behind the bar was taking a bloody liberty. No one who knew Billy the Kid would ever suggest, 'I'm afraid you've had enough, sir.' Addressing him as Sir had been the final sarcastic insult.

Wanker.

'Billy, come on. The boss won't be happy if you cause mischief in his club, will he? And look, Red's here. You know Red, don't you?'

'Red?' The name was familiar.

Billy released his grip on the barman, shoving him away so that he collapsed into a shelf, glasses crashing to the floor as a singer belted out, 'All right now, baby, it's all right now.'

Billy recognised it as a popular song by a band called Free.

'Hey, man, bring us a pint of Double Diamond and two rum and cokes please,' the newcomer said to the barman as he steadied himself. 'We're at the table over there, dig?'

'I'm sorry, I can't serve him, he's…'

'Oh?' said Jerry. 'Do you want to explain that to Jack Hathaway? That you refused to serve one of his close associates.'

Now Billy was able to place the geezer who had him in a bear hug. It was that coon who hung around doing odd jobs for Blaize. What was his name? Bollocks, his mind wasn't working tonight.

The barman grunted, then turned to fix the drinks. Billy shrugged off his captor and wandered in the direction of the ginger bird. Oh, yeah…her. He slumped into the chair opposite.

'Everything OK, Jerry?' said the girl, looking over Billy's shoulder.

Jerry! That was it – like Mungo Jerry, the band who had that singer with the funny hair.

'In the summmerrrtime!' he wailed, just as the music stopped and his voice echoed off the walls.

'What do you think?' Jerry said as he sat down next to Billy.

Cheeky cunt. He was cruising for a bruising.

'He'll be OK once the show starts, I'm sure.'

Through his alcohol-fuelled haze, Billy could sense the room filling up. A new song erupted from the speakers, Dave Edmunds telling some bird that he heard her knockin', but he wouldn't let her in.

That will be my answer to the cops, Billy thought with a smirk.

'What's he laughing about?' said the girl.

'Ehhh, Treacle!' he shouted across the table. 'You performin' tonight then? You got a nice little...'

'Hey, be nice,' said Jerry.

'Was I talking to you, Sambo?'

The black guy clenched his fists.

Oh, here we go. Let's 'ave it!

At that moment, the barman turned up with the drinks.

Saved by the fuckin' beer, thought Billy, grabbing a pint pot from the table and throwing some of the medicine down his throat. With any luck, a few more of these and he would have completely obliterated his memory...particularly the image of that old lady.

12

THEY WERE PLUNGED into darkness. Then a spotlight hit centre stage and a man in a gold waistcoat stepped into it. 'Good evening, ladies and gentlemen, and welcome to the Glamour Puss.' His words were accompanied with shouts and whistles. 'Tonight, we have some fabulous dancers for your delectation with some very special talents.' There were hoots and jeers.

One wag shouted, 'Get 'em off!'

The host played up to the crowd. 'I don't think you're here to see me without my clothes, dear,' he said in a camp voice. 'It's the Pussy Cats you want, am I right?'

The crowd erupted with a unanimous 'Yeah,' the whistles and catcalls reaching a crescendo.

'Then, without further ado, let's get the evening off to a flying start. Performing for you now…the one and only Juanita!'

The lights dimmed, and the music started up. Red recognised the song as one of her stepfather's favourites. A gently flowing keyboard permeated around the room as the percussion tapped out a Latin rhythm.

On the stage, the spotlight picked out a raven-haired girl wearing a mask and dressed in black apart from a red cloak. She strode across the stage in thigh-length boots encrusted with jewels, carrying a cane in her hand. As the music intensified, her arms weaved in the air to a haunting guitar melody.

Red surveyed the faces around her, wondering if any might be undercover police officers. The packed audience was almost entirely male, and all eyes were on the stage. She made out a few shadowy features in the reflection of burning cigarette ends, the second-hand smoke invading her nostrils and making her eyes sting. Looking back at the stage, the woman threw her cloak to the floor, revealing a black, sequined bra exposing an ample cleavage. Walking in Red's direction, she reached out from the stage edge, her fingers moving like those of a fisherman retrieving a net. The singer on the backing track was telling of a Black Magic Woman who was trying to make a devil out of him.

Santana.

The artist's name came to Red in a flash. She could picture her stepfather sitting in his favourite chair, looking at the album cover and telling them all about how Carlos Santana was the best guitarist in the world. Red smiled. Then a faded memory of Marc laughing sprang into her head. He said the old man knew nothing and Eric Clapton was the undisputed king. Guilt gripped her insides, but she dismissed it immediately. Who had deserted whom?

The girl on stage interpreted the music with sexuality and grace, but Red couldn't shake the feeling there was something familiar about her. As she watched more closely, the dancer whipped off her skirt and dropped it to the floor. An elaborate rose tattoo peaked out from her left leg, just above the ankle. Red had first seen it in a police cell in Brixton.

This was no mystery Spanish stripper. It was her new "best friend" Kat.

'What did you think?' Kat had swapped the long black wig for a blonde bob, her exotic underwear replaced with jeans and a T-shirt.

'You were amazing!' said Red. 'If I hadn't seen the tattoo I never would have guessed it was you.'

'My mum was half Spanish as it 'appens and she loved flamenco,' said Kat. 'When I was young, she taught me some moves. Then she enrolled me in dance classes and I graduated to ballet, tap, and that – one of the girls in the class said I should try out for Blaize. Hey, maybe you should give it a go. You've got a nice figure.'

'Oh no…I'm no dancer. Mam says I've got two left feet.'

'You don't think this lot watch your feet, do you?' She laughed.

'Maybe not. I haven't got your confidence though.'

'I don't know,' said Kat. 'You've got a bit of sass. Look at you...you've got two blokes in tow.'

'Eh? Oh no!'

'Methinks she doth protest too much.'

'What's that mean?'

'I dunno. Shakespeare, I think.' Kat studied the two young men. 'You gonna introduce us?'

'This is Jerry,' said Red, 'and that's Billy.' She lowered her voice and leant over. 'He's a bit pissed, like.'

'Hang on...that's Billy the Kid, ain't it? I've heard a lot about him.'

'Really?'

'Yeah,' said Kat, moving her hand to cover her mouth and leaning in. 'One of the girls had a one-nighter with him once, said his thing was the size of a baby's arm.' The mad cackle emerged for the first time.

'You're shockin'!' said Red.

'It wasn't me that said it – I'm just passing on the information ain't I, darlin'? Mind you.' Kat looked over at Billy, who was tapping a cigarette against the ashtray and glancing towards the bar, wondering whether another drink might be on its way. 'I wouldn't mind finding out!'

Red slapped her arm. 'He's married, like, and he's got two boys and a girl. The eldest one is two years younger than me.'

'Probably fancies a bit of variety then.' She cackled, making the two men look up. 'So, are you buying me a drink or what, girl?'

'Oh yeah, sure,' said Red. 'Blaize gave me my wages today. I'm not sure I deserve them, mind.'

'Don't worry, love,' said Kat. 'You'll have earned them five times over by the time she's finished with you.'

Red watched Kat in intimate conversation with Billy, amazed at how she was able to get any sense out of a bloke who had practically bathed in alcohol. She was a bit surprised her friend had deserted her so quickly, but at least Jerry was decent company. A clock on the wall indicated it was gone half eleven, and she felt nervous. It was hard to shake the habits of a lifetime and she couldn't get used to the idea she wouldn't be going home to a rollocking, a face inches from hers, boozy breath invading her nostrils. She nudged Jerry.

'You must be worn out after the week you've had.'

'I'm sweet, girl, but I can see your peepers are weighing heavy,' he said. 'Fancy heading back?'

'If you're sure,' she said. 'Maybe we can have a nightcap there.'

'Cool.'

Kat was so close to Billy now she might as well have been sitting on his lap. They were engrossed in each other, but Red didn't want to leave without saying goodbye. She leant over and tapped her friend on the shoulder. Kat patted Billy on the knee and said something, then turned to Red.

'All right, girl?'

'I'm a bit knackered to tell you the truth,' she said. 'Jerry and I are calling it a night but going to get a drink in the Cat first. We wondered if you'd like to come.'

'Ahhh, Billy's just invited me somewhere else,' said Kat. 'It's a popular late night drinking den where you sometimes bump into actual TV and music stars. Why don't you tag along?'

Though it sounded a genuine invitation, Red didn't wish to cramp her friend's style. 'It's fine.'

'OK. Night, then!' Kat leant in and planted a kiss on her cheek. 'Have fun and don't do anything I wouldn't do.' She nudged her head in Jerry's direction and gave Red a wink.

'What? No, mun!' said Red in horror. Fortunately, Jerry was already sauntering towards the door.

13

'ANOTHER OF YOUR sources, old man?' WPC Irene Brockman raised her eyebrows and tutted. 'Why did you never put in for CID? You'd have solved more major crimes than that bunch of thickos put together.'

Cliffy Simpson was used to being teased by his younger partner. Irene was a smart girl, but sometimes she just didn't get it. He expected she was destined for bigger and brighter things – like his many partners before her. The young WPC had moved from Bradford to join the Met and if she was prepared to make such a leap her ambition wouldn't stop there.

'Less of the old man,' he said. 'I'm not handing in the badge just yet. Anyway, it's got nothing to do with personal glory. I joined the force to help people from backgrounds like mine.' He'd given the explanation a thousand times and had to commend her for being so restrained in her mockery. 'I grew up on a rough estate and when I was about 12, I got caught shoplifting. Instead of taking me to the station, the neighbourhood copper made me apologise to the shop owner. He explained that by stealing her sweets, I might as well have been taking money out of the till and food off her table. I never forgot.'

'Wow, a modern-day Robin Hood,' said Irene.

'No, I work within the law. Those cocky blokes in plain clothes just want to climb the greasy pole and make a quick buck. They don't have empathy. Fair enough, but it ain't for me.'

'You don't want a better car, a nicer house, and some dapper clothes?'

'Have you got something against my brown cords and Woolworths T-shirts?' He laughed. 'Look, it's nice to be able to stroll into the local pub or newsagents and have a natter without everyone thinking you've got an ulterior motive. Of course, I'd like to do better, but in this game, everything comes at a price.'

'Don't you get free pints as a reward for that "integrity"?' she teased. 'I'm pretty sure that's against the rules too, Cliff.'

'Think of it this way…it's amazing what you can find out if people treat you as one of their own. I was having a pint in the Bullfinch at Leytonstone last night and picked up some interesting snippets.'

'About the bank job?' she said.

'Biggest story of the moment, isn't it?'

She nodded, and he fell silent, earning a cuff on the shoulder for his pains. 'Come on then. What "snippets"?'

Cliffy grinned. 'OK, well apparently there was this bloke in there just days before the Sperlings raid who was boasting about having a big job lined up.' He told her about his conversation with the barmaid and how she'd tipped him off about a couple of chancers called Arthur Lee and Billy Dolan. Then he produced the paper bag from his pocket as if it was a conjuring trick.

'You been at the sausage rolls again?' she said.

He rose to the bait. 'It's not mine, dummy. He left it with the barmaid, didn't he? Scrawled his number on it.'

'You're telling me this bloke was showing off to a bit of skirt? Wow, that's a first – a bloke exaggerating his abilities to get in a bird's pants.'

'OK, funny girl, but listen to this…I checked out the bakery and there's a flat above it. Guess who rents the flat?'

'No!'

'Yeah. Only Arthur Lee.'

'You jammy sod!'

'Funny you should say that. It's true. That bakery did have some lovely jam donuts.'

'Ha bloody ha.' Her laugh was heavy with sarcasm.

'Joking aside, I spoke to the owner, Mr Kyrios, who said young Arthur was his tenant. He told me some very enlightening things, including the fact that early on the morning of the raid he was up making fresh loaves for his customers when he heard noises outside, so went to the window out of curiosity. He saw his tenant cross the road and jump into this blue van with two other geezers. A naturally suspicious man, our Mr Kyrios studied the van. He couldn't make out the number plate but recalls a sticker in the back window with numbers on it: 2, 6 and 7 he thinks.'

She stopped walking. They were right below a streetlamp, and she squinted as she looked up into his face. 'Right. Well, I'm sure that narrows things down. There are loads of vans with stickers on in London...and why are we here exactly? This information should have gone straight to the serious crime mob.'

'And allow them to put their size 12s in it?' said Cliffy. 'That's a good way to ensure our old lady's killer goes scot-free. I can't have that. I want it all wrapped up in a pretty bow before they get their mitts on it. The sarge understands.'

'Bloody hell, your little "mate". You talked him into giving you this beat, didn't you? How did you manage that?'

He ignored the question. 'We're here to see a grocer I know, Polish fella, name of Krakowski,' said Cliffy. 'Flew for the RAF in the war and afterwards stayed on and set up shop, literally. He heard a vehicle haring down this street that morning, brakes squealing and engine revving. He rushed to the door just in time to see it disappear into a side road.'

'So? There have been hundreds of witness reports and the robbery squad has been going through them one by one, logging everything—'

'Look, Krakowski has been reliable in the past. What he has told me led to a few collars. He also sells a mean Polish sausage...'

'DO YOU KNOW who owns the garage, Jakub?'

'No, Cliffy, my friend. The first time I saw anyone there was when someone drove a green car in there a few days ago.'

'Any idea of the make?'

'It might have been a Ford, but I couldn't swear to it.'

'OK. So, you don't know how we could get hold of the keys?'

'Sorry...look, though, I have some nice Kielbasa here. You can eat it cold or maybe Mrs Simpson can make you a nice meal with it, eh?' The grocer grabbed a pack from the glass display beneath his counter, placed it in a brown paper bag and handed it over. 'And what about your friend?'

'Umm, no thanks...you're all right,' said Irene.

'She'll take some,' said Cliffy, ignoring her confused look. 'And thanks again, Jakub, I'll see you soon...and if you need any help in the future, just give us a call or let Jackie know in the Star and Garter.'

'Will do, friend.'

The policeman turned and walked out of the door with Irene close on his heels.

'Bastard!' she muttered, slapping him on the back.

'Well, you didn't want to be rude, did you?'

'How do I explain that? You've compromised me now. I'm complicit in the crime.'

'Don't sweat it,' he said, taking the package from her. 'The Sarge likes his Polish sausage, so he'll take it off your hands. Now, let's have a peek at this garage, shall we?'

'And add breaking and entering to our list of misdemeanours?'

'If you don't tell, I won't.'

He set off at pace and she followed him past terraced houses dimly lit by sporadic street lighting. After 300 yards, a lane appeared which had previously been hidden between two sets of houses. It was wide enough to fit the average van and at the end of it stood black metal gates which had seen better days. Eroded by rust and decorated with graffiti, they didn't quite meet in the middle. He immediately dismissed the idea of squeezing through the gap himself, knowing that if his bulky frame became stuck, he wouldn't hear the end of it. He nodded in the direction of the gap.

'Do the honours then, WPC Brockman,' he said.

'You're jokin'!'

Her expression was a mixture of shock and outrage. 'There could be a guard dog strolling around in there waiting for a nice, tasty dinner.'

'Don't be daft,' he said. 'The thing would have been out on the streets long ago judging by the state of those gates...and if by some dreadful misfortune I'm wrong, we'll just feed him your sausage.' He paused and sunk to his haunches, pointing at the ground. 'Skid marks. Someone left in one hell of a hurry.'

'Shit!' she mumbled under her breath. 'Well, don't leave me here if something happens, you promise?'

He nodded and watched as Irene reluctantly removed a torch from her waistband and flicked it on. Turning sideways, she put one foot through and breathed in to make herself thinner. Seconds later, she was gone.

Cliffy waited.

Nothing.

Then he heard a yelp.

'Irene! Irene! You OK in there?'

'Fuckin' hell man!' she shouted. 'We've only gone and struck the jackpot.'

Cliff heard the scraping sound as one of the black gates moved towards him. He raced forward to lend a hand and soon there was a gap wide enough for him to join his colleague on the other side. The sight that greeted him produced an adrenaline rush unlike any he'd experienced before.

In the middle of a small yard stood a shabby looking blue transit van and attached to the back window was a sticker advertising *Piccadilly Radio: wavelength 261*.

14

WHEN BILLY AWOKE, it was as if some crazy psycho had taken a jackhammer to his skull. Waves of pain crashed against his cerebral cortex, and he slipped beneath the sheets, shutting his eyes to the glare of a bright morning.

'Hello, lover.'

Shit. That wasn't Jean. What the hell had he done now?

He tried to piece together the previous 24 hours, remembering the supermarket run then picking up Cilla from school. After that, he'd gone into the city to make collections for Jack and heard the news on the transistor radio in one of the porn shops. The old woman from the bank had died. How could that be? They'd used rice specifically to avoid something like this. Had that demented fuck Arthur Lee gone against his instructions? It wouldn't be the first time. At that moment, he knew only a stiff drink would straighten him out.

The weight of a body slumped down beside him on the bed and a pale arm reached across his belly. Cheap perfume, cigarettes, and some sickeningly sweet women's tipple – Babycham or

Pony – invaded his nostrils. He had to swallow hard to prevent last night's booze making a reappearance.

'Not feeling so good, honey?' said the girl. 'Can't say I'm surprised. You had a right shed full. I got you here in a taxi, then you passed out on me. Hardly romantic. You were nattering away to yerself last night; seemed in a right state, even came out in a sweat. I couldn't be doing with all that chatterin', not to mention the snoring, so I slept on the sofa.'

She let rip an annoying cackle as a slender leg shot out, wrapping itself over his midriff. He felt her nose nuzzle his neck.

At least he hadn't done the dirty deed. Jean would be furious if she thought he was up to his old tricks. He didn't want to add to her worries with everything else that was going on. She'd been diagnosed with breast cancer and had just gone through a mastectomy. They hadn't touched each other for months. He loved her but, hell, what was a red-blooded male supposed to do? Working for Jack, you got wall-to-wall skirt thrown at you every day. You would have to be a eunuch to turn it down.

Even though his brain was planning a quick getaway, his body had other ideas. It didn't seem to matter what situation he was in or what size the hangover, it was impossible to tame his rampaging libido. Jean had always been his be-all and end-all. They'd known each other from kids. But he couldn't turn off the tap just like that. He had full-on morning glory.

Turning to face his willing hostess, he recognised the big brown eyes looking out at him from beneath a blonde bob, her exposed breasts peeping through a red babydoll night dress. His hand grabbed her around the back of the neck and pulled her onto his lips, thrusting forward with his hips as he did so. What choice did he have? She was begging for it.

After they'd done the deed, he lay back and asked her to pass his cigarettes. She gave him one of the Woodbines then handed over a lighter. It was one of those throwaway jobs that were cheap as chips in the West End gift shops, an image of Big Ben plastered across it. 'What's this?' he asked.

'Your lighter innit?' she said. 'It was wiv your fags on the table in the club. You would have forgotten it, so I scooped it up and put it in me handbag.'

He looked at her. 'Not mine, love...There are so many of them little match books lying around Jack's clubs I don't need one.'

'Never mind,' she said. 'Consider it a prezzie.'

He glanced at the bedside clock. *Shit.* He had things to do for Jack before heading home and facing the firing squad.

'I got to go,' he said, jumping up. 'I'll see you about...' He left the sentence hanging in the air. He was damned if he could remember her name.

BILLY WAS TUCKING into his favourite tea of pie,

mash, and liquor when he heard a loud banging. He thought maybe it was local kids playing knock-out ginger, bashing at random doors then running away before the householder answered.

'Can you get that, Jeanie, love?' he shouted.

He heard his wife's footsteps on the stairs.

'Why do I have to drop everything and answer when the door goes? You got two feet ain't ya?' She was still moody because he'd stayed out a couple of nights earlier. He couldn't really blame her.

'Don't be like that, love, you know I'm having me scran,' he said.

He heard the rattle of the chain then the sound of boots on the hallway tiles. Moments later, two hefty men in suits walked into the kitchen. 'Billy Dolan?'

'Who wants to know?'

'Detective Sergeant Martin Withers, and this is DC Phillip Burns,' said the man in front. His shoulders were so broad it was a squeeze for him to fit into the room. 'We believe you can help us with our inquiries. Would you kindly accompany us to the police station?'

'Nah,' said Billy. 'You're all right. I ain't done nothin'.'

'Play it your way, then. DC Burns, cuff him and read him his rights, would you?'

Before Billy could put another scoop of mash into his mouth, the other copper, a gangling character of well over 6ft, dragged him from the chair.

Of all the bleedin' cheek.

He kicked the officer in the shin, then lifted the table and turned it over. Plates, cups, saucers and condiments went flying. The temporary barrier gave Billy the opportunity to fling open the back door and hurtle into the overgrown garden, ducking under a washing line and getting some of Jeanie's smalls wrapped around his face. Pulling them away with a grunt, he made a determined dash for the back gate as his mind formulated escape options. A neighbour's dog growled to set off a cacophony of barks.

What Billy hadn't factored in was the coppers might not be alone. Two bobbies in uniform burst through from the alley at the back of the house, an Alsatian straining at the leash in front of them. Its handler leant forward and whispered something into its ear before unhooking it. The dog leapt up and bowled Billy over before taking his arm between its teeth and biting into the flesh.

'Fuckin' 'ell, call it off – no need for that!' he shouted. The policeman laughed but obliged, ordering the dog away now it had done its duty. The whole incident had taken barely a minute. Billy cursed again as the other officer rolled him over and applied the cuffs.

THE BROAD-SHOULDERED detective sat opposite, his dark, slicked-back hair reflecting the bright, uncovered bulb overhead. There was a cassette recorder on the table and to the right of the copper sat another man Billy didn't recognise. He'd decided he wouldn't make it easy for the mugs and intended to hold out until he could make a call to Jack. His boss wouldn't be thrilled about the situation because he didn't want the police's attention focused on his Soho businesses. Jack would find him the best legal advice, though. That walking clothes rack Scott Woodman was on a retainer.

'I'm Detective Chief Inspector Marcus Braddings and you've already met my colleague here, Detective Sergeant Withers.' The man in front of Billy had salt and pepper hair and a moustache to match. He read Billy the normal spiel about anything he said being used in evidence against him. 'Where were you on the morning of the twenty-first of February, Mr Dolan?' he asked.

'Shagging your mrs,' said Billy.

'Well, that's amusing, because she tells me you left early to rob Sperlings Bank in Walthamstow.' DCI Braddings was unfazed by Billy's crude attempt at defiance. 'Maybe we'll call her as a witness.'

'It would be just like you lot to fit me up,' said Billy. 'Talking of phone calls...where's mine? It said out there in the corridor I'm within me rights to call someone if I'm in bother.'

'Look, Mr Dolan, we know it all anyway. You'll feel a lot better when you get it off your chest,' said DS Withers.

'Phone call,' said Billy, stretching out the words as if his interviewers were hard of hearing.

'Arthur and Geoff Lee are down the hall,' said DCI Braddings. 'If I was a betting man, I would say

Geoff is the weak link and will pin the blame on you in order to do a deal.'

Billy drew his lips together and focused on a spot on the wall behind his inquisitor's head. The DCI wanted a reaction. He wasn't going to get one. He continued regardless. 'Brothers stick together, see, and I've no doubt they'll hand your arse to us in order to protect themselves.'

'Phone call,' Billy repeated.

'We've got the van,' said DCI Braddings. 'Had a right party in there didn't you? Were you off to a wedding? There was rice all over the place – just like on the counters and the floor of that bank. Why not tell us what went down? The forensics report will be back soon, and I expect our guys found your dabs all over it.'

'Phone call.'

'Let him have his call,' DCI Braddings told his colleague. 'Can't see it making any difference. He's banged to rights, and he knows it. Just a matter of time now and he'll be up before the beak on robbery and murder charges.' He looked at Billy. 'A little old lady killed...that's a life sentence right there.'

15

'HOW THE BLINKIN' Nora did you pull that off, Woodsy?'

The solicitor shook his head, opening the car door for Billy to climb in. 'Nothing to do with me, son,' he said.

'Then what the 'ell happened? I thought I was toast I tell ya. Those rozzers meant business.'

'Don't say any more,' said Woodsy, starting the car. 'I don't want to know.'

'Sure.' Billy sat back, still trying to come to terms with the fact that twenty minutes ago he'd been sitting in a cell, expecting he wouldn't see the London streets again for years. Now he was being driven through them like royalty – in a Jag. He rested his feet on the dashboard, eliciting a withering look from the lawyer.

'Jack wants to see you,' said Woodsy. 'I don't think this is over by a long chalk, so don't get too damn cocky...put your feet down and shut up.'

Billy got on OK with Woodsy most of the time, but always felt the man treated him like a bad smell he couldn't escape. *Fucking ponce. He thinks he is better than me.* Billy had a good mind to punch him out, but two factors stopped him. One, Woodsy was driving and, two, Jack wouldn't appreciate it. The rest of the journey took place in an uneasy silence.

When Billy stepped into Jack's office ten minutes later, he experienced yet another shock on a day full of surprises.

'What the fuck is he doing here?' he asked. The fat copper he'd been introduced to as Foggy was perched on the edge of Jack's desk, smoking a cigar. 'Has he come to arrest me again?'

'DCS Fogarty is the reason you're not in a cell now,' said Jack. 'So play nice.'

The desk groaned with relief as Foggy stood up and wobbled across to them. He took a long drag and blew smoke directly into Billy's face. 'I had a feeling we'd meet again, son, though maybe not quite so soon,' he said. 'I had you pegged for a wrong 'un from day one.'

'What's he on about, Jack?' said Billy. 'I'm out on bail and when they don't find nothing linkin' me to this robbery caper, I'll be free as a bird, and they'll owe me an apology.'

'Free as a bird?' repeated Foggy. His booming laughter ricocheted off the walls. 'The only bird you'll be seeing is the inside of The Scrubs for the rest of your days. They have forensics from the van, fingerprints off the radio tuning button, two witnesses ready to put you at the scene...you're totally fucking fucked, mate, and one call will have you back in the nick as fast as your plates will carry ya. Don't believe me?'

Billy didn't. What was the guffawing lump of piss and wind on about?

Foggy produced a brown folder from behind his back, his hand encased in a black glove. 'You can see the report yourself,' he said. 'It's all in here. But first, let me give you an alternative scenario.'

Billy couldn't take his eyes off the folder. He wanted to wrestle it out of those fat fingers and burn it. Trouble was, there would be other copies.

'Be nice to me, help me out with a few little favours, and this all goes away,' said Foggy. 'In fact, alternative evidence turns up to point the finger in another direction, understand? And you'll be doing your muckers a favour. Those two brothers will be back on the streets in no time. They'll owe you because you saved their skins, understand? Luckily for you, things go missing in the cop shop...More tea leaves work for the Met than we have in the cells.'

The copper was speaking Billy's language. For tea leaves, substitute thieves. It was some twisted boast. Though Billy maintained his baffled look, the truth was dawning on him. Foggy was as bent as a nine-bob note. He was being told the evidence could disappear...for a price.

'Listen up, kid,' said Jack. 'I don't want you to go down and poor Jeanie needs you, what with her condition and three nippers to look after. What happens...'

He left the question open, but Billy wasn't stupid. The implication was they could end up in care if no mother or father was around to look after them.

'Foggy's offering you a way out. Not just that, but he can protect you in the future.'

The obese cop put an enormous arm around Billy's shoulder and blew smoke rings in the air. The body odour poured from his armpits like sewage from a blocked drain, and Billy wanted to gag.

'You understand, don't you, son?' he said. 'Do me a few little favours and I can guarantee that if you get nicked anywhere in London at any time, I'll be on the blower to someone who will know someone who can sort it out. We're a firm, you could say, just like your darlin' Krays, but tougher and more organised...and we got the law on our side.'

Billy thought it an idle boast. Even though the twins were serving time, they were still able to pull strings from the inside and many of their foot soldiers had stayed loyal. He pulled away from the steely grip of the bear-like beast. 'So how exactly do I return this "favour"?'

Foggy put his hand up and turned to Jack. 'Sorry, Jack, can you...?' He indicated towards the door.

'I have things to do in the bar,' said Jack.

Foggy watched the door close behind the club leader, then breathed in the tobacco-infused air greedily. 'The beauty of it is, Billy boy, that you carry on doing exactly what you do. You continue with your little adventures but instead of splitting the proceeds three ways you hand a little donation to the police benevolent fund...in other words, me.'

Billy nodded. Teaming up with a copper? he thought. Never in a million years. For now, though, the bloke had him by the short and curlies. He either accepted the proposal or spent the next few years eating porridge. He would think of a way out later.

'It gets better,' said Foggy. 'Do you know how much information crosses my desk in a single day, telling me all sorts of stuff your average, down-at-heel thief or armed robber would pay to know? I'll not only turn a blind eye to your little escapades, but I'll also tip you off about who to hit and when. I can let you know who is moving jewellery, how much and where, or which companies are in possession of a full payroll in preparation for wages day. A mine of information, me, so between us we'll make an unstoppable team.'

'I get what you're saying,' said Billy. 'You're the little piggy who wants to put his snout in the trough.'

Without warning, a heavy fist rammed into Billy's kidneys, sending him to his knees. As he hit the floor, a heavy weight landed on his back as if a wardrobe had fallen on him. He felt a searing heat against his cheek and tried to cry out, but the air had fled his lungs.

'Don't make an enemy of me, boy.' Foggy's voice was a hissing whisper, the message clear. 'Maybe you need a constant reminder of who I am. Perhaps I put this cigar out on your face and when reinforcements turn up, I tell them I was simply defending myself against a vicious armed thug who killed an old lady. Then I show them the folder. How do you think that would play out?'

Billy thought about how he could get the big lug to release the pressure but was stuck like a fly to sandpaper. He let the tension seep from his body, hoping the submissive act would force his attacker to release him.

'Do we have an understanding, you little shit?'

Billy grunted. 'Good. Then I'm gonna release you now. Give me time to make a few calls, set the wheels in motion, and by tonight you will be free as a bird and back with the trouble and strife.'

Standing slowly, the policeman breathed out, his face red from his exertions. He looked like a nailed-on cert for a heart attack. Here's hoping, thought Billy. Walking back over to Jack's desk, Foggy picked up a china saucer and stubbed out the cigar. Billy rose to his feet slowly, noting that the cop was now holding the folder in one hand and tapping it with the other.

'What are you gonna do with that?' he asked.

'It will find its way to the right people,' said Foggy. 'With a few alterations, of course. What I need to know from you is if there's anyone who might have an inkling you were behind the Sperlings job. I'll do what I can, but we both need to cover your tracks. It's damn important. We can't have anyone crawling out of the woodwork and making damaging statements, right?'

Billy looked at the ground and mumbled, 'OK.'

'I'll be in touch,' said Foggy, walking to the door, opening it and disappearing into the usual hubbub of night club activity. As Billy watched, he caught a glimpse of the girl Red with her black boyfriend, Jerry. Deep in conversation, they didn't notice him.

Suddenly, the flashbacks came. Two nights earlier, a few drunken hours in the Glamour Puss. Red and the bloke had been there and, feeling sorry for himself, he'd ended up in bed with one of Blaize's tarts. Shit. What had been said? Might he have divulged anything about the robbery? He didn't think so. Then again, he could remember barely anything of that night's activities.

He took the object from his pocket and turned it over in his hand. Big Ben sat proudly on the front of the lighter – a reminder that the clock was ticking.

16

A HAND SHOT out and forced the lift doors open. To Cliffy's surprise, a figure he recognised from TV stepped inside, nodding politely and lodging himself against the back wall. Even though the lift said it could take six people, he wondered if the installers had taken into consideration that two men of their proportions might be thrown together in such a confined space. He felt claustrophobic.

'Clifford, isn't it? Clifford Simpson?' The question shocked the constable. The last thing he expected was for this celebrity cop to know his name.

'Sorry,' continued the head of the Flying Squad. 'I didn't mean to shock you. I'm not a weird stalker, I'm DCS Gordon Fogarty.'

Cliffy grasped the proffered hand and felt a thumb press down on his second knuckle. He didn't respond. The 'special' handshake was exclusive to members of the secret society known as the Freemasons. Many in the Met had joined the clandestine group, but Cliffy had turned down the chance. There was something about it that didn't sit right with him.

'DCI Braddings gave you the news?'

Cliffy nodded. He was still reeling from shock after an earlier phone call telling him his theories on the Sperlings Bank job had proved groundless. Forensics had found no evidence linking the transit van to any of the suspects, and they all had solid alibis. He'd been convinced he was onto something. Barmaid Flo's tip-offs about Arthur Lee and Billy Dolan seemed to fit so well.

'Knocked you back a bit, I'm sure,' said Fogarty, as if reading Cliffy's thoughts. He offered up a sympathetic smile. 'We were very grateful for the hard work you put in, but things rarely turn out the way you think in serious crime. It can be a real bitch. This setback can't put you off, though. Eventually, you'll get your reward. Here, take this...' He dug into his jacket pocket and pulled out a business card. Cliffy looked at it. It contained Fogarty's name, rank, and a couple of phone numbers. 'If you fancy some proper detective work, give me a call and we'll set the wheels in motion. OK?'

The circumstances seemed bizarre, but Cliffy realised he was being invited to take his first step on the CID ladder. 'Th...thanks, sir.'

'No problem and look...' With his other hand the elite officer pulled a small brown envelope from his inside pocket. It was identical to the ones in which Cliffy received his wages. The DCS reached over and slipped it into the uniformed officer's pocket.

'Have a little drink on me to wash down your disappointment.'

The lift stopped, the doors slid open and DCS Gordon Fogarty headed for the exit. 'Take care,' he shouted, without looking back. The main doors to the HQ slid open and in seconds he was gone.

Cliffy stood frozen to the spot until the lift doors began closing again. At the last moment, he shoved out an arm to stop them. A couple of policemen he knew from sight were milling around in the foyer, and he felt a hot sensation spreading across his face. Why was he blushing? He realised he was embarrassed without understanding why. Everything about the impromptu meeting with Fogarty had seemed surreal, from the handshake to the brown envelope.

Once outside, he walked 100 yards along the pavement to a lane which cut between two large buildings. Looking both ways, he then disappeared into it and removed the envelope from his pocket, twisting it a couple of times in his hand before running his finger under the flap and ripping it open. There were three shiny pieces of paper neatly folded inside. He pulled them out and spread them like a fan in front of him. The purple-coloured bank notes bore the image of the monarch Queen Elizabeth II while on the other side was a drawing of a gentleman standing at a lectern decorated with three heads, one of which was wearing a crown. Below the figure, in small writing, it said *William Shakespeare 1564-1616.*

The notes in his hand were light, but he sensed an extra weight because of their value. 'I promise to pay the bearer on demand the sum of £20.'

Realising he'd been holding his breath for longer than normal he let it out slowly, a whistle escaping his lips. DCS Gordon Fogarty had handed him the astonishing sum of £60. A drink? Cliffy could put a substantial down payment on a scruffy East End boozer with that sort of cash.

17

'YOU'VE DONE WELL since you've been with us and it's got me thinking, sweetie,' said Blaize. 'At your age it's difficult to give you, umm, certain jobs around the clubs, but recruitment might just be your bag. You're a people person at heart and you work well with Jerry.'

'Thanks, Blaize.'

The girl watched her boss pick at some foreign speck on her expensive red trousers. 'You like the flares? They're Mary Quant, darlin', very expensive, but if you play your cards right, you could be dressing in somethin' similar before long. I can see good things coming to you with the initiative you've shown. For the moment though keep your head down, do what is asked of you and let's see how it goes. I hear it's your birthday today. Fourteen, eh? I'm gonna start you off on £10 a week, OK? We'll continue to take care of your board and lodgings, and you pay for your food.'

Red found it difficult to hide her delight. This was exactly what she wanted. She now had a job with decent money, a place to put down roots and friends. She wanted to tell her mother and stepfather, letting them know she wasn't as useless as they suspected. That would be stupid, though. Any contact would put her new life in jeopardy.

'You won't regret it, Blaize,' she said, a slight look of confusion on her face.

'What is it?' said Blaize.

'Well, it's just...what do I tell people my job is?'

'Call yourself a junior assistant if you like,' said Blaize. 'Now, why don't you toddle off? I saw Jerry moping around downstairs. I reckon he's got a crush on you.'

Red felt a wave of embarrassment break over her and turned quickly to avoid Blaize's penetrating stare. At no stage had she thought of Jerry as anything other than a new and slightly unusual friend.

As she walked down the stairs, she recalled the nice night they'd spent at the Glamour Puss and on subsequent days since.

Romance, though?

'Penny for 'em?' She looked up to see Jerry leaning against the wall at the bottom of the stairs. He was dressed in jeans and a yellow and green striped tank top. He looked smart, not a hair out-of-place even though she imagined the afro took ages to tame each morning.

'What?'

'You were miles away,' he said. 'Just wondered what you were thinking.'

'Oh...sorry, mun.' She felt his dark brown eyes on hers, waiting for her to elaborate. There was a moment of awkward silence. 'Well?' he said. 'Don't keep me in suspenders.'

'What?'

'Suspenders? Suspense? It's a joke. Never mind. Jus', you look like the cat that's got the cream.'

'Oh, right,' she said, 'but if I tell you, you have to take me somewhere to celebrate, right?'

'Deal,' said Jerry, 'So...?'

'Blaize has given me a job! I'm going to be a junior help...assistant.'

Before she knew what was happening, he'd wrapped her in his arms, and they were jumping up and down. When they brought their joy under control, he leant forward and kissed her on the lips. It took a moment for each of them to register what had happened. It was nice, but...she pulled away. 'What are you doing?'

He stood back, holding his hands up in surrender. 'Sorry, doll,' he said. 'I got carried away, understan'? I like you and...well...it's great news.'

'Oh,' she said warily. 'I guess I'll let you off then.'

He gave her an elaborate bow, as a servant might give the lady of the house in a different era. 'Thank you, your majesty,' he said. Realising he was off balance, she rushed forward and pushed him so he ended up spread-eagled on the floor of the Cat and Fiddle corridor. 'Why you little...?'

As he stumbled to his feet, she realised it was time to make her getaway. Turning to run, she bumped into something hard and fell back into Jerry's path.

'Having fun, are we?' said Billy the Kid, looking down at them.

'Sorry, Billy,' she said. 'We were just messin' about. I've got a job. We're celebrating.'

'Congratulations,' he said.

'How are you?' said Red. 'You, OK? There was a rumour…'

'I'm fine,' he said. 'You don't want to listen to rumours, gal, they can get you into trouble…Ain't that right, Martin Luther Coon?'

Red looked at him, her mouth wide with shock as she realised what he'd said. Pushing herself to her feet, she marched up and looked him straight in the eye. 'You don't call him that,' she said. 'That's disgusting!'

'Out of the way Princess,' said Jerry, thrusting her aside. 'I fight my own battles.'

'Yeah?' said Billy. 'Let's see you try.' He swung a punch, which Jerry ducked. Red moved quickly between them again, her palms out towards the aggressor.

'Stop!'

Billy stood still, fists raised, looking at her with a mixture of surprise and contempt. The shout had come from behind him. As he turned, he was smashed across the top of the head by an open palm. 'You're supposed to be keepin' your fackin' nose clean,' said his boss.

'Bleedin' 'ell, Jack!' Billy clenched his fists again.

'Want to try me for size?' said the club owner. 'Where d'you reckon that would get you, kid? Now, listen, all of you...I don't know you, Jerry, you're Blaize's boy, and you're new, Red. I'll say this just once, though. We are a family and fighting amongst each other gets us nowhere. It's a battle every day just to keep our heads above water when the police, the council and the government would love nothing better than to close us down. Indulge in this sort of stupid behaviour again and you're finished here, right? All of you.'

He waved his arm around to indicate not just the Cat, but his empire. No one spoke.

'Red?' he said. 'Congratulations on your new job – and happy birthday. If the boys are gonna fight over you, though, I can't see we'll be keeping you long.'

'It wasn't like that!' she protested, pointing a finger at Billy. 'He was rude to Jerry. He...'

'I heard and I'm sure there was nothing serious intended,' said Jack. 'Hell, I bet Jerry gets called far worse on the streets every day of the week from complete strangers. It's the way it is, I'm afraid. The good thing is, we look after our own. I'd hope Billy would stick up for Jerry if the chips were down.'

Red looked at the man they called The Kid. His expression was blank. She couldn't imagine him raising a finger to help her friend. 'Now come on,' said Jack. 'Get back to doing what you do best...helping to keep this place afloat. Before I go, I want to see you two boys shake on it.'

Billy and Jerry stared at each other from a distance, neither wishing to make the first move. In Jerry's eyes, Red saw something she hadn't witnessed until now. Hate. Billy's expression was simply unreadable. Fed up with waiting, Jack nudged him forward and he shoved his hand in Jerry's direction. Red's friend kept his fists balled at his side until she gave him a nod of encouragement. After rubbing his hands on his jeans, he reached out and shook Billy's hand.

'That's better,' said Jack. 'All friends again. Now I've got things to do, so I will love you and leave you.' He winked at Red, then waved a hand and turned back the way he'd come. Although the altercation had crushed her good mood, Red vowed she wouldn't let it spoil her day. She linked arms with Jerry.

'How about you buy me breakfast at the Soho Grill?' she asked. 'A birthday treat.' He nodded, though she could tell his mind was elsewhere. As they started to walk off, Billy barged past them in the other direction.

As he did so, he muttered, 'It ain't over. You'll see what you get when you mess with Billy the Kid.'

18

'WHAT D'YA THINK, girl?' asked Jerry. Her friend stood in front of her, arms wide open, twirling like a fashion model on a catwalk. He wore an expensive looking Afghan coat, stylish leather boots poking out from beneath brown velvet loon pants and a multi-coloured tank top in red, yellow and green. His wiry frame made him look like a child wearing adult clothing and his hair was twisted in tight plaits which ran down his back.

'Very colourful,' said Red. 'What have you done to your hair?'

'They're me dreads,' said Jerry. 'You know, dreadlocks? Rastafari?'

'Rasta what?'

'Oh, come on, girl, I know you're from some little speck on the planet, but surely you're joking with me now.'

'Honestly, I've never heard of it. What did you say it was called, Rustyfurry?'

'Man, Rastas are all over the world, you dig? Preaching peace and love, sticking up for a man's rights.'

'What about women, then?'

'Aye, women too. Sure.'

'We do make up half the world's population, you know?'

He looked confused for a second, then his face lit up again. 'Let me tell you more before you go off all half-cocked,' he said. 'The word comes from our spiritual leader Haile Selassie, emperor of Ethiopia. He united all the African nations and black people together with the same goals and desires.'

'OK.' She was still confused, though. 'His name's Hiley something – where did Rasta come from?'

'Haile Selassie was not the name he was born with, dig? His name was Tafari, and he was born an Ethiopian prince. The word for prince, duke or lord in that language is Ras. So, he was...'

'Prince Tafari, or Rastafari. Right!' A light bulb switched on in her brain.

'That's my girl,' he said, grabbing her by the forearms and shaking her. She smiled at his infectious enthusiasm.

'What does a Rasta do exactly?' she asked, pulling herself free.

'We promote one love and peace and harmony in his name. Though black people are spread across the world we originate from Africa. The white people came and stole mothers and brothers and children then transported them to the four corners of the earth to sell as slaves. Families were torn apart, but Rastafari says, in spirit, we are together. This is why days like today are important. I want to share that joy with you.'

'I don't know,' said Red. 'It doesn't sound like I should be there. For God's sake, mun, I'm as white as a ghost and have bright ginger hair. I'll stand out like a sore thumb.'

He chuckled, which quickly turned into big belly laughs, the pleasure on his face so infectious it made her giggle too. 'No one's going to mistake you for Aretha Franklin, that's for damn sure,' he said, patting her on the shoulder affectionately. 'You're Jerry's girl, though, so nothing to worry about. Besides, I'm sure there will be other white people there. Many politicians support our cause, dig?'

Before he was aware of what was happening, she smacked him hard on the arm, not with the palm of her hand but with a closed fist. He yelped and rubbed at the tender area.

'Damn!' he said. 'What you go and do that for?'

'This time you're the stupid one,' she said, her face close to his. 'However much you might like it to be true, Jerry, I'm not your girl, dig? And how are you going to defend me when you can't even take a punch from a weedy woman?'

For a moment, he looked hurt, only to burst out laughing again. 'Now that's why I like you,' he said. 'You've got fire, like a true Rasta girl.'

'I'm worried there might be trouble, though,' she said. 'I've seen these street protests on the news. They don't always end well.'

'Hey, if it all gets a bit mad, we sneak off and leave it to the Panthers.'

'Who?'

'You ain't heard of The Black Panthers neither?' he said. 'Man, they're big in America and there's now a branch over here. They've organised this meeting with the Black Liberation Front and a few other guys. They don't take no shit. If affirmative action's needed, they're first in the queue. Truth.'

Red grabbed his hand. 'Come on then,' she said, tugging him in the direction of the door. 'If it's gonna be that busy, we don't want to be late and we can pop to Brixton on the way to see if we can find that squat and get my bag back.'

RED FELT A strange tingle in her stomach as she stepped out into the mass of people milling around the Oval Underground station entrance. The sight was intimidating, scary, and exciting in equal measure. She clutched Jerry's hand.

As he walked, he nodded greetings to people as if he'd known them all his life, occasionally raising his fist and shouting things like 'Freedom for the Oval House warriors' and 'Black Power!' All around there was music, kettle drums banging out a colourful beat while the tenants of surrounding flats opened their windows to add their musical tastes to proceedings.

The crowd became denser the further they walked and for every colourful tunic she saw, there now seemed to be a brother dressed head-to-toe in black, carrying a placard and shouting a slogan. She struggled to make out the words but heard several references to "Pigs".

'Sorry we couldn't find your bag,' said Jerry. 'It looks like the police and council shut down that squat, man, and everyone moved on.'

'I guess it was a long shot,' she said, looking around her. 'Jeez, I don't think I've ever seen so many people in one place, mun. It's scary.'

No sooner had she spoken than stumpy, hard fingers dug into her arm. Spinning around, Red encountered a thick-set man staring at her. Stepping forward, he invaded her personal space. 'Sorry,' she mumbled, assuming she'd trodden on his toe without realising. His response came in the form of a growl, any words lost in translation. Jerry was still nosing forward, oblivious to the escalating problem. Feeling petrified, she pinched her friend's arm.

'Careful girl!' he said, swivelling around. 'That hurt.' She nodded in the direction of the big man, whose large fist encased her other arm.

'What's up, big man?' Jerry asked the stranger.

'Why she here?' The imposing figure's nostrils flared, eyes burning into Jerry's.

'She's come to support the Oval House Boys like everyone else,' said Jerry.

'And what does a honky whore know about our struggle?' The big man leant down and spat the next words in Red's face. 'You sure she ain't no undercover pig?'

Feeling under attack, her regular defence mechanisms clicked into place. She didn't even hear Jerry's reply. Fists balled at her sides, legs braced to resist the tug of the aggressor, she got ready to launch herself.

'Hey, Benjamin, man!' Another voice broke the tension. A boy stepped forward, tugging a girl behind him. He looked strangely familiar and when he spoke, she realised she'd met him before.

'Leave the girl alone, irie? She's OK. Serious. She's from my yard.'

'Hmph.' Her aggressive interrogator flicked his head into the air, released Red's arm and set off through the crowd.

'Thanks, man,' Jerry said to the boy before introducing himself and Red.

'I met you in Brixton, didn't I?' said Red.

'Yeah. Donavan, remember?' The kid grinned, then wiggled in the small space around them, showing off some well-coordinated dance moves. 'You were with that geezer Chancer, who lived in the squat down the road from me. He came over because he like the music. We were dancing to the great man Jimmy Cliff.'

She nodded. Though it was six months ago, the episode was clear in her memory because she recalled feeling slightly intimidated by the number of black faces on the streets, having heard rumours at school about criminals 'invading' Britain with a reputation for causing trouble. Her friendship with Jerry had shown her how silly she'd been to listen to myths spread by ignorant teenagers. 'What about my sister Chandice?'

'Of course.' Red smiled at the young girl who stepped forward. She responded with a shy grin.

'Sorry about my cuz there,' said Donavan, nodding his head in the direction her interrogator had taken. 'He comes across a bit fierce and spends too long in the gym. I reckon he's on them pills that make your muscles grow and your dick shrink.' He laughed, and Jerry joined in. 'No one better to fight your corner, though...'

His words were drowned out as the public address system burst into life. There was a short burst of static and feedback before a man's voice boomed out around them. 'Plenty of room down the front, brothers and sisters. Can we move forward a bit? It's great to see such an overwhelming demonstration of support but we don't want no one crushed, you hear?' His words were greeted with a mixture of whoops and hollers. Whistles and customised percussion penetrated the air, reinforcing the party atmosphere.

'This way,' said Jerry, pulling Red onto a small section of pavement to their left. 'This will be perfect.'

She beckoned to Donavan, and he and Chandice mounted the pavement alongside them. 'Good spot,' he said. 'This should be an entertaining evening.' A couple of loud booming noises projected forth from the speakers followed by the familiar sounds of a microphone being tested 'One two...one two'. Around them the chatter became louder, more urgent, hundreds of different voices speaking at once.

'Did you ever see Chancer after that?' she asked. 'I'm wondering what happened to my friend Marc, who was with us.'

'To be honest, I still bump into Chancer sometimes. He's moved in with all these left-wing political types. They're Communists I think – at least they have this commune. I didn't see the other boy again, though. Sorry.'

'That's OK, I think he went home,' she said.

STANDING ON TIPTOE, Red occasionally got a glimpse of the speakers. Around her, people shouted support while others chanted slogans at regular intervals. One was quite clearly aimed at the police with a section of the crowd baiting, 'Calling All Pigs, Calling All Pigs...Freak Out or Get Out'. Though there was a sizeable, uniformed presence, they seemed content to keep a low-key watching brief from the edge of the crowd.

'Brothers and sisters.' A tall man stood centre stage with a microphone in his hand. 'We are gathered here in our thousands to show the powerbrokers of this country that we, London's black community, will no longer stand for the sort of harassment carried out against us by the Metropolitan Police. Acts which seem to be condoned by the legal sector.' He walked forward to the front of the stage and leant forward, scanning the crowd and picking out various people to engage in eye contact. 'Despite these unlawful acts being reported to the Home Office on numerous occasions there has been no response, leaving it up to us, brothers and sisters, to defend ourselves against these inhumane and racialist attacks by those who wish to oppress us...'

Jerry put fingers into either side of his mouth and let out a loud wolf whistle in the direction of the stage. 'Who is that man?' Red shouted in his ear.

'His name is Jeremiah Kikolome,' he said. 'He is a legend, a member of the BBPM. Apparently, he smashed a chair over a racist copper's head once when the bastard was trying to arrest a young mother at a wedding party last year.'

'BBPM?'

'The British Black Panther Movement.'

The speaker was warming to his task.

'It's so good to have you come out today in your thousands. This protest is necessary, people, as all other methods have failed to bring about change and the new racist immigration bill is only going to make things worse. It will be a license to intimidate and beat down on the black people of Britain. That's why it's the duty of all of us to continue to protest until we're treated justly by both the police and the courts.'

The speaker finished to a rousing ovation, the spectators showing their support in different ways, shouting and catcalling, jumping up and down, beating drums and blowing whistles, banging metal cans together.

Red had never seen anything like it before. Rather than a protest meeting, it was more like a carnival celebration.

The crowds stayed on after the speakers had gone, transforming the event into a party, while enterprising characters with rucksacks on their backs drifted through the ranks, selling cans of beer and other alcoholic beverages. Jerry bought a can of lager for himself and a cider for Red, warning her to use her discretion and keep an eye out for the police. They wandered around sampling the atmosphere, Jerry occasionally engaging a fellow protestor in conversation.

As the light began to fade and the temperature dropped, people ebbed away, keen to continue their conversations in the warmth of the nearby pubs and bars.

19

RED BOMBARDED HER friend with questions on the way to the Tube station. She'd been intrigued by the sheer passion of the people, finding the event exhilarating and intimidating in equal measure.

'Who are the Mangrove Nine?' she asked.

'The Mangrove is an all-night restaurant in Notting Hill,' he said. 'Two years ago, the cops launched a drugs raid and found nothing...Not a dodgy cigarette butt, a crumb of grass, nothing.'

Red linked arms with him, immersing herself in his softly spoken voice. She felt tired but exhilarated from her experience.

'No one was arrested?' she asked.

'Nah,' he said. 'But the pigs weren't satisfied with that. A few weeks later, the same thing happened again, and again, nothing was found. Even so, they came up with an excuse to shut the place down early, which seriously impacted the owner's livelihood. It was very popular with the black community because before then it had sold food and drink after eleven. What made people annoyed was that white establishments in the area could remain open until the early hours.'

'They must have had a reason for closing it,' said Red.

'You see, you see!' He was becoming so animated she had to pull her arm away, struggling to equate this new, aggressive Jerry with the convivial and peace-loving boy she worked alongside every day. 'That's prejudice. The pigs don't need no reason to do things like this to the black community. The government and the courts simply take their word over us every time.'

After entering the Tube station, Jerry jumped on the escalator with Red following close behind.

'Who are the nine, then?' she shouted at his back.

When they arrived on the platform, he turned to face her. 'Look, eventually the relationship between cops and local people became so bad a protest march was organised and almost 200 people turned up. It was peaceful enough until the protesters clashed with the Pigs at Notting Hill police station.'

Though Red was hanging on his every word, she paused briefly to look over his shoulder, wondering if anyone was paying attention to his one-sided rant. A few protesters were milling around while some well-dressed men with short haircuts looked like they were heading into the West End for a night out. She'd seen plenty of their type during her evenings working in Soho.

'Before long it got out of hand, dig?' said Jerry. 'But no one was arrested until nine weeks after the march. The police had filmed the entire thing and early one morning they started knocking on doors and dragging out the people they suspected of being ringleaders. Seven men and two women were charged with assault and affray.'

'And that's why we came here today?' said Red, hearing a faint whistle from the rails to indicate the approach of a train.

'Partly,' he said, 'but, personally, I came cos of the Oval t'ing. I was at that wedding party I told you about. The pigs burst in and accused random people of stealing a boy's watch. They lined us all up against the walls to search us. Nothing was found, but it spoilt a happy occasion...'

'Sure.' Red could see a pattern emerging.

'There were some Black Panthers at the party who weren't happy – they were chanting "Fuck the Pigs", and "Kill a Cop". It turned nasty, and the pigs retreated to lick their wounds. A big cheer went up, but later three people were charged with inciting a riot.'

Jerry stopped talking as the train pulled into the station. 'Edgware,' he said. 'This is our ride, girl. I'm shattered, man, so if you don't mind, I'll save the other horror stories for later.'

THEY WERE DELIGHTED to find an empty carriage. Red propped herself in a corner, leant against the window and closed her eyes, trying to let her mind drift with the clickety-clack of wheels on the track. She couldn't switch off though, her brain conjuring up images of pitched battles between police and angry young black men on London's streets. Next to her, Jerry was engrossed in a pamphlet he'd picked up at the rally.

Amid the chaotic frenzy of her dream, she heard a door slam, followed by pounding footsteps. She only opened her eyes when Jerry barged roughly against her and yelled, 'Hey, man, watch the threads. What are you doing? Hey!'

She took vital seconds to process what she was seeing. Jerry was bent over in front of her, his right arm forced high up his back by one of the men she'd seen on the platform. Pushing herself to her feet with the intention of protesting, she then felt a large hand thud into her back, sending her crashing back down.

As she tried to push herself up to a sitting position, another man arched back and head-butted Jerry in the nose. Blood gushed from the wound, down across his lips and onto his chin. He spat something on the floor and to her horror Red realised it was a blood-stained tooth.

'You can't do that!' she protested, looking along the carriage for assistance. There was no one around other than the aggressor's two identikit mates.

'Who's gonna stop us then, bitch?' said one of the men. He held Jerry in position while his clone went to work, pummelling fists into his stomach and chest. 'We saw this fucker passing through the crowd pilfering people's wallets and valuables. Like a bit of black, do ya, darlin'? I hear they're big down below.'

The clone responded by ramming his fist into Jerry's groin. He screamed and Red leant forward, dry heaving.

'Oh, we got a dribbler,' said the other man, wrestling to contain the writhing, anguished Jerry.

'Just in case you were wondering, you dirty tart, we're the police and your friend here is bang to rights.'

Red sucked in the musty air of the Tube, trying to bring her shakes under control. She realised that in her panicked state she was no help to Jerry at all.

'He...he's not a thief,' she said, squeezing the words out. 'I was with him all day. He hasn't stolen anything.'

'We'd expect you to say that ginger pubes.' The foul chuckle that followed ignited Red's angry streak. She felt blood rush to her face, not through embarrassment but through undiluted fury. A succession of do-gooders – parents, siblings, friends, aunties, uncles, and teachers – had told her that one day her combustible nature would get her into serious trouble.

Now was as good a day as any.

The speaker was unaware he was poking a bear. 'These fuckin' immigrants are like the pied piper. They enlist young slags like you as accomplices. You distract the mark while old Noggin' the Wog here can use his big dipper fingers...'

Ignition! Red flew from her seat, hands out in front of her and nails extended, the third finger on her left hand connecting with an eye and sending her tormentor reeling. Seeing his opportunity, Jerry launched an elbow into his captor and was rewarded with a satisfying shriek. The big thicko in front of him was cursing and holding his injured eye, so Jerry took advantage by kicking him on the knee. For a moment, the Pig stood there before the pain registered and his leg gave way.

Red turned her attention to the man who had been holding Jerry. As he struggled to get up, she jumped at him feet first, angling a heavy boot into his solar plexus. If he had hair, she would have grabbed it and dragged him around the train. Instead, she drew her fingers down the side of his face, producing a squeal of pain.

'You bloody freak!' he shouted. 'Jonny, Jonny...fuck me she's a mental case. Help us, would ya?'

The third man, slow to react at first, moved forward, swiping around with a metal stick he produced from his belt. His first blow struck Jerry across his broken nose, sending him crashing to the carriage floor, his head bouncing on impact. Moving forward like a farm worker scything through a wheat field, he then caught Red on the elbow, followed by the leg, the strength from her arm draining instantly. She tried to make a run for it but fell over Jerry's prone body and ended up spread-eagled on the ground.

The man called Jonny had given his dazed mates time to recover. He jumped on her back and wrestled her wrists around so that he could slam on handcuffs. Leaning forward, he whispered, 'What you could do with is a nice bit of truncheon meat up you.'

Shit. She knew that voice. If she wasn't mistaken, it was the policeman who'd molested her in Brixton.

20

JERRY WAS HAVING great difficulty in focusing. His eyes were puffy and painful, one lid so swollen that he couldn't see out of it. The overall effect was like peering into a bottle of swirling smoke. He continually touched his right cheek to check on the giant lump which had sprouted under his skin. A tear trickled along his swollen nose, and he wiped it away, hoping the police didn't think he was crying and take it as a sign of weakness. A police doctor would later reveal he'd ruptured a tear duct.

Biting on a loose piece of skin inside his lip – something he always did when he was nervous – the Rasta leant forward on the scratched wooden table, trying to focus on his surroundings. The room was small and square, with a blue metal door opposite him containing a rectangular post-box window halfway up. The walls to his right and left were bare and painted in drab magnolia, the odd telltale stain indicating that more than talking had taken place here on previous occasions.

'Well?' The interviewer had introduced himself as Detective Sergeant Martin Withers and another officer sat alongside him.

'I told you,' Jerry slurred. 'I was there for the march, that's all.' Every time he made the 's' sound air pushed through the gap where a healthy incisor should have been, producing a strange whistle. As he spoke, he winced, the nerve hanging down and exposed to the elements, so he tried to keep his lips as close together as possible. As a result, his answers emerged as a mumble.

'Hmmm. You're not very clear about any of this,' said the detective sergeant. 'Seems like you need us to refresh your memory.'

The other policeman put down his pen and reached under the desk. Jerry watched in confusion, wondering what sort of stunt they were about to pull. He'd heard plenty of stories of police underhand tactics from his friends, some of them recounted earlier that day.

'Catch!' He was ready for most things, but not the bulky projectile sent on a collision course with his face. At the last minute, he flung up his arms and grabbed the grey duffle bag by a strap, preventing the object causing him further damage.

'What the hell is this, man?' he spluttered.

'Oh, come on,' said the officer with the stripes. 'It's your bag. Our men rescued it from the Tube train.'

'I...I've never seen it before.'

'Really? The officers who brought you in said that after you resisted arrest, this was found under your seat. Maybe what's inside will refresh your memory. Pour the contents on the table and let's see if something rings a bell.'

Jerry lifted the bag then dropped it to the floor. 'Tol' you, it ain't mine.'

'Jesus!' shouted the sergeant. 'DC Burns, do the honours, would you?'

The other officer wandered around to Jerry's side of the desk and retrieved the bag. He was wearing plastic, transparent gloves. Tipping it upside down, the contents spilled onto the table, a pen rolling away and landing on the floor.

'Recognise anything?' said the sergeant.

Jerry studied the jumble of miscellaneous items. There was a set of keys, a cassette tape, a couple of bank notes, some coins, a map book, a pack half full of cigarettes and a lighter. 'For fuck's sake!' he sat back and laughed. 'Are you suggesting I stole these things during a protest march?'

The DS leant across the table, his eyes burning into Jerry's. The boy was used to the stereotyping, though, and refused to take the bait.

'DC Burns,' said DS Withers. 'Please take it to the lab and let our boffins have a look at it.'

Jerry let out a troubled laugh. 'Shit, you know it ain't mine. What's all this about?'

Suddenly he found himself falling backwards, cracking his head against the floor as the copper called Burns kicked the chair legs from under him. He let out a startled yelp, then lay there feeling helpless, his head spinning and provoking a nauseous reaction in his stomach. He rolled over and puked on the floor.

'Dirty bastard,' said Burns, leaning over and spitting the words in Jerry's face.

'Leave him,' said DS Withers. 'The man says this stuff ain't his, so we should establish the truth. Let me speak to the lab.'

'Yes, sir,' said the constable. Jerry saw his own battered face reflected in the pig's shiny boots.

HAVING CLAMBERED BACK into his chair, Jerry was then forced to sit in one place for so long it made him irritable. 'I told you, man, that ain't my bag,' he reiterated to his minder, DC Burns. 'This is a fit up. No wonder we're out on the streets protesting when you pull stunts like this. It's discrimination, man.'

'And that sort of talk, "man", will earn you another sore head,' said DC Burns.

The conversation stopped abruptly as the door banged open. DS Withers was still displaying his poker face, but Jerry thought there was something different about him...a confident swagger. The constable stood, giving priority to rank.

'You're a dark horse, son, I'll give you that,' said the DS, taking the seat opposite Jerry. 'And before you protest, I'm not referring to the colour of your skin. I just never thought you capable.'

'What you on about, man?' Jerry stuttered slightly, a hint of uncertainty creeping into his voice. 'Capable of what?'

The senior detective read some papers in front of him. It was all part of the act. Make the accused sweat. At last, he delivered the words deadpan. 'Are you Jeremiah Sanka Oyawale of Dean Street, Soho?'

'You know I am,' said Jerry.

'Answer yes or no.'

'Yes.'

'Jeremiah Sanka Oyawale, you are not obliged to say anything unless you wish to do so, but what you do say may be put into writing and given in evidence. Do you understand?'

'What's this? I tol' you, I never nicked those things.'

'Mr Oyawale, please could you to tell me where you were on the morning of Monday, February 21, 1971?'

'February? This is July, man...How am I supposed to remember that? I don't even recall what I had for breakfast yesterday, dig?'

'Well, perhaps it's slipped your mind, Mr Oyawale, but there are people who won't forget that day in a hurry. I'm talking about the family of Gladys Matthews, or Grandma, as some heartbroken kids knew her. She was the woman who collapsed and died during an armed robbery at the Sperlings Bank in High Street, Walthamstow, where she'd turned up to deposit her pension in a savings account.'

'Hey, hang on...what's this shit? Robbery? Nah. What have I—'

'Shut up!' Withers slammed his fist down on the table, forcing Jerry to jump back. A moment's silence followed. 'You need to listen very carefully, Jeremiah son, because you are in a whole heap of trouble. Our forensic team has been all over that bag of yours and tell me...'

'It's not—'

'...That not only are your fingerprints all over it, but there's this...'

He produced the lighter again and having taken little notice when it was emptied from the bag, Jerry now took a closer look.

Damn. Big Ben.

He'd seen it before.

'Well...yeah, I had a lighter like that, but I lost it ages ago. Hang on, what trick is this? It may have been in that bag, but that ain't my bag. This is a fit up! I want a solicitor.' Jerry's voice was injected with fear.

'...And I want answers,' said Withers. 'It will take at least 10 minutes for a solicitor to get here and in the meantime, I'm quite within my rights to interview you because I consider any delay would hamper my investigation. Now answer my questions, Mr Oyawale, and I'll see if we can find you a brief this late on a Sunday night.'

'That's wrong man, I need—'

'There's not only rice in that bag, which we are informed was used to replace the explosive charge in the shotgun cartridges, but the serial number of a bank note found inside matches one of those stolen in the raid,' said DS Withers. 'For this reason, Jeremiah Sanka Oyawale, I am charging you with…'Jerry felt himself go cold. He began to stutter, unable to protest his innocence, his breath catching in his throat as his airwaves constricted.

'Burns, get the prisoner a glass of water, would you?'

Before the constable could move, Jerry collapsed forward, banging his head hard on the desk and falling to the floor, his legs kicking out of control as froth appeared at the corners of his mouth. DC Burns held back at first, thinking it was some kind of ploy. Then he looked into the bulging eyes and realised he was wrong. Jeremiah Sanka Oyawale was in the middle of a full-blown seizure.

21

RED HAD BEEN shut away in a small room for almost two hours without anyone coming to speak to her. She feared that at any moment her stepfather would turn up to negotiate her release before dragging her back to Wales. That would be disastrous after the good progress she'd made in recent weeks.

She was tired and achy, her legs and elbow badly bruised from the one-sided dispute with the copper's truncheon. After she and Jerry had been overpowered, they'd been taken from the Tube, then marched up an escalator and bundled into the back of a van. On the relatively short journey at breakneck speeds through London streets, they'd been subjected to occasional short bursts of carefully targeted violence. Finally, they'd arrived at an unfamiliar police station where they were ushered through the back entrance and questioned by a custody sergeant before being separated, Jerry going one way and she the other. She hoped he was OK. The police had reserved most of their vitriol and savagery for him.

She was just about ready to settle in for the night when she heard noises – footsteps running here and there while people shouted at each other. Banging on the door, she demanded to know what was happening. *Was there a fire?* She didn't want anyone to forget they'd locked her in here. Just as she was starting to despair, a key rattled, and the door squeaked open.

'What's happening?' she asked.

'You're getting out of here, that's what,' said the policewoman, standing in the doorway.

'I'm free to go?' She was confused.

'Appears so,' said the WPC. 'Ten to one, the blokes who bought you in can't be arsed with the paperwork. They weren't after you, anyway. You just got in the way. Gosh, you have been in the wars. I suggest you put some ice on those injuries when you get home.'

'Have you seen my handbag?'

'I'll check with the desk sergeant. I wasn't here when you arrived.'

'It was a small, red bag, you know, not much bigger than a purse. There was a note inside and all my money—'

'OK, well, we have to sign you out anyway, so come this way.'

'Where are we exactly?'

'Marylebone Police Station, love. You were brought here from Tottenham Court Road Underground.'

'How do I get home?'

‘Not my problem, I’m afraid. If you have some money, you could jump on the Tube again, you might catch the last one. Where are you heading?’

‘Leicester Square.’

‘Well, if you miss the Tube, it’s a bit of a walk. Perhaps get a taxi.’

‘What about my friend?’

The policewoman looked at her and Red sensed her unease. ‘Forget him, love. Between you and me, he’s going to be spending some time with us.’

‘Why? We went to a protest march, that’s all!’

‘I’ve said enough,’ replied the policewoman. ‘Serious crimes would tear a strip off me. Now, head out the door and keep walking. You seem a bright young woman. Some in here are just seeking an excuse to add to their arrest records.’

Red did as she was told. The officer on the desk said no bag had been handed in at the time of her arrest, but at least she got back her bracelet. Once out on the pavement, she looked from one direction to the other, trying to identify a familiar landmark. Normally, she would follow Jerry around like an eager puppy, taking scant notice of her surroundings.

Poor Jerry.

She felt she was abandoning him, just as his father had done. What was the alternative, though? She had no idea when he would be released and could have been waiting around all night. Only one person would know what to do in these circumstances: Woodsy. She needed to contact him fast.

Red knew Oxford Street wasn't too far from Soho, so when a London bus passed with the name of the famous shopping thoroughfare on the front it seemed logical to head in the same direction. Falling into a steady pace, she saw a large department store called Selfridge's and crossed the road, pausing briefly to admire the window display. Mannequins dressed in the latest fashions had her dreaming of one day being able to afford such luxury clothing. For months she'd relied on Blaize's generosity, suspecting some of the other girls were calling her a tramp behind her back because of her limited wardrobe.

What time was it? There was plenty of traffic about and late-night revellers passed her at regular intervals, some of them giving her strange looks when they caught sight of her bumps and bruises. They probably assumed she was a street dweller, high on drink or drugs.

Distracted by her thoughts, she almost missed Duke Street, at the last moment turning back when the road sign sparked a glimmer of recognition. She was pretty sure she'd been here before and that it wasn't too far from her current 'home'. Believing she'd hit upon a shortcut back to Soho, she turned off the main road and into the quieter street, the noisy chatter of some passing tourists disguising the sound of heavy boots settling into a steady rhythm behind her.

THE STREETLIGHTS BECAME more sporadic the farther Red got from the main road. It was quieter, too, and she felt suddenly exposed, an icy chill running through her as if someone had trampled across her grave. She couldn't explain her anxiety and it crossed her mind to turn back, but she took a deep breath and quickened her step, focusing on the brighter lights at another busy traffic intersection a few hundred yards ahead.

Suddenly, she registered the second set of footsteps, out of sync with hers but approaching rapidly from behind. For a crazy moment, she thought it was the police arriving to re-arrest her having realised they'd made a mistake letting her go. Spinning on her heels, she wasn't quick enough to avoid the heavy weapon, its dull thud echoing off the high walls as it struck her on the temple. A large, gloved hand grabbed her upper arm to prevent her falling while the other snaked out to mute any screams. Even though she felt woozy and disorientated, her survival instinct kicked in and she tried to dig her feet into the ground. Her attacker was strong and motivated, though, and dragged her backwards into darkness.

Red tried to commit things to memory. There was a smell of leather mixed with a strong, musky scent, woody like cedar, the aftershave providing her with the first indication her attacker was male. The man was so confident in his movements that she suspected it wasn't the first time he'd attacked someone in this manner. Some of the girls around the clubs had regaled her with stories of sexual predators cruising London's streets looking for women on their own, and slowly it dawned on her she was going to be raped. How could this happen in the centre of one of the busiest capitals in the world, just yards away from bright, tourist-laden thoroughfares and a busy police station?

Her attacker pressed his weight down on her shoulders and she collapsed to the ground. Instantly, she was aware of loose stones digging into her shoulders and buttocks. As he straddled her, his well-built torso cut out the light. All she could see were dark, malevolent eyes studying her through slits roughly cut from the balaclava covering his face. His thighs squeezed into the bones of her hips like metal clamps, making her gasp as the pain kicked in. With his face inches from hers, she recognised the familiar, unpleasant odour of stale alcohol on his breath, which brought swift flashbacks from home which she found hard to eject from her mind.

She tried to turn her face away, but he mirrored her movements, his cold stare devoid of any trace of humanity. The sound of material ripping was followed by an icy blast of night air, and she wondered if this was her punishment for not wearing a bra that day. With one glove still clamped to her mouth, she felt daggers of discomfort rip through her as his other hand probed and pinched with all the callous disregard of a clumsy doctor. A flicker of excitement flashed across his eyes as he sensed her fear, and the attacker shifted his weight with the intention of loosening his trousers and taking advantage of her unease.

Big mistake.

Red had been waiting for just such an opportunity and didn't hesitate, raising her knee into the soft tissue of his groin and forcing him to overbalance. 'Bitch!' he squeaked, the first words escaping his mouth in a strangled cry as he tried to reassert control, his hand releasing her mouth to hold down her arms.

'You're gonna get much worse for that.'

Did she know the voice? She couldn't be sure. As she tried to analyse it, her attention was stolen away by another excruciating jolt of pain as sharp, feral teeth penetrated her tender flesh. Then, from nowhere, two bright lights pierced the darkness, the spotlight falling on the bodies writhing on the ground. There followed the sounds of tyres screeching across gravel, then skidding to a halt before a door banged open.

'Hey! What the sweet Jesus do ye think yer doing?' The voice echoed off the surrounding walls and within seconds, she was free. Pushing herself into a sitting position, she covered her exposed flesh with her arms and peered in the direction of the lights, watching her attacker barrel his way past the new arrival, who fell back against the side of his van. From the passenger side, a young man climbed out and walked around to join the prone figure.

'You OK, Dad?' he asked.

The man nodded. 'No bother, son. Fackin' perv was in a hurry, that's for sure.' He looked over to Red. 'You all right there, girl?' he asked. 'I'm Paddy and this here's my boy, Stanley. I'm guessing you're a bit shook up right now. Come see us when you're ready. Yer safe now.'

Red recognised his Irish brogue. He spoke like several punters she'd encountered in the Soho clubs. 'I'm f…fine,' she said, her mind a blur.

'Stanley, yon Colleen there could do with a blanket. Fetch one from the back of the van, would ye?' He looked over again at Red. 'Your parents will be worried sick, love. Tell us where you live, and we'll drop ye home. We were only here to pick up stock for the market from that warehouse.' He pointed at one of the buildings. 'Lucky for you, it seems.'

Suddenly, she felt a panic setting in and studied her wrist. 'My bracelet,' she said, 'it's gone. It's got sentimental value.'

'Bastard,' muttered Paddy. Then he brightened up. 'Hey, it's just occurred to me. Marylebone nick is around the corner. We should report it. He might not have got that far—'

'No!'

The older man flinched, shocked by the panic in her voice. 'Entirely your choice,' he said, turning to his son. 'What are you waiting for, boy? This young lady will catch her death while you're mooning around. Now, get that blanket and I'll stick the van's heating on. We need to get her home.'

Five minutes later the three of them were squeezed into the front bench seat of the van, winding their way through the streets. Mam had always told her never to accept lifts from strangers, but Red figured she would have to be damn unlucky to bump into two sexual deviants in one night. Anyway, the driver was getting on a bit and looked harmless. He introduced himself as Patrick Marshall and said he'd arrived in England from Ireland in the 50s. He met his wife Celia at a dance hall in Bow and two years later they'd married with their only son Stanley coming along soon afterwards. Over the years, he'd established a market stall in Walthamstow and it was when they'd turned up to the warehouse to restock for Monday morning that they'd come across the attack on Red.

'That bastard made a right mess of that pretty face,' he said.

The young lad with black curly hair and chocolate brown eyes was perched between them on the bench seat and she noticed a flicker of a smile playing around his mouth.

'You're beautiful,' he said, seeming not to register all her bumps and bruises. 'I like the colour of your hair.'

She was used to Jack's boys handing out compliments like sweets, but they never sounded as sincere as this young man. She thought him pretty good looking, too, though he was two years younger than her. Her thoughts immediately switched to her younger brother at home. They would be roughly the same age.

'Don't fret about him,' said Paddy. 'He fancies himself a bit of a ladies' man and has got the hots for ye, I wouldn't wonder.'

'He's very sweet,' she said.

There was something about the grin Stanley gave her that made her feel warm and just a little bit tingly.

22

RED STOOD BACK and admired the imposing Edwardian Baroque building. Its intricate carvings and statues loomed ominously above her in the shadow of the morning sun. She'd seen it on TV before, but up close it appeared far grander, particularly with the 12ft gold statue on top, glinting in the sunlight.

'Ahhh, Lady Justice.' Woodsy appeared at her shoulder. 'She stands with her arms out like that to appear perfectly balanced, the left hand holding scales and the right a sword. She stands on a globe to signal justice straddles the world. Who better to say, "Welcome to the Old Bailey"?'

His eyes focused on hers as he played with the cuffs on his trademark silver jacket.

'How are you holding up?' he said.

She shrugged. 'I just want to make sure he's OK.'

'He's been in a cell for three months,' said the solicitor. 'No one's going to be a bundle of joy in those circumstances.'

People milled around them, holding separate nervous conversations. Occasionally, a group would split off and pass through the door beneath a stone sign informing them they were entering the Central Criminal Courts.

'You'll have to prepare yourself for the worst, Red,' said Woodsy. 'I've discussed it with his brief and the evidence sounds damning. His fingerprints are all over the bag used to move the loot and they've recovered a bank note which has been traced to Sperlings through the serial numbers. On top of all that, there's a lighter with his fingerprints all over it, and those same fingerprints were found on a transistor radio in the van used for the escape.'

Blaize and Kat ran up to join them, dressed in designer clothes more in keeping with dinner at the Dorchester or a day at the races. Their excited greetings suggested they hadn't seen each other in weeks, when the truth was they'd been together just the previous night mulling over what the day would bring. Red wriggled away from their hugs and turned her attention back to Woodsy, the anger bubbling inside.

'It's ridiculous!' she said. 'You know Jerry wouldn't be involved in anything like this. Those racist pigs planted the stuff on him.'

'Do you know where Jerry was on the morning of the robbery?' Woodsy looked stern. 'None of you do, which is why he doesn't have a bloody alibi.'

'He was still recovering from that beating he got from the cops when the robbery took place,' said Red. 'He was in no condition to...'

'Rob a bank?' Woodsy finished her sentence. 'How do you prove that? Were you there when he was beaten up by the cops?'

'Well, no, but—'

'Exactly!' said Woodsy. 'We only have his word for that, too. We saw the cuts and bruises, sure, but proving what happened without eyewitnesses is impossible and, in my experience, making allegations against the police causes more harm than good. The judges think the boys in blue are above reproach. Smearing them tends to backfire. He could end up with a bigger sentence if the judge believes he lied under oath.'

'Can't I testify on his behalf?' said Red. 'I was there when he was arrested and can still feel their kicks in my bloody ribs, mun. I know what they said. They had it in for him before any of this evidence miraculously appeared.'

'You're thirteen...'

'No,' she said. 'I was fourteen a few months ago.'

'Sure, so shall I get in touch with your parents? You need a responsible adult to give their permission.'

'Blaize could vouch for me.' She looked hopefully at the woman with the extravagant bouffant hairstyle, only for her boss to refuse to meet her eye.

'How would that look?' said Woodsy. 'Soho strip club owner is character witness to 13, sorry, 14-year-old runaway.'

'What about me?' said Kat, jumping in to spare Red's blushes. 'I don't know the full story, but there are far more credible candidates than Jerry when it comes to robbing banks. It's not in his nature. I know the police are looking in the wrong place.'

'You know?' Red's raised eyebrows invited her friend to continue.

'She knows nothing!' Woodsy seemed keen to shut down the conversation.

'But surely, if Kat's got vital information—'

'Kat's put two and two together and come up with five,' said Woodsy, raising his voice in anger. 'She's been listening to Soho tittle tattle, I expect. Hell, most of the people we bump into will say anything to relieve someone of their dosh. The last thing we need is another one of our guys being put in the frame by idle gossip and rumour. We're a family, as Jack always says. This conversation stops now.'

Kat's mouth was hanging open, but she closed it in response to Woodsy's glare. He was silent for a moment and when he eventually spoke, he sounded calmer.

'Listen,' he said to Red. 'You're upset. Jerry's your friend, I get that, and I know things haven't gone well for him in the past. But you can't just throw allegations around. You were confused, remember? You were arrested and manhandled on a train, cuffed and taken to a police station where you were kept for hours. Then when you were released, some sicko attacked you. All that can play on your mind. Let's face it, how well do any of us really know Jerry? Even you. How long have you been here – six months? He's been in trouble before, you know.'

'It's true,' said Blaize. She gave Red's arm a gentle squeeze. 'We all love Jerry, but Woodsy's had to get him out of plenty of scrapes in the past. Fights, nicking stuff, you name it...and if Woodsy tells us the evidence is stacked against the boy, then, I'm sorry, but it's difficult for us to argue.'

Woodsy looked at the expensive gold watch on his wrist. 'Time's getting on,' he said. 'We'd better go in. He's in court four – Judge Stringer. That's not good either. They call him Judge String 'em up.'

'I NEED ANOTHER pee,' said Red. 'It's my nerves.'

'Go now before it starts,' said Blaize. 'I'll keep your seat.' The club owner stood and shuffled out of the wooden pew so that Red could squeeze past. 'The loos are just outside and to your left. Don't worry, you won't miss anything. I've been to trials like this before. The barristers say their piece then call witnesses and eventually Jerry gets a chance to give his side of the story. It could go on for a couple of days.'

Red left through the public gallery exit and emerged into the corridor, her stomach doing somersaults as she passed benches full of people waiting to be called for their moment in court, oblivious to their magnificent surroundings. With its stained-glass windows and high-vaulted ceilings, they could have been inside a cathedral rather than a building in which judgment had once been passed on Britain's most notorious criminals.

Woodsy, keen to keep Red's mind off Jerry's situation, had taken great pleasure in describing some of the high-profile cases that had taken place in the notorious No.1 Court. There was the American doctor Hawley Harvey Crippen, who stood trial in the early part of the 20th century for poisoning and dismembering his wife, not to mention John Christie, the serial killer who hid the bodies of eight women at his home in Rillington Place, Notting Hill. Both had received the death penalty. More recently, Woodsy had helped in the defence of Ronnie and Reggie Kray though his work had been in vain with the gangster twins sentenced to long prison terms. What was lovely, gentle Jerry doing in that sort of company?

Red pushed through the door into the ladies and absent-mindedly entered a cubicle, her brain playing the night of Jerry's arrest over and over on a loop. She wished she'd been able to visit him, but Blaize and Jack had strictly forbidden it, fearing some do-gooder would start asking questions about her and inform social services. Reluctantly, she'd accepted a compromise and wrote a letter to him in Pentonville Prison, where he was on remand. She had no idea if her friend had read or even received it because no reply had been forthcoming.

Exiting the toilets, she was greeted by raised voices and was astonished to see the doors to Court Four burst open and people pour out. How could it be over already? Red knew she'd been daydreaming, but a look at the clock on the wall told her she'd been gone barely five minutes. Perhaps there had been a bomb scare. The Irish Republic Army had threatened to attack, and she imagined the Old Bailey was a legitimate target.

'What happened?' she asked, running to fall in step with Kat as her friend emerged.

'It was mental!' she said. 'I don't understand.'

Woodsy emerged with Blaize and immediately grabbed Red by the elbow, shepherding her away from the other human traffic. His usually unflappable demeanour had completely deserted him, replaced by an expression conveying both shock and concern.

'What on earth got into him?' said the solicitor.

'Who?' she said.

'Jerry,' said Woodsy. 'He tried to attack the judge! One minute he seemed normal, a bit tired and he'd lost some weight, but that's to be expected. Then the clerk asked everyone to rise, and Judge Stringer took his seat behind the bench. That was when your friend lost the plot. He bombarded the judge with a mouthful of insults and tried to climb out of the dock. Stringer looked genuinely perturbed. Thankfully, a couple of officers restrained Jerry for long enough to get the judge back to the safety of his chambers. Police and court officials then hustled Jerry out of the dock and down to the cells. He'll face contempt charges now and God knows what. He's been a silly, silly boy. None of this can do him any good.'

'Is he OK?'

'The judge? Just a bit shaken—'

'Not him, you daft lemon...Jerry!'

'I honestly don't know,' said Woodsy. 'By the look in his eyes he's gone completely insane. Maybe none of us know him as well as we thought we did.'

'Sorry to butt in,' said Blaize, appearing at Red's shoulder. 'I've got to go. I suspect you will need a rest, too, before you perform tonight, Kat.'

It was said in a friendly manner, but they all knew it was an order rather than a request. The boss wanted her back in Soho. 'I feel bad leaving you like this,' said Kat, giving Red a hug. 'I can see you're upset and...'

'You go,' said Red. 'I'll be fine. I'll wait with Woodsy and see what he can find out, like. He'll drop me off later.'

'Don't rush back,' said Blaize. 'Take the evening off. You've had enough trauma today.' She leant forward and planted a kiss on Red's cheek, then took a handkerchief from her pocket, spat on it and wiped away the lipstick imprint she'd left behind. The action reminded the Welsh girl of her mother – it was the way Mam reacted when she returned home dirty after playing outside or people were coming to visit. After watching her friends disappear down the staircase, she turned back to see Woodsy walking towards her after holding a brief conversation with one of the court ushers.

'What's happened?' she asked.

'They're holding Jerry in the cells and waiting for a van. The bloke said he was like a man possessed.'

'Well, if there's anything wrong with him it's because of those bastards.' She nodded in the direction of a group of men in suits holding a whispered conversation in the corner. They all had neatly cropped hair, and she recognised a couple of them from the incident on the underground.

'SPG,' said Woodsy.

'What's that?'

'Special Patrol Group. If the cops think a protest might get out of control, they call in those thugs to restore order.'

'They were the ones who arrested us!' said Red.

'Were the Black Panthers at the protest you went to?'

'Jerry said so, yes.'

'That would have been enough to alert the SPG's interest.'

As they watched, another figure sauntered over to speak to the men. He was imposing, tall and hefty, with a shirt straining to keep his large belly contained. 'Interesting,' said Woodsy.

'Who's that?'

'The head of the Flying Squad, Gordon Fogarty. He's always giving Jack grief over his clubs. Bent as a butcher's hook. I'm not sure what business he has with those boys, but I'd bet the Jag it's something iffy.'

From outside came a dim wail of sirens. Neither of them flinched, imagining that a guarded vehicle was in a hurry, probably carrying a big-name criminal to Court One for trial.

'I want to speak to him,' said Red.

'Fogarty?'

'No, of course not!' said Red. 'Jerry. I'm sure he'd tell me why he lost it in court. He won't talk to any of them fancy court people, but we've been through a lot together.'

Woodsy shrugged. 'I very much doubt they will change their regulations for that.' He paused. 'Maybe I can grease the wheels a bit, though. If I speak to the right people, perhaps I could take you in with me. Let's go. Presumably he's on his way back to Pentonville by now. Might as well try our luck. What have we got to lose?'

JERRY FELT THE walls closing in. He was sitting in a small cubicle in the paddy wagon, the gate secure in front of him. He wasn't good with confined spaces and had lost it on a couple of occasions in custody, his pleas for help only bringing laughter and more beatings from those who had been entrusted with his care. Now he had new aches and pains to add to his previous injuries after a couple of heavy-handed police officers had laid into him following the incident with that bastard judge.

'You can't do that sort of thing in this country, Sambo,' one had snarled. 'They might accept it in bongo-bongo land, but we're civilised over here.'

He wanted to laugh at the irony. He had the bruises to prove exactly how 'civilised' the British police force was.

Nothing had prepared him for what he'd seen that day. He'd been looking forward to clearing his name with the help of an experienced and bright legal team, which Jack assured him was the best money could buy. The people judging him were 12 of his peers and he trusted those ordinary people to dig through the lies and uncover the truth.

While on remand he'd been visited by a woman and her male companion who told him his case was not unique. They represented a group called Release and were intent on getting fair trials for those they suspected had been 'fitted up' by the police. The woman, Jackie, felt he had a strong case, and they would search for evidence to exonerate him.

That morning, he'd been briefed about court procedures and was pretty sure he knew exactly what to expect. His heart had leapt at the sight of Kat and Blaize in the public gallery and he even received a smile and wink from the solicitor Woodsy, sitting at a bench behind the barristers in their wigs and gowns. The one face he wished to see though wasn't there. He'd been sure his friend Red would turn up, even though she hadn't visited him in prison. Having seen her take quite a beating herself, he hoped she was all right.

'Court 4 is now in session, His Honour Justice Judge R Stringer presiding'.

Jerry had looked straight ahead, feeling hot and uncomfortable in the ill-fitting suit and noose-like tie Jack had loaned him. He involuntarily lifted his hand to fit a finger between the shirt collar and his chafed neck, stretching it to find some minor relief. It was when he returned his eyes to the court bench that his brain froze in horror and sweat started pouring down his forehead. Inside, his bowels twisted and turned in fear. The man sitting in front of him might have been wearing a wig, but his face was etched vividly on Jerry's memory.

'No...no,' he stuttered, falling forward. It was as if he was trapped in a straitjacket, helpless to move. This couldn't be happening. At any moment, he expected to wake from his nightmare and find himself back in his remand cell. Shutting his eyes, he willed it to happen, but when he peered out again, nothing had changed.

After that, he'd completely lost it, and now everything was a blur. He remembered he'd tried to climb from the dock only for a mass of bodies to jump on him, poking and grabbing and pushing and punching. The last words he heard were those of the figure who had elicited such a combustible reaction from deep within him. 'We will adjourn until another day when the accused has learnt to show some restraint. Take him down!'

Jerry was still cuffed when the prison van sped away through the London streets, heading for the Holloway Road and Pentonville two-and-a-half miles away. It meant he was unable to loosen his tie and he could hear his breath coming in intermittent bursts, punctuated by wheezing gasps.

'What's the matter with him?' a voice said from outside the cage.

'Withdrawal symptoms,' said another. 'Fuckin' nigger junkie.'

The words faded in and out of Jerry's mind as he battled to cling on to consciousness. The walls of the van were throbbing, his surroundings spinning like those shapes in a kid's kaleidoscope when you twisted its base. Lurching forward, he grabbed for the bars, shouting, 'Help! Let me...out...can't breathe—'

'Fuck off, Rasta,' said the older of the two guards.

'Oh fuck,' said the other, lurching forward.

'Don't you dare...'

Too late. A stream of bile and puke shot from Jerry's mouth as if some neighbourhood washerwoman had dumped filthy green water from an upstairs window onto the two prison officers.

'You fackin' dirty cunt!' shouted the older guard, charging forward and unlocking the gate on the cage. Jerry fell through the door, wobbling on unsteady legs, his hands grasping for anything which might help steady him. The younger officer lurched out of the way, sticking out a careless foot to send his prisoner crashing forward into the side of the van. He rebounded back, eyes wide with shock, before slithering to the floor and coming to rest in his own vomit.

His humiliation didn't end there, though. Suddenly the two men were upon him, turning him over and raining down blows. One of them put a hand over his mouth and began spitting threats in his face, but by that time he was too far gone to understand. A heavy punch connected with his temple, and he zoned out, the blackness swooping in and taking him, transporting him somewhere else, somewhere quieter and more peaceful...and empty. Submitting to the inevitable, he flopped back and let it all go.

RED'S BEST-LAID plans hit the buffers before they got to the prison. Woodsy had to bring the Jag to a standstill with the traffic nose-to-tail on the Caledonian Road. Sirens filled the Islington air, the high-pitched two-tone squeal of a rushing ambulance followed by the nee-naw, nee-naw of two police cars. Spinning blue lights reflected from the windows of nearby shops to leave no one in any doubt that someone, somewhere, was in trouble.

'Must be a bad accident,' said Woodsy. 'Shit! I'm supposed to be visiting clients this afternoon and I'm back in court at 3.30.'

'What do we do?' asked Red.

'Hang on!' When the traffic edged forward, he swung the car into a narrow side street and pulled to a halt next to some large bins piled high with used packaging from the shops. 'Wait here. I'm going to have a chat with a few people, then I'll let you know what's going on. All being well, you'll be able to ask your friend why he went all Robert Mitchum in court this morning.'

'Robert, who?'

'Robert Mitchum. Don't tell me you've not heard of him. *Cape Fear?* It's this film where a guy has a personal grievance against the judge who sent him down. Mitchum plays the lead. He's a famous actor.'

'My stepfather wouldn't let me watch that sort of thing,' said Red. 'He said I was too young.'

'I forget you're thirteen sometimes.'

'I told you. I'm fourteen!' She felt her temper rising again.

'Sorry. To be honest, you do look older than you are, what with the clothes you wear and the company you keep.'

'Thanks, I think. Anyway, Jerry's nothing like that bloke in the film. He's not the vengeful type at all, he just sticks up for those who can't defend themselves. If he thinks this judge has done somethin' wrong, you can bet the arsehole's done somethin' wrong.'

Woodsy sniggered. 'You could be a lawyer,' he said. 'You make a good case.' He climbed out, closed the door, patted the window as a farewell gesture, and headed off in the direction of the large stone edifice that was Pentonville Prison. She watched him go, then wondered what she could do to take her mind off the gnawing anxiety creeping through her body.

Taking a quick inventory of the car – the plush red leather upholstery, the shiny handles and window frames, the walnut dashboard – she spotted the radio and was grateful that Woodsy had left the key in the ignition. When she turned it, lights flared on the dash. Leaning forward, she carefully twisted the radio knob and sound burst from the speakers. It was the kind of classical music her stepfather loved, which meant it was something Red detested. She lurched forward and adjusted the dial until the sound of a well-known DJ's voice filled the airways.

'Now, here's a song flying high in the charts to tickle your delectables,' he said. 'It's Greyhound, and it's "Black and White".'

The tune was familiar, and she recalled singing along to it with Jerry in her bedroom when it was on *Top of the Pops*. It was a happy memory, so she turned up the volume. Her favourite style of music might be hardcore rhythm and blues or heavy metal, but this sort of music relaxed her, helping to ease the tension from her shoulders. Leaning back, she let the gentle introduction of the clarinet wash over her, shutting her eyes as the strings of a harp joined in to add to the overall effect. Then, from nowhere, a chugging reggae beat was added before the singer joined in.

Remembering the words, Red whispered them to herself, forgetting for the moment the sirens and traffic mayhem all around. They were beautiful, a lament about how black and white kids could learn together to read and write, and what a wonderful sight that was.

Before she knew it, tears were rolling down her cheeks, joyful images swimming around her brain of good times with Jerry. She might have known him for less than six months, but their bond was strong, living proof that people from different backgrounds could embrace each other's unique qualities and overcome petty prejudice. In fact, digging deeper, they were on identical wavelengths, sharing a mirror image sense of humour and moral compass. They also could empathise with each other over unhappy childhood memories.

That fateful night on the Tube had been an eye opener. In one fell swoop, they'd gone from dancing in the street with like-minded people to experiencing at first hand the destructive nature of certain elements in a so-called civilised society. From the moment the police officers waded in, the lies she'd been sold in her childhood about a fair and just world were laid bare. It was OK for these singers to serenade her about Black and White being in perfect accord, but the reality was altogether different.

When the song finished, she turned off the radio, sat back and shut her eyes, thinking deeply about the lessons she'd learnt since moving to England's capital city. In many ways she wished she could unlearn them, return to Wales and slip comfortably into her old world, but she knew the genie would never fit back into the bottle.

It seemed she'd been wallowing in her thoughts for hours, seeking different solutions to the many problems rolling around in her head, when the driver's door opened and Woodsy slumped back into the car. She looked at him and immediately knew something was wrong. His face was bleached of colour, as if he was sick.

'What is it?' she said.

When he turned to face her, Red realised the solicitor was in shock.

'I'm so very, very sorry.' He reached out and held her hands in his.

'What?' she said. 'What do you mean? I'm guessing they said "no" did they?'

He was silent again, a vague shake of the head the only impression she had that she'd been correct. She'd been half expecting the answer anyway...

'It's OK, Woodsy man,' she said. 'I understand.'

'No, you don't, Red,' he said. 'You really, really don't. And neither do I. It's Jerry...He's dead.'

23

'WELL DONE, MY lovely, lots of happy punters tonight,' said Blaize as Kat walked out of the dressing room at the Glamour Puss.

'Thanks,' said Kat. 'Any news of Red? I thought she'd be 'ere tonight.'

'I've not seen her,' said Blaize. She wasn't ready yet to tell one of her top dancers the sickening news about Jerry. Woodsy had only divulged it to her a couple of hours ago, and the nightclub owner needed to think about how the whole Soho dynamic might be affected. They were a tight-knit group and if one got hurt, they all suffered. She wanted to spare Kat that pain, particularly in view of how radiant she looked. She obviously had a special night planned.

'Who's the lucky fella, then?' she said, changing the subject.

'Oh, no one, just...'

'Well, you don't have to tell me, but I thought we were mates.' Blaize liked to tease her girls with emotional blackmail. 'He must be a bit special to deserve that tonight, anyway.' She looked Kat up and down approvingly.

'Bloody 'ell you make it sound like I don't always make the effort, boss!'

'For the punters, yeah, but you tend to prefer jeans and a T-shirt after the show's over. Yep, this bloke must be special. Got money, has he?'

'It ain't all about money, you know.'

'Isn't it? Silly me,' said Blaize. 'And there was I, thinking it made the world go around. Look at me and Jack. It cushions you when everything else turns to shit.'

'Well, I guess this bloke ain't doing too bad as it happens,' said Kat.

'Good. Well, don't let me hold you up. Off you go and have a nice night...and don't do anything I wouldn't do.'

'That gives me plenty of scope, then.' Kat pushed herself off from the wall and walked down the corridor towards the back exit, her expensive new heels click-clacking into the distance.

KAT LIKED A stroll to freshen herself up after spending the entire night inside a smoky club. It enabled her to get her thoughts straight and switch back to her real persona, having dressed up as a variety of different characters to please the punters. She guessed it was like being an actor really, without having to deliver any words. She lit a cigarette and strolled through the bright lights of Chinatown on her way to the rendezvous with her new man on the Embankment. There were plenty of people around and she was quite happy to walk among them on her own.

Unlike her young friend Red, Kat was streetwise and knew not to stray from the beaten path. She passed through Leicester Square and on to Trafalgar before cutting across to the Strand, witnessing the punters racing to make their last trains from Charing Cross. She wouldn't need the Tube tonight. He told her he was picking her up in his brand-new car.

Leaving the main thoroughfare, she cut down Villiers Street and, feeling the anticipation building, she dropped her cigarette in the gutter as she approached the rendezvous. Turning right at Embankment station, she walked on, the Thames sparkling under the lights from the nearby bridges, unaware of the car tracking her until it drew up beside her and a man wound down the window and asked for directions. The noise of the other traffic made him difficult to hear, though, and she was unable to make out his features because of the large-brimmed hat pulled down over his face. Moving closer, she bent over and was taken completely by surprise when the door opened sharply and knocked her to the floor.

When the man in the hat leant down, she thought he was going to help her up. Instead, he clamped his hand over her mouth and she was overcome by a powerful smell which made her feel dizzy and lightheaded.

By the time she realised what was happening, it was too late.

A RETIRED COUPLE walking their border collie beside

the River Thames west of Hammersmith Bridge found the naked body early on Sunday morning. The police arrived promptly, roping off the area and calling in the forensic team. At first there was a suggestion the victim had been skinny dipping after a night out and got into trouble. That theory was laughed off though – no one in their right mind swam in the Thames. The medical examiner said marks on the neck were consistent with strangulation.

Gordon Fogarty, head of the Metropolitan Police Flying Squad, arrived on the scene to announce, 'He's back.'

The more grizzled veterans on the investigation nodded knowingly.

'Jack the Stripper,' Fogarty told the team. 'Bastard gave us the run-around for two years in the 60s then...nothing. We thought he'd gone abroad or was doing a stretch inside for another offence. The last one he bumped off was in February 1965 – Irish girl, name of O'Hara. Her body was discovered in a storage shed in Acton and we sussed she was one of his because of the industrial paint marks found underneath the body. It was the same paint found on six other victims. We reckon he kills them and stores them somewhere until the coast is clear, then dumps 'em.'

'It's a long time between the two deaths, isn't it?' said one of the other detectives.

'Like I say, he might have been inside for something else and now he's out on our streets again,' said Foggy. 'Hammersmith and Chiswick were chummy's favourite dumping grounds. Pound to a penny she's a hooker. Start making inquiries around the Soho area...see if she attended any *private parties*. If anyone can identify the victim, they'll be working there.'

A few days later, the squad had a name. Kathleen Juliet Rose had been an exotic dancer at several Soho night spots, including the Glamour Puss. The victim was known to the police, having been pulled in on a couple of occasions under suspicion of soliciting in a public place for the purpose of prostitution. She'd never been charged though, and further inquiries revealed there was a lack of evidence in both cases.

Murder detectives found plenty of resistance to their inquiries. Soho workers knew that providing help to the rozzers could result in them being thrown onto the streets. The people who owned businesses there – both legal and illegal – ran a tight ship and didn't need the extra publicity a murder hunt generated.

RED PEERED THROUGH the grime London had deposited on her small bedsit window, her mind as morbidly grey as the bricks of the tenements opposite. She felt so alone. In a matter of days, her two closest friends in London had been stolen from her.

Jerry's inquest had returned a verdict of natural causes. A forensic pathologist regularly recruited to investigate deaths in custody told the jury that the teenager had suffered an epileptic fit and choked on his own vomit. Despite the concerted efforts of those travelling in the prison van with him, he was dead by the time they reached Pentonville. What had caused the fit in the first place was undetermined, though there were rumours he'd ingested a large quantity of illegal drugs. A search of Jerry's cell uncovered a small bottle of pills, which would have produced the desired effect.

Red was dubious about the whole process. She'd never seen Jerry consume anything stronger than cannabis and had been witness to his treatment at the hands of the police. She was still confused over his attempt to assault a High Court judge, but guessed she might never get answers to her questions.

Jerry's loss had hit Blaize's team hard. The club owner had said she would pay for a burial plot in a small, peaceful area of Highgate Cemetery so that Red and his other friends could visit any time to pay their respects. The pain of his death had barely subsided when Kat's body was officially identified three days after her brutal murder and knocked them all sideways.

The evening before Kat's disappearance, Red had helped her friend pick out an outfit for a 'Hot Date' she'd arranged after the show. Now the youngster wished Kat had trusted her enough to reveal the name of her mystery suitor. There was every chance that man was her killer. For the first time since arriving in the smoke, Red was ready to admit defeat, pack her meagre belongings and head home to Wales. Both victims had close links to her, and she was beginning to wonder if the two deaths might be connected. People might see them as random events, taking place in different areas in entirely different circumstances, but Red was unable to shake off the fact they were her closest friends and had lost their lives within days of each other. Could she be next in line, for a reason she was unable to comprehend?

An urgent tapping at the door made her physically jump.

'Who is it?' she whispered.

'Come on, love, open up!' *Thank God, it was Blaize.* 'Can't have you moping around here all day and all night, can we now?'

Red unhooked the chain, turned the key in the lock, and threw open the door.

'What is it, Blaize?' She felt uneasy. The last time her boss had knocked on the door it was to tell her the awful news about Kat.

'With everything that's been going on, we're a little bit stretched,' said Blaize. 'Bearing that in mind, I am going to need you to step up. You're fourteen now, still a bit young I guess, but I started in this game young, too. From this moment, you aren't just my gofer, you are officially my personal assistant. I need help to manage the clubs, book acts and everything else besides. Think you can handle it?'

In the time it took Blaize to ask the question, Red had dismissed from her mind all thoughts of returning to Wales.

PART TWO

1973

24

South Wales, March 1973

'GO ON, ELF, son. Run with it. Oof! Unlucky.'

Osean Rhys stood on the touchline, his sensible slip-on shoes caked in mud, the rain dripping onto his face from his blue and white bobble hat. He was oblivious to the atrocious conditions, so completely was he wrapped up in a rugby match between Croesybont Youths seconds and Pontyprenis Boys.

His youngest son – stepson, officially – was doing him proud. Though he was only fourteen, Elfyn was already competing with boys up to four years older than him. His size helped, no doubt. He was a mountain of a kid, having passed the six-foot mark shortly after his thirteenth birthday and continued to grow from there. His nickname, Elf, seemed the ultimate irony.

At that size, he was ideally suited to the second row. He was an asset in the line out and quick on his feet, too, while not afraid to barge into some of the heavier units on the field. If he had a fault, it was that he could be clumsy and, some might say, accident prone. It was these disappointing character traits which Osean feared might prevent him reaching the very top. It was a pity, because the boy was also educationally challenged and though, as deputy headmaster at the local school, Osean had done his best to provide extra tuition he knew Elf's future would not be defined by academic achievement.

It was strange, really. Elf's sister Megan, who ran away from home in February 1971, had been quick on the uptake and, at times, too clever for her own good. Eldest boy Owen was a bright spark, too, though he didn't always use his talents wisely and if two words summed him up, they were "sly and untrustworthy".

Like biological father like son, he thought.

Those inherited defects weren't exclusive to Owen. They'd shown up in Megan's personality too, her running away the culmination of a series of problems the headstrong girl had heaped on her parents. To this day, her mother, Doreen, was consumed by guilt and worry. Osean had done his best to convince his wife the girl would return one day, but that seemed less likely as time wore on. In the weeks leading up to the second anniversary of Meg's disappearance, his wife's morale had sunk lower and lower, to the point where she couldn't get through the day without taking the 'happy pills' the local GP had prescribed.

Like any good husband and father, Osean had been in touch with the authorities regularly in the hope of discovering Megan's whereabouts. He was a regular visitor to Croesybont Police Station, driving Sergeant Harris and his team barmy with his incessant questions. He'd been in touch with missing person's helplines and charity organisations, too, without any luck.

'Yes...go!' he shouted as Elf received the ball from one of the nimble backs playing alongside him. He barged through the first tackle, virtually ran over the next boy in his path and then haired off over the twenty-two. Suddenly he was in the clear with the Pontyprenis defence split asunder. Elf took a brief glance over his shoulder to admire the scene of destruction he'd left behind, lifted his knees and charged for the line.

He was just 10 yards from the whitewash when it happened. With the ball tucked under his arm and a clear field in front of him, his attention to detail let him down. The laces of one of his boots had been unravelling for some time, but he'd ignored it. As he attempted to switch direction and evade a last desperate tackle, he tripped over his own feet and crashed face first in the mud.

'Bloody 'ell, Elfyn, you stupid big tart!' shouted Osean, unable to contain himself. It earned him admonishing looks from the parents around him but how was he supposed to react? The boy had once again embarrassed him in public. Laughter rippled all around him, and there were more chuckles from players on the pitch. Even the referee was struggling to contain his amusement. After enduring sixty minutes of taunts like 'You need glasses, referee' and 'That wasn't a straight line out, you biased bastard', it came as welcome light relief. Moments later, he blew his whistle and brought the game to an end, the final score being 16-14 to Pontyprenis. Elf's missed opportunity was the difference between success and failure. He received some consoling pats from those around him as he trudged off the field, but Osean knew it would do no good to mollycoddle him.

'Am I going to have to give you a refresher course in tying your bloody boot laces again, mun?' he said, feeling the glow spread across his face as he struggled to contain his anger.

'Sorry, Dad,' said Elf, his crestfallen face feeding Osean's contempt. He didn't want sulks; he wanted the kid to learn from his mistakes. *Hell, if Elf could only iron out flaws like that, greater things might await.* He had everything going for him in terms of physique, speed, strength, and determination. It was just his innate ability to bugger everything up that let him down. Wales Schools were poised to select a squad for their upcoming trials soon, too. He hoped the scouts had left early.

'Where's Kez?' Elfyn looked around.

'She got bored,' said Osean. 'Went for a walk with your brother.'

Kerry Ellis was Elfyn's girlfriend of nearly two years. They had a lot in common. Not only had they lost a parent at a young age but also a sibling, Elf's sister having disappeared with Kerry's brother Marc. Osean suspected the boy was the ringleader and was convinced that if it wasn't for him, Megan would be still at home.

'I'm gonna find her, OK, Dad?'

'Eh? Oh, sure,' said Osean, taking a moment to realise the boy meant Kerry. 'Don't worry about me. I'm happy to stand on the side of a pitch in filthy weather, watching you perform week after week only for you to disappear at the final whistle.'

'Aww, don't be like that.'

'Well, I thought you were coming down the club,' said Osean. 'I was gonna buy you a shandy. All the other boys and their parents will be there. There's a big match on the telly.'

'Sorry like,' said Elf. 'But I promised Kez we'd go into town. She's seen this dress, see...'

'She's got you wrapped around her little finger, that one. No doubt you'll be spending all your paper-round money on her again. You've got a lot to learn about women, boy. She'll suck you in and blow you out in bubbles.'

Osean noted the strange looks he was getting from some parents nearby. 'What?' He turned to confront them. 'I wasn't being literal, was I? God, some people...' He decided to stop before the complaints rolled into the headmaster on Monday morning. Bloody busybodies.

'Go on then, boy, off you trot,' he said. 'I'll see you at home for tea. Don't be late.'

'OK, Dad,' said Elf, a smile creeping across his face. 'Thanks!'

Young love, thought Osean. It's bound to end in tears.

'BLINKIN 'ECK, MUN, you're nearly as dirty as me.' Elf found Kerry behind the clubhouse. She had a strange look on her face, which morphed into a scowl.

'Thanks very much,' she said. 'Flattered, I'm sure!'

'I didn't mean...Why is there mud down the back of your jacket, like? Did that brother of mine trip you? I'll bloody sort him out...'

He noticed Owen had one of those annoying smirks on his face. If he wasn't a gentle giant by nature, he would have knocked that look off his older brother's face. The boy might have been three years his senior, but he was a few inches shorter and not as well built. The two of them shared a bedroom and squabbled incessantly, particularly now Meg wasn't around to keep the peace.

'It wasn't his fault Elf, you silly apoth,' said Kerry. 'You were the one who brought me here. Just look at the state of the ground around yer. I come out to watch you in the wind and rain, having to walk across thick mud which nearly sucks my bloody boots off, and for what? Rugby's boring! I don't mind watching Wales play cos they knows what they're doing, like, but you lot...Lost again, isn't it?'

'Some bloke said your boyfriend fell over and missed a sitter.' Owen made sure he was at a safe distance as he delivered the put-down.

'I don't suppose they mentioned I ran half the length of the pitch past three or four of their boys, did they? You would know if you'd been watching. What were you up to, anyway?'

'Your brother needed a pee, and I needed some shelter, that's all,' said Kerry. 'When I turned the corner I slipped and fell on my arse, didn't I? Looks like we're all at it, eh? Now, are we going shoppin', or wha'?'

ELFYN AND KERRY spent the day visiting department stores and women's fashion outlets in Cardiff's Queen Street. Kerry had birthday money burning a hole in her pocket and Elf had saved up some of his wages from the local newsagent to buy her something. They settled on a ring with a shiny stone from a jewellers in one of the small alleys off the main shopping area. She'd waved it in front of his face and teased, 'I'll expect something a bit more extravagant when you propose proper, Elfyn Prince.'

Though it was meant as a joke, it sent a tingle up Elf's spine. Was this wonderful, whacky, outgoing girl suggesting that one day they might marry? He was bubbling with excitement all the way home on the valleys' bus. After dropping her off and being promised a 'fashion show' the following day, he walked up the hill towards his house, whistling a happy tune under his breath, something about tying a yellow ribbon around an oak tree. Despite his rugby slip, it had been a good day.

When Meg's friend Wanda stepped out in front of him waving a piece of paper, he almost collapsed in shock.

'What you got there, Wand?' he said after taking a moment to bring his heart rate under control.

She passed him the envelope. It was addressed to Miss Wanda Williams of 15 Plaes-Y-Parc, Croesybont, Rhondda, Wales and he could see it had been opened. He lifted the flap. 'No one else can see, right? It's for you only,' she said.

'OK.' He moved to a small grass area which housed a large sycamore tree, playing his part in the cloak-and-dagger game. Wanda followed. Rain drops fell on them occasionally from the branches, a stray drip smearing the ink on the front of the envelope. He recognised that handwriting.

'Careful!' she hissed. He held his hand up to quieten her and then removed a small package from inside the envelope, together with a slip of paper which read: *Dear Wanda, please pass this on to my brother Elfyn. I've sent it to you rather than home because no one else must see it. Thanks for keeping this secret, your friend, Megan.*

'Thought she might have said more, to be honest, like,' said Wanda. 'Best friend? After she took off, I never heard another peep until now.' Looking up, she saw Elfyn was holding a model of a red bus in one hand. In the other was a postcard. 'She all right, is she?'

'Shhhhh,' he said, reading the message written on it. 'I'm trying to concentrate. Yeah, she's OK, but I can't say any more.'

'It was sent to my address, though,' she whined. 'Bloody hell, I could have opened it and read it myself, Elf mun. I did you a favour.'

'Yeah, but...' He wasn't sure how to proceed. He didn't want to betray Meg's confidence, but Wanda had a point. 'OK, well don't tell anyone, right? Not your mum or dad, and certainly not your classmates. She'd kill me...'

'OK, OK, just read it like, Elf mun.'

He'd never been able to resist this kind of pressure. He took a deep breath and read the words which had been composed carefully in his sister's neat handwriting. Afterwards, they stayed silent for a moment, assessing the implications.

Eventually Wanda broke the silence. 'She's in London, then?'

'Sounds like it.'

'And she is safe and has a job but doesn't say what it is. What are you gonna do?'

'I dunno,' said Elf. 'She says not to look for her, so I guess I should stick to that.'

'Why send the postcard, though? She ain't sent one before. If you ask me, she wants you to find her.'

He just shook his head in response.

'And what does she mean when she says, "Things happened that made it impossible for me to stay"?' asked Wanda.

'Dunno,' he repeated. 'I guess there was the odd family squabble, you know, and Osean was a bit fierce with her, placing strict curfews and stuff, but he was the same with all of us. I can't think it was so bad that she had to run away. She would have known how worried we would be, particularly Mam. Christ, Meg had promised she was going to help me with something, but then she was gone.'

He felt tears gathering but didn't want Wanda to see.

'I got to go,' he said, quickly turning away, the postcard and gift clutched in his hand. He would have to hide them well.

More importantly, he needed to speak to Kerry.

She would help him sort through his feelings.

25

'IT'S BEEN EXACTLY two years now...shouldn't we start another appeal? I mean, you haven't heard anything in that time have you, Ose, butt? No clues as to their whereabouts? What about the police? Are they still looking? You'd tell me if...'

'Of course, I'd tell you, Aaron mun!' Osean's face became animated, his complexion red. He could exhibit a detached coolness with most people on parents' night, but when it came to Aaron Ellis, it was impossible. Osean was a big man, but Ellis towered above him, his muscles bulging beneath his shirt sleeves. The father of Marc and Kerry Ellis worked in a steel foundry in Port Talbot – Swansea's unfashionable neighbour – and Osean could only imagine the kind of heavy lifting the job entailed. In his spare time, Aaron was a key forward in the Croesybont first XV and was often seen holding court in the clubhouse. It was common knowledge that he'd been a useful back row with Pontypool in his younger days and even earned a call up to a couple of Wales training sessions before injury halted his progress – a metal bar falling from a crane at work and striking his right leg.

The damage to his knee was so bad, doctors feared he would never play again, but Aaron was made of sterner stuff. His Wales ambitions might have been crushed, but he was determined to play his beloved rugby and went through the rehabilitation process from hell in order to resume the game at club level.

'It's gutting,' he said, leaning towards Osean with his elbows on his thighs. 'Marc had everything he could have wanted at home. I never put pressure on him to do anything – not like other people who demand their offspring follow the path they've selected. I pledged when Ruby died I would let him and his sister plough their own furrow, and I was true to my word until...'

'Don't torture yourself, Aaron,' said Osean. 'Thousands of kids like Marc run away from home every year. He was at that age where he thought, rightly or wrongly, that he could do better if he branched out on his own. He obviously needed a bit of adventure injected into his life. Losing your mother is tough at a young age. You don't know how a person will react. He's a sensible kid, though. I'm sure he wouldn't do anything silly.'

'He's a very shy boy, though,' said Aaron. 'He wouldn't say boo to a goose, mun, you know that. There's always someone going to take advantage of a trusting, gentle nature like that. Now, our Kerry, that's a different kettle of fish...'

'And Kerry is why we're here,' said Osean, seizing on an opportunity to change the subject. 'You are here to discuss her progress with her form tutor and teachers.'

'Is there a problem?'

'Not really,' said Osean, his expression hinting at something different. 'She's a very popular girl.'

'You mean with the boys, don't you?' said Aaron. 'It's difficult, for both of us. She's growing up and changing, physically and mentally. I never expected to be left in the position to have to bring up a teenage girl on my own.'

'Look, as teachers, we're here to help. From what I understand, she contributes to topics in class and has plenty to say for herself – which we like to encourage.'

Kerry's father leant back and studied the polystyrene ceiling then sighed loudly. 'You don't need to pussyfoot around the subject, Ose. If she's an unruly influence, then she needs to be brought into line. Your Elfyn seems a nice lad. Hopefully, his good manners will rub off on her. I'm not really in the business of encouraging boyfriends, but if it's a choice between him and some of those "rebels" who strut around acting like extras in a James Dean film, I know who I prefer.'

When Aaron finally wandered off to find Kerry's English teacher, Osean headed back to the staffroom and an ambush from a deputation of school governors. In fairness, they'd always been supporters of his, particularly when the news that his daughter had run away had spread through the valleys.

'How are you and the family, Osean?' asked a woman with an extravagant blonde perm. A local GP, she wore a houndstooth jacket and matching skirt. She patted him gently on the hand. 'We are aware of what time of year it is. It must be tough. If there's anything we can do...'

'It's not easy,' he admitted, his fingers caressing a pack of cigars in his pocket. He longed for a nicotine hit but had to play the game. 'Doreen still expects her to walk through the door any day.'

'I'm sure.'

He rubbed the back of his neck. 'Megan was never easy to communicate with, you know? I tried my best but after what happened with her father...Maybe I arrived too late to make a difference.'

'You've been a rock, Osean. We all know that. I'm sure Doreen's grateful...and the boys have done so well. I suppose daughters and their fathers don't have quite the same bond, y'know?'

'I know I could have done more,' he said. 'Meg was old before her time. Very clever, but with a vivid imagination.'

'How do you mean?'

'Well, her storytelling was getting out of hand,' he said. 'It was like she locked herself into a fantasy world and turned her back on reality.'

'It's tough enough to be deprived of a parent when you're a full-grown adult but at five, well...'

'Her real dad walking out was a massive contributor, no doubt,' he said. 'Whether it was because she was ashamed to admit the truth, I don't know, but the tales she came up with...do you know she told some members of a visiting drama group that he died in a pit accident?'

'Gambler, wasn't he?'

'...And the rest: Drinker, thief, philanderer...ran off with some bird from Newport and never bothered with the kids again. Still, I suppose if your dad deserts you like that, you're bound to feel embarrassed. Maybe the best solution is to make up a story to help you cope. To suggest he'd been a victim down the mines, though, is just a bit disturbing. I found some 'deepest sympathy' cards among her belongings when I searched her room. Never in a million years did I imagine she'd run out on her mam and brothers the way she did, but I suppose she was a bit screwed up. Maybe she went to look for her real dad. Who knows?'

'How is poor Doreen?' The man sitting in the other visitors' seat spoke for the first time. Strands of thin, silvery hair sat precariously atop an egg-shaped head. Some of the kids had given him the nickname Bobby Charlton after the Manchester United and England footballer who had a similar comb-over. Ivor Williams was a clerk in the local branch of a well-known bank by day, but treated his governor role very seriously. Osean had known him for years and was grateful for his support on both a professional and personal level.

'The wife's struggling,' said Osean, his voice cracking as he rubbed at one eye. 'Megan's her baby. I used to listen to them talking sometimes, and it was like a friendship rather than just a mother-daughter dynamic which is why it was cruel for the girl to leave the way she did.'

'Yes, well, I'm sure Megan is safe and sound, wherever she is,' said the GP. 'At least she's with a friend – they'll look out for each other.'

'Hmmm,' said Osean, indicating he had reservations. 'I always found Marc a bit of an oddball, very unlike others in his peer group. For them, it was all about girls, sport and generally mucking about. He was a loner and a butt of their jokes at times. I had to personally counsel him on several occasions.'

'Was he bullied?'

'Hell no!' said Osean. 'Have you seen his dad? I was with him just now – a steelworker who spends his spare time bashing up people on the rugby field. No one would dare bully the son of Aaron Ellis.'

'Well, no matter what trials you're going through, we think you're doing a splendid job,' said Dr Brown. 'The setup you have here is great, and you have a very good disciplinary record. I'm sure it won't be long until you get a school of your own.'

26

'HOW LONG HAVE you been keeping this from me?' Kerry asked, her eyes boring into him.

'I'm telling you now, aren't I?' said Elf. 'I didn't want you flying off the handle, and our Meg had begged me to keep it a secret.'

She didn't speak for a moment while her intense gaze continued to lock him in place. Then she asked, 'Why doesn't she mention him?'

'It's just a postcard, Kez,' he said. 'You can't write everything down on it and her handwriting was always big.'

They were sitting on Kerry's single bed surrounded by posters of every schoolgirl crush imaginable from David Cassidy and Donny Osmond to David Essex, Robert Redford and George Best. Barely an inch of wall space remained uncovered. A portable record player, some make-up and a packet of Bazooka Joe bubble gum sat on a dressing table to the right of them.

Occasionally, Kerry would blow a bubble, one expanding to such an extent that when it popped the elastic pink substance ended up spread across her mouth and nose. She pulled it all together and pushed it back into her mouth. Elf found it hypnotic and sexy, his teen male urges rising at the sight of Kerry's rapidly developing bust peeping out from her low-cut white dress. He was sure she dressed that way to tease him while simultaneously keeping him at arm's length.

'Funny, she had time to write all this shit about how important it is not to tell nobody.' She continued to pick at the scab. 'Doesn't she realise we need to know our Marc is OK? All she's done is made up my mind. I'm going to that London to look for him.'

'No, Kez,' he moaned. 'You can't. She'll go crazy!'

'We ain't even going to look for your Meg, though, are we?' She poked him in the chest with a long-nailed finger. 'What are you, man or mouse, Elfyn Prince? We know she's OK, but I got a horrible feeling about my brother. He ain't like your sister. He's always been a bit soft. Can you imagine him all by himself in that big place? It's dangerous. There was this film on TV the other day about a girl who runs away with her bloke and ends up living on the streets there. She was called Connie I think – no, hang on, it was Cathy. I couldn't help thinking about our Marc. If you love me like you claims to, you'll help me find him.'

She was calling on all her tricks now, giving him the sad puppy-dog eyes, her bottom lip pushed out in his direction. 'I...I don't know,' he said. 'I'm not being horrible. It's just...'

His sentence was cut off as chunky fingers gripped the back of his neck, pulling him forward onto her. He smelt smoke from the sneaky Players no. 6 she'd puffed out of the bathroom window while he stood guard at the door. When their lips collided, she thrust her tongue into his mouth, playing it around his teeth. He could taste the peppermint and smell the powerful citrus and peach odour of the Rive Gauche perfume her father bought her for Christmas. He felt lightheaded and when she pushed hard against him, his strength deserted him completely.

'Please...' she whispered in his ear as her other hand rubbed at the outside of his trousers. 'I'll let you do that thing you wanted to, you know...?'

His breathing sounded loud in the still room. 'Really?'

'All the way. You'll have to be quick, though...our dad's only at the school open evening. He'll be back soon.'

He felt her unzip the fly of his light blue Oxford bags and slip her hand inside, pulling at the elastic waste of his y-fronts until...ohhh, ohhh, he was so aroused he feared he would spoil the big moment there and then. She interpreted the signals just in time, releasing her grip and flopping back on the bed. Lifting the hem of her dress, she then worked his belt loose and pulled the trousers down over his muscle-bound thighs.

It was all teenage awkwardness, clumsy and rushed. His hand travelled up her blouse before twisting and pulling at something behind her back.

Impatiently, she slapped his hand away, snapping, 'I'll do it.' He sat back like a schoolboy admonished by a teacher, watching as she undid the buttons on her dress then unhooked the bra. He couldn't help gawping at the way the chunky nipples protruded from her pale, freckled breasts. It made him think of the Walnut Whip chocolates Mam brought every Christmas.

'You want an official invite, like?' she said. He reached out and ran his hand gently over her cool skin, goosebumps appearing on his arms as he caressed her. 'Stand up,' she ordered breathlessly. He shuffled awkwardly to do her bidding, and she worked the trousers down until they nestled at his ankles. Then she sat back, slid her underwear off, and kicked it across the room. 'Go on then,' she said. 'Or do you plan to be a virgin all your life?'

In a few seconds, it was over, but the memory would last far longer.

Afterwards, she was like a villain cleaning a crime scene, using scent and tissues to destroy the evidence. When they were both fully dressed, they sat on the bed, awkward in each other's company. 'I...I thought it would be harder than that,' he said.

'Seemed pretty hard to me,' she said, giggling. Then her expression changed, the space between her eyebrows puckering in a look of concern. 'Hey, you ain't saying I'm a slag, are you?'

'N...no, I didn't mean that. It's just, you know, some of my mates told me I'd have to really push to get it in, like.'

'Yeah, well, I ride horses, don't I? It makes sex easier, apparently. I read it in a magazine.' He nodded. It seemed a reasonable explanation. 'Now, we got things to do before the old man gets home.'

'Eh?'

'We need to look for the clues if we're gonna find Marc in London.'

Belatedly, he realised he'd fallen blindly into her trap. Damn, she was a clever bird.

ELF FELT LIKE a criminal breaking and entering. Marc's bedroom door had been locked for as long as he could remember – ever since that day the police had performed a cursory search in the hunt for clues to his whereabouts. Kerry said her dad had insisted the room remained untouched, so that when Marc returned, it would be exactly as he left it. Tonight, Kerry had retrieved the key from a kitchen drawer and hoped that by breaking the taboo she could unlock the secret to her brother's disappearance.

Peering inside, Elf saw the usual array of posters on the wall plus a pile of 45rpm vinyl singles stacked on a dressing table next to a record player, its needle thick with fluff. Opposite was a white-painted wardrobe yawning open to cough a variety of clothes onto the floor. The curtains were closed to the outside world and had been for a long time. A musty smell stuck in the back of the throat.

'Come on, scaredy cat,' urged Kerry, marching into the centre of the room. Elf watched her lift a dog-shaped lamp from the bedside table. When she flicked the switch, everything became enveloped in a green glow. 'Spooky, eh?' she said. 'Right, you start on the bedside drawers.'

He crossed the threshold slowly, his ears finely tuned to detect the sound of keys turning in the front-door lock. There was nothing other than the distant cry of a baby permeating through the walls from the next-door house in the terrace.

He saw Kerry pull a stool from inside the wardrobe, climb up and start rifling through the top drawers. Her mini skirt rode up and Elf got a tantalising view of the top of her thighs. It made him think of the earlier events and he felt aroused again. 'Hey, perv...I can't hear no search going on,' she said, without turning. Did she have eyes in the back of her head? Blushing, he turned and eased open the top drawer to reveal assorted socks and y-fronts.

'Flippin' 'eck, Marky, what a weirdo you are,' she said. When Elf looked over his shoulder, he saw that his girlfriend was holding a pair of glittery hot pants between two fingers. 'Do you think he's worn them? Yuk!'

Elf said nothing. He'd often thought that Marc was a bit strange. He'd overheard the boy talking to Megs in glowing terms about some of the items in his mother's catalogue. What teenage boys spent time discussing women's fashion? Returning to the task at hand, Elf found the contents of the second drawer far more random. There was a broken watch, a stapler, a packet of chewing gum, a couple of springs, one of those shooters that delivered little flavoured bricks known as Pez sweets, still loaded, a yo-yo and a collection of blackjack and fruit salad chews still in their wrappers. He wondered how long it took for them to go off.

'Jackpot!' said Kerry. She climbed down from the stool and walked across to the bed, a rucksack in her hands. Kneeling, she then emptied it onto the eiderdown. They stood side-by-side admiring the big find. It contained an eyeliner pencil, a small bottle of glitter, a make-up box with eye shadow in bright colours, a small container of mascara, some stick-on stars, a box of tattoo transfers, a pair of purple velvet loon pants and some white platform boots.

'Hang on,' said Elf, casting his eyes through some pieces of card in his hand.

'Found somethin'?'

He shuffled the cards and held one out to her. 'Tyrannosaurus Rex.'

'So, he went to some bleedin' dinosaur exhibition,' she said stroppily. 'Probably got it from a school trip, mun. How does that help us?'

'It's not an exhibition,' he said, enthusiastically pointing to one of the posters on the wall. A man with wild corkscrew hair half covering his face was sitting on a stool playing an acoustic guitar. 'You know who that is, don't you?'

'Fuckin' 'ell, Elf mun, I'm not thick. It's Marc Bolan, innit?' She paused. 'Jesus...T. Rex...'

'Who were once called Tyrannosaurus Rex,' said Elf, his face brightening as he realised Kerry was finally on the same wavelength. 'And this is a ticket for a gig in Cardiff two days before Meg and Marc disappeared...which could also explain the stuff in that bag. I remember now, a couple of days before she left she gave me some drumsticks.'

Kerry was biting her bottom lip, thinking. He found it endearing and quite sexy. Then the light bulb came on again. 'Bolan dresses up in sparkly clothes, wears glitter and make-up, sticks stars to his face...Hell, you think our Marc wore this stuff to the gig?'

'Yes.'

She was silent for a moment, then the hope in her eyes faded. 'It don't mean nothing, though. He came home afterwards and was here all Saturday. He seemed a bit dozy but didn't he always?'

Elf thought about what she was saying. 'Well, I s'pose. But he obviously put these things in the bag because he didn't want your dad to know about them...how would he have reacted?'

'He'd have been well angry. Marc would have been grounded and told he couldn't go to another gig until he was a bleedin' adult, and not even then if he was still living here. "Not under my roof, you don't".'

It was a good impression of Aaron Ellis, he had to admit.

'So, what if your dad did find them?' said Elf. 'You weren't here all day, were you?'

'Umm...no. I went to Pam's party. Pam Williams, y'know? It was a bloody Barbie doll thing and I had to dress in a stupid pink dress. Her entire bloody house was pink, mun, made me...—'

'OK. So, your dad finds out. They have a big row when you're not here and...—'

'...Marc runs away.'

'Yes.'

'What about Meg, though? How does she become involved?'

'Maybe he asked her to go,' said Elf. 'They were inseparable, like. Whatever happened, it was a quick decision. Meg had promised to do something with me on the Sunday but when I woke up in the morning, she'd gone. I think she had a bit of a row with our dad on Saturday morning. I could hear them going at it, but there was nothing unusual in that, so I thought nothing more of it.'

'What was the argument about?'

'Getting in late. So must have been something to do with that gig.'

She shook her head. 'London though? That's quite a step for her, particularly knowing how your dad would react.'

He went silent for a moment, choosing his words carefully. 'Meg hated Osean,' he said. 'I don't know why. He tried his best with her, but she wasn't happy at home. He'd told her off a couple of times recently and Mam refused to get involved. Our sis had even taken to barricading her door at night because she told me he used to go in there and have a go at her after he'd been to the pub.'

'I had no idea,' she said. 'Whenever I saw her she seemed fine, but I expect she's good at hiding her true feelings. You don't think... You hear stories don't you?' He wasn't sure what Kerry was babbling on about, and she picked up on his confusion. 'Forget it,' she said. 'Let's keep looking. Finding that's a great start...'

She turned away and started moving objects around on the bed. He could tell by the way she bit her bottom lip that she was at the peak of her powers of concentration. He turned to replace the ticket stub in the drawer and stopped. 'Kez?' Excited, he waved his latest find in her direction.

Before she could answer, a door banged downstairs.

27

'S...SORRY, DAD, I didn't hear you.' Kerry looked down from the top of the staircase. 'All OK?'

'Come down,' said Aaron Ellis. 'We have stuff we need to talk about.'

'OK, I'm just finishing my homework with Elfyn.'

'He's here? Well, it's time for Elfyn to go home. It's a school night.'

'Hello, Mr Ellis.' The boy emerged at Kerry's shoulder.

'Grab your stuff, please, Elfyn,' he said. 'I need a word with our Kerry about her report. I expect your mum and dad will want to do the same with you.'

'They've done it already, Mr Ellis,' Elf replied. 'Dad being the deputy head and all, they know exactly what's happenin'. I see him every night, innit?'

'In that case, you're a lucky boy,' said the older man. Elf didn't think it lucky to have an inquest into your school performance every day. 'For some of us, it can be a bit of an eye opener, meeting the teachers.'

'Just give us five minutes, Dad...pretty please,' said Kerry. 'We got to pack our books up. I don't want to find I'm missing a textbook when I go to school tomorrow, do I?'

The old man nodded slowly. Elf could tell he was on a slow-burning fuse and an explosion wasn't far away. 'Five minutes, not a second more,' he said. 'Then I want both of your arses down here pronto, right?'

'Yes, Dad,' said Kerry, turning and leading Elf back towards her bedroom. On the way, she stopped to lock her brother's door. 'Phew,' she whispered, turning to him. 'Quick! What were you about to say? Did you find something else?'

As she guided him through the door to her room, he took the concert flyer from his pocket and turned it over, so they were now looking at the back. There was a name scrawled on it in ink: Greg Chance, c/o Roadie Life London. Next to it was a phone number.

Before he knew what was happening, she'd grabbed his face in both hands and kissed him sloppily on the mouth. 'You're a genius,' she said. 'This could change everything.' Her hand strayed downwards and gave him a squeeze, bringing him instantly erect. 'When all this is over, you will get a big reward, but before then I have to face the music,' she said, nodding in the direction of the stairs. 'I'll see you at school tomorrow. We can ring this Greg Chance character from the phone box by the shops and find out what he knows. OK?'

He nodded, his eyes shutting as she gave him a few more rubs for good luck, her tongue caressing his neck. He bit his bottom lip in an effort to regain his equilibrium.

'On my way, Daddy,' she shouted.

'And Elf?'

She restrained a giggle. 'He's just coming, Dad!'

LOOKING AROUND MARC'S sacred chamber had brought memories flooding back for Elfyn Prince and as he walked home, he tried to fit together all the pieces, his mind replaying the day his sister and her friend had disappeared – Sunday, February 13, 1971.

He'd awoken that morning to the strains of a harmonica wheezing out from Mam and Ocean's state-of-the-art clock radio in the next room. Chugging Rhythm and Blues guitar chords followed, and he leapt from bed, grabbing the drumsticks Megan had brought back from a rock gig in Cardiff two days earlier. Crossing to the dressing table, he'd then hammered out a rhythm on an old metal tray which provoked a groan from beneath a pile of sheets on the top bunk.

He chose to ignore it but was unable to do the same when a gruff voice bellowed through the wall, 'Elf, stop that racket now!' In truth, he'd felt it a bit rich coming from his stepfather who, the previous night, had disturbed the entire household by crashing through the bins because they stood on a direct path between pub and bed. At the time, Elf had been in a deep sleep and leapt up petrified, fearing a clumsy burglar had targeted their house.

The guttural shout from outside had immediately put him straight. 'Dor, Dor…let us in, Dor, would you? Can't f…find the…f'ing keys. Must've dropped 'em outside the chippy. Come on Dor, love, it's freezin'.'

After a brief delay, Elf heard the window in the master bedroom open with a squeak. 'Bloody hell, Ose, you'll wake the entire street up, you silly fool,' Mam shouted. 'Thought you said you were only having a couple of soft drinks tonight, so you'd be tip-top for the darts game?'

'Don't be like that, Cariad…We won, so we had to celebrate, didn't we? Open this door now, would you, before I catch me death?'

'Freezin', is it? At least you've got a bloody great big coat on. Didn't occur to you how cold it was when you turned the heating off though, did it, you tight git? I've a mind to let you sleep in the shed.'

Despite her protests, Mam had eventually padded down the stairs and unlocked the door – just like she always did at the end of what had become a weekend ritual. Elf wished she would just let his stepfather in first time to spare everyone the back-and-fore drama. He remembered thinking of his English lessons at school. At the time, they'd been reading Romeo and Juliet, where the infatuated boy visited the girl of his dreams and wooed her on the balcony. The Croesybont equivalent was as far removed from that tale of star-crossed lovers as it was possible to get.

Deciding not to bait the bear, Elf put down the drumsticks and went in search of Megan. In his hand he clutched the Valentine's Card he'd designed. It needed the final seal of approval from his big sis. She'd promised to accompany him when he went to deliver it to his crush Kerry Ellis. It was strange, though. Megan was an early riser and normally bounced through his bedroom door the moment he opened his eyes.

He recalled pulling on his dressing grown with the dragon on the back, before forcing his ungainly size 8 feet – out of proportion to his 12-year-old body – into his Wales rugby slippers, which bore the muddied face of legendary international outside half JW Owens. Satisfied he was ready for the world, he'd then levered open his door and padded past his parents' bedroom, his ears detecting the all-too-human sound of puffing and panting, accompanied by the creaking of bedsprings.

Meg questioned what Mam saw in the bloke, but Osean had always played fair with Elf. A former PE teacher, he'd encouraged the boy's ambition to be a professional rugby player, driving him to matches and backing him vocally from the sidelines, whatever the weather. To Elf it had seemed logical for Mam, having been left to fend for herself with three kids, to seek out a partner to help raise them. Not that he particularly wanted to hear them doing the dirty deed, of course.

Meg had clashed with Osean on numerous occasions. 'The girl's got to learn,' Osean would bellow if Doreen Rhys questioned his methods. The harder he'd pushed though, the harder Megan pushed back, and Elf could only admire his sister's bloody-minded bravery. At school, fellow pupils shook with fear if they were summoned for a private meeting with the deputy head, intimidated by the legendary traffic light system outside his office. When the light was red you knew someone else was in trouble and entry was forbidden. If it was green, it was most likely your turn for punishment. Meg was perhaps the only pupil who refused to cower at the altar of his reputation.

Bounding downstairs, Elf had knocked at the reception room where Megan slept. The homemade sign on the door, meticulously constructed with a variety of coloured felt tips, warned: Megan's room, keep out if you value your life! He knew it didn't apply to him, though. Meg would never deny access to her favourite brother. Taking two steps back, he'd waited for the summons.

Nothing.

At the time, he'd thought it odd but suspected she was playing a joke on him. 'Megs,' he whispered, then 'Megs!' loud enough so that even if she was in the deepest sleep his shout would prove difficult to ignore. When there had still been no answer, a worm of worry began to grow inside his stomach and, after an internal debate lasting all of 10 seconds, he had reached out and pulled the handle downwards. The warped wood scraped against the stone tiles of the hallway, producing a screech, and he had to administer an extra thrust to navigate the obstacle. Finally, the door flew open, leaving the room in full view. There was an unmade bed, but no sign of Meg.

Once he'd alerted his parents to her absence, his stepfather called a family meeting around the dining table. 'You're sure she didn't say anything to you about staying over her mates?' asked Osean. 'She can be a bit sneaky.'

The forensic stare of his stepfather penetrated deep into his soul. It was no wonder he got kids to own up to their worst crimes. If he'd been born in Germany fifty years earlier, he might have found a place in the Gestapo as one of those scary interrogators Elf had seen in films.

'Leave the boy, Ose, he obviously doesn't know anything,' said Mam. 'Let's call the police. God, she might have been taken! She's only 13 and you hear such terrible things. I always think about them two up north who used to take kids, Brady and Hindley...'

'Not in front of the boys, Dor,' said Osean. 'I'm sure this is nothing like that. You know how headstrong Megan is. My bet is she's taken off on a whim and forgot to tell us where she's going. Didn't you say her favourite boots were missing, and some perfume and make-up? Probably met some bloke and...'

'Not our Meg,' said Mam. 'She would never do something like that without telling me.'

'She's getting older,' said Osean. 'They change. Hormones. She can't have gone far, though. She hasn't got any money.'

'Ahh...'

'What?'

'Sorry.' Doreen's face had creased up. 'You know gran left her a little something in her will? It was for a trip to see Trooping the Colour at Buckingham Palace, and there was a bit more besides. You know how my mam used to tell her all about The Queen. I was going to go with her – make it a mother and daughter trip. Anyway, our Megs asked if she could have some now. She wanted to buy some new clothes and tickets to a jig.'

'The word's gig, woman.'

'Yeah, one of those,' she said.

'How much?'

'Eh?'

'How much did you give her?'

'Look, I warned her it wouldn't last long, and she'd have to look after it, maybe put it in a piggy bank or somethin'.' Elfyn had looked at Osean at the time and known he wouldn't accept her wishy-washy answer. 'Sixty pounds,' she admitted.

'Jesus!'

'I know, I know. It's a lot for a 13-year-old but, well, she is growing up and I thought it would be good practice for her to manage her money. Hey, maybe she went into Cardiff...'

'Well, the shops ain't open on a Sunday.'

'There's the market.'

'She would have told you if she was going there, wouldn't she?'

'I don't know.' Mam looked about to cry. She took a tissue from her cardigan sleeve and blew into it. 'Yes, or at least she would have left a note. Anyway, the buses don't run this early on a Sunday, do they? Oh hell, we must call the police.'

Elf could tell Osean was thinking things over. Silences like this were either the prelude to an ugly explosion or a logical conclusion.

'What?' Doreen's resolve cracked first.

'You know what those coppers are like, barging around everywhere in their big clodhoppers,' he said. 'The first thing they'll ask is how long she's been missing. What do we tell them – between three to six hours? They won't be too chuffed. They'll want to know that we've contacted everyone she knows before launching a missing person inquiry.'

He placed a pair of large, hairy hands over Doreen's and gave them a squeeze. 'What are they gonna do, Cariad?' he said, his tone softening. 'They'll go door-to-door talking to family and friends. We can do that ourselves, now. It's not like it's a busy weekday and everyone's at work. We can split up and ask our own questions.' He turned to the boys. 'Elf and Owen can help,' he said. 'And if she doesn't come back, well, I'll make an appeal at school tomorrow, see if her mates know where she's gone.'

'I'm not sure,' said Mam. 'The police are the experts. They handle things like this all the time.

They will get to the bottom of it quicker than we ever could. We aren't detectives, Ose, love.'

'And what happens when they do?' Osean had argued. 'They'll most likely get social services involved. Do you want them nosing into our business, Dor? It wouldn't look very good, particularly with me holding a position of responsibility at the local school. And you know what she's like, she tells tales. She hates me and with her vivid imagination…' He looked around for his packet of mini cigars, picked one out and lit up.

'Oh, Ose.' Mam nodded slowly as she weighed things up in her mind. He rubbed home his advantage quickly.

'Christ, I might get the sack! As soon as we hand the reins to the police, it opens a whole new can of worms.'

Suddenly Elf had a brainwave. 'I'll run across to Marc's! I bet he knows something.'

'Good idea, son,' said his mother.

'Take your older brother along, too,' said Osean. 'That lazy, good for nothing needs to get out of the house.'

28

ELF AND KERRY sat opposite each other on the 9.15 Great Western Railways train from Cardiff Central Station to London Paddington. The rest of the Women's Institute members were spread around the carriage, happy to leave the youngsters to it. 'We don't have to stick with them, do we?' asked Kerry, indicating two women further down the carriage with grey perms and hideous floral dresses.

'Course not,' said Elf. 'Mam said it's up to the individual what they do as long as people are back at the station by five.'

'It was kind of her to get us on the trip with her WI,' said Kerry. 'It doesn't leave us much time, though. We've got to get across London yet, mun, isn't it?'

'We've got that A-Z guide and we're meeting this bloke close to a Tube station so we should be OK,' said Elf. 'How did you get hold of him, anyway?'

Kerry's face broke out in a cheeky grin. 'Let's just say it's lucky you have such a smart girlfriend.' He felt her hand rub his leg under the table and a warm sensation flooded his cheeks. 'I rang that number on the postcard and spoke to this bloke, didn't I?'

'Greg whatsisname?'

'Not him. Some other fella answered. He said his firm arranged roadies for gigs. When I asked to speak to Greg, he said he didn't work there but was one of the regular casual staff they supplied. He also told me that on one or two occasions this bloke – Chancer they call him – brought a friend with him...and guess what? He had an accent like mine.'

'You think Marc did some roadying, too?'

'Maybe. Anyway, Greg didn't have a phone unfortunately and this bloke Ricky told me he lived in a squat, like.'

'What's that?'

'It's an abandoned property that homeless people take over so they can live rent free and not have to worry about bills and stuff.'

'How did you get in touch with him if he didn't have a phone, then?'

'Well, this Ricky was a real sweetie,' said Kerry. 'A few days after we spoke, he got a call from Chancer about a gig and told him I wanted to get in touch. He gave Chancer my number and later he rang. We agreed to meet in this café called The London Grind in Brixton.'

'How will we know which one Chancer is?' he asked.

'Apparently, he'll be wearing a David Bowie Aladdin Sane T-shirt he got from one of his gigs.

You know, the one with the lightning bolt across Bowie's face?'

Elf couldn't fault his girlfriend's tenacity. Every day, he was finding more compelling reasons to love her. They'd been together for almost two years now and it was strange to think that if Meg and Marc hadn't disappeared, their relationship might never have got off the ground. Sitting back in his seat, he flicked through the rugby magazine he'd bought at the station while his mind drifted back to the time he and his brother had called at the Ellis household on that fateful Sunday morning.

When he'd answered his front door, Mr Ellis had looked down at them from the raised step which led straight onto the pavement and asked, 'Where's the dirty stop out, then? I'm guessing he stayed at your house last night. Well? Cat got your tongue, lads? And where's your sister? She's norma—'

'Meg's missing,' said Owen. 'We were hoping she was at yours.'

'Oh,' Mr Ellis had looked shocked. He stepped down onto the street, looking both ways as if the two youngsters might suddenly appear. The Ellis family lived halfway up the hill leading out of town and their pastel-green house floated in a sea of brightly coloured terraced properties. 'You'd better come in,' he said finally. 'Trust that pair of adventurers. I'm sure they'll be together somewhere, thinking they're clever.'

Despite discussing the situation at the Ellis's dinner table, no significant clues emerged until Elf approached Kerry the next morning and summoned up the courage to present her with the homemade Valentine's Day card.

'I had no idea you were such a soppy sod, Elfyn Prince!' she'd exclaimed on opening it and seeing the red heart on a white background with BE MINE VALENTINE stencilled across the top.

'Don't you like it?'

'I'm not saying that, am I?' Kerry had said. 'It's quite sweet that you've drawn something just for me. Why didn't you leave it at the house yesterday, though? I heard you talking to my dad.'

'We were looking for Meg,' he said. 'You should have come down.'

'I was busy...homework.'

'Oh.'

'You could have come to see me, though. Given me the card and said hello. I would have shown you my bedroom.'

It was the first of many occasions on which she'd made him blush. 'I had to get back, didn't I? Mam and Osean were waiting for news.'

'Liar,' she said, a teasing smile dancing on her lips. 'You were scared, weren't you? I don't bite, do I?'

From the outset, he'd liked the way Kerry often finished off her sentences with a question. He also enjoyed her teasing. It was Meg who had said that if a girl teased a boy, it normally meant she had a sweet spot for him.

'Hey, you should have asked me about Marc and Meg,' Kerry had said, her face lighting up. 'I know things you don't. Marc talks to me...more than he does Dad, anyhow. And when he doesn't, well, sometimes I hear him chatting to your sis. His bedroom is just across the landing, isn't it?'

'You know where our Meg is?'

'I didn't say that did I?'

He shook his head. The girl was talking in riddles.

'Look, our Marc was quiet on Saturday,' she'd continued. 'There was somethin' different about him. He was on edge. Then Meg came around. Her hair was all over the place like she'd been running. They went to Marc's room, and I heard them talking about needing transport and money. I thought they were just fantasising about a holiday.'

'Flippin' hell...you think they planned this?'

Rather than give him an answer, he'd felt her slim, cold fingers come to rest on his chin, exerting pressure and turning it so that their eyes met. Hers were a pale, cool blue colour, reflecting the cold sun that peered through the darkening clouds above them. Before he knew what was happening, her lips were on his, moving in a circular motion, her tongue pressing against his teeth. He wasn't sure what to do. The only lips he'd connected with before were Mam's lipstick-caked ones and the dry, stubbly ones of his grandmother.

Kerry had pulled away. 'Loosen up,' she said. 'It's better with tongues.'

The second kiss was much better and went on for some time. It was so good he almost forgot his surroundings, the other kids, the noise...even the teachers keeping a beady eye out for any wrongdoing. When they broke apart, they were both in dire need of oxygen.

'You ain't a bad kisser,' she said. 'You going to ask me out then, or what?'

'Ummm...'

'There are plenty of other...'

'Will you go out with me?'

'Well, say it like you mean it.'

'But I do!'

'Get down on your knees, like they do on the telly. I saw it happen in Crossroads, see, this bloke proposing to his girl on one knee. Dead romantic, don't you think?'

He'd looked around. His mates were taking turns kicking a football against a wall and didn't seem to be paying them any attention. Satisfied, he bent his leg and sank to the floor.

Rip!

Oh fuckety, fuck. Cold air rushed into the newly rendered hole in the seat of his pants.

'Bleedin' hell!' said Kerry. 'Have you ripped your flippin' trousers, Elf Prince? That's just embarrassing, that is! Get up, mun, some of the other kids are coming over. Shit, I must go...It's French soon.'

Without another word, she'd picked up her satchel and scuttled off in the direction of the main school doors, the card falling out of her bag and landing on the gravel floor to be stampeded underfoot by a group of kids running in his direction.

Damn!

'Elfyn's ripped his trousers, Elfyn's ripped his trousers la la la la, la la la la,' some of the boys sang to the tune of the *Conga*, while children of all ages surrounded him, laughing and pointing.

He'd felt his face flush red as he got to his feet, his hand covering the offending hole. Then he scuttled off like a crab in the direction of the boys' toilets.

Why did things like this always happen to him?

29

GETTING ACROSS LONDON wasn't easy. A couple of times they got off at the wrong Underground stop and at one stage even ended up travelling in the wrong direction. By the time they reached their destination, they were 10 minutes late. Walking through the entrance to the coffee shop, Kerry was in such a hurry that she bumped into someone on their way out and murmured 'Excuse me'. Elf, trailing through the door, stepped aside. He caught a glimpse of blond shoulder-length hair resting on the collar of a leather jacket as the figure headed in the direction of the Tube station.

Kerry looked around the room. There were only three seats occupied: an old lady with a small poodle, his leash wrapped around the table leg, and two workmen in hi-vis jackets with close cropped hair. 'Looks like he hasn't turned up,' she said.

'Hang on.' Elf spoke to the girl in the apron behind the counter then turned on his heels and darted for the door.

'What the hell, mun?' said Kerry, but he had no time to explain. Outside, he saw a crowd of people entering the station and thought he was too late, only to catch a glimpse of blond hair and leather. Barging past people as if heading for the try line in a game of rugby, he then reached out and grabbed his target's shoulder.

'Excuse me, mate?'

The next few seconds were a blur. The man swivelled quickly and swung a fist into Elf's face, forcing the schoolboy to fall backwards. In doing so, he took some innocent bystanders with him. As he gathered his senses, Elf heard a scream and saw someone hurdle him and dive on his assailant.

'Hey, that's my boyfriend you're punching, you bell end!' shouted Kerry. 'He's only a kid.'

Grabbing her victim by the hair, she then pulled his head down onto her knee. When she let go, he staggered for a moment, then rallied to thump her in the stomach. Losing her balance on flowery platform shoes, she grasped the cuff of his leather jacket and clung on desperately as she fell. As the man tried to shake her off, she caught a glimpse of the T-shirt: A portrait of a man with bright glowing hair and blue and red zigzag stripes shooting diagonally across his face. 'You're Greg?'

The words slipped out as the two of them landed in a bundled heap on the pavement.

Five minutes later they were sat at a table in the café, nursing their various wounds and sipping at cups of tea. 'Sorry about the misunderstanding,' said the roadie. 'I've lost count of the times I've been jumped around here – if you don't act quickly, you get a reet beating.'

'Elfyn's only 15 though, mun. What were you thinking?' said Kerry.

'Big lad, though, ain't 'e? No one that size went to my school. He's got whiskers on t'chin, look – that's the start of a beard if you ask me. Lucky I didn't bray him.'

'Do they all talk like that around here?'

'Ahh, I'm not local.' He dabbed at the cut on his lip with a tissue Kerry had retrieved from her bag. 'I'm from Leeds. If you cut me, you'll find the word Yorkshire runs through me like a stick of rock.'

'So why are you here like – I mean, in London?'

'For the same reason your kid came here I expect. The freedom to be myself.'

'Our Marc was OK where he was – Dad gave him all the freedom he wanted.'

'So how did it go down with your folks, eh? Your Marc being a friend of Dorothy...'

'What you on about, mun? Who's Dorothy?'

'I mean that your beloved sibling was a queer, dear...a fag, a pooftah.'

'You can't say that!' Kerry's raised voice caused other customers to turn in her direction. Elf grabbed her by the forearm and squeezed.

'Calm down, Kez,' he said. 'The bloke's only trying to help. We have to face up to the fact Marc ran away for a reason. I always wondered...'

'Oh, so now you think my brother's a poof, too, do you?' she said. 'Thanks a lot, Elfyn Prince. You're supposed to be on my side!'

Despite her anger, Elf couldn't dismiss the voice inside his head – the one that had always suspected there was something different about Marc. He'd heard boys directing jibes at him in the playground, but assumed he was being picked on simply because he had no interest in rugby and football. When they searched Marc's bedroom, though, Elf's suspicions had hardened. It wasn't just the hot pants and the boots, but the giant film poster on the back of the bedroom door. It featured Judy Garland with her arms around her three famous friends – the Lion, the Scarecrow, and the Tin Man – from the *Wizard of Oz* musical. She was dressed in her blue and white pinafore dress over a white cotton blouse with bunched sleeves. On her feet were sparkling ruby slippers.

In the film, the character Judy played was named Dorothy.

He grabbed Kerry under the chin and turned her to face him. 'Of course, I'm on your side, Kez, but we came here for answers, and not necessarily the ones we want to hear. Let the man speak. You want to find Marc, and I need to know what's happened to my sister.'

She sat back and blew out a breath, trying to contain her anger.

'Reet enough,' said Chancer, interrupting the lovers' tiff. 'I'm guessing you're Red's brother?'

Elf shook his head. 'My sister's called Megan.'

'Whatever,' said the Yorkshireman. 'I knew her as Red. Seems like someone else who was trying to invent a new identity.'

'Well, she's got ginger hair, so I suppose it makes sense. Did she mention me? They call me Elf.'

Chancer laughed. 'By eck, pal, you're a bit bloody big to be an Elf ain't you?'

'Elf's short for Elfyn,' he explained. 'It's a Welsh name.'

'Right. You should just call me Chancer...everyone else does.'

'When did you last see them, Chancer?' asked Elf.

'I saw Marc at a gig not that long ago,' said the roadie. 'I ain't seen Red, I mean Megan, since that first day. I thought she went home.'

'They aren't together?'

'No, man,' said Chancer. 'At least they weren't the last time I saw him. Marc and I lost her after this café incident and I assumed she went home.'

'What incident was that?'

'Let's get another brew and I'll tell you about it,' said Chancer.

'SO HOW DID you meet in the first place, mun?' asked Elf.

Chancer looked out of the window as he considered the question. 'I was one of the roadies at a gig Tyrannosaurus Rex played in Cardiff,' he said. 'You would know them now as T. Rex, but this was just before they changed their name. I saw this bloke at the front of the stage, and he looked great – he was wearing these red velvet loons and knee-length white boots with a huge heel and he was really going for it – into the music.'

Kerry's mouth fell open in shock. 'Our dad would never let him go out dressed like that.'

'If that's the case, I doubt he would have approved of the mascara and black eyeliner either, or the glitter on his face. That was how I first saw him, though.'

'Remember the stuff we found in his bedroom?' said Elf, raising his eyebrows in Kerry's direction before prompting Chancer to continue his story. He feared that at any moment the roadie would cut off the conversation and disappear and sensed this was the only chance they would get to question such a transient character. 'What happened?'

'I fancied him a bit,' said Chancer, 'so I decided to chat him up. It's easy in my job because these mad fans see you as a route to the band. They think you know the stars personally and so you use it to your advantage.'

'Ah, I see what's going on yer,' said Kerry. 'You tricked him.'

'No, not really,' said Chancer. 'Your brother wasn't like the others in that respect. He was a bit shy but very nice and easy to talk to. He seemed to know exactly where I was coming from and was interested in me, not the band. He introduced me to Red – sorry Megan – and it went from there. I was staying overnight with a mate in the valleys, so we gave them a lift home and I invited them to my Valentine's Day party at the squat on the

Sunday night. It was the sort of thing you say, but I didn't think in a million years they would come. I rang Marc the following day, though, and he was right up for it. My pal picked them up early on the Sunday morning and drove us to London. Red only had a small rucksack, though, and he came in the clothes he was dressed in…I certainly didn't expect them to stay.'

'You said there was an incident – was this at the party?'

'No, that went great,' said Chancer. 'The following morning, though, we all went for breakfast. I remember it clearly because it was Valentine's Day. Not only that, but I went to buy some fags and found it reet weird because it was the day decimal currency was introduced, y'know? I showed Red the change I'd been given, and we all discussed how difficult it was going to be to get used to it. I remember Red being fascinated and telling me her mum worked in a bakery and would struggle working out what change to give out. While we were on the subject of money, I decided it was best to own up and tell them I was skint. I hadn't been paid for the gig yet, but Red volunteered to pay for breakfast. She had a bit of dosh…'

'Nana left it to her in her will,' said Elf.

'Sure. Anyway, in the café we ordered the full English, but when the owner came over, Red couldn't find her purse. I didn't stick around long enough to see the outcome – I legged it and Marc came with me.'

'You ran off and left my sister in the bloody café?' It was Elf's turn to get annoyed. He could feel the muscles in his body tense, the thought of his sister being abandoned lighting a spark inside him.

'You have to understand, around here it's every man for himself,' said Chancer. 'You look after Number One.'

'Except she wasn't a man, she was a 13-year-old girl,' said Elf. 'And in Wales, we stick together, mun.'

'Marc didn't seem too bothered. He said she was a resourceful kid.'

'It sounds like you didn't give him much choice,' said Kerry. 'You grabbed him by the arm and forced him to run. This is your fault.'

'Woah!' Chancer pushed his chair back. 'I don't have to speak to either of you, y'know? Don't start on me.'

'Wait!' Elf shouted as the roadie headed for the door. 'You're right...we're sorry. We just want to track down the people we love. What happened next? Where did you go?'

Slowly, Chancer returned to his seat and continued with his story. 'Marc and I ran down the high street and tried to lose ourselves in the crowd. Unfortunately, we attracted the wrong type of attention. There were these skins over the road and, I don't know, they just sensed we were queer, right? I have a nose for trouble, so dragged Marc into this alley between two shops. Unfortunately, we got cornered. It was a dead end, and we got the shit kicked out of us. I can look after myself so gave as good as I got, but Marc was laid out by this big bastard who was kicking him when your sister turned up.'

'Oh no.'

'Credit where credit's due, she shouted at this thug, telling him to leave Marc alone,' he said. 'Unfortunately, the bloke wasn't one to respect women. He punched her, and she fell. That was the last I saw before the police turned up.'

'You didn't help her?' Chancer looked sheepish. 'For fuck's sake, are you telling me you left her in the shit a second time?'

'Look, I ain't here to be put on public trial,' he said. 'I feel guilty enough as it is. I think I've said all I have to say. I never saw her after that, and I haven't had much to do with Marc since then, either. I got him a roadying job, and he paid me back by copping off with the bass player from the band. Since then, I've just seen him now and again at gigs.' The roadie jumped up again, his chair clattering to the floor. Then he headed for the door.

'Hey!' The shout came from behind the counter. 'You ain't paid for that tea yet, mate.'

Chancer looked at the woman in the white apron who was coming out from behind the counter. 'My friends will take care of it,' he said, opening the door and stepping outside. As he turned in the direction of the station, Elf crashed into the back of him, sending him flying to the pavement again. The Welsh boy then twisted him around and sat astride him, eyes red with menace as he drew back his fist.

'Should have marked you down as another queer basher,' said Chancer.

'No, he ain't. He's my bloke,' said Kerry, joining them outside. 'We're both kids and we don't have much money so the way you're acting takes the piss. Pay the lady or I'll break every one of your flamin' fingers.'

The woman emerged from the café. 'That's 20p you owe me mate – two cups of tea,' she said, leaning over the prone figure. 'And if you are paying for theirs as well it will cost you half a nicker.'

'Hold on,' said Kerry, dipping a hand into the pocket of Chancer's leather jacket. She pulled out a colourful small pouch and opened it up, handing the woman a 50p piece.

'That's perfect, love. Thanks. We're always getting tea leaves in here.'

'I'm not surprised. You're a tea shop.'

The girl laughed. 'Bless you, love, ain't heard cockney rhyming slang, 'ave ya? Tea leaves means thieves.'

Kerry laughed and expected Elf to join in. When she looked at him, though, his face had drained of colour.

'Bloody hell, have you seen a ghost, mun?'

'It's Megan's,' he mumbled.

'What is?' she asked.

'That purse you're holding,' he said. 'It's hers.'

30

ELF DRAGGED CHANCER to his feet and stood him against the wall. 'What are you doing with this, eh?' He waved the small, knitted object in the air.

'I was looking after it for her,' said the roadie. 'She left it at the squat.'

'I don't believe you, mun. I think you're a thieving ratbag. Megan would never have run out of a café without paying. Our mam always says if you steal something, someone else will suffer, like the shop assistant who gets sacked if the till doesn't balance at the end of the day.'

'You ain't got a clue about real life, have ya?' said Chancer, the sneer returning. 'It's all right living in a cosy little village in Taffy land where nothing happens, but here on the streets is different. Every day you fight battles to make ends meet while trying to survive constant attacks from queer bashers, cops and the posh city bastards who take advantage of the poor while supplementing their lavish lifestyles. Marx said—'

Crack! The sharp slap in the face took the roadie completely by surprise and made his eyes water. He looked to his right where Kerry stood, fists balled, ready to resume the attack. 'You know nothing about us, you stuck-up prick!' she said. 'My mam died young from some terrible infection brought on by damp and cold when I was two, like. Our dad said it was down to the shit conditions we lived in and worked every hour God sent in searing heat down the local steelworks to get us a better home. There ain't many around our way that haven't lost a loved one through tragic circumstances like pit accidents and the like, see?'

Chancer stood, mouth open, defenceless against the verbal attack. 'It's all right for you in your fancy clothes, leather jackets and stuff, spouting off about things and quoting this fuckin' Marx fella,' she continued. 'I just think "What a prick". You ain't got a clue about hardship and poverty. We struggle every day just to get up in the morning. You wouldn't know struggle if it jumped up and punched you in the face, see?'

'Which it just did!' said Elf, never feeling more in love with this girl than he did now. He didn't even think Kerry was listening when Chancer had been talking about life in his current squat, which he shared with a collective of gay Marxists. He'd waffled on about anarchy, freedom of speech and solidarity to such an extent Elf had zoned out. He thought Kerry had, too. It wasn't the first time he'd underestimated her. To think some kids referred to her as a "dumb scrubber" in the playground.

Who were the dumb ones now?

'I can't help you anymore,' said Chancer. 'I ain't got a clue where your sister is. I admit I had a bit of a fling with Marc but, like I say, he fucked off with someone more "interesting".'

'My brother ain't like that,' said Kerry. 'You obviously never bothered getting to know him. He's the sweetest, kindest, caring person. So where can we find him? You said you see him at gigs. Which gigs and when's the next one?'

'You think you know him, but he's changed,' said Chancer. 'I doubt he'll give you the time of day now he's gone up in the world. You'll cramp his style.'

'What are you talkin' about?' she said. 'He's my brother. Of course, he'll want to see me again. I don't know what you mean about going up in the world. I just want to know where to find him.'

'You could start by looking behind you,' said Chancer.

It was the oldest trick in the book, but they were distracted long enough for Chancer to wriggle free of Elf's grip, scramble up and run off.

'Shit!' said Elf.

He turned to give pursuit, expecting Kerry to have a similar reaction. Instead, he saw her standing stock still; her face white and her eyes drawn hypnotically towards the wall opposite. On it, half hidden in shadow by a railway bridge, was a poster. It featured a singer, pouting at the camera, dark make-up framing eyes which stared out from a chalky white face. Jet black hair rose in spikes from the singer's head while he was dressed in a glittery red vest top and knee-length leather trench coat. Suspended from a wrist held above his head was a microphone. Underneath the picture were the words The Cashmere Criminals followed by a list of dates and venues.

Before Elf could stop her, Kerry bounded across the road, the loud horn of a bus blasting through the London hubbub as it braked to avoid her. Running across the nearest pedestrian crossing, he caught up with his girlfriend as she reached the other side. 'Bloody 'ell Kez, mun, you could have been killed!' he said. 'What's so interesting, anyway? You know this band? I've never heard of them.'

'It's not any band, Elf,' she said, pointing her finger at the singer on the poster. 'It's Marc's band…And that's our Marc, right there.'

31

'WANDA WILLIAMS!'

The exclamation boomed across the playground and reached its intended target on the netball court.

Oh Christ. She dropped the ball to the floor and looked in his direction. The beckoning finger told her she wasn't mistaken. She was in for a bollocking. She thought she'd got away with applying a minimum amount of blue eye shadow in the bogs 15 minutes before the final bell. Make-up was banned, of course, but the girls had learnt to bend the rules over time. 'Yes, sir?' she mumbled as she walked towards the deputy headmaster, eyes fixed on the floor.

'Come with me.'

'But, sir, it's home time.'

He ignored her plea, turning and pacing in the direction of the main school building. It could mean only one thing. She felt her skin prickle as she realised they were heading for the vice-principal's office. The eyes of her fellow inmates followed her walk of shame. A summons from Mr Rhys had to be viewed with trepidation.

Above his office door was a light which, when red, glared at the passers-by with demonic intensity. It meant some poor kid was in trouble. Myths were rife, mainly perpetrated by older pupils who had either survived to tell the tale or simply felt it their duty to scare the living daylights out of the younger ones. Wanda had heard all the stories: 'He smack's your bare arse with a stick with a rusty nail poking out', 'He ties you to a chair, removes your socks and holds a lighter to your bare feet', 'He makes you eat dog food from a tin that he keeps in his cupboard'. The fact she was aware those telling the stories were wind-up merchants didn't make them easier to swallow.

One girl claimed he'd touched her private parts. When people suggested she report him, though, she quickly withdrew the allegation. 'He would come after me in the night if I grassed him up,' said Karen Major. Her friends dismissed her story as pure fantasy.

'You wish,' said one of the cattier members of her class. 'That's the only way you'll get anyone to touch you. I bet you dream of Mr Rhys when you're flicking your bean at night.'

Harsh, but Karen was no school beauty.

Once inside the building, Wanda saw the door ajar at the end of the corridor. There was no one on reception and she passed empty classrooms, looking out of the window to see the other girls in the school team practising. A tall girl, she had high hopes of getting a first-team spot when the South Wales schools championships started in a few weeks' time. It was a good way to guarantee exemption from double maths.

Reaching the open door, she paused briefly to stare up at the light, which was now green. 'Come!' The command made her hands shake and her stomach flip. She desperately needed a pee. Not now! Closing her eyes and drawing in a breath, she put one foot in front of the other and entered his lair. 'Shut the door behind you.'

She did as she was told, turning and gently pushing it, hoping that it might remain ajar. No such luck. It speeded up as if his mind alone was controlling it, slamming shut behind her. Twisting her fingers behind her back, she turned to face him and watched him press a button on his desk and guessed the red light would now be on.

'There's something different about you today, Miss Williams,' he said, walking around the heavy wooden desk to make a closer inspection. A tingle of alarm crept up her spine. 'Hmmm. When did your eyelids turn blue? Did you inadvertently stick your hand in some paint during art class, then rub them? Noooo. How about I ask you to empty the contents of your bag on the table? I wonder what I might find?'

'Dunno, sir.'

'Then that makes two of us. Shall we do that then – solve the mystery?'

Now Wanda was worried. The make-up wasn't the only contraband stashed away in her satchel. There was also the spliff her boyfriend had given her after sneaking into school at lunchtime and feeling her up behind the bike sheds. She had to stop the line of questioning going any further.

'It's make-up, sir,' she said. 'A bit of eye shadow. I only put it on in the toilets before netball practice. I didn't wear it to class, honest.'

He put his hand on his chin and moved closer, his face inches from hers. She could smell his breath, a rancid mixture of garlic and strong cigar smoke. 'Hmm,' he said. 'You should know the rules better than anyone, though, with your father being head of the governors. No cosmetics are allowed on the school grounds. The question is, do I search your bag, or do I take your word for it? In my experience, if a pupil breaks one rule there's a good chance they've broken others, too.'

She stayed silent, trying to remain cool under his piercing stare.

'How do you think your father would react if I told him you were acting like a cheap tart for the benefit of a certain type of boy…the type of boy who has one thing on his mind? A certain boy like, well, Melvin Hughes perhaps?'

Fuck. How did he know about Melv? She'd tried her hardest to keep their liaisons a secret.

They'd only started seeing each other a couple of weeks ago and she knew her parents wouldn't approve. Melvin was two years older than her – 17 almost 18 – and had been expelled from school the year before. He rode a motorbike and her friends said he had a reputation. Even so, when she caught his eye as she stood with a group of classmates, including his sister Marjorie, she thought she was going to faint. Flicking the bike onto its stand, he'd walked confidently up to her, looking so sexy in his leathers that she almost wet herself.

'I ain't seen you before, babe,' he said. 'What's your name, eh?'

When she stuttered in response, she thought she'd blown her chance, but he simply laughed and offered her a backie on his bike. A week later, they were driving into the countryside and finding secret locations where they could "get to know each other better". This meant a lot of fumbling and a brief amount of fucking which he called "making love". He told her she was the only woman for him, but deep in her heart she knew it wasn't true. It was good for her feelings of self-worth to take him at face value, though.

'Sir, I...look please...'

'Open the bag.'

'I know where Megan is.'

Shit. Wanda had blurted it out before she realised what she was doing. Biting her lip and fighting back tears, she issued a silent apology to her missing friend.

'IT'S ME.'

'Yes.'

'I need a favour.'

'Oh?'

There was a pause followed by a sequence of loud pips.

'Damn! Stupid new money.' Finally, the coin dropped.

'New money? We've had it for more than two years now. You should be used to it. Or has decimal currency only just reached the valleys?'

'Funny. Listen, I haven't got long.' There was a sigh, then silence on the other end. He decided the best thing was to blurt it out. 'It's about my daughter.'

'The one who did a bunk with lover boy?'

'Yes...she's back in circulation.'

'Like the currency.'

'If you're going to make that analogy, you could say she's turned up like a bad penny.' There was a moment's silence, so he realised he should carry on. 'She sent a postcard.'

'You have it?'

'No, it wasn't sent to me but to someone else, and has since been thrown away, I understand. Apparently, it had images of Piccadilly Circus, red buses, the bright lights...'

'Hardly unique then. You can get them anywhere.'

'Yes, but the person who received it said it had a London postmark. I think she's on your patch.'

'And what would you like me to do about it?'

'Find her...well...find them both. I'll post you a photograph. It makes me nervous thinking of them wandering around, telling people God knows what. You, more than anyone, should know the implications, judge.'

'It's been two years since they went missing,' said the man. 'Nothing has come out yet, so why worry now? And there's a good chance they might have changed a great deal. They are two years older.'

'True. There's one thing that makes her stand out in a crowd, though.'

'Oh?'

'Her hair. You won't see it in the pictures, but it's bright red and...unruly. And she has freckles to match.'

'Typical Celt,' the Judge said. 'There are thousands of you lot here in the smoke, though, not to mention the jocks and the paddies. I can't make any guarantees. Leave it with me and I'll put out some feelers.'

'It needs to be a priority. For all of us. If those pictures get into the wrong hands...'

'Don't say any more.'

Click.

Osean Rhys stared at the mouthpiece for some time after the phone went dead. Eventually, he replaced it on its stand, turned and left the box. He would have to play the waiting game.

32

ELFYN WATCHED HIS paper dart perform a couple of loops before landing in the donut-shaped bun on top of Angela Watkins' head. She turned and glared.

'Attennnnnshunnn!'

The noise in the hall died instantly, heads turning towards the main doors. Elfyn's stepdad stood there, feet apart, his eyes scanning the gathered assembly. Next to him was a man dressed head-to-toe in khaki. There was a beret on his head decorated with the three-feathers emblem.

In complete silence, the two men marched down the corridor dividing the ranks of pupils, the soldier's boots beating out a rhythmic tattoo on the parquet floor. Climbing the stairs, they then walked to the lectern in the centre of the stage. Behind them stood a large screen.

The deputy headmaster scanned the pupils to make sure he had their undivided attention. Satisfied, he finally spoke. 'Boys and girls, we are honoured today to have with us Corporal Barry Webster from the Welsh Guards. Corporal Webster has kindly agreed to talk to you about the abundant careers available in the armed forces and, in particular, the army. Before we hear from him, however, there will be a short film. If someone could dim the lights...you boy, Jenkins, you'll do.' He pointed to a fair-haired pupil in the back row who stood and carried out the task.

'Thank you.' The deputy head looked down at a nervous woman in a tweed skirt, white ruffled blouse and tortoiseshell spectacles, a tangled mass of grey hair sitting on top of her head. 'Would you kindly do the honours, Miss Barrett?'

Splodges like gravy stains appeared on the canvas followed by a row of dots before an image sprang to life of a tank rumbling across bumpy ground accompanied by a dramatic soundtrack. A posh, clipped voice spoke over rousing classical music.

'The modern army has many roles in the world today. Rather than on foot, the infantry now travels in fast, armoured personal carriers, giving them protection and mobility. All men, vehicles and weapons are formed into combat teams.'

The tank rumbled on, firing its big guns before the camera panned to explosions in the distance. Elf was mesmerised as the narrator informed him that Britain's Chieftain was the finest battle tank in the world, capable of phenomenal accuracy. He could just imagine the thrill of driving it through countryside and destroying specific targets far away. Words like rapier and blowpipe poured through his brain as he learnt of the anti-tank weapons Britain could employ to protect their own troops. Elf could see himself shouldering one of those big guns and destroying an enemy vehicle. It was the sort of dream he'd harboured since those primary school days playing soldiers with his mates at break time.

The narrator explained that the British army's worldwide responsibilities gave recruits the chance to travel. The film flashed from one exotic place to another before settling on a less glamorous scene. A group of ragamuffin kids not much older than Elf were throwing missiles at British soldiers. Stationary cars and army vehicles burst into flames and the pupils were informed about the army's massive job maintaining security in Northern Ireland.

'To accomplish these tasks and man all equipment, the army is on constant lookout for class recruits, intelligent men from all walks of life with an active interest in the many specialised branches of the service.'

Elf looked around, feeling proud, though he couldn't say why. His eyes focused on Angela Watkins, who was playing with something in her hand and paying no attention. He wasn't surprised she was bored. This was a man's work.

'We need men of quality, not those who have failed in civilian life,' said the commentator. *'When recruits come forward, we train them to be fitter, more disciplined and schooled in a variety of equipment.'* Some of the boys looked at each other, trying to work out which were the failures and which represented quality material. Elf thought

his performances on the rugby field left no doubt as to where he fitted into the grand scheme of things.

'Responsibility, even at the lowest level, can be high and therefore has to be reflected in the soldier's salary', said the clipped English voice. Elf realised this meant he might have enough money to meet his and Kerry's needs and send a decent wedge back to Mam. Yes, it was his dream job.

'In a six-month tour of duty, it might just take one slip on the soldier's part or a moment of forgetfulness and his whole section could be at risk.'

Elf looked over at Colin Mablethorpe. That accident-prone loser would get his platoon killed without a doubt.

Now on the screen, fit young men were smashing a tennis ball back and forth across a net, cycling through beautiful countryside, hitting the hell out of each other in a boxing ring and scampering around a cricket field. Then the film switched to a man with a ball tucked under his arm, evading tackles then diving over a white line. They even had rugby!

'The facilities for sport in the army are first class both at home and overseas, and few civilian firms can match them,' explained the narrator. This no longer sounded like work to Elf, just one extended adventure holiday. He had made up his mind, his imagination already scrambling up walls and traversing rope bridges over ravines. He didn't even hear the bit where the voice mentioned that,

'Soldiering means risks to life and limb if the occasion demands.'

The film ended with a still of a shopfront on a normal British High Street, the sign above the doorway announcing it was a British Army Recruitment Office. He wondered where he could find the nearest one.

'IT WAS FANTASTIC, Mam, see. This bloke, well, he is a corporal like in the army, the Welsh Guards no less, see, and I spoke to him after and he was sure I could be one. Guess what? They play rugby! I could even end up parading in front of The Queen.'

Mam smiled. Her youngest boy was so excited he could hardly get the words out fast enough. 'I'd be so proud of you, Elf, son, not that I'm not already. Your sister and I…' Doreen Rhys paused. Elf saw a tear roll down the side of her nose before she wiped it away with her hand. He put a large, comforting palm on her shoulder.

'I miss her too, Mam, but she'll be back one day,' he said. 'You never know. She might see me in one of them parades and get in touch.'

'I was always…' She cut off the words and sniffed. Elf knew what she was going to say. For as long as he could remember, it had been her plan to take Megan and his grandmother to see The Queen in one of those marvellous spectacles of pomp and ceremony. He felt awful using his mother's sentimentality to push through his plan.

'Mam, this soldier said he was so impressed with my enthusiasm that he invited me for a weekend in London with other potential recruits. You go to Trooping the Colour and learn more about the job. They put you up for two nights and...'

'That's a long time to be away from home for a boy your age,' said Mam. 'You're still only 15 and I worry every night about Meg, like. If she's safe or sleeping in a cardboard box on the streets. I wouldn't want—'

'Mam, look,' he said. 'I'm almost a grown man and I can look after myself. Ask Dad.'

'What was the date?'

He sensed she was weakening. Just a few small twists...

'It's Saturday June 2. The 1st Battalion of the Welsh Guards is performing the ceremony to mark The Queen's birthday. It's going to be special.'

'And you say your father knows about it?'

Elf knew Mam wouldn't sign off on chips for tea without Osean agreeing. That's why he'd planned like a true army officer would. Making sure his stepfather was watching, he'd engaged the corporal in conversation and put his name and address down on a form requesting further information about the services. Then he'd asked the corporal about the possibility of attending Trooping the Colour and the soldier had said he would inquire. There had certainly been no personal invite and an offer of accommodation, but Elf had spun the story to his stepfather once the soldier had returned to barracks.

'Dad said I'm big enough and daft enough to look after myself,' said Elf.

'Well, I guess if he thinks it's OK...' She didn't finish the sentence before he flung himself at her and engulfed her in his arms. When he put her down, she reached for the bakery calendar hanging from the pantry door frame, removed the pen from the coil at the top, and scribbled down a reminder against June 2. At that moment he knew he'd won. If it went on the calendar, it meant it was happening.

IN THE RED phone box two streets away, Osean was speaking to his London contact again.

'You're a bit impatient,' said the judge. 'I won't hear for a while yet.'

'I've got something that might help.'

'Oh?'

'My youngest boy is coming up in June. Says he's on an army training weekend, but he must think my head buttons up the back. I know his real intention is to look for her.'

'Not soldier material?'

'It's not that...he told me an army recruitment officer had invited him to watch Trooping the Colour, but when I checked with this bloke, he said it was just a tentative suggestion. I think Elfyn has a secret agenda.'

'He's looking for big sis. You think he saw the postcard?'

'I wouldn't be surprised. I'll scout around when he's out just in case it's in his room.'

'We'll keep an eye on him.'

'I'm pretty sure he won't come alone...'

Peep...peep...peep...peep...

'Oh, for fuck's sake...there...got it...'

'You were saying?' asked the judge.

'I fully expect my boy to be accompanied by his girlfriend, Kerry. She's the sister of the boy who went missing.'

'You bloody Taffs,' said the man from London with a chuckle. 'Like to keep it in the family, don't you?'

Part Three

April 1973

33

Soho, London, March 31

THEY FELL SILENT at the sound of the door opening. A head appeared around it, looking into the room nervously.

'Sorry,' said Red. 'I was told you wanted me.'

'Not me,' said Blaize. Then she looked wide-eyed at Jack. 'Am I missing something...?'

'Not a bit of it, my lovely, I know she's your girl,' he said. 'She just places some bets for me sometimes. It's the National today.' He opened his bottom drawer, removed an envelope, and handed it to the younger woman.

Blaize swivelled and looked Red in the eye.

'Don't worry, Blaize. I've done it before,' said the girl. 'The bookie knows me.'

'Does he now? Well, I suppose...'

With a subtle nod of the head, Jack dismissed her, and the two club owners watched her leave.

'Did she hear anything?' said Blaize.

'Doubt it,' he replied. 'The walls are pretty thick.'

'Good. The fewer people that know, the better. It's highly illegal, y'know, and if we get caught, you might as well say goodbye to the club business once and for all…let alone your freedom. Now you've got me involved. I'll be neck deep in the shit, just like you. You're a selfish prick, Jack.'

'Love, we can clear 20 grand.'

Her eyes opened wide. 'Nah,' she said. 'Too cheap. It's worth 30 at the very least. We're taking all the risks. That lot – this "club" as they call themselves – is good for it and can wriggle out of anything. That's the power they wield, so even 30 grand is chicken feed. If it goes wrong, it will be you and I that pay the consequences.'

'I've already agreed the price with Foggy, though.'

'That bloody man,' she said. 'Sometimes I think he's got his hand up your backside, pulling all the strings. Get back to him. He of all people knows the risks. Imagine if this got in the papers…we're talking kids and that's a jail term right there. It's bad enough if you're the law and you end up inside, but being a nonce, too? Good luck with that.'

'OK, OK,' he said, wishing he didn't have to include Blaize in the venture. Their relationship was such, though, it was virtually impossible for one of them to keep a secret from the other. Buying each other birthday presents was a nightmare.

RED WAS ENTERING the betting shop when someone

called her name. The voice was familiar, and a smile crept across her lips.

'Well, fancy seeing you here,' she said.

'All right, gorgeous? Thought you might have a friendlier greeting for me than that, seeing as I'm your number one bloke.'

'In your dreams.'

'Very much so.'

She punched him on the arm. 'You're gross!'

'I know,' he said. 'That's why you love me.'

The banter had become a tradition between the two of them, ever since that first night when Stan Marshall and his father Paddy had rescued her from a masked attacker in the heart of the West End. She was so grateful it would have been rude to decline when the youngster begged to see her again. Anyway, he was mature for his age and where was the harm?

Stan's regular appearances in Red's company hadn't gone unnoticed by some of the other girls. One or two of them were even quite taken with Stan's charm and liked to mother him, slipping him sweets or cigarettes and draping themselves across him, teasing him that they couldn't wait until he was 'all grown up'. He gave as good as he got.

'What are you on?' he asked her.

'What do you mean?' she said.

'Which horse?'

'Don't be daft, it's Jack's money ain't it?' she said, noting the cockney twang to her accent and wondering when that had started to take over.

'You know he gets me to put his bets on when he's too busy to do it himself.'

'In that case, do us a favour would you, Princess?' He fumbled in his pockets and came out with two-pound coins. 'I've got a hot tip – Red Rum. Two pounds on the nose. I got a good feeling.'

'Why?'

'Obvious, isn't it?' he said. 'Anything with Red in the name is good enough for me.'

She felt her face burning. 'Why don't you put the bet on yourself?' she said.

'Have you forgotten how old I am?' He gave her his best pleading look, his brown eyes reminding her of a puppy one of her friends used to have back in Wales.

'I'm not that much older,' she said.

'Yeah, but that bloke Jack vouches for ya,' he said.

'Come on then, give it here,' said Red. 'But if you win, you're taking me out for a slap-up meal.'

'Deal,' he said. 'Now, where can we watch the race?'

'NEVER MIND, STAN, you did your best. I hope you could afford to lose all that money.'

'It's not over yet, darlin', honest. It's a long race, the National. Anything can happen.'

'Seriously?' said Red. 'Jack's horse is strolling it. What did the commentator say? He's 33 clear. Not that I have a clue what that means.'

'He's 33 lengths clear...each measure is the length of a horse. Hold up, mine just got a mention. There. Listen!'

Sure enough, the famous BBC commentator Peter O'Sullevan said Stan's horse was emerging from the pack and giving pursuit, though she thought there couldn't be far to go. They'd jumped 28 fences and time was running out. Not that Stan seemed deterred. He jumped up and down as if he was on the horse's back, and Red feared he would attract attention to them.

Stan had dragged her into a full Soho bar so that they could stand at the back and watch the race without being questioned about their age. He was wearing a cheerful light blue cravat with a paisley pattern on it, insisting it made him look older.

'Look! Look!' He grabbed her arm and pointed. The big horse was gobbling up the ground now, closing on Crisp with every stride. Jack's horse leapt the 30th and final fence in the lead but was tiring badly. *'Just a furlong to run now, 200 yards now for Crisp, and Red Rum is still closing on him!'* shouted the excited commentator.

'Oww! You're hurting,' said Red. 'Your nails are digging into my arm!'

'Shhhh!' said Stan. 'Come on Red!'

'...Crisp is getting tired, and Red Rum is pounding after him. Red Rum is the one who's finishing the strongest. He's going to get up! Red Rum is going to win the National. At the line, Red Rum has just snatched it from Crisp!'

Red felt herself pulled into a strong embrace, the young boy ecstatic as he shouted in her ear, 'We did it! We did it!' Holding her face in his fingers he bent forward and gave her a long, minty kiss. She was so stunned she didn't know what to say. She had to admit, though, it felt nice. Even so, she knew she was expected to register some sort of protest, so smacked him across the cheek. In response, he stared back at her, a big smile attached to his face.

'Worth it,' he said.

'What do you mean?'

'I've wanted to kiss you for ages and this time I had the perfect excuse. The good thing is I know exactly what I want to buy with my winnings.'

'And what's that?'

'An engagement ring,' he said. Though he was still smiling, he had a determined look in his eye.

'Dreaming again, Stan,' she said. 'That's a *Jackanory* idea, if you ask me.'

He laughed at the reference to the popular TV programme in which well-known personalities read bedtime stories to a young audience.

'We'll see, Cinderella,' he said.

34

WHEN RED GOT back to Jack's office, a familiar figure was waiting outside. Billy the Kid Dolan was dressed in an expensive pinstripe suit and tie, his pair of highly polished black brogues glinting in the corridor lights.

'All right?' he asked.

She nodded. Just speaking to Billy made her feel unclean these days, as if she was disrespecting the memory of her dead friend Jerry. It was almost two years since his death, and she still suspected foul play despite the coroner's suicide verdict. Her scepticism had grown when one of the dancers at the Cat had told her Billy had spent 24 hours in the cells accused of the robbery before her friend was arrested and charged. Since that time, Billy's fortunes had been on a remarkable upward spiral. He swaggered around the corridors with his head held high, dressed in the finest clothing, with jewellery dripping from his wrists and a top-of-the-range sports car at his disposal. Someone had dubbed him the new Reggie Kray, and though rumours of his criminal activities were rife, he seemed untouchable.

'What are you here for, Red?' he asked. 'Maybe I can help?'

'I've got to give Jack his winnings,' she said.

'He's busy. Give 'em here and I'll pass 'em on.'

She tightened her grip on her bag. 'I'd rather do it myself.'

'Please yourself,' he said. 'Remember who you are talking to, though. I'm Jack's number one man. Christ, me and you were mates once.'

No, we weren't, she thought. You gave me a lift once, and we shared a drunken evening in a strip club, that's all. 'Look, I'm not being funny, but Jack likes me to hand it to him personally, right?' she said.

He sniggered.

'What?'

'I didn't have him down as one of them that fancies them so young. How old are you? Fifteen? I guess you learn somethin' new every day.'

'I'm 16 and, anyway, I don't know what you're talking about.'

'You're a big girl, you figure it out.'

Before she could respond, he turned and began walking towards the far end of the corridor. 'Anyhow, I'm a busy man,' he said. 'Things to do, people to see. I ain't got time to shoot the breeze with a young slapper...but I hope you enjoy yourself with the old man.'

He winked at her, and she shuddered, as if ants were crawling across her skin. As he walked away, she put her hands flat against the wall, feeling the cold plaster against her fingers. Bringing her breathing under control, she looked back down the corridor after him, noting that Billy was engaged in conversation with another man she vaguely recognised.

As he talked, the new arrival hoisted his belt up around his enormous belly, the loose folds of skin around his mouth wobbling as he spoke. The two men obviously had a close connection. The older man reaching out to pat Billy on the arm as he made his point.

Red rifled through her memory banks and when she came up with the answer, her hand shot to her mouth. It was the same man who had spoken to that group of SPG officers in court on the day Jerry died two years ago. At the time, Woodsy had told her he was some kind of bigwig in the Met.

What could a top London police officer have in common with a scumbag like Billy Dolan?

'YOU GOT MY cut?' asked Fogarty.

'I've been waiting for the dust to settle,' said Billy. 'Won't be long.'

'Good.' The cop took in his surroundings, his eyes settling on the girl at the end of the corridor. As he watched, she pushed herself from the wall and disappeared into Jack's office. He was starting to realise he couldn't be too careful these days. There had been a reporter from *The Sunday Times* investigation team knocking about and asking questions in recent weeks. Fortunately, Foggy thought he'd covered his tracks well. He'd kept his team in bungs so that none of them could speak out against him without incriminating themselves.

'Any more jobs like that?' asked Billy.

'Greedy little fucker, ain't ya?' said Fogarty. 'It took all my ingenuity to set up that newspaper payroll job. I heard you pulled more than 200 grand, so I'm expecting a nice little drink out of it. They've appointed a top cop to investigate police corruption in the city. Nothing I can't handle but we need to be patient. In the meantime, I'll give him some of the smaller stuff to distract him. It's all about arrest figures at the end of the day. Hopefully, he won't put two and two together. D'you know, I got 500 boys in blue off the streets for that "training day" so that you could pull off the newspaper thing without hassle? Bet you didn't see anyone out on the job from start to finish.'

Billy shook his head. 'Thanks for that. Look, I got bills to pay too, though. Takes a lot of preparation, lot of mouths to feed, a job like that...'

'I'll keep my ear to the ground for a nice little touch. You do the same, won't you? And if this corruption tsar, as they call him, starts sniffing around here you'll let me know, right?'

'Sure.'

'Who's the tart?'

'Which one?'

'The one you were talking to. Red hair.'

'One of Blaize's birds.'

'She didn't hear anything?'

'Doubt it. Simple little Welsh bint she is. Wouldn't spot something amiss if it bit her on the aris, if you get what I'm saying.'

'Of course,' said Fogarty. 'How old is she? I know someone who's partial to a bit of ginger.'

'You're out of luck there. Blaize keeps a close eye on her – Red is her personal assistant. She doesn't get involved in that side of the business.'

'We'll see about that,' said Foggy. 'Some of my connections are wealthy people and money talks.'

'Ain't that the truth,' said Billy.

35

THICK, SANDY HAIR unfurled in waves down the back of an Afghan coat as the girl in front stood up in response to the sound of a tinny bell. 'Camden High Street!' the conductor announced. A bony elbow clattered into Elf's ribs, forcing him to cry out.

Kerry sniggered. 'Big poody!' she said. 'I thought you were going to be a soldier, like? You won't be much good to Her Majesty if you can't take a little dig in the ribs from a girl, will you? Come on, this is our stop.'

'Bloody hell, Kerry mun, you caught me unawares.' He rolled up the army pamphlet he'd been reading and got to his feet. Grasping her hand, they ran towards the exit and jumped from the back step, turning to watch the red London bus depart, the conductor hanging from a pole like a dancer in a strip club.

'This lot seems to know where they're going,' said Kerry as she fell into step behind Afghan girl and her posse of gaily clad friends. They passed a succession of grubby premises, second-hand shops and tobacconists followed by a bookmaker and a cobbler. Everything was grim and grey. After being overtaken by the initial thrill of their adventure, they fell silent, wondering if they'd made a mistake and climbed off at the wrong stop.

A jumble of derelict buildings sprang up to their left, hidden behind dilapidated wooden barricades. There were words painted in white hinting that behind the obstruction was a timber yard, but at various intervals someone had pasted random posters on the fence. Various musicians and bands were featured, some they'd heard of and others, who were a complete mystery. It wasn't until they saw Marc in a familiar pose with his guitar that Kerry clasped her boyfriend's hand and hissed, 'Told you'.

The crowd in front of them was rapidly expanding, with people flowing from every direction like tributaries feeding a main river. For a while, they allowed themselves to be carried along with the tide until they found themselves on a cobbled street surrounded by tables hidden under giant tarpaulins. 'This must be the market,' said Kerry.

'Oops sorry!' Failing to realise the crowd had come to an abrupt halt alongside a long, narrow building running through the middle of the site, Elf had clattered into the person in front of him. A young man turned and jabbed a finger in his direction. Elf stepped backwards with surprise, not from the aggressive reaction but because the kid's face was split down the middle, one half painted black and the other white.

'Watch where your big boots are treadin' would ya, mate? Or I may have to stick me own boot where the sun don't shine, awrigh'?'

Kerry quickly moved forward. 'Sorry, mate, he can be a bit clumsy.'

The kid looked her up and down and smiled. 'OKaaay, sweetheart, whatever you say. Bit simple, is he? Poor bloke. Ain't seen you at Dingwall's before. This your first time? It only opened a month back, but it won't remain a secret for long. Best music venue in London.'

'Sounds great, mun, like, seen anyone good then?'

'Sure. The DJs play some top stuff – not your chart shit, y'know, and tonight's headline act, Kilburn and the High Roads, are well worth seeing. They've got this weird, crippled guy singing for them called Ian Dury – some of his lyrics are a bit close to the bone, but he's a lot of fun.'

'Shit, mun, bouncers,' said Elf, leaning forward and whispering in her ear. 'What if they ask us for proof of age?'

'Don't worry about it, mun,' she said. 'We're on the guest list, right? Come on…' She grabbed his hand and started leading him past the waiting queue. 'How did you manage that?' he asked.

'Ricky, that roadie fella who put us on to Chancer,' she said. 'He couldn't have been more helpful. I had to agree you'd help move some gear, but you don't mind, do you?'

Even if he did, Elf knew it was too late to change things. It was one of his girlfriend's annoying traits that she made decisions for him, then presented them as a done deal.

'THIS USED TO be stables, y'know?' The boy with the two-tone face appeared at Kerry's shoulder as she stood in the middle of the venue, looking around. 'They were two storeys and to get horses from the bottom to the top stables they used those steps outside. By the way. I'm Mike,' he said. 'And you are...?'

'Kerry. Friends call me Kez.'

'I love the Welsh accent. Where's that bloke you were with? The simple one. I'm guessing you're his care worker. I s'pose it's all voluntary, too. I got a lot of respect for people like you.'

Kerry felt no obligation to put him right.

'Thanks,' she said. 'He's just gone to the loo. Listen...I'm told The Cashmere Criminals are good, like. Have you seen them?'

'Ha!' He looked at her as if she'd just told him she'd won the football pools. 'My mate's only the bleedin' drummer. Alfie. Good lad he is. Good band. They're about to release their first album for EMI Records and two weeks ago they did a session on John Peel's late-night show. Their lead singer, Marky Cross, is a bit of a showman. They might even be on the *Old Grey Whistle Test* soon, that TV show with 'whispering' Bob Harris.'

She'd vaguely heard of the programme, but the only music show that interested her was *Top of the Pops*. Kerry had dreamt of being a member of their resident dance group Pan's People and flaunting herself around a stage in provocative gear, knowing every girl would be envious and every boy would fantasise about her.

'...The band, I'm sure it wouldn't be a problem.'

She realised Mike was still talking.

'I'm sorry,' she said, cupping her ear. 'I didn't catch that.'

'I just said that if you want to meet the group, I can arrange it. We could go for a drink after the show.'

'Wow, I'd bloody love that, mun! Serious.'

'Great! Now, I'm just gonna wander off and find my mates. I'll come and get you after the Criminals have played their set.'

Kerry said goodbye and peered out over the growing crowd in search of Elf, noting for the first time that there were hardly any windows in the stuffy building. It made her feel claustrophobic but also excited, a feeling which intensified as the lights dimmed and she was engulfed by darkness, just a few psychedelic patterns moving around the walls, providing any source of illumination.

Her ears were assaulted by an incessant soundtrack of loud chatter, snippets of different conversations fighting for her attention across a crowded room. On the stage to her left, a few people were busy wiring up microphones and connecting instruments to amplifiers while on her right a gaggle of people were fighting for the attention of the bar staff.

'Good evening, Dingwalls!' a voice boomed out, and all eyes turned to the stage. Kerry's stomach churned at the prospect of seeing her brother again, and she almost jumped out of her skin when a hand landed on her shoulder. 'Bloody hell, Elf mun, you scared me!'

'Sorry.'

'Everything OK?'

'Gagging for a beer,' he said. 'Lugging all that gear is thirsty work, mun. Do you want anything from the bar?'

'Sure,' she said. 'Get me a vodka and orange, would you? Hurry, though. I think it's about to start.'

Kerry briefly monitored his progress as he pushed his way effortlessly through the crowd. She found it amusing to see people step hurriedly out of the way as they caught sight of the giant teenager lumbering towards them, many doing a double take once he'd passed.

'Right, you bastards! We're the Cashmere Criminals and we don't give a fuck who you are.'

The voice interrupted her thoughts and made her instantly transfer her gaze to the stage. Under a single spotlight, his hand wrapped around the microphone and his face staring menacingly out into the crowd, was the band's lead singer. Though he was wearing an outrageous outfit of sparkling red shirt open to the navel, figure-hugging black jeans, and thigh-high platformed white boots, the sight of him pierced her like a rapier to the heart. He might have been taller, thinner and displaying a disturbing arrogance, but beneath it all he was the same boy she'd grown up with back in the quiet Welsh village of Croesybont.

Her brother Marc. Or Marky Cross, as he was now known, apparently.

His outrageous greeting to the crowd brought catcalls, shouts, boos, and cheers. From behind her, a plastic bottle shot over her head and landed at Marc's feet, spraying liquid over the stage. She turned to see if she could identify the culprit, but the crowd was now dense with all eyes focused on the stage, questioning what would happen next.

All eyes barring those of one person, who instead focused on the blonde teenager looking around the room. The man, who wore a denim jacket and jeans and had a peaked cap pulled tightly down to shade his face, leant against a pillar and puffed on a Players No. 6. He'd found it easy to keep tabs on the Welsh boy and girl but so far they'd met no one resembling the person in the photograph.

'ENJOY THE SHOW?'

'Fantastic, mun,' said Kerry. 'Your singer's a bit of a loose cannon, mind. Can't believe he called us all bastards the minute he took to the stage.'

'He likes to get a rise out of the audience,' said the drummer she'd been introduced to as Alfie. 'It doesn't always make him popular, hence the bottles and cans that got thrown at us. All adds to the spectacle, though, I guess. What was your favourite song?'

'I liked the last one...I think it was about an ogre, or something.'

'Yeah,' said Alfie. "Red Light". Best thing Marky's ever written.'

'Made you sound like a real band, like.'

'Jeez, thanks for the compliment,' said the drummer. 'That's because we are a real band. We've got a manager, are about to sign for a record company and that's gonna be our first single. Hell, Mike, where did you find her?'

'Wales, Alf.' The boy with the two-tone face stepped forward. 'She's in London with this mate of hers...' He twisted his head to indicate Elf, then leant forward and whispered, 'He's a bit slow. I think she's his nurse or somethin'.' He touched his nose.

Kerry shot a glance at Elf, but he was busy watching a cripple with a Teddy-boy hairstyle hobbling onto the stage for a sound-check.

'Is he OK?' asked Elf, turning in their direction. 'I could help. He doesn't look like a roadie to me.'

'That's cos he ain't,' said Alfie. 'That's Ian Dury. He's somethin' else. I reckon if he hadn't suffered polio as a kid, he could have been a big star. Let's go through, shall we?'

He pushed a door open to their right and led them into a small, jumbled dressing room – clothes, underwear, instruments, cigarettes, beer bottles, and other detritus were strewn everywhere. A sea of faces looked up to greet their arrival, but one person remained perched on a chair in the corner, his head bowed forward, his eyes barely open...

'Marc!' said Kerry, a look of confusion on her face. The boy with the curly, long hair didn't flinch. 'What's wrong with him?' she asked. 'Is he drunk?'

'Shit!' said Alfie. 'Wanker's been chasing the fuckin' dragon again. Bollocks! Sorry, guys. You're gonna have to leave.'

He turned to usher them out of the door, but Kerry stood firm. 'Come on, girl, you ain't gonna be trouble, are you? Marky needs his privacy. You got no right to be here, anyway—'

'I have every right, boy,' she shouted, thrusting the drummer out of the way with a well-directed elbow. 'He's my brother.'

36

THE SELECT GATHERING in the dressing room froze, no one sure what to do. Kerry span and locked eyes with Elf. 'What's wrong with him, Elf? He looks—'

'Stoned,' said Alfie tentatively, unsure whether getting involved would be good for his health. 'Your brother's a heroin addict.'

'What?' Kerry stared at him. 'How the fuck did that happen? He didn't even smoke or drink when he was at home, which must mean one of you bastards decided it was a good idea to feed him poison.'

She poked an angry finger at each of the band's entourage in turn forcing them to back away hastily, not wanting to be the next victim if the mad Welsh girl decided to lash out. Looking around, Elf realised he was the only person capable of intervening. He lunged through the group and wrapped his large arms around her. In response, she wriggled like a demented worm, beating her fists against his chest. Gearing himself up to resist the assault, he then felt a sharp pain as the toecap of her boot connected with his shin.

Biting his lip, he swallowed back a curse and stuck to the task, calling on some of that famous resilience his stepfather urged him to muster on the rugby field.

'Get off me, you big lemon!' she shouted. 'Marc needs me.'

'Calm down first,' said Elf, keeping his voice low and measured. 'I know how you feel, Kez. Honestly, I do, but acting like a raving banshee will only scare him off. You wouldn't want that when it's taken all this time to find him, would you?'

He sensed the tension ease in his arms as her body slowly relaxed. He was relieved. She was a handful on most days, but when her temper was up, Elf hated to think what harm she might do. 'OK?' he said, taking the risk of releasing one arm so that he could turn her to face him and plant a soft kiss on her cheek.

'We've got to get him out of here, Elf,' she said. 'It ain't no good for him.'

'I know,' he said. '...but we can't just kidnap him, mun. You're his sister. You need to persuade him all will be fine if he comes home.'

'Hey!' They turned to see an older man with greying sideburns and long, floppy hair pushing his way towards them through the crowd loitering in the area. 'What's going on here?' he asked. '...And who are you?'

'I'm Marc's fuckin' sister, that's who I am,' said Kerry. Elf tensed. This new clown was about to light the touch paper again.

'That's nice...and I'm his manager.'

'So, you're responsible for the bloody state of him, are you?'

The new arrival looked at the figure slumped in the chair. 'Oh fuck, no...Bloody hell!' He sank to his haunches in front of the inert figure, then span around to scan the audience. Alfie and Mike had disappeared into the backstage labyrinth, while others began to disperse as if they'd wandered unintentionally into an area where an unexploded bomb was about to go off. 'No one wants to tell me where he got this shit?' he shouted after them. 'For Christ's sake, we've been trying to wean him off the stuff. If I find out one of you...'

'You're his manager?' Kerry seemed to calm down once the man had demonstrated he shared her concerns.

'That's right. I'm Simon. Simon Anthrobus. I'm both his manager and, err, landlord. We share a house together, work together...but we don't do drugs together. The sad truth about this scene is there's always a dealer lurking around somewhere, ready to grab the chance of a quick killing – financially I mean, not...anyway, it's an illness and I've made it my job to find the cure.'

He looked from Kerry to Elf, who thought that if this man was lying, he'd perfected his act extremely well. 'We've tried drug substitutes, cold turkey...I even locked him in a room at our house, only entering to give him his meals,' said Simon. 'I thought that had done the trick, but Marky has hundreds of tricks up his sleeve when he's desperate to score. This' – he pointed to the slumped figure – 'is a massive kick in the balls.'

'Maybe he shouldn't be on this "scene" then,' said Kerry. 'He needs to come home to his family. He doesn't belong up yer.'

'You're Kerry?'

She nodded.

'Christ, he talks about you all the time,' said Simon, getting back to his feet and walking over to her. 'Unfortunately, you seem to be the only good thing about his time in Wales…you and a girl called Megan.'

'Meg's my sister,' said Elf.

'Right,' said Simon. 'Look, I can't say I know much about his background because whenever I bring it up, he changes the subject or clams up.' He turned to Kerry. 'Very occasionally he lets things slip, which is why I've heard of you and Meg. If I try to get him into anything else, though – his home, his school, his parents – there's just a cold silence. I suggested once we travel to Wales to exorcise those demons, but he looked petrified at first then stormed off. I found him two days later in some drugs den at Kings Cross.'

The groan from the corner was totally unexpected, and all heads turned to look at the figure on the stool. A hand waved in front of the drugged teen's head as if to remove imaginary cobwebs, then a face plastered in foundation and blusher peered out from between curtains of tangled jet-black hair.

'Si? Sorry, man, didn't know you were here. It, umm, went well, yeah? The gig?'

'Where did you get the shit from, Marky?'

'Up your bum!' The Welsh boy let his head fall back and expelled a hysterical cackle. Elf thought he sounded like the Joker, a character from his favourite TV show *Batman*.

'Don't, Marc,' said Simon. 'You're showing yourself up in front of your sister.'

Marc shut one eye; his confusion evident from the lines forming on his face.

'Sister? No…I don't…'

'Hello, lovely,' said Kerry, moving forward to embrace him. 'It's just me and Elf. We're gonna take you away from this hell and deliver you back to those who love you.'

'Nooooo!' Marc sprang to life suddenly, making them pull back in shock. Pushing himself to his feet, he then looked imploringly at his manager. 'I can't go back, Si. Don't let them take me.'

Simon put his arms out and Marc Ellis clung to him like a human life raft, his only protection from the whirlpool intent on dragging him below the surface. 'Of course, I won't,' the manager said in a soothing voice. 'You don't have to do anything you don't want to, but…look. Your sister and her friend have come a long way. The least we can do is show them the courtesy of listening to what they have to say. They've probably been worried to death about what happened to you. Don't you want to put their minds at ease?'

An hour later, Simon stood with Elf at the bar. Kerry had insisted on sitting with Marc, who was recovering on a camp bed they'd erected backstage. The venue was emptying out now, the crowds moving on to late opening pubs and clubs having enjoyed the bands on offer.

'What did you think of the gig?' asked Simon.

'Loved it, mun,' said Elf. 'They're, umm, unusual, aren't they?'

'You've got that right,' said Simon. 'Marky's not to everyone's taste, I'll grant you, but it's better to go out on a limb than copy someone else.'

Simon leant over the counter and ordered two pints of bitter, handing one to Elf then taking a big gulp of his own. 'Marky got the idea for the band at a Faces gig at Wembley last year,' he said. 'It was the support act which really resonated with him. Believe it or not they went on stage in dresses, and I think the whole "fuck you" attitude was what impressed him. Someone called them punks and if that's what they were, then I reckon we need more punks.'

He took a packet of cigarettes from his pocket and offered Elf one, which he declined. 'Not a smoker?'

'No, it's not very good if you play sport,' he said.

'Good for you,' said Simon. 'How old are you?'

'Nearly 15.'

'Ahh, better not let the barman know, eh?' Simon gave him a conspiratorial wink. 'Anyway, this band wasn't your normal rock act...there were no 10-minute guitar or drum solos. Every song was beautifully succinct, maybe less than four minutes long, but had maximum impact.'

'Would I have heard of them?' asked Elf.

'I doubt it,' said Simon. 'They're called the New York Dolls, and they went back to America straight after that gig. Can't say I've heard a peep from them since. Still, I think music like that will be the next big thing. That's why Marky and the Criminals are ahead of the curve. People don't know how to take them at the moment. Sometimes they're cheered to the rafters and others they have stuff chucked at them. Some dirty bastards have even been known to spit at them. I'm convinced they'll get it eventually, though. Now, let's go back and see how Marky is doing.'

'YOU DON'T UNDERSTAND.' Marc Ellis waved a finger in his sister's face. 'There are things tha—'

'You're a homo.'

Marc's head fell back against the cot, Kerry's words stunning him into silence. The door banged open, and Kerry looked up to see Simon and Elf enter the room carrying drinks.

'Have I interrupted something?' said the band manager.

'No,' said Kerry. 'You need to be part of this conversation, too. It's obvious what's going on yer, isn't it, like?'

'What do you mean?'

'I'll just come out and say it shall I? You two are bum chums.'

'Kerry!' Elf couldn't believe his girlfriend's lack of candour.

'What?' She turned, anger flaring in her eyes. 'You think I should be pussyfooting around this for their bloody benefit, Elfyn Prince? Look at 'im!' A red, painted middle fingernail was pointing at Simon.

'What about me?'

'You must be 30 if you're a bloody day, mun. Get off on molesting boys, do you? You're at least 10 years older than him. It must be illegal, that.'

Marc snorted, and she turned her venom on him. Elf shifted his weight from one foot to the other, feeling uncomfortable at the surprise turn of events.

'Oh,' said Kerry, 'Funny, is it? I expect our dad will crack up when I tells him, don't you?'

Marc's expression changed in an instant, the grin disappearing as quickly as it appeared. 'Y...you can't!'

'I bloody well can,' she said. 'Have you forgotten what I'm like? Our dad deserves the truth. I wonder how he'll react when he knows you left home and ditched your family only to shack up with an old poof.'

'Hey!' said Simon. 'Carry on like that and you can bloody well fuck off.'

'Fine,' she said. 'Come on, Elf, let's go, mun.' She jumped up from the sofa and grabbed her boyfriend's hand. He knew from one glimpse at her face it wasn't time to argue. 'I saw a police station down the road. I'm sure they would be...'

'Stop!' said Marc, jumping to his feet, his face animated, the effects of the drug no longer evident in his movement.

He grabbed his sister's arm, the bony fingers digging into her flesh. Elf had never seen him act so aggressively.

Marc had always been the sweet-natured boy from down the road in direct contrast to his more robust, pugnacious sibling. 'You don't understand, Kez…really, you don't. Tell her, Elf!'

The schoolboy was baffled at why Marc would bring him into the conversation and unsure how he was supposed to respond. 'Oh, never mind,' said the singer, greeting the silence with a look of resignation. 'Before you storm off to the cops, though, Kez, there are things you need to know. I'm 17 now and they won't just waltz me back to Wales. What they will do is make our lives a misery. We already suffer enough prejudice, living as a gay couple in Hackney.'

Elf handed Kerry the drink he'd bought her before they left the bar, hoping it would calm her down. 'Maybe the police are right,' she said, taking a sip as she fought to bring her temper under control. 'Ever think of that? It just doesn't seem right.'

'Let him speak, Kez,' Elf said, gently resting his hands on her shoulders as she sat in a chair by her brother's side. 'We've come all this way to see him.'

She tossed her head in irritation, but her silence was an invitation for her brother to carry on talking.

As he carefully considered his words, he played with a heart-shaped box in his hands.

'Two years ago, I was in a dark place, sis, and I mean really dark,' he said. 'I honestly couldn't see a way out. When I got invited to this party in London, it seemed a way to escape for a few days and I persuaded Meg to join me. I realised I was homosexual and didn't know how I could tell our dad with him being such a man's man. Even when I was a little kid, I knew there was something different about me, but the older I got the more I began to understand. I found it hard to fit in.'

'Are you sayin' you were bullied?' asked Elf. 'Because I'll sort out—'

'No...well, no worse than anyone else. Other kids just thought I was a weirdo. That's not to say that if the rugby boys had found out the truth, they wouldn't have made my life a bigger hell than it already was. The truth is, there were other things going on. I felt trapped by both my sexuality and my circumstances. Every day was torture. I had to leave.'

'No one knew?' asked Kerry.

'Well...It doesn't matter.'

'Seems to me you didn't give our dad enough credit,' said Kerry. 'He loves you and even though it would have been a shock, I'm sure he would have found a way to get over it.'

'People are narrow minded,' said Marc, his hands delicately caressing the prop in his hand.

'When I first came to London things weren't great either. The bloke who invited us to this party said he wanted me, but it was all about him, really. It was his fault I got separated from Meg, but at least I didn't have to explain to her I wasn't going home.'

'You know Meg didn't come back either?' said Elf.

'What?'

'No one's seen her since the day you left. The bloke you're talking about is a roadie called Chancer, isn't it? We met him. He stole Meg's purse, which is why you had to do a runner from that café, mun. He brought it to our meeting not realising I would recognise it. He couldn't tell us where she was, though. I was hoping you might.'

'I've no idea,' said Marc. 'The day after the party was the last time I saw her. On Valentine's Day.'

'You got beaten up, didn't you?' said Kerry. 'Surely that persuaded you it was best to come home.'

Marc curled his lip into a sneer. 'If you met Chancer, you'll know how persuasive he can be,' he said. 'He wanted me to join him in some gay liberation organisation, moving into squats and the like. I've no interest in politics, though. For me it's always been about the music. When he got me a job roadying at this gig, I met members of a band and sang with them for a while, before forming my own group. Then Simon came along.'

Kerry looked over her shoulder.

'But, Marc...can't you see? He's no better than Chancer.'

'You're wrong,' said Marc. 'Simon's the best thing that's ever happened to me. He's kind, generous, helpful, supportive, caring and...well, he's my rock. We were just friends for, what, a year? I was his lodger, but over time we became close. To be honest, when I was first getting to know him, I didn't even realise he was gay. Being a big wheel in the local music scene, he had girls fawning all over him to the point where, I guess, I was jealous – of them, not him!'

'Really?' Simon spoke for the first time. Elf had almost forgotten the older man was still in the room. 'I had no idea you thought I was straight, Marky. I thought it was obvious which way I leant.'

'Yeah, but everyone in the industry sounds, I dunno, "theatrical",' said Marc, bending two fingers of each hand in the air to form quote marks. 'You were just another of those types.'

'Oh purleeeze, darling,' said Simon, and they both burst out laughing. Elf couldn't resist smiling, too. Their good humour in a trying situation was uplifting and indicated a strong bond. As if to reinforce the point, Simon sank to his knees next to Marc, leaning against the bed. They were like any ordinary loving couple.

Simon took up the story. 'One night we had a few drinks and opened our hearts to each other,' he said. 'I told him how, as a young man, I was virtually forced into marriage by my parents because they were so eager for a grandchild to extend the family line. The pressure of living a lie was too much, though, and a year later I walked out on my wife and headed to London. I'm not proud of the fact, and my parents will certainly never forgive me because they will never understand.'

He ruffled his lover's hair. 'I'd been quite a successful DJ north of the border,' the manager said. 'I worked on a popular radio station, and when I came to London, doors opened for me. By the time Marc came along, I was already mixing in the right circles and with his obvious talent I thought I could help his band find gigs. It wasn't just because he was cute – though that played a part – it was because I felt the music was vibrant and alive. When I found out he'd been dossing on friends' sofas, I offered him a room at the house, no strings attached.'

Marc twirled the box in his hand, studying it closely. 'It was this "mysterious" gift that turned up outside my door on Valentine's Day that changed everything. It was meant to be anonymous, but I recognised the handwriting on the little note attached to it was the same as that on my monthly rent receipt.'

'You surprise me,' said Kerry, a smile creeping across her lips. 'To be honest, Simon, our Marc's never been quick on the uptake.'

At that moment, Elf thought everything was going to work out.

He couldn't have been more wrong.

37

RED CLUTCHED THE brown package under her arm and climbed the familiar stone steps. She rang the bell and moments later there was a rattle of chains.

'Well, 'ello stranger, ain't seen you for yonks,' said Maisie Goulding after throwing open the door. 'You come bearing gifts I see.' She reached out and removed the package from beneath Red's armpit. 'You OK, honey? Come in and take the weight off...cup of tea? I'll just see what we have here, then I'll give you a note to take back with you.'

Red watched her go, the clack of her heels bouncing off the Victorian Grasmere-patterned tiles, short skirt swishing around black fishnet stockings. Billy the Kid had described her as a right sort, and the Welsh girl imagined plenty of men would desire a night with Maisie.

Following for a short distance, Red then pushed open a heavy door to the right, entering a large room containing bookcases, an imposing Welsh dresser and a large bay window. She chose a chair with an expansive view of the street so she could people-watch. This had been Jerry's favourite pastime, and she'd never been more content than when she was wiling away the hours with him giving various characters imaginary names, jobs, titles, and back stories.

As she watched, the front door rattled again, and a familiar figure emerged before walking off along the street.

Odd.

Her thoughts were interrupted by the door squeaking and in strode a scruffy-looking girl with long, unkempt silver hair carrying a teapot, china cup, and plate of biscuits on a silver tray. 'I was told…' She stopped suddenly, her mouth falling open. There was the trace of a scar above her right eye. She placed the tray down, turned, and bolted from the room.

Red knew she'd seen the girl before but was finding it difficult to place her. After the briefest hesitation, she came to a decision, leapt up and gave pursuit, following the sound of heels echoing off wooden stairs.

'Hey,' she hissed at the girl's back, keeping her voice low. There was no reply. When her quarry reached the first landing, she broke off down a corridor and disappeared through a doorway.

'Wait!' cried Red. 'I need to speak to you. Please!'

Taking off at a sprint, she wedged her foot through the gap in the door just before it closed. Applying pressure, she forced it open and came face to face with the girl, who was visibly angry about the intrusion.

'What do you want?' she demanded.

'Don't we know each other?'

'What gives you that impression?'

'I don't know. You look familiar, only...'

'Older. Uglier. More decrepit?'

'No, of course not. I...'

The girl lurched forward and pulled her through the entrance by her arm before slamming the door shut behind them. Inside, the room was small. An unmade double bed stood against one wall with a vanity table and a large mirror at right angles to it. Peeling wallpaper added to the impression of neglect while a small door to the side led to an en suite bathroom. There was a putrid smell, sweet and sour at the same time. Red held her breath and wondered if she was making a mistake. This small, wiry female might be dangerous.

The girl's throaty voice interrupted her thoughts. 'My place not good enough for you? You should walk out then. I wouldn't blame you.'

'N...no,' said Red, 'I just...'

'That's your game, isn't it? Interfering,' said the girl, who up close looked younger than she first appeared. 'I'm surprised you don't remember me. You were all over me the first time we met. Still, I guess I've changed a lot – goes with the lifestyle. You look the same – smarter clothes, maybe. Life been treating you kindly, has it?'

The penny dropped. 'Babs!' Red walked forward with the intention of giving the runaway a hug.

'It's Barbie now,' said the girl, swerving away from Red's outstretched arms.

'It's good to see you...look, I'm not sure what I've done to upset you,' said Red. 'If it's because I didn't recognise you, well...'

'I've changed,' interrupted Babs. 'That's probably down to the fact I don't really get enough beauty sleep, y'know? Which is odd because I spend most of my life in bed.'

Silence fell uneasily between them.

After a moment, Red tried again. 'Do you remember I saved you from the clutches of a pervert?'

'Oh yeah, thanks for that. Saved me from one and kept me fresh for thousands of others. Well done. Have a house point. Sorry, I know I really should be grateful. Maisie has been like a mother to me...a mother who rents her daughter out to every Tom, Dick, and fuckin' Harry with dick being the key word. Some of the fellas are even older than my own father.'

The horrible reality dawned on Red. 'Oh God.' She felt her eyes watering.

'If you want God, he don't spend much time here,' said Babs. 'I used to think my mum's preaching was the worst thing a child could tolerate. She would drag me to church every week to confess my sins when I didn't even know what sinning was until now. I guess that's another debt I owe you.'

'I'm so sorry,' said Red. 'I was told I was helping youngsters, getting them off the streets and finding them work – a way to earn their own money. Rescuing runaways was the first job I did for Blaize. I had no idea...'

Conflicting emotions were flooding her brain, and it was impossible to process them all. The fact she'd plunged this girl into the depths of a personal hell worse than the one she'd fled was awful; the image of Babs being used to service a revolving door of men too horrific to contemplate. Perhaps the biggest kick in her guts, though, was that Maisie and Blaize were responsible and had pulled the wool over her eyes. They'd done it for personal gain and Red had indirectly benefitted, too. She chastised herself for not seeing the signs earlier. It seemed so obvious now.

The Welsh girl's stomach was performing somersaults. Without saying anything more, she turned and barged her way into the small toilet cubicle, leaning over and sending a jet of bile plunging into the pan, all the while thinking that Blaize, her friend and mentor, was nothing more than a whoremonger and pimp. 'Didn't like the tea?' Babs stood behind her in the doorway, cruelly taunting. 'Spit it out, love.'

'I want to help you,' said Red, fighting to bring her body under control. 'Do you need money? I can...'

'You've helped enough I think, so clean yourself up. Maisie's shouting your name and I don't want her to find you here or I'll be in trouble. Wash your face and go downstairs. Probably best we don't see each other again.' Walking out into the bedroom, she then set about pulling sheets from the mattress and leaving them in a crumpled heap on the floor.

Red walked to the sink, poured cold water into her hands and wiped her mouth. Turning to seek a towel, she spotted a small green one on the radiator. Lifting it, she heard something tinkle and drop to the floor. Bending over, she discovered a small silver object under the sink. Holding it in her hand for a closer look, her stomach did another flip, her mind freezing and spinning, her fingers going numb as she lifted the item of jewellery and dangled it in front of her face. Tears began forming as she read the inscription.

Closing her hand around the silver bracelet, she dropped to her knees again and emptied the remaining contents of her stomach into the bowl.

38

'ALL RIGHT, HONEY? You're back early. How was Maisie? Everything OK?'

Blaize was sitting at the empty bar of the Cat, drinking coffee. Without speaking, Red handed her the envelope. Blaize nodded and opened the flap, pouring two photocopied sheets onto the counter. Red could see the pages were filled with monochrome pictures of girls, many of them young. Taking a sip of her coffee, the boss began to study them closely.

'Your whores, are they?' asked Red.

Blaize looked at her from below pencil-drawn eyebrows, her forehead creasing in a show of concern.

'Remember who you're talking to, honey...Is there a problem?'

'No problem,' said Red. 'Only that for two years I've been treated like a complete dummy.'

'Oh?' Blaize directed a glare at her. It made Red feel uncomfortable, as if the woman could see into her soul. She'd never managed to get on the club owner's bad side before. 'That's obviously a reference to what I've been asking you to do since you've been here. Well, if you've a bee in your bonnet you'd better get it out of your system.'

'The girls,' said Red. 'The ones I used to take off the street and promise free meals, a room and a job. I thought I was helping them, but I was recruiting them to go on the game.'

'Ahh, you've got a conscience.' Blaize lit one of her cheroots, leant back, and blew smoke in the direction of a giant ceiling rose. For a moment, there was silence between the two of them. Then the nightclub owner spoke again. 'I wish I'd realised that when I got you released from the police cells after you got caught stealing. Can I ask what you thought I was doing with those girls? Did you think this was a charity, or I was grooming them to become the next Prime Minister – if a mere woman could ever climb to such lofty heights, of course? Girl, you can't manage a successful business on charity. My name's Blaize, not Barnardo.'

Red wasn't sure how to answer. Perhaps it was her fault for being sucked in by the lies. Blaize had cut an impressive figure to a 13-year-old girl and had treated her as if she was the greatest thing since the pop-up toaster. If Red was blaming Blaize, she also had to apportion some level of guilt to Jerry for persuading her she was doing the right thing.

'I thought you were giving out jobs as dancers and waitresses,' she said.

'...And I was,' said Blaize. 'Plenty of girls came off the streets and ended up working behind the bar or taking part in cabaret. That doesn't suit everyone, though. Some of those that end up here just don't possess the talent, the brains, the looks or the coordination for that sort of work, so I give them a chance to earn in other ways. Then it's up to them. They can stick around or go back to the streets where you found them. I guarantee that in a few months they'll be addicted to drugs, abused by perverts or, most likely, dead. Some just can't look after themselves. They don't have natural survival instincts. At least I look after them. What would you have me do?'

Red fell silent, thinking over the options. 'Some of these girls feel exploited. I met one today who says...'

'Oh yeah, which one?' Red kept her mouth shut. 'Ahh, a secret, is it?' said Blaize. 'This girl has plenty to say about how badly she's been treated but isn't prepared to speak out about it. Maybe she's trying to give you a guilt trip. Think about that? Perhaps she was going to tap you up for money. Honestly, they might not be bright in some ways, but they are streetwise in others. If she has a grievance, tell her to come to me...if she doesn't feel she can do that? Tough.'

She looked down at the contact sheet in her hands.

'Is she one of these?'

Red walked across to cast her eyes over the faces. Eventually she spotted a girl with platinum blonde hair cut into a bob which curled gently under her chin. She looked like one of the stick-thin models who shot to fame in the 60s, girls with one syllable names like Twiggy. The giveaway was the fading scar above her eye. Even though she was wearing a wig, Red had no trouble in identifying Babs.

She handed the contact sheet back to Blaize. 'Can't say.'

'Have it your way then, Red,' said Blaize. 'I can hardly help this girl if I don't know who she is. Now, what about you? If you want to leave, the door is over there. I'd miss you, but that's life and you've already pointed out there are others who would jump to get your role. Of course, I don't want you to go because it takes a while to train someone to do the job the way I want it done. That's why it comes with a good salary.'

Red realised their relationship was at breaking point. Just as she was about to answer, the nightclub owner cut in again.

'I don't get it,' she said. 'You've met plenty of Maisie's girls in the past. Do they all seem fed up to you? Some of them have thanked me for giving them the chance to rebuild their lives.'

'You make money from them,' said Red in a last act of defiance, though she could sense her resolve slipping. 'They go out and risk disease and beatings and all sorts while you sit here and rake in the cash.'

'Beatings and disease? Not if we can help it. They get regular checks from a doctor and if we hear of someone getting heavy with the girls we step in. I foot their medical bills, and how do you think I use the rest of the cash? Look at it like this...I pay you, for starters. They could work for less caring employers.'

The words struck home like a poison-tipped arrow to Red's heart. She didn't know what else to say. There was still one thing she had to get off her chest, though, if they were laying all their cards on the table. 'Remember I told you I was attacked?'

Dark lines formed on Blaize's temple. 'I suppose that was my fault too?' she said. 'Christ, Red love, that happened a long way from Soho. I like you, honey, but today you are testing my patience...'

'I'm not saying it had anything to do with you, but you know the person responsible.'

'Really? Noooo.' She started shaking her head. 'That can't be right. Jack has a few loose cannons, but I can't think of anyone capable of that. Jump a girl in the dark and try...bloody hell! We'd be down on them like a ton of bricks.'

She thought about it.

'Give me a name,' she said. 'Then leave it with me. This bastard will never work for us again. One of the bouncers, was it?'

Red ignored the question. 'I want to confront him face to face,' she said. 'I haven't slept properly since that night, you know? All I see is this masked bastard in my dreams. Now I know what I know, I reckon the nightmares might go away if I confront him.'

'Give me a name then,' said the nightclub owner. 'I'll bring the fucker down here and we'll do it together...I'll stand by you all the way.'

Shutting her eyes, she spoke it out loud.

'HAVE YOU GOT those pictures for me, darlin'?' asked Jack. 'I got a big cheese calling around in a minute to have a shufty at 'em.'

'Here.' Blaize passed over the contact sheets. 'Thanks.' He started walking towards the door.

'Jack?'

He turned. His wife had an unusually stern look on her face. 'You remember when Jerry got banged up?' she said.

'Hmmm, vaguely.'

'What did you do that night? To help him, I mean.'

'Well, the call came through late. There was little I could do, to be honest.'

'What about Red, though? She was at the police station as well. Did you know she was there?'

'Sure. A friendly copper I know rang me. Told me all about it.'

'A fellow Mason, no doubt. What did you do? I don't believe you would leave it at that?'

'Of course not. She's your girl, ain't she, Blaize? I knew you wouldn't forgive me if I didn't do somethin' to get her out. Jerry was beyond my powers. Somethin' real serious was going on there that I couldn't affect. Red was a different matter, though, so I made a quick call.'

ARCHIE, THE BODYGUARD in the penguin suit, stood in the shadows at the rear of the bar area, awaiting a signal. Blaize had bought him in just in case things got out of hand. What Jack had told her had reinforced Red's words. As she thought about them, one of the big wooden doors creaked open.

'You wanted me, Blaize?'

'Not me. It's Red. She has a serious matter to discuss with you.'

'Oh?'

Red got up from her seat and walked across. 'Recognise this, mate?' she said, dangling the bracelet from her hand.

Woodsy's eyes flitted between the two women before settling on the club owner.

'What is this? *Going for a Song*?' he said, chuckling uneasily over his reference to the popular antiques show on TV. 'It looks like an item of jewellery, but I'm not Arthur Negus.'

'You haven't seen it before then?' Red maintained a stony expression.

'Don't think so. No.'

'Liar!' said Blaize.

'What?' Woodsy was visibly stunned at the speed the conversation had taken a nasty turn. 'Why would you say that Blaize?'

'Because we know you gave this bracelet to one of Maisie's girls as a gift. Girl by the name of Babs. Ring a bell?'

Now the lawyer was rattled. 'Seriously? I don't think...'

'We've heard it from the horse's mouth,' said Blaize, omitting to mention the information had come to her through Red. 'Babs had this piece of jewellery in her possession and said it was a present from her boyfriend – you.' Woodsy stared at her unable to speak. 'What's more alarming to me, Woodsy, is that this bracelet belonged to Red. It was given to her by her father and has sentimental value.'

'OK, well honestly I...'

'...It was stolen from her when she was the victim of a frightening sexual assault just around the corner from Marylebone nick. And in an amazing coincidence, you were in the area.'

'Hold on,' said Woodsy, his composure deserting him. 'This makes no sense.'

'It does to me,' said Blaize. 'It makes perfect sense. You get Red released from jail. She doesn't know where she is and has no money for a lift. You follow her, knowing she's going to be emotionally drained after spending the whole evening in a cell. Where did the balaclava come from, Scotty? Is it something you keep in the boot of the Jag just in case such an opportunity arises?'

'What balaclava? Honestly, Blaize, I've no idea what you're talking about.'

'Don't play dumb. Giving Babs the bracelet was a big mistake. Have you never heard the phrase that you don't shit on your own doorstep?'

Red had never seen the cocky lawyer reduced to so few words. Satisfied she was now in full control, Blaize continued, 'Now listen. Archie over there is getting twitchy. He's not broken any bones lately, and he's been having withdrawal symptoms. He's got two little girls himself, so hates things like this even more than I do. Let's not antagonise him, shall we? Instead, we can sit down like grown-ups and get to the bottom of the whole sordid business.'

WOODSY TOOK A gulp of whisky, then looked Red in the eye. 'How long have we known each other, love?' he asked.

'Don't call me love,' she said. 'I'm not your love.'

'OK, but do you seriously think I'm capable of something like this? We've been in each other's company often enough – surely you would have identified me as a dodgy character before now?'

'Isn't that how blokes like you operate?' she said. 'They sneak below the radar, then strike when their victims least suspect them. You certainly had me fooled.'

She watched his reaction, and he genuinely seemed scared. Despite her earlier conviction, she was starting to have doubts as she studied him up close. Woodsy wasn't a muscle-bound gym regular, yet the man who'd forced her to the ground had been immensely strong, pinning her arms down and making escape impossible. During the attack there'd been a strong smell of musk, too, a cheap brand she could never imagine being worn by the slick, impeccably dressed lawyer opposite. She'd been pretty confused on the night in question, though, and the evidence itself seemed irrefutable.

'This bracelet was given to me by my real father…on my fifth birthday,' she said. 'The inscription on the back here is from a famous Welsh poem: "Myfanwy".' She turned it over and held it in front of him. 'Translated, the words mean My Golden Flame. My mother told me it was a reference to the colour of my hair. It's unique. I don't reckon there can be another bracelet like this in the world. You gave it to Babs after ripping it…'

'No!' His voice squeaked with alarm. 'It honestly wasn't me. Like you said, Blaize, I'm not stupid. Do you think if I had done this thing I would give it to someone who lived and worked alongside you? The truth is, I bought it at a police charity boxing night weeks after you and Jerry were arrested. This young copper was trying to make a few quid and offering it around. I liked it so I bought it from him. I didn't see the inscription at the time and was happy to take it off his hands for a good cause.'

'Does he have a name, this copper?' asked Blaize.

'All I know is his name is Jonny, and he was transferred from Brixton to the SPG.'

Flashbacks came to Red now, making her feel faint. She remembered the incident on the Tube, the merciless attacks she and Jerry had been forced to suffer. Woodsy had told her in court the men responsible were members of the police

Special Patrol Group. Maybe he wasn't spouting lies after all.

39

'ANYONE TAKE YOUR fancy?' asked Jack, the nerves creeping into his voice. This man was a step up from the boys in blue. Even Foggy was a lightweight in comparison.

The visitor scratched his chin as he studied the menu. 'You've nothing, ummm, fresher?' he asked. It was the response Jack had feared. Blaize had been willing to push the boundaries, but had insisted they didn't break the law. She'd chosen the youngest-looking girls, but none of them was under 16.

'I'm sorry,' said Jack. 'I made your requests clear, but this is all we have available...'

'Right.' The man put the sheets on the table. The girls' faces looked up at Jack accusingly.

'I guess...well, there's this one. She reminds me of someone. She won't be any trouble?'

Jack took a closer look. 'Good choice. She's only been with us 18 months but there have been no complaints. She's the youngest we have.'

'Is that a scar?'

'Just a small one but there are plenty...'

'It's not a problem,' said Jack's visitor. 'The odd blemish adds, umm, character, I always think.'

The words sent a shiver down Jack's spine. The bloke gave him the creeps. Talking of scars, his visitor would know all about them, having one that stretched the length of his face from eyebrow to chin. Not for the first time, he wondered how he'd obtained it. Perhaps he'd been attacked by one of those he sent down.

Pulling on white gloves, the visitor asked, 'Can I use your phone?'

'Of course,' said Jack, knowing exactly what was expected of him. 'I'll wait outside. I should really check the staff are ready for lunch. I look forward to seeing you all on Thursday.'

'Yes,' said the VIP guest, walking to the desk and lifting the receiver. He stood there with it in his gloved hand, looking at Jack. The porn baron was being dismissed from his own office.

'HOW DID IT go?'

'Sweet as a nut, guv,' said the voice on the other end of the line. 'But listen...this is the third time you've called on my services and it ain't no stroll in the park. The more of this I do, the greater the risk, right? I'm a police officer, for God's sake. I think you need to show a bit more appreciation for my efforts.'

'Ahh, I see,' said Jack's visitor. 'You're trying to extort me, you little shit? Well, let me tell you, others would snap my hand off for the chance to make that sort of cash. You either put up with it or...'

'Or what?' The person on the other end of the line raised his voice in anger.

'Let's not get things out of perspective,' said the VIP. *Did the little shit not realise who he was addressing?* 'You aren't in danger. As far as Joe Public is concerned, these were just sad cases who fell victims of their own, umm, peccadilloes.'

'You keep talking posh, your honour, and I'll keep thinking about how things can get into the wrong hands. A word in certain ears would bring all that wealth and those fancy titles crashing down around you. Right?' His voice was laced with disrespect.

Exactly what was the toll now, anyway? There was the black kid, the dancer and now this latest loose end. Did this ignorant foot soldier not realise that some of his orders had been rubber-stamped by the very same people to whom he was now threatening to snitch?

Judge Stringer liked the role of puppet master. Unfortunately, when the puppets began dreaming of a life of their own, it was time to snip the wires.

WOODSY WAS STILL talking as they stepped out onto the busy streets of lunchtime Soho. Red no longer felt uneasy in his presence, realising she'd jumped to the wrong conclusions. It wasn't that she trusted him exactly, but she knew he wasn't the man who attacked her. He'd promised to make inquiries and track down the police officer who had sold him the bracelet.

'How long have you been seeing Babs?' she asked.

'Aaah.' She could see he was embarrassed. It was a little secret he wanted to keep to himself. 'I first met her about a year ago. I bailed a few of the girls out for Maisie. She seemed brighter than the others. We got talking...'

'You took advantage, you mean?' Red wasn't going to let him off lightly. She stopped walking and turned to face him. 'Bet you have a wife of your own...kids too.'

He shook his head. 'Never happened.'

'Girlfriend?'

'Josephine,' he said. 'She's a university professor. Cambridge. We've been together for a couple of years.'

'At least she's a grown woman. Not like Babs. For heaven's sake, Woodsy, she ain't much older than me.'

'She looks older.'

'Tell that to the judge.'

She thought for a moment he was ignoring her last remark, but his attention had been distracted by a figure in a coat leaving through the back door of the Cat.

'Speaking of judges...'

'Who's that?' she asked. The mystery visitor looked strangely familiar. 'One of Jack's pals, by the look of it.'

'You don't recognise him?' said Woodsy. 'Of course, you weren't there, were you? That is the honourable Judge Royston Stringer, the guy Jerry tried to attack. You know on the day he—'

'Died.' The Welsh girl completed his sentence as an icy chill travelled through her body.

40

'YOU'VE DECIDED YOU'RE going to be a little toy soldier, then? That's nice for you, innit?'

'I'm just saying I had a great time, like,' said Elf. 'Seeing The Queen on horseback, watching the Welsh guards performing in front of her...magic.'

'Very exciting, I'm sure,' said Kerry. 'And how do I fit into this grand scheme of yours, eh? If you fuck off into the army, you'll be away all the time, mun. You can't expect me to sit at home waiting for my hero to return.'

'I'll get plenty of leave, look, and the money's good. We could get married.'

'Married, is it?' she said. 'You haven't even asked me yet. Mind you, I can imagine you coming back from playing your little war games in that uniform. Ooh, I'd have it off you in no time.'

Elf felt his face colouring and noticed the taxi driver taking a special interest in them, his eyes locked on the rear-view mirror. 'Don't, Kez!' he said. 'Can't you treat me seriously for once? I feel like a...a sex object.'

'Oh, spoil the fun why don't you, Elf mun?' she said. 'Plenty of others would relish the idea. Hey, what's happening?'

Elf looked through the windscreen and saw flashing lights up ahead.

'It's London, Kez,' he said. 'There's always somethin' going on, you know that from the telly and the papers. We'll just have to find a way around it, won't we? Hey, drive,' He leant forward and pulled back the sliding panel. 'Can you—'

'Sorry, mate.' The driver pulled the car to a halt and looked over his shoulder. 'This is as far as I go. You asked for Victoria Park Road. Well, this is it. Let's call it a fiver for cash, shall we? If I act quickly, I can get away before the traffic gets too clogged up.' Elf pulled a handful of coins from his pocket then separated them out before adding a small tip. He was glad he had plenty of change from the money Simon Anthrobus had given him for the taxi home the previous night. 'What's going on, drive?' he asked.

'Your guess is as good as mine, me old China,' said the driver. 'Pound to a penny it's some darky stabbing another in a row over drugs, or the Turks getting out of 'and with the Greeks. Not my favourite neck of the woods. Always someone getting lairy with someone else in Hackney. They should send all these foreigners back where they came from.'

Elf sat there for a minute, looking out. He felt a long way from his comfort zone. People in the big city were a lot quicker to take offence than they did back home. They also seemed to have little conscience when it came to the way they treated others as long as they got what they wanted.

'Come on, Elf, mun, let's go,' said Kerry. 'We're late already, isn't it?'

Reluctantly, he pushed the window down, reached out and depressed the handle. The door swung open, and he unfolded his large frame, decanting onto the pavement. Straightening his back with his fingers pressed into his hips, he turned to see Kerry grinning at him. 'Bloody 'ell, Elf, think of yourself as a soldier? Sometimes you're like an old man. Got some aches and pains have you, gramps?'

'Oh, shut up, mun,' he said. 'Them taxis ain't designed for tall lads like me.'

'Better stop growing then,' she said, one eye on the street scene in front of them. An ambulance and two police cars had drawn up at the kerb halfway down, officers on the street roping off the scene with tape. 'Which one's Marc's again?'

'Thirty-three,' said Elf. 'Up there.' He pointed in the direction of the emergency vehicles, his stomach doing flips. 'Maybe you should wait here.'

'What are you talking about?' asked Kerry. 'I'm here to see my brother and no bloody cops and nurses are gonna stop me, OK?' She marched up the street in the direction of the house. He knew she was counting off the numbers as she went because her lips were moving. When she reached 27, a police officer in a bobby's helmet saw her and approached.

'No way through I'm afraid, love, you'll have to find another way. We're dealing with an incident here.'

Kerry put her hands on her hips and leant forward to give the officer an eyeful of her cleavage. 'That so, is it, love? Well, my brother lives four doors up that way and has invited me to tea. What should I do – starve?'

He looked over his shoulder. 'What number is he?'

'Number 33; It's the one with the lime green door. Wouldn't have been my choice of colour, mind, but...'

'Name?'

'Kerry.' She gave him her best smile.

'Not yours!' he said.

'Oh, umm, sorry. Yer, it's Marc Ellis, though people call him somethin' different around here.'

'Marky Cross.'

'How did you know?' said Kerry. 'Fan of the Cashmere Criminals, are you?'

'Wait here.' The officer turned and walked back to a group of people milling around further up the road. Before Elf could stop her, Kerry had wriggled her way beneath the police tape and was walking in pursuit of the copper. The schoolboy had no option but to follow, feeling a twinge in his back as he copied her movements.

'PC Gregson! Bloody hell, didn't I ask you to stop the public coming through here?' An older officer in plain clothes stood in front of the uniformed policeman and pointed at the two

Welsh teenagers. PC Gregson turned to see Kerry walking towards him followed closely by her boyfriend. At the same time, a hubbub of activity broke out behind the officer.

Men in green uniforms were bringing a stretcher out from one of the properties and, as Elf watched, there was a flash of movement to his left, and he turned to see Kerry dodge under the constable's arm and race forward. 'Jeez, Elf...Elf!' she called back to him. 'It's our Marc on the stretcher. For fuck's sake, what's going on?'

Before he could answer, his girlfriend was submerged beneath a wave of bodies. Momentarily, Elf wondered if there were enough people to restrain her. Catching up with PC Gregson, the officer shook his head, a stunned look on his face. 'Bloody hell,' he said. 'First it's the whirling dervish then you turn up,' he said. 'Please can you...'

'That's my girlfriend,' said Elf, pointing at the scrum which had formed. 'And the person on the stretcher...That's her brother, mun. Will someone tell us what the fuck's going on, like?'

'Look...' PC Gregson drew Elf to the side of the road and pushed him up against a garden wall. He was a good six inches smaller than Elf and had to look up at the Welsh boy to make eye contact. 'Your girlfriend's brother is very unwell. We think the drugs he has taken may be from a harmful batch circulating in the London area. He needs all the medical attention he can get. Do you think you could calm your girlfriend down and let everyone get on with their jobs? It's imperative we get him to a hospital pronto.'

'I can't guarantee anything,' said Elf.

ELF AND KERRY sat side by side in the police car as it raced towards the nearest hospital. They could see the ambulance in front of them, its lights flashing as the convoy careered through the traffic. Eventually, they were dropped at the doors of A&E and as they walked through, they encountered a room full of people in various states of disrepair. The policeman who had accompanied them pointed to some seats in the corner.

'Let me just speak to the people on duty,' he said. 'I'll try to find out what is happening.'

'But Marc needs me!' shouted Kerry.

'Kez.' Elf spoke calmly into her ear even though he was gripped by the overwhelming tension of the occasion. 'We ain't going to get to see him any quicker if we cause a scene. They'll just arrest you, cariad. You know that.'

'Shit.' Her head dropped, but she didn't raise an objection, worn out from her struggles. Elf had just managed to calm the situation when Kerry was up again, her platform shoes squeaking on the tiled floor as she rushed forward. 'Simon!' she shouted.

Elf watched her and Simon Anthrobus swap a few words then grab for each other and morph into one, inconsolable in their grief. He knew from their reaction.

Marc Ellis was dead.

41

'I'D ONLY LEFT him for ten minutes,' said Simon. 'He wanted me to cook a bolognaise – said it was your favourite, so I went to buy some mince. When I left for the corner shop, he was fine.'

'It's all our dad can cook,' said Kerry. A small laugh caught in her throat, and she fell into Elf's lap again, tears soaking into his black Fred Perry. There had been plenty of inconsolable crying since Simon had imparted the news. Kerry's brother had died from a massive heart attack, which was almost certainly brought on by a fatal dose of heroin.

'Wh...where did he get it from?' said Kerry. 'You said you'd searched the house top to bottom.'

'I did, but addicts are clever...ingenious even. Getting a fix is all they think about. Though I believed I'd done everything in my power to straighten him out, somehow he must have slipped something by me.'

He got out of his chair and walked across, sinking to his haunches and grabbing Kerry's hands, his earnest eyes locking onto hers.

'I can understand you want to blame me, love. Hell, I blame myself. I was the adult in this relationship, for God's sake. He was only 17. I thought I'd be able to guide him away from this evil, arrogantly assuming I could change him. But some people have a defence mechanism buried so deep that however hard you try you can't get through.'

'Our Marc wasn't like that, though,' she said. 'He was a very open and honest boy.'

'Well, he didn't tell you he was running away,' said Simon, tilting his head in a questioning manner. 'Then when he got here, he didn't tell you where he was or anything about his real life...' He waved his arm to encompass the room. 'Y'know...his sexuality. His relationship.'

'Did he kill himself because he couldn't come to terms with being gay?'

'No,' said Simon. 'Marky wasn't suicidal. If anything, living here made it far easier for him to accept who he was.'

'Maybe I was to blame, then?' she said. 'I mean...he was fine until we turned up.'

'No, Kerry, you can't think that,' he said. 'It was much deeper than that. There was stuff he wouldn't even tell me, though, God knows, I did enough prying. We'd get to a certain stage in our honest conversations then, bam, he would close it down, change the subject...it was as if a drawbridge went up when you got close to the truth.'

'So how do we find out then?' asked Kerry.

'There's possibly one person in the world he might have told the entire story to...but even then, I'm not sure.' He looked at Elf. 'Megan. Your sister.'

'Meg?' Elf was surprised. 'She was younger than him, though.'

'Whenever we had deep discussions, he told me his biggest regret was parting from Meg the way he did,' Simon revealed. 'He said she was the only one who understood him.'

'I wasn't a good sister, that's for sure,' confided Kerry. 'I took the mickey out of him all the time. Me and the other girls at school teased him rotten about being too soft. We even did hurtful impressions of him. Most of it was purely to impress other boys, but it was nasty, like. Marc was an easy target, see? He'd wander around the playground on his own, never part of the in-crowd. If he was ever with someone, it was always Meg.'

'Don't worry,' said Simon. 'He spoke fondly of you. He just said you were different characters. That sometimes he wished he had your courage. I think he was brave in his own way, though...to get up on stage every night, to face the abuse of some crowds who didn't like you, who might even spit at you and chuck things at you, then do it all again the next night. And to write the powerful songs he did, to open his mind and let it all out on the page...'

'Why can't I see him?'

'I think it's because your brother's body is actually, ummm, evidence now.'

'Evidence of what?' said Kerry. 'It was a drug overdose.'

'Yes, but who gave him the drugs?' said Simon. 'They've already said they want to interview me. It's probably best you don't get involved.' He thought for a moment. 'To be honest, something has been nagging me. When I got back from the shops, the back door was unlocked and all this drug paraphernalia on the table...I found him in the chair in the front room, out for the count. I tried to wake him without luck, then his whole body began shivering and he was violently sick. His eyes rolled back in his head, and I was scared. I knew instantly this was something bad, that he'd OD'd or something, so I phoned an ambulance. What I can't quite grasp is that normally he would have gone out of the way to hide the evidence rather than leave it out for me to discover. That was why I broke all my own rules and rang the police. If someone's hawking dodgy gear, they need to be stopped.'

'Shit!' Kerry looked at Elf. 'How do I tell Dad? He thinks I've only come up here to keep you company, mun. The news is going to cripple him.'

'The police will let him know,' said Simon.

'No,' she said, her mouth tightening with resolve. 'He needs to hear it from me first. He's gonna be ripped apart, mun. First you lose your wife, then your son. It's like the family is cursed, isn't it? We need to go, Elf. I don't want him hearing this on the news or learning it from no local copper. I must be the one to tell him.'

'We've missed the train, Kez,' he protested.

She looked at the clock on the waiting room wall. It had gone one on Sunday morning.

'We could hitchhike?' she suggested without conviction.

'I'll drive you,' said Simon. 'Marc would want me to help you as much as I can.'

'Well, I don't know. Our dad...'

'Don't worry, I won't come in,' he said. 'That would trigger some awkward questions I don't feel in any state to answer right now. At some stage, though, his lifestyle will come out into the open.'

She nodded, a tear running down her face.

'You're kind,' she said. 'I'm glad Marc spent his last year with you. Listen, our dad ain't a bad bloke. All he ever wanted was for Marc to be happy. He knew he loved his music, so the fact he played in a band, and you arranged that...well, it's bound to help.'

Simon nodded, then his face became animated. 'I've just remembered,' he said, jumping to his feet. 'There are some things Marc wanted you to take back to Wales and other things I know he would like you to have.'

'Oh.'

'I'll go home and get them. Have you left anything at the hotel?'

'Our bags.'

'OK, we can pick them up on the way.'

42

'WHAT'S THIS?' KERRY leant forward from the back seat, waving something in her hand.

'Kez, he's drivin' mun,' said Elf. 'He has to concentrate!'

They were travelling at a steady pace down the middle lane of the M4, the car having joined the motorway at Chiswick. At that time, it had been dark but now the first glimpses of a new day were breaking on the horizon.

'It's what Marky calls his brainwave vault,' said Simon, unable to refer to the love of his life in the past tense. 'It looks like a load of old scribbles and bad poems, but he uses that book to write down his ideas for songs and stuff. He used to cut phrases out from newspapers and magazines and stitch them together into lyrics. It was a skill he learnt from David Bowie. People wondered what sort of genius could come up with that level of inspiration, not realising he'd just been shuffling cuttings around on the dining table until a phrase fitted the tune in his mind.'

'Shit! Look at this, Elf.'

The Welsh boy leant across. There were pages and pages, covered completely in words, doodles and drawings of different shapes and sizes. Some writing was in pen and some sections had been stapled to the page. Scribbles and doodles covered every white space available. Yet despite the random nature of it, there was not a hint of colour anywhere. Everything had been scrawled in black ink or pencil, making some of the drawings appear macabre and even gruesome.

'How could anyone work out song lyrics from that?' said Elf.

'Maybe it takes a troubled mind,' said Simon. 'A couple of his songs referred to his addiction. He was letting his demons loose in order to warn others.'

Kerry put the book back in the carrier bag and lifted out a big, square object with buttons and sliding controls. 'Cassette player?' she asked.

'Yeah, I needed to put it in because there are tapes he would want you to hear,' said Simon. 'One of them is what we in the business call a demo. It was the last number Marky and the band played on Friday. We were sending it to the label they were about to sign up with.'

Kerry delved into the bag again, eventually pulling out a small case of hard plastic with some paper inserted. She recognised the writing immediately as her brother's. It simply said: *Red Light. Written by Marky Cross; Music: Marky Cross, Ethan Rendell.* She pulled at the flap and a small rectangular item fell into her hand.

'I prefer records,' she said, twisting the tape around in her fingers. 'These things can be so fiddly, and if it all spools out you're fucked.'

'Well, I've got copies and if the worst happens just grab the nearest pencil.'

Kerry's look reflected Elf's own confused feelings.

'Ahh, you guys have a lot to learn,' said Simon. 'The cassette tape is the future of music. Sure, they have a bit of a bad rep for twisting up, but if you're patient and insert a pencil in one of the wheels, you can usually wind the kink out and it will play again, OK? I'm sure they'll find a better solution eventually and once they do that; it'll be the age of the tape.'

'Tidy,' said Kerry.

KERRY WAS PREPARED for the most difficult conversation of her life.

Pushing open the back door, she found her father in the kitchen making a cup of tea. He always rose early. It was a habit he'd got into because of his shift work.

'Hello, lovely,' he said, sounding in a particularly good mood. 'I wasn't expecting you this early. How did you manage that?'

When he turned to look at her, he immediately knew something was wrong. Rivulets of salty tears were cascading down her cheeks, her lips contorted in an agonised, silent cry. She ran to him, and he barely had time to put down the scolding tea before he was entangled in her arms. She felt like a child again, safe in the cocoon of his muscular chest. It was a side of her she rarely showed to the world, preferring people to think of her as a tough cookie.

'Oh no,' he whispered. 'Elfyn isn't with you. Have you two—'

'He's dead, Dad.'

'Elfyn's dead?'

'No…no…Marc. Our Marc. He's gone.'

'Wait. No. What are you talking about? I'm sure he's…'

'I found him. In London. It was one of the reasons Elf and I went there. I didn't want to tell you until I knew he was OK. I was with him on Friday night only…' She tried to get the words out, feeling her father's hold tighten to the point where she feared her ribs might snap. 'Dad!'

'S…sorry, love.' He released his grip suddenly, as if he'd been holding hot coals. Then he stood back, put his finger under his daughter's chin and raised her face to look at him. She could see the whites of his eyes were bloodshot from years of hard work, enhanced by the effects of alcohol. He'd always enjoyed a drink, but was never an angry or miserable drunk. It just helped him forget some of the pain buried in his past.

'Let's sit down and you can tell me all about it,' he said, swallowing and shutting his eyes to filter out his daughter's pain. This was the father Kerry knew – calm, soothing, kind and in control – and all she wanted to do was break down his defence mechanisms and tell him, *Come on, Dad. Scream, shout, thump the wall, smash a window, go berserk for once in your soul-destroying life! I've just told you your son is dead – just like your wife. You've had more than your fair share of pain. It's time to let it out.* Swallowing down her anguish, she gripped his hand and let him lead her into the living room, stopping briefly to grab his tea from the counter on the way.

When she was seated on the edge of the two-piece maroon sofa, he handed Kerry a handkerchief. She dabbed at her eyes, then held the saturated rag between her knees. He sat on his favourite chair and leant towards her, enclosing her hands in one giant fist. She realised he was looking over her shoulder, focusing on the school picture that took pride of place on the Welsh dresser, the most up-to-date one he had of his boy.

'How did it happen?'

'He died from an overdose, Dad,' she said. 'Our Marc was on drugs. Bad drugs. Heroin.'

'N...no...That can't be...'

She could tell his mind was trying to digest the information but struggling to understand, so she began to recite the whole story, from the meeting with Chancer to the moment her brother was transferred to the ambulance on a stretcher. As the tears flowed again, her father moved across, perching on the arm of the sofa and wrapping her head in his burly arms, running his fingers through her hair as if her grief was a knot that he could remove with careful grooming.

'There's something else you need to know about Marc, Dad,' she said, pulling away from his embrace. 'I think it may be why he left us.'

'He was homosexual,' said her father, stunning her with the calm assurance in his voice. 'I guess I knew but didn't want to embarrass him...I was worried I'd got it all wrong and didn't want to cause a scene. I was waiting until he felt ready to tell me. To be honest, I thought it was a phase he was going through and he would grow out of it. I mean, he liked Megan, didn't he?'

'Yes... but not in that way,' she said. 'The bloke Marc shared a house with in London was not only the manager of the band but also his boyfriend. His name's Simon and I think they were very happy together. He's a lovely bloke...you'd like him. He gave us a lift all the way home even though he was grieving himself and had things to do.'

'You should have brought him in,' said Aaron Ellis.

'It didn't seem right,' said Kerry. 'I needed to tell you first.'

'Is he a junkie, too?'

'No, Dad. In fact, Simon knew Marc was wrestling demons and did his best to wean him off the drugs. Marc fooled Simon, though...He somehow got hold of his dealer when Simon was out at the shops. By the time he got back, it was too late.'

They sat in silence for a moment.

Kerry felt her father's gnarled, thick fingers running gently through her hair. For a big man, he had the softest touch. She looked down at the carpet, recalling lying next to her brother as children, taking turns putting stickers in an album. Tears were brewing again.

'I messed up badly, didn't I?' he said. 'I should have kept him safe, but I didn't have the guts to ask him about his feelings.'

'Don't blame yourself, Dad,' she said. 'He was troubled, but I'm sure it had nothing to do with you. You were the best father anyone could have.'

'I don't know.' He lapsed into silent contemplation; his eyes fixed on the patterns of the Laura Ashley carpet. Then out of the corner of his eye he saw it.

'What's in the bag?' he said.

'Oh...' She'd forgotten about Simon's parting gift. 'It's some of Marc's stuff, like. There's a book in there where he jotted down song ideas. He was in a band, you know, and doing very well. Simon said they were destined for big things. There's a tape, too – a recording of one of his songs. They sent a copy to a top record producer and had just been given a recording deal.'

He raised his eyebrows. 'I always thought he showed promise on that guitar, but I know nothing about music,' he said. 'Tone deaf, me.'

She tried to stifle a laugh, and it came out as a snort, causing her nose to run again. 'Yes,' she said. 'I had to listen to you singing at Christmas after a few bevvies. Terrible it was, mun. And when Auntie Hilda joined in it was the Cats' choir, remember?'

He thumped her playfully on the arm. 'Flippin' cheek,' he said. 'My 'Wonder of You' was right up there with the king himself.'

'Yes,' she said. 'If Elvis was a cat.'

'May I?' he asked.

She handed him the bag, and he reached in, pulling out the book.

43

THEY LINED UP for inspection like squaddies on parade with Blaize the drill sergeant. The eight girls wore scholarly glasses, short tweed skirts and white blouses unbuttoned to reveal just enough cleavage. None of them looked older than 15 thanks to the work Blaize and some of her team had done behind the scenes.

Barbie had arrived late but looked perfect for the role. She stood at the end of the row; her legs encased in black fishnet stockings with suspenders just visible under the hem of a miniskirt. She could have been auditioning for one of those popular *St Trinian's* movies, her mouth moving as if she was chewing gum. Like the others, she wore a mask. Through the slits in it, her eyes nervously focused on the door as the punters filtered in.

The honoured guests were resplendent in black tuxedos and matching bow ties. Their ages ranged from mid 40s to late 60s and they were talking loudly, laughing at each other's jokes, as if attending a formal dinner rather than preparing for a night of debauchery. Barbie estimated the ages solely on their gait and their hair – and in several cases lack of it. Their faces were also covered as part of the 'game'. Among them were rumoured to be a cabinet minister, a newspaper proprietor, and a High Court judge.

There was no mystery to why they were there, though. They expected a good time, and the girls had been briefed on exactly how to provide it. The upside was that they could make more money in one evening than they might in any normal week. The downside was they would be made to earn it. They began to giggle and whisper like schoolgirls, just as they'd been instructed to do.

Blaize cracked a leather whip against her hand, and they shut up immediately. For a moment Barbie teetered on her new heels and feared she might keel over face first, ruining the entire evening. Scrambling to regain her balance, she breathed a sigh of relief when the troublesome footwear remained rooted to the varnished wooden floorboards. Blaize shot her a glance and pointed at her own temple. Barbie mouthed 'sorry' and adjusted the silver wig.

Jack stood at the entrance like an obedient butler. He nodded to Blaize, bowed to his guests and left the room, pulling the double doors closed behind him. Taking her cue, his wife approached the men, tapping the whip against an open palm behind her back.

Tick, tick, tick.

'Gentlemen,' she said. 'It's time to get the evening's entertainment under way.'

They broke from their individual huddles and eagerly formed a line. Their eyes were bright, their libidos no doubt lubricated by whatever fine wines and spirits they'd been served earlier in the restaurant. Barbie suspected that to enhance the feel-good effect some of them had taken drugs. One particularly overweight individual still had some white powder smeared across his septum, and she imagined he'd been taking cocaine in order to boost his sex drive. The man in question had sweat glistening on his top lip and she felt nauseous thinking about this unattractive specimen slathering over her, consoling herself with the thought that back in the day she'd had worse.

Tick, tick, tick.

'Right then, naughty boys, when I tap you on the shoulder you will step forward, select the girl you have chosen and leave via the door on your right. You will then be guided to a room for your date. Is that understood?'

They nodded as one.

Tick, tick, tick.

'I said, is that understood?' She smacked the whip against her hand and let a note of simmering disdain enter her voice.

'Yes, ma'am,' they said.

'Good,' she said. 'Now, in the privacy of your own room you can ask the girls to do whatever your heart desires, but please do not treat them badly. They are eager to please, but don't overstep the mark. Other than that, there are no taboos.'

She walked forward and stopped in front of a man who had a black toupee nestling on his head like a lazy cat. He bowed carefully, as if he was about to receive a knighthood from The Queen. Barbie wondered if he might indeed have one.

Tick.

Blaize tapped him on the shoulder with her cane and he walked along the line of girls, casting his eyes up and down approvingly until he saw what he wanted. Stopping in front of Barbie, he put his arm out. She took it and they headed for the exit.

'LET'S HAVE A drink and get to know each other better.' The tall man's piercing dark eyes seemed to take in every inch of her at once. Barbie felt uncomfortable, but knew she had to bite back her reservations and play the game.

She looked around the room. It was set up in the exact same way as when she'd first seen it. There was a king-sized bed against the wall, a thick mauve carpet covering the entire floor and a rather clichéd animal print rug lying on top of it. Opposite the bed and butting up against the far wall was a sturdy oak desk. Upon it sat a decanter and two glasses on a silver tray.

'I'll get them,' she said, walking slowly towards the desk so the man had ample time to admire the view. Pouring the drink, she bent over in such a way that he was afforded a glimpse of stocking top and pink knickers.

'Ice?' she asked.

'Ummm, yes, please.' He was so close behind her she could feel his breath on her neck. 'Excuse me, but I must ask...have we met before? I feel I know you from somewhere.'

'Well, what do you do?' she asked.

'Ahhh, I'm afraid I can't answer that.'

'Oh,' she said. 'Then...no, I don't think I...'

'Ice would be great. I have to say, your picture doesn't do you justice. How old are you?'

'I'm fourteen, sir.'

'Ohhhh.' She turned around. Behind the mask, his eyes had come alive, and she battled to bury a feeling of nausea. Carry on with the job or there will be no reward, she told herself, picking up the drinks and handing him the one with the ice. He rattled it before taking a swig. 'Hmm, perfect,' he said. 'Now Miss...?'

'Barbie.'

'Of course. Barbie. I hear tell you've been a rather naughty girl. You were seen fornicating with grammar-school boys during lesson time and you must realise that sort of behaviour has ramifications.' He put his hand down to his waist and she thought he was going to unzip his trousers. Instead, he unhooked a black leather belt and began to pull it through the loops. For the first time, the adrenaline took hold, freezing her to the spot. Perhaps he just needs to remove the belt so that he can take off his trousers, she told herself. Deep down, though, she knew that wasn't the case.

'Bend over the desk,' he said. 'You must be taught that acts of gross indecency in a public place are shameful.'

'But, sir...I'm sorry, sir. It won't happen again. Maybe I can, umm, do something to make it up to you. Perhaps...'

She reached for his zip, but he slapped her hand away.

'You don't fool me,' he said, his voice slurring the words slightly. 'You're that little bitch – the one who escaped me in Leicester Square. Some black...boy and his t...tart came to your rescue. Well, no one's gonna help you this time.'

The hand without the belt crashed against her face and she felt her skin burn with pain and shame. It was beginning to dawn on her that she might have made a mistake.

'I don't know any black boys,' she protested.

His head wobbled, but the hairpiece stayed in place.

'I recognised you immediately from your picture. Something's different though, but that...Two years ago, it was when you...he...spoilt my fun. At least I got...him.' He twisted the belt in his hands, his knuckles turning white.

For a moment, she felt trapped and afraid. It wasn't as if she needed to be here. She could have gone anywhere, done anything...

'Uurgh.' His groan gave her hope.

'Look,' she said, seizing her chance. 'You've had too much to drink. Let's lie on the bed – it will give you a chance to get your strength back.'

Not waiting for an answer, she grabbed his hand, finding him strangely compliant as she guided him away from the desk. The belt was wrapped around his right hand, but he no longer seemed sure what he was intending to do with it.

'What happened?' she said.

'Mmm?' He was fading now, his eyes blinking slowly as his mind struggled with the question. Not now, she told herself. Not yet.

'The black boy. You saw him again?'

'In...court. Bugger tried to attack...me. Me!'

'And?'

'Dead.' He slumped back and landed on the bedspread, his eyelids fluttering.

'What do you mean?'

He snorted, but was losing consciousness. It was too early. In desperation, she removed his mask and turned him towards her, slapping him across the face to keep him awake. The cat slipped and fell off, the red outline of a scar immediately visible. She remembered it so well.

'Wha...? Bitch!' It brought him briefly to his senses.

'The black boy died, you said. How?'

'Easy when you know...people.'

She grabbed him by the shoulders but could barely lift him. He was so heavy. The scar on his face was livid where she'd struck him. *Good.*

Barbie climbed from the bed and retrieved the ice bucket from the table. Perhaps a cold shock would revive him just enough to keep him talking.

Then she saw the small plastic vial and cursed herself for being careless. Picking it up, she then dropped it into the top pocket of her blouse. It took so much concentration that when a hand grabbed her by the hair and pulled her backwards, the attack caught her completely off guard.

The silver wig slipped from her head to expose the bright red hair beneath.

'You!' he shouted.

44

RED FELT THE heavy belt buckle crash against the back of her knees. The next moment she was on the floor with a great weight pressing down on her. This was the last thing she'd expected. Woodsy had told her the drug acted as a sedative and was supposed to last for at least a couple of hours.

The lawyer had obtained the pills from a doctor friend who used them to help patients with sleeping problems. It was officially called Methaqualone but as it became more popular users shortened the name to Quaaludes. Partygoers were taking the pills in night clubs and calling them *Disco Biscuits*. When mixed with alcohol, they could encourage people to lose their inhibitions and talk about things they wouldn't usually discuss.

Red had assumed Judge Royston Stringer had passed out under their influence, so had felt no qualms about leaving him on the bed. She was planning to rouse him later by throwing iced water in his face as she sought answers to the many questions she had. Now she suspected he'd known about her plan and faked unconsciousness. Had someone tipped him off?

'You're not Barbie, you little bitch,' he said, lowering his face to hers, his eyes ablaze with rage and lust, his bald head reflecting off the overhead light. 'You stole her away from me, didn't you, while your bastard boyfriend had the temerity to fight me in the street? Well, I'm sorry you little bitch, but if this was your plan for revenge you should know Royston Stringer doesn't cower from street hooligans.'

It felt like her ribs were in a vice, being squeezed from both sides by his knees.

'You're the bastard!' she said, the Welsh inflection emerging. 'People like you are meant to protect youngsters like Jerry, not kill them, like.'

'Me?' he said. 'I didn't kill anyone. I might have whispered a few words in the right ear, but that's the luxury of being "respected". People will do anything to keep you happy. I guess someone must have forgotten to lock that nasty little oik's cell door.'

'You got someone to poison him,' she spat out the words, knowing her chances of survival depended on being able to keep him talking. 'They injected him with drugs that killed him.'

'Oh, don't waste your tears. He was the type who would have died from a drug overdose sometime down the line. All we did was speed things along and put him out of his miserable existence. It's amazing what the police had access to in their evidence locker – some of the things they confiscate can turn out to be deadly. Still, I doubt the likes of him could envisage a better way to go.'

He watched her with an amused detachment as she wriggled beneath him, her anger taking hold. The more she struggled, though, the more she would tire, so she soon gave in, opting to conserve her energy.

'When you think about it, you're no different from me,' the judge said. 'You tried to harm me with illegal drugs, but should have read the label properly. I would have expected more from someone whose father is a deputy headteacher.'

Red froze. It felt like someone had just poured ice cubes down her top. How did this despicable man of her nightmares know her stepfather? He'd inserted the throwaway line into the conversation as if it was the most natural thing in the world. 'You know Osean?'

'We've crossed paths, yes. He's been looking for you. We first met when he worked up here and became part of my little club. I didn't put two and two together until he called the other day asking me to keep an eye out for you. He mentioned your distinctive hair colour and sent me a picture. The cogs clicked into place...the red hair, the rudeness, the shocking attitude and lack of respect for your elders and betters.'

She felt his weight shift as a dry, coarse hand reached underneath her skirt, bony fingers and sharp nails probing and prodding. Suddenly, there was a rip and her underwear fell away, leaving her dreadfully exposed to the disgusting pervert. Though she couldn't see, she sensed he was fumbling with his own zipper. She almost gagged when she felt the thick, curly hairs on his inner thighs push against her and a firm, fleshy object brush her leg.

Stay calm.

He still wasn't in prime position to perform and expressed his irritation in a mumbled curse. Red realised it was now or never. When he briefly turned his face away, she jerked forward and clamped her teeth onto the lobe of his ear, biting down as hard as she could.

Judge Royston Stringer screamed, his coolness evaporating instantly. He shook his head like a wounded animal, ripping his ear free so that the blood flowed. Scrambling to get to his knees, he then made a grab for the discarded belt, but in shifting his weight, he gave Red the opportunity she craved. In an instant, her knee crashed hard into the judge's exposed genitals and as he screamed and fell backwards, she scrambled out from under him and climbed to her feet.

Disorientated, she tried to get her bearings. The door was just a few steps away and she immediately set off towards it only for something to take hold of her foot and drag her back down to the floor. Looking over her shoulder, she saw the belt looped around her ankle and felt the carpet slipping through her fingers as he reeled her in like a fisherman landing a prized catch. Her hope of escape diminishing, she reached out, praying her hand would fall on something to help facilitate her escape.

There was nothing.

He twisted her onto her front and re-established control. She smelt the leather but was unable to react quickly enough to prevent the belt slithering around her neck and tightening to cut off her airways. The scream died in her throat and her lungs expanded under the pressure to such an extent she feared that at any moment they would shatter like crystal.

Crystal.

Glass.

Summoning her last ounce of energy, she kicked out fiercely, her leg connecting with the desk and sending the decanter, glasses and ice jug flying. As he turned to see what she'd done, the pressure on the belt weakened. Red heard the sound and knew it could mean the difference between life and death. Reaching out, her right hand closed around a shard of broken glass.

PEERING INTO THE corridor, Red breathed a sigh of relief when she saw the way was clear. Thankfully, all her fellow actors in this sordid play were squirrelled away in their separate rooms. She felt the sticky, treacle-like substance coating her face and hair and soaking into her school outfit. Creeping along the wall, she reached the emergency exit, pushed on the bar and threw the door open, then stepped into the alley. When she saw that her escape vehicle was in position, as promised, she almost cried with relief.

Stan Marshall sat astride a blue Honda SS50. 'Fuck, what happened?' he said. 'You're covered in…is that blood?'

She ignored the question, taking the helmet off him and putting it on. 'Are you old enough to drive this thing?'

'Of course not.' He grinned. 'It's my mate's moped and luckily for me he does a good deal on fake licences, too. Are you gonna answer my question?'

'Later, Stan,' she said. 'We have to go…now!'

'We'll go to mine.'

'But your da—'

'He's in Ireland on a bender. You can have a bath and we'll get rid of them filthy clothes. What the hell are you wearing? Luckily, my mum's about your size.'

He twisted the throttle and when the engine reached a certain pitch, he released the brake and the bike rose on its back wheel before shooting out through a gate into one of Soho's many lanes. Soon they were travelling past the busy theatres of the West End, the streets packed with revellers too busy to notice a young blood-soaked girl in school uniform riding pillion on an under-aged boy's moped.

As Stan weaved expertly in and out of traffic, Red cast an eye around her home of the last two years; the bright advertising hoardings for drinks like Cinzano, the department stores full of mannequins dressed up to the nines, and the billboards outside the gaily lit theatres.

Her gaze settled on an advert for a popular show. It featured a glamorous young blonde woman and seeded the germ of an idea in her mind. Why couldn't she become a good actress and switch to a new role? After all, it wasn't something particularly novel to her. Over the past two years, she'd been Megan, then Red, and finally Barbie. This time, she would need a total transformation. The name she saw on the poster seemed entirely appropriate. Sheila. She would become a Sheila, too.

45

'FUCKIN' 'ELL, JACK, how the blue blazes could you let that 'appen?'

Gordon Fogarty's face was bright red as he leant in, invading the club owner's personal space, spittle flying from his wobbling jaws. Jack Hathaway imagined the cop's blood pressure had to be through the roof. For a moment, he allowed himself to dream about the fat man keeling over with a heart attack. Would that ease his stress levels or add to them? Whatever happened, though, he knew another Gordon 'Foggy' Fogarty was just around the corner.

'What could I have done, Foggy?' he said. 'The judge, God rest his soul, brought it on himself. When I walked into that room, it looked like all hell had been let loose. Seems to me he attacked her and got more than he bargained for.'

'Fuckin' 'ell! She slit his throat like a professional killer.' The policeman pulled back, then slumped into a chair. 'What I do know is this episode had the potential to cause us all a great deal of grief; a full-scale investigation would have led to an in-depth look at everything you and your lady friend do, Jack. It's lucky I could call in some favours.'

That luck doesn't come cheap, thought Jack. 'I'm in your debt,' he said.

'Yeah well,' said Foggy, reaching into his coat pocket for a cigar. 'We should probably talk about that. I had to get guys to remove the body and dump it back at his house where it was found by cleaners the following day. They set it up as a suicide, though how you slit your own throat, I have no idea. Still, that's for the coroner to establish and as he's one of ours, I don't envisage a problem. Then there was the clean-up operation. I'll give you credit. The fire alarm was genius. We were able to get our important guests out without too many questions. Who was the girl?'

'We're investigating,' said Jack. Even now, he was finding it difficult to believe Red could have pulled off such a deception. When he'd questioned Blaize, she denied all knowledge of the switch. She said the lights were low and the glasses she was wearing were cheap props, which prevented her from seeing the girls clearly. What was even more difficult to explain was why her assistant would walk straight into the lion's den, swapping places with a prostitute and leaving herself at the mercy of a vile and powerful paedophile.

Jack had discovered the tape machine on the antique desk before Foggy's crew arrived and shoved it in his pocket before returning to his office. From listening to the recording at home later, he was able to glean that the judge had Jerry killed, Red having trapped him into a full confession. Hearing the man boast about his awful deeds had made the porn king physically sick.

It was now three weeks since the incident and Foggy had kept himself at arm's length in case any intrepid investigators put two and two together. There would be an inquest into the victim's death, of course, but if Jack had learnt anything from his 15 years mixing with the rich and well connected, it was that the truth would remain buried. Too many people had a vested interest in letting dead judges lie.

'GOOD AFTERNOON, PETE. How are you?' Woodsy held his hand out and Marylebone Police Station's veteran desk sergeant Peter Davenport shook it.

'Very good, Mr Woodman, sah, thank you sah,' said Davenport, raising his arm and saluting. It was a passable impression of panicking Corporal Jones from the popular *Dad's Army* TV series, and the solicitor decided the polite thing to do was laugh.

'You should be on the stage, mate,' he said.

'I am,' said the policeman. 'My lot, the Hammersmith Players, are doing *Blythe Spirit* next month. I'm playing Dr Bradman. You've got to love a bit of Noel Coward, haven't you? Could I interest you in some tickets?'

There was nothing the solicitor hated more than amateur dramatics, so it was some sort of twisted irony that he had to play the diplomat. He needed information, and being rude wouldn't help his cause. Even though Red had disappeared immediately after that fateful night at the Cat, Woodsy still felt he owed her one, and was determined to uncover her Marylebone attacker. Having spent years perfecting the art of pulling wool over the eyes of jurors, he hated the fact that in this case it was he who had been duped. He also knew that if he could provide Red with answers, the Welsh girl might refrain from revealing his part in the judge's murder. Not that he ever could have envisaged a scenario like the one that played out at the Cat that night.

In the first instance, Woodsy had become involved with Red's scheme out of a misguided feeling that he was in her debt. Having heard her plan to get to the bottom of Jerry's death, he'd spoken to a friend from the security agencies who had given him a reel-to-reel recording device with a battery life of more than six hours. The spook explained it had been successfully used by MI6 in the entrapment of Russian spies so, having found out which room the judge would be in, he'd set the recorder running half an hour before the evening's entertainment began.

That wasn't the full extent of the solicitor's involvement, either. He'd also sourced the quaaludes, which put him firmly in the dock for aiding and abetting a cold-blooded murder.

'I'm in a bit of a hurry to be honest, Pete,' he told the desk sergeant. 'I'll get those tickets some other time, but while I'm here, I could really do with your help. I've been trying to track down a guy I met at one of those charity boxing nights a little while ago. I owe him some money from a small wager we had that night. From what I recall, he was recruited by the SPG from Brixton. Blond boy. Dyed-in-the-wool cockney. First name might be Jonny?'

The desk sergeant looked as if he'd seen a ghost. 'You're talking about Monkton,' he said. 'Always chasing a quick buck, that one, not that it did him any good. Your money's safe mate.'

'Oh?'

'Turned out he was a real bad apple,' said Davenport. 'Salient tale, really. They dug his corpse out of the Thames a few weeks back, down Wapping way. Rumour has it he double-crossed some crims he had some dodgy dealings with. I guess if you lie down with dogs you end up getting fleas.'

'Jeez,' said Woodsy.

'Yeah. What is it that mafia guy says in the *Godfather* movie when that big bloke gets bumped off? "He sleeps with the fishes".'

46

WHEN KERRY OPENED her eyes, she took a while to get her bearings. She must have dozed off on the sofa.

Ever since her brother's death her body clock had been erratic. She would find herself staring into the darkness in the early hours of the morning while her mind sifted through the events of the last few weeks.

She'd been granted a period of compassionate leave by the education authorities, but after the funeral her father insisted they got back to normality.

It was easier said than done.

Looking over, she saw her dad sitting cross-legged on the lounge carpet, flicking randomly through the pages of Marc's Brainwave Vault.

When at home he seemed to do this most of the time, as if the answer to his son's untimely death was hidden among those pages. 'Not again, Dad,' she said. 'That book's going to turn you screwy. It's Sunday, mun. Why not go down the club for a lunchtime pint? You used to love doing that. It's you who says we should get back to normal.'

'I know, angel,' he said. 'It's difficult, though. Everyone has questions and I just think I'll have the answers if I understand him better. Every day, I learn a bit more about who my son really was. It's like we're finally having an honest conversation.'

She stretched forward and stroked his close-cropped head. He leant towards her like a cat yearning for contentment. 'There's one thing that worries me, though...'

She pushed herself into a sitting position, then dropped to her knees next to him. 'What do you mean?' she said. 'It's just mad scribblings and drawings, different ideas he had for songs, Dad. I don't think you'll find...'

'You know that tape?'

'Yeah.'

'Who do you think it's about?'

She shrugged.

'Look,' he said. 'The same thing is written here...and here...and here, too. It's a message, I'm sure. I can't help thinking there's something vaguely familiar about it.'

'Dad, your mind's just playing tricks, mun. It's the grief, I'm sure.'

'No,' he said. 'Listen again.'

He grabbed the machine and pressed the play button.

Instantly, jangling guitar chords filled the room, a heavy drum beat and thudding bass maintaining a steady rhythm. A short lead guitar riff then overlapped, adding melody to the pumping rock beat.

A plaintive cry broke the air as if the singer was in terrible pain before Marc's gravelly voice sprang out of the tinny speakers, each word laced with venom.

'Why do you play this game? You ain't cut out for that. Instead, just come and play with me. We'll call it tit for tat; You can be a whore for me, a filthy little slut; When the red light's on, you know it's time to keep your sweet mouth shut...'

As Kerry listened, her mouth dropped open. She still found it hard to equate her brother's gentle demeanour with his alter-ego spitting out words like 'whore' and 'slut'.

She'd always teased him for being a goody two-shoes, so when she'd seen him on stage, it was like he'd invented a totally different persona.

Which, in Marky Cross, she guessed he had.

The chorus of the song was delivered in such an angry manner it was as if every syllable was a smack to Kerry's face. Her hands curled into fists and she drilled them into the carpet, feeling the sound fill every empty cavern of her being. It made her angry, and she didn't know why.

'There,' said her father, jabbing his finger in the air as his son sang to them from the grave:

'You can tell yourself it's over,
There's no such thing as ogres,
But in the cold light of day,
He'll spirit your soul away.
The Ogre's just so greedy,
He leaves you feeling needy,
Until there's no escape,

And love gives way to hate.'

'He seems fixated with this Ogre,' said Aaron. 'He's scribbled the word in the book too, over and over. Could it be a real person?'

Before she could answer, the letterbox rattled in the hallway. Kerry jumped up. She expected it would be another condolence card from the neighbours, but instead she found a white envelope on the mat with her dad's name typed on the front. There was no stamp, so it had obviously been delivered by hand. Taking it through to the front room, she then handed it to him.

He read the front, then slid his finger under the flap and tore open the envelope. Kerry noted the letter inside bore the school masthead followed by several neat lines of type. She feared it might be another complaint about her missing a homework assignment or bunking off domestic science.

'The school is holding a special assembly for Marc,' her father informed her as he quickly scanned the letter. 'It's on Thursday and they plan to play some of his favourite music. They want to know what he liked.'

'I can tell them that,' said Kerry. 'Lots of T. Rex and David Bowie should do the trick.' She felt herself tearing up again.

'That will be nice, won't it? The trouble is they want me to say a few words and I...you know I'm not a public speaker. I'd rather shove my hand in a hot kiln. Perhaps I should ask his favourite teachers. They'll be much better at that sort of thing.'

'I think you should say something, Dad, even if it is short,' said Kerry. 'Come on, I'll help you work something out.'

Silence. She thought for a moment she'd upset him. 'Dad?'

When she turned towards him, she saw that his hands were balled tightly into fists; the knuckles turning white as he gripped the paper. His mouth was drawn into a thin line, his face a macabre mask as he stared at the letter held at arm's length in front of him. Then his body began to tremble and for a horrible moment she thought he was suffering a seizure.

'Dad? Dad? Bleedin' hell, Dad, what's wrong?'

He turned his head slowly in her direction, mouthing words she was struggling to hear. She leant in to get a better idea of what he was saying.

'Him,' he mumbled, shaking his head as if the information was impossible to digest. 'Good Christ, the answer has been staring me in the face. It's all about him.'

47

OSEAN RHYS WAS spending a typical Sunday in the rugby club bar, holding court among friends, neighbours, and fellow drinking buddies. He was in a particularly good mood because Glamorgan Schools had informed him Elf had been selected for their Under 16s rugby team. He still had the letter in the pocket of his jacket and planned to tell the boy about it when he turned up for a birthday drink later.

At the bar, he encountered his friend Ivor Morgans, the local butcher, who was kitted out in his Sunday best, a tweed suit, brown tie and matching shoes, having accompanied wife Janice to chapel earlier that day. In front of him was a pint of his favourite stout beer.

'Ose, mun, what will it be?'

'The usual, Ivor, thanks,' said Osean. 'How did it go? Did she give you a hard time?'

'Nothing unexpected, mun,' said Ivor. 'I've done my penance though, and this is my reward.' He took a sip of the dark liquid. 'Fancy a game of dominoes?'

'Why not?'

The butcher leant across the bar. 'Hey, Lisa,' he shouted. 'Can we get the dominoes and cribbage board, please?' A young barmaid in a low-cut white top gave him a big smile and walked to the far end of the bar, returning moments later to hand over a wooden box and a pegboard with burnt matches inserted in some of the holes. Flicking her blonde hair back, she then flashed a smile at the deputy headteacher. 'Hello, Mr Rhys,' she said.

He screwed up his eyes to take a closer look.

'Well, well, if it isn't Lisa Morgans,' he said. 'All grown up and all. I barely recognised you. Working here now, are you? Glad to see that maths O level is being put to good use.'

'The till does all the hard work, sir,' she said.

He smiled. 'No need to be formal. I'm no longer your teacher, am I? I'm just an ordinary punter and you're a grown woman, as I can see. It makes me proud to see pupils going on to bigger and better things. We'll be seeing a lot of each other if you're going to be working here on a regular basis, lovely.'

'Yes, s...Mr Rhys.'

'Why not call me Ose or even Geraint if you prefer? Some of my friends do. It's my middle name.'

'Never knew that, sir,' she said. She looked slightly uneasy though, and he realised he was probably overstepping the mark a bit. The kids were conditioned to show you respect at school and it was difficult to break the habit once they'd left. Of course, some rebels never adhered to the rules, which was why they spent their adult lives banged up in criminal institutions. Osean followed Ivor across the room and stopped in his tracks when he spotted something through the panoramic main window. His youngest boy. Looking at his watch, he checked to make sure he hadn't lost track of time. Nope. It was just gone 1.15. Elf must have caught an earlier train, having been to the recruitment office in Cardiff for a special open day.

'I'm sorry about this, Ivor old son,' he said, catching up with his companion as he placed the peg board and domino's box on a corner table. 'Hate to keep you waiting, but the wanderer has returned. I need a chat with him and owe him a congratulatory drink. Did I tell you he was enlisting?'

The other man shook his head. 'No, but that sounds great, mun. Better than the rubbish jobs on offer around here.'

'I know, and they pride themselves on their sport facilities, so he'll be able to play his rugby. I've just heard he's been picked for Glamorgan Schools, you know? Stick around and I'll be back in two shakes of a lamb's tail.'

Walking out into the lobby, Osean then approached the man sitting at a table checking memberships. An acquaintance of the deputy headteacher, the man had a list in front of him and a plastic tray full of coins together with the odd bank note. Visitors were required to pay a small entrance fee and had to be accompanied by a member. 'Hey, Jim, my lad's on his way,' said Osean. 'OK if he comes in?'

'Of course, mun, he's one of our players, isn't he? Strapping lad, too. Can't imagine the boys in blue challenging him for his ID.'

'He's just been picked for the county U16s you know,' said Osean.

'That's marvellous, mun! You must be very proud. Buy him a pint from me, would you?' The committee man handed him a couple of coins from the tray.

'Sure.' Osean walked past the table and bounded towards the door. When his son came through, though, he felt the smile slip from his face. He'd lived with the family long enough to know when something was wrong. 'Elf, boy, you all right?' he asked. 'Ain't split up with Kerry, have you?'

'I don't know where she is, Dad,' said the boy, swinging his rucksack in his hand. 'I called her this morning, but no one answered. Ever since the business with Marc, I think she's been trying to avoid me.'

'She's just upset, is all,' said Osean. 'She needs time to process it. As soon as she needs you, she'll be around. Let's go and have a quick chat, shall we?' He smiled and turned to the doorman. 'Any committee rooms free, Jim? Me and the lad just need a quiet chat about things before we join the hordes.'

'Sure, Ose,' he said, retrieving a key from a drawer in the desk. 'Room 3, down the corridor.'

He handed it over and Osean reached for Elfyn's bag. The boy switched it to his other hand. 'I can manage,' he said.

'Of course, you can,' said Osean. 'This way then, son.'

He led the way past doors marked HOME and AWAY into a separate block containing the women's toilets, stopping at a door on the left-hand side. At the end of the corridor was a glass window framing a pair of white posts in the distance. This was the route the teams took every weekend on their way to the playing fields. He'd watched Elf make the journey countless times over the past five years, and the act always filled him with pride. Unable to contain himself any longer, he said, 'I've got some good news for you.'

He entered the room and Elf followed. Inside, there were several chairs set out in front of a chalkboard which had diagrams plastered across it, arrows pointing one way and another. 'This is where the firsts discuss tactics,' said Osean.

'Dad, sit down please,' said Elf.

The deputy head teacher did as he was told. 'OK,' he said, 'I'm all ears. What's this about?'

Elf seemed unsure how to begin. He twisted in his chair and shifted his bag from one side to the other before looking out of the window at the rugby field where two boys were throwing a stick for an energetic small white dog. 'I'm sorry for lying to you about the London trip,' he said. 'I went up there because I was hoping to find our Megan, and I didn't even manage to do that. All we discovered was...well, you know.'

'Yes, of course,' said Osean. 'It must have been a terrible shock.'

'It was.'

'Did he mention Meg before...you know?' asked Osean.

The boy shook his head. 'Marc hadn't seen her for two years. He thought she'd gone home.'

Osean put his hand to his mouth. 'Have you told your mother this?'

'Don't worry,' said Elf. 'I wanted to talk to you first.'

'Leave it to me. Obviously, when I tell her, she'll need our support. Just when it seems like she's recovering, the whole saga raises its ugly head again.'

'Why did they leave, Dad?'

'Well, that's the million-dollar question, isn't it?' said Osean. 'I've been trying to work that one out for two years and have been up and down to that police station a hundred times trying to get to the bottom of it, as you well know. I've asked her friends, as you have...' He stared out at the field for a moment, his mind wandering. 'I blame myself, you know? I never connected with her properly. I should have been more understanding. Meg was older than you. She was of the age where she'd formed a solid bond with her real dad – your biological father – and saw all his good bits but none of his faults. Your brother was old enough to realise he was a bit of a wrong 'un but Meg didn't see it. When I came along, all I wanted to do was make life better for your wonderful mum, but in Meg's case I think I made things worse.'

'Was she frightened of you?'

Osean chuckled. 'Meg? You heard the way she spoke to me. That wasn't fear I can assure you.'

'But you argued a lot. I guess I'm asking if something particularly bad happened between you in the days before she left?'

'Absolutely not. I don't know what Marc said to you, but the trouble with your sister is she is prone to fairy stories, as you well know.'

They fell silent for a minute, Osean tapping his feet impatiently as he waited for a response.

Suddenly, the door flew open with a crash and Aaron Ellis stood there, his hands balled into fists and his eyes blazing.

48

THE MUSCLE-BOUND steelworker was across the room in seconds, propelled by fury and adrenaline, his swinging right hook connecting with the left cheek of the schoolmaster, sending him spinning to the floor. 'Murderer!' he screamed.

Elf leapt up from his chair and stood to one side, staring at the confused tangle of limbs. He'd seen fights on the rugby field before, but there was always a referee to jump in and save players from serious damage or parents ready to intervene from the touchline. He wanted to respond but felt frozen and disconnected from his nervous system. Watching his girlfriend's father rain blows on the person he thought of as his dad was surreal and he wasn't sure how he should react. He thought he should pull the steelworker away but didn't want to upset Kerry by manhandling her father.

Voices in the corridor were the prelude to a group of well-built men bursting in and rushing towards the fight. Elf recognised some of them as first-team rugby players. The person who was in front, a bloke called Jeremiah Snow, had a fearsome reputation as a hard-as-nails back row forward. He arrived at the melee first and attempted to grasp Aaron Ellis only to receive an elbow in the face.

'Aaron man, stop now for God's sake, he's had enough!' said another of the new arrivals, the club captain Miles Chuparek. He nodded to another man, and they grabbed an arm each. Like a wild beast ridding itself of a couple of irritating flies, Aaron Ellis shook them off before raising a blood-soaked knuckle and bringing it crashing down again on his dazed victim's face.

Elf felt the bile rise in his throat. He'd seen plenty of blood spilt, even at his young age, but the sight of his stepfather's nose spread across the middle of his face like a lump of gristle made him feel sick. The schoolteacher's left eye was shut and there was an ugly-looking gash across his right eyebrow which would have forced a seasoned boxing referee to call the fight off. Here, though, there were no Queensberry Rules. The law in evidence was that of the jungle, with only the strongest likely to survive. Elf realised his stepfather was trying to say something, but only bubbles of blood emerged from his swollen lips.

'Dad, Dad...stop!' Elf turned to see his girlfriend barging her way through the audience gathered in the entrance to the room. 'Leave it to the police...please! You'll bloody kill him. And then what happens to me? You're all I've got.'

When she reached Elf, he anticipated her first words before she said them, her eyes appealing to something deep inside him. 'Do something, Elf mun. Please! If he carries on, there won't be any justice. It will be my old man serving time, not yours.'

'What the hell is going on?' he asked.

'I'll explain later, but that bloke ain't the father you think you know.'

Though confused, for Elf it all came down to love and trust. He and Kerry had endured traumatic times together but had stayed united and strong through them all. Taking a deep breath, he threw himself on the steelworker, who bucked and twisted beneath him like a fairground Bronco. Avoiding a flailing arm, Elf took hold of the man's jacket collar and, using all his strength, rolled from the melee, dragging the attacker with him. Aaron Ellis twisted his head in Elf's direction, the glazed look in his eyes betraying his confusion. 'You're gonna protect him? After what he's done?'

'Sorry, mun, I'm doing this for Kez. You must think of your daughter. She doesn't want you ending up behind bars, Mr Ellis.'

The man's reaction was instant, the mask of fury ebbing away at the mention of his girl. He opened his mouth as if to say something, then spotted two local bobbies approaching. One of them rushed across to help Elf while the other made aggressive hand signals, ordering those surrounding the inert body to move away. When they reluctantly parted, the officer sank to his knees and put an ear to the victim's bloated and deformed mouth. 'He's breathing,' he said. 'It's erratic, but if we're quick, he should be OK. Call an ambulance, someone. Now!'

'I HAVE TO go with him,' said Kerry to the policeman who was putting her father in handcuffs.

'I'm afraid that won't be possible love,' he said. 'We'll be in touch as soon as we have spoken to him. Our boss needs to ask Dad some questions first.'

'But I can explain...'

'Well, if you know something to throw light on what's just happened, we'll be in touch.' The policeman gave Elf an apologetic look before marching Aaron Ellis out of the door.

'He'll be fine, I'm sure,' said Elf. 'Are you going to tell me what's going on?'

She sighed. 'Don't you need to speak to your mam?'

'She'll find out soon enough from the gossips and when she does, she'll want me home. Before then, I need to know why your dad went mental and pounded mine.'

'Come on then,' she said. 'You need to see something.'

As they headed for the door, people barred their way, shouting questions from every direction. 'What the hell was all that about kid?' said the local butcher Ivor Morgans, a big drinking mate of Elf's dad. 'Your crazy old man went at Ose for no reason. He should be locked up.' Kerry raised her head from beneath Elf's arm, her eyes bright with anger.

'What do you know then, mate?' she demanded.

'Save it, Kez,' said Elf. 'Ignore them. They're just busybodies with nothing better to do than meddle in other people's business.'

Pushing past the butcher and some of his mates, they stepped out into the corridor, where more nosey onlookers stood. Feeling invigorated by his active display of defiance, Elf pulled Kerry closer to him as if she was a colleague in a rugby scrum, barrelling through the pack until they emerged into the sunshine of a crisp autumn afternoon.

49

IN THE ELLIS sitting room, all Marc's worldly goods seemed to be strewn across the floor. There were T-shirts, socks and pants together with some records, magazines and random personal possessions, including a collection of snow globes, a copper engraved lighter with a wick, a rolled-up poster of his band and the heart-shaped box. In the middle of it all was the cassette player.

'You've been listening to the tape,' said Elf. 'I guess that's enough to...'

'Sit down.' She directed him to the two-seater sofa. 'I'm so sorry, Elf, I wish this wasn't happening, but it is, mun. I think I know why my brother and your sister ran away.'

'Oh?'

'Dad spotted the connection. Remember, we thought Marc was just letting off steam in the song. We guessed maybe he'd read something in the papers, but Dad was convinced there was some kind of message in those lyrics. He said something kept nudging his memory, something about this ogre Marc sang about. He said my brother was sending us a message through his music. Then when the letter arrived…'

'What letter?'

'The one from the school. I'll show you in a minute.'

'OK.'

She pressed the play button on the cassette recorder and the familiar opening bars started up again. 'Think now, cos this is important,' she said. 'Have you any idea what this could be about?'

He listened to Marky Cross forcing out the words again, his voice low and menacing. 'It's not a love story, that's for sure,' he said. 'I dunno, I thought it was about a pimp, like? He keeps mentioning sluts and whores. Maybe they're people he encountered when he was sleeping rough.'

'OK, and who's the pimp in the song?'

'He doesn't say…well, I guess…'

'Go on…'

'This ogre character. But surely that's just Marc pinching lines from a fairy tale. Hans Christian Anderson and those Grimm brothers didn't always write nice stories, mun? Look at Hansel and Gretel. They were kidnapped and—'

'Right, so you thought it was make believe. So did I.'

She switched off the tape and handed him the school letter. He read it slowly, trying to digest the overall message. 'That's good, surely. An assembly in honour of Marc is a great idea. Why would it make your dad react like that?'

'Bloody hell, mun, it's staring you in the face!' said Kerry.

'Hell, Kez, I'm no good at puzzles.'

'The signature,' she said. 'Look at the signature.'

'I know, but that's the way he always signs his letters...with the...'

He stopped suddenly as the world span out of control.

O.G.R.

Osean Geraint Rhys.

Deputy Headmaster, Croesybont Secondary School.

Stepfather to Owen, Elfyn, and Megan.

To Marc Ellis?

The Ogre.

'Maybe Marc just didn't like our dad...he's a strict teacher.'

'Remember the small key taped inside the front cover of his Brainwave Vault? The one that had the words to a song called Key to My Heart underneath? We thought it was just symbolic, but it was another of Marc's clues. Dad looked through all Marc's things again and found this...'

Kerry picked up the heart-shaped box. She turned it over and inserted the key into a small hole in the back. Turning it, she then removed the back and pulled some folded pieces of paper from the secret compartment. She handed them to Elf. On the front was written, *To Dad. Hopefully, this explains everything...* Elf noted that the neat, even script was in sharp contrast to the crazy scrawling throughout the Brainwave Vault. He opened the folded sheets and began to read, feeling a shiver run through him. It was as if Marc's voice was whispering to him from the grave...

50

Dear Dad,

If you're reading this, it's because something bad has happened to me. I don't want you to feel guilty for the rest of your life or blame yourself for my disappearance, as none of this was your fault. In the event of my death, I know you will be clever enough to follow the clues and find this confession. Deal with it as you see fit.

At the outset, I need to admit a simple truth. I am homosexual. For the past two years, I have been living openly as a gay man in the heart of London, where I have met some wonderful people who have cared for me and not rushed to judgement. For the most part, my life has been far happier and more fulfilled than it ever could have been in Croesybont, though I admit I have made mistakes. People will tell you I was a drug addict, and this is true, but there are deeper reasons for this that you deserve to know about.

The unhappy situation I found myself in began some time ago but came to a head two days prior to my disappearance. Even though I managed to create a new life for myself, I constantly lived in fear that my dark secret would come back to haunt me. When I lived in Croesy there were times when I felt lost and alone, despite the love of you, Kerry and my best friend Megan. All the time the truth was eating away at me inside, but I was too ashamed to tell anyone. I also didn't think the words of a schoolboy would hold much weight when measured against a person so respected in the community. In fact, that person had told me as much on many, many occasions.

Anyway, I am rambling, and I should get on with things before my courage deserts me. My story begins on what was promising to be the best day of my life...

FRIDAY, FEBRUARY 11, 1971

WHAT A GIG! Marc Ellis was still elated when the car pulled to a halt. He'd just been blown away by the glittering talent of Marc Bolan and delighted with the freedom he'd felt in his new glam rock gear. There was still some glitter and make-up stuck to his face, but much of it had been washed away by perspiration as he boogied on the dance floor.

On arrival in Cardiff earlier that night, he'd performed a magical transformation, entering a public convenience in jeans and T-shirt and exiting in a sparkly blue top, red crushed velvet loon pants and white platform boots. His best friend Meg had been lost for words at the sight of her usually reserved friend. When they reached the venue, there were plenty of others in similar outfits gathered outside and, for once, he felt he was able to be himself, not the odd one out.

Having danced wildly to the exciting electric bop music Bolan was experimenting with, it was towards the end of the gig that he became aware of a good-looking roadie standing at the side of the stage. When it was over, the original intention had been for Megan to pay for a taxi home out of her grandmother's inheritance, but that all changed when Chancer introduced himself. Before long the Valleys' schoolboy was engrossed in colourful stories about life in London and the grandiose house the roadie shared with a group of "like-minded individuals".

All the time the two boys were talking, Megan had stood at Marc's side looking bored. 'Oh, sorry,' he said to his roadie friend after getting one of her trademark stern looks. 'I should introduce you to my friend Meg.'

Struggling to catch the name against the noisy background, Chancer had responded with, 'Your name's Red? It suits you! Matches your hair.'

Marc was about to correct him when Megan's heavy boot connected with his ankle. He opened his mouth to scream, then stifled the sound with his hand, not wishing to look like a wimp.

'That's right,' Meg had agreed. 'I'm Red. Nice to meet you.'

Chancer had looked her up and down and said, 'Wow, I get the feelin' you're as fiery as your barnet, duck. Is it dyed?'

'No, it's natural,' she snapped. 'Now we must get home, Marc, or Osean will go mental.'

Chancer asked where they were going, and when they told him he offered them a lift. His mate Brad, who had been born and brought up in a nearby Welsh village, was putting him up for the weekend, and it wasn't a massive diversion to drop them off. By the time they pulled up outside Croesybont Park, it had gone midnight.

The area, with its lake, open expanses of grass and dark, brooding trees, was a good half-a-mile from Marc's house, but that was fine because he still needed to clean up before going home. He couldn't face the thought of his dad reacting with one of his throwaway remarks like, 'Are you auditioning for the Danny La Rue show?' The reference to Britain's most-famous drag performer might seem harmless, but it was the type of casual prejudice which hurt Marc deeply.

'Anywhere here's fine,' he told Brad. 'I need a walk. Can you drop Red home? Her dad will cause a scene if she's late.'

'Stepdad.' She corrected him. 'Anyway, I want to come with you.'

At that point, Chancer intervened. 'Marc's right,' he said, leaning over from the front seat and holding the door closed. 'It's dark and you're a young lady on your own. I'd never forgive myself if anything happened. It's no trouble for us to drop you right to your door.' Meg would normally have put up a bigger fight but was too tired to argue.

As Marc climbed out and started to walk away, the roadie wound down the passenger window and shouted, 'Hang on!' The Welsh boy's heart began pounding in his chest, but he continued walking, listening to the running feet closing in. Fuck, he thought. What is this? He'd never felt such anticipation and exhilaration before. As he turned a corner, his enigmatic new acquaintance caught him by the arm. 'I've got something for you,' he said.

Marc could see the lights of The Cross Keys pub burning brightly over Chancer's shoulder. Another lock-in, he thought. Often his dad took advantage of old Roger Melbourne's flexible opening hours as a member of the revered darts team, but his Friday night plans had been thwarted tonight because he was on the rota for an early Saturday shift at the steelworks.

'You seem distracted,' said Chancer. 'Look...' His arms reached out and grabbed the park railings, neatly trapping Marc in place. The roadie's electric blue eyes were like magnets, making the Welsh boy's heart palpitations go into overdrive.

'Come to London on Sunday. My pals have organised a Valentine's Day party. It would be great to get to know each other, wouldn't it? Bring Red if you like. Brad and I are leaving early Sunday morning and can give you a lift.'

He waved a scrunched-up piece of paper in Marc's face, then pulled it away like a bad magician attempting a vanishing trick. The next thing Marc felt were fingers slipping into his back pocket, kneading his left buttock then slapping it as he removed his hand. 'That's the invite, OK lover?' He slumped forward as if he'd been pushed by an invisible force, his mouth clattering into Marc's, the teeth clashing. Marc could taste a mixture of beer, cigarettes, and marijuana but didn't consider it unpleasant. In fact, it added to his sense of arousal. It was the first time he'd been kissed by a boy.

He was still trying to process what had happened as Chancer ran back to the car. He felt elated, confused, excited, and scared all at the same time. A horn beeped, and he jumped out of his skin as he watched the car shoot past, Megan waving from the back window. 'See you tomorrow, Marc!' she shouted. 'We can go shoppin', like.'

'Yeah, sure,' he mumbled. He was still waving, his mind suspended in the moment, long after they disappeared.

THE DROP IN temperature was a reminder he needed to change out of his party gear. There was a bowls pavilion in the park he could hide behind and he tried the gate, but it was locked. Walking on, he spotted an area in the fence where the links were broken and there was a hole big enough for someone his size to squeeze through. Once inside, it was dark, just one streetlamp lighting a small section of the path as he picked his way through the trees.

Hearing a car, his heart lifted for a moment at the thought maybe Chancer had returned for him. The engine sound wasn't the same though – more a throaty growl than a contented purr. The car was climbing the hill slowly from the direction of the Cross Keys, and curiosity got the better of him. When he turned, he was dazzled by a full beam of headlights as it pulled into the kerb. Though he couldn't see the driver, that driver must have been able to see him.

Moving out of the streetlight's glow, he began walking in the other direction, but could barely see a hand in front of his face. He heard the click of a door opening then a soft thud as it closed again, followed by the sound of a hard-wearing shoe displacing gravel.

Go away, go away, go away, he pleaded silently, fearing the car might contain local thugs intent on having fun with the boy in the prissy clothes and poofy make up. Plenty of rough lads had left school without qualifications and now spent their unemployment money in the local boozers, emerging later to pick on anyone they viewed as an easy target. He knew he fitted the bill perfectly and every muscle in his body was telling him to run.

'MARC MATTHEW ELLIS.'

Those words, delivered in a biting, deep tone, made Marc realise he was in far greater trouble than he at first feared. His name had been spoken that way many times, by the same voice, and never with a positive outcome. He imagined his personal demon looking through the bars and trying to make him out against the dark background. The hair on his arms rose in response.

The time for running had arrived, but Marc's legs felt weighed down by the heavy boots, as if his feet were cemented to the ground. He recalled a lesson in school about the theory of fight and flight, but in this case neither seemed an option. He was stuck in a trap of his own making, knowing that struggling would only make things worse. He had an urge to pee, his stomach doing somersaults propelled by fear.

Rattle, rattle...Crunch, crunch, crunch.

The figure had negotiated the hole in the fence and was now walking towards him along the path. 'I can give you a lift home, boy. My God, what are you wearing?' His demon started closing the gap, the smarmy arrogance rising to the surface. 'You must be cold in that...creation. What would your father say? Maybe I sh...should...'

'No!' The moment Marc opened his mouth he regretted it, his words betraying his fear and vulnerability.

'Then I suggest y...you come here, boy, and he'll be none the wiser.'

Strange.

There was something slightly different about the voice this time and he should know: it regularly camped out in his nightmares and daydreams.

Crunch, crunch…clump.

The stumble gave the new arrival away. The speaker sounded different because he was drunk! It put a whole new complexion on things. A drunken man stumbling around a dimly lit park should be no match for a young kid with the perfect incentive to escape. Marc felt in his back pocket for the piece of paper Chancer had given him and quickly transferred it to the rucksack. Then, summoning new levels of courage, he broke into a jog, his eyes looking back in an effort to spot the demon.

Clunk! Hope evaporated as rapidly as the air rushing from Marc's lungs. When he'd arrived at his equation for escape, he hadn't factored in that he, too, had been drinking that night. What made things worse was that he was relatively new to alcohol and the idea he had control of his limbs was an illusion. How stupid was he to think he could outrun his demon? His flimsy hopes rolled on the gravel path alongside the cheap plastic rubbish bin he'd stumbled over.

A quarter moon made its entrance from behind a cloud only to disappear immediately as an imposing silhouette loomed large above him.

'LOOK AT YOU,' sneered the Ogre. 'You really are disgusting, Mister Ellis. Do you think people don't see you for what you are? That they can't recognise a depraved mind harbouring filthy urges? I was watching, you know. I saw you by the railings, with your dirty tongue inside the mouth of that...that creature. How would your father feel about that, I wonder? To learn that the son he idolises is nothing but a degenerate. It would kill his spirit as readily as that foul disease that took your mother...'

Marc had been threatened by the Ogre a thousand times. The only difference on this occasion was he'd been caught in the act of kissing another man, something that would be added to his exhaustive list of misdemeanours. Tuning out of the monologue, his mind recalled how he'd first fallen into the Ogre's trap shortly after he'd moved to the big school.

A shy and nervous child, he soon recognised the yawning gulf between him and other boys his age. While they gathered in corners to talk about members of the opposite sex with lustful bravado, he preferred to sit on his own with a book or some music magazines. The feeling of separation grew when he had to attend games lessons. Macho masters prowled the touchline like caged tigers, reserving praise and consideration only for those who excelled in the sphere. It took little time for Marc to realise he didn't fit into that category, but it was difficult to hide away in an environment that cruelly exposed the limits to his sporting talent.

Before long, he was dreaming up ruses to avoid the weekly ritual of torture and humiliation.

First, he simply 'forgot' his kit, which backfired spectacularly when he was forced to wear ill-fitting garments from lost property which smelt awful and left others with the impression his family couldn't afford to clothe him. Then he tried keeping his head under the pillow at night to create the impression he'd a temperature. Unfortunately, the thermometer always told the truth. The catalogue of failures led to his most desperate ploy yet, and it was this that let the Ogre into his life.

'LET'S GET THESE disgusting clothes off.'

Rough hands clawed him back to the present. Marc opened his eyes to find the Ogre's face inches away, the smell of stale alcohol, pipe tobacco and halitosis producing a puke-inducing aroma from which there was no escape.

'But...sir, it's...c...cold,' he stuttered.

'Perhaps you should have realised that when you came out dressed like this.' A claw-like hand ripped downwards from his collar, the flimsy material falling away to expose Marc's scrawny chest and arms to the chill morning air. He shivered, though the goose bumps criss-crossing his body had nothing to do with the sub-zero temperature. He tried to move, but the weight of his nemesis pressing down on him kept him pinned to the stony ground.

'I don't know what that bloke saw in you,' said The Ogre, referring to Chancer. 'You're all skin and bone, hardly a pin up.'

Don't listen. Tune out. It will be all over soon, Marc told himself. Empty your mind. He couldn't clear the memories though – awful reminders of three years in hell, which had begun on a crisp Autumn Thursday morning when he took the misguided decision to 'bunk off' games. Having planned his absence like a military operation, he'd sneaked out while the teachers on playground duty were busy organising the dinner line. Then, via gulleys and back roads, he'd made his way to the woods less than a quarter of a mile away.

Everything had been going perfectly until the French teacher Mrs Pettigrew drove past him. Stopping the car, she'd ordered him to climb inside and interrogated him. The flimsy excuse that he felt unwell and was going home might have worked if he hadn't been heading in entirely the opposite direction. After explaining that she often drove around that area because it was a common destination for skivers, she told him he would be presented to the headmaster for punishment.

It seemed hard to believe now, but at the time he'd felt relieved when he learnt the school principal was away on business and Mr Rhys would see him instead. The deputy headmaster was stepfather to his best friend Meg, and he'd thought that alone would guarantee him favourable treatment.

When he first saw the illuminated red light above the door, he was intrigued. He watched it for a while and when it flickered and died, a boy emerged from the office looking suitably chastened. He'd thought about that moment regularly since and come to realise the boy's reactions were brought on by degradation and shame.

Having watched the scrawny frame disappear, Marc turned to see Megan's stepfather emerge through the doorway and beckon him forward. Ordered to sit on a wooden chair, he then watched as the deputy head flicked a switch on his desk to turn on the red light.

Then it was just him and The Ogre.

Alone…

JUST LIKE IT was now in the park.

Osean Geraint Rhys grabbed him roughly, turned him onto his front and pressed his head into the moss, grass and stones with such force Marc could barely breathe.

His arms were pulled back, and plastic ties applied so that he couldn't struggle while stubby, savage, ruthless fingers poked, prodded and pulled at him.

It was an alien feeling, but at the same time, horrifyingly familiar.

51

IN THE FEW weeks after Osean's arrest, it dawned on Elfyn Prince that he, too, was a victim of one of the vilest sexual predators in British history. The Ogre hadn't touched him physically, but it was as if the close-knit community of Croesybont had labelled his family guilty by association. It made his skin crawl to think of the lies being spread by those who once claimed to be friends. All he could do was bow his head and walk on, reciting his mother's mantra that gossips bored easily and soon moved on to other targets.

He was amazed at the resolve Mam was showing, particularly as many villagers were determined to hold her accountable for the actions of her husband. She had to be under intolerable stress, but maintained her dignity for the boys' sake. The backlash had begun shortly after Aaron Ellis was released and Elf's stepfather taken straight from the hospital into custody. A day later, the first parent came forward to report their child had been abused.

Turning up at the bakery shop that afternoon, Mam had been informed her services were no longer required. The owners bleated meekly about a downturn in the economy, but their true motivation was obvious. The presence of Mrs Doreen Rhys behind the counter would put mothers off buying their children tasty after-school pastry treats.

As the days went by, the full story of his stepfather's depravity was unravelled piece by piece. Elf learnt that The Ogre had preyed on the more troubled children – those who were consumed by anxiety and known as class loners. He offered them sanctuary, giving them '1-2-1 sessions' in which they could discuss their hopes and fears. Once he knew the source of their problems, he groomed them, building barriers between child and parents and laying them open to his sordid secret agenda.

His modus operandi was clearly outlined in the black book scribbles and unpublished music of Marky Cross, AKA Marc Ellis. The boy's hatred of games lessons and attempt at truancy had lit the touch paper, together with his inability to bond with his testosterone-fuelled peers. Once in his clutches, The Ogre's grip tightened to such an extent that only drugs had been able to set Marc free. Over a period of three years, the boy's psyche had been carefully deconstructed to a point where he found it impossible to repel the deputy head's sexual advances.

At the centre of The Ogre's scheming had been the relationship between boy and father. Having quickly established the youngster was homosexual, The Ogre constructed a scenario whereby a burly, testosterone-fuelled steelworker would disown his only son if he learnt of his secret 'depraved' thoughts and feelings. When Marc voiced reluctance to perform increasingly sordid acts, the older man hinted he might have to reveal the boy's secret at a forthcoming parent-teacher evening, a blow from which Aaron Ellis might never recover following on from the loss of his young wife.

If feelings of intolerable guilt weren't enough, Marc was continually told about how his father and the deputy head were on good terms outside of school. They drank together in the rugby club and played for the same pub darts team. Marc was convinced his dad would believe anything the teacher told him.

Like other pupils similarly manipulated through psychology, Marc allowed the abuse to escalate until that fateful night when he'd been pursued into the local park and raped by the paedophile Osean Geraint Rhys. Afterwards, the victim, in considerable pain, had stuffed the ruined, flamboyant clothes he loved so much in his rucksack and made his way home. The contents of that bag had remained hidden in Marc's wardrobe for two years, until it had been discovered by Kerry the night, she and Elf had searched his room for clues. Only one thing had been missing – the ripped sparkly blue shirt.

That was discovered by police in the garage where Osean kept his beloved car. It was buried in a barrel full of "souvenirs" the deputy headteacher had kept of his conquests, which included a collection of depraved black and white photographs. Elf overheard one copper say during a search of the Morgans Park Road property, 'The arrogant bastard dumped them in plain sight because he never suspected he would be caught.' His colleague simply nodded and said, 'A man like that? His wife was bound to know what was going on.'

It wasn't just the victims' parents who had the wool pulled over their eyes. Before the full paedophile history of the deputy headmaster's reign emerged, the school governors had dismissed the vulgar accusations as frivolous and libellous, believing them to have been fabricated to sell papers. There were even discussions about raisings funds to fight a vigorous court defence. After all, the national press was only interested in the events in Croesybont because a budding pop star called Marky Cross was involved. Yet, like many of his ilk, he was a heavy drinker and serious drug addict and hardly the most reliable source. It was only as Marc's fate became common knowledge around the village that current and former pupils emerged to confess to receiving similar treatment.

There was one positive to come from it all. Rather than driving a wedge between them, the trauma had brought Elf and Kerry closer together. Where there could have been simmering animosity between the families, Aaron Ellis gave their relationship his blessing because of the way Elf had supported Kerry throughout the trauma.

The two of them would sit in her brother's old room, reading parts of the journal to each other and discussing what they meant and what he must have been going through. It wasn't until a good month after The Ogre's arrest, though, that they plucked up the courage to listen to the song 'Red Light' again. As they huddled together around the cassette player, it became obvious that Marc had used music to exorcise his demon.

'Why do you play this game? You ain't cut out for that. Instead, just come and play with me. We'll call it tit for tat...'Kerry had looked at Elf, shrugging her shoulders. 'It's about the rugby,' he said. 'That's the game. Why does he play it when he isn't any good? It was how The Ogre coerced him from the rugby field into his office.'

'You can be a whore for me, a filthy little slut?' Elf said, 'I wondered at first if that referred to our Megan, y'know? That maybe he'd abused her, and that was why she ran away. I don't think she would have kept something like that a secret, though. She hated him. I think he was only interested in boys...not one girl has come forward since his arrest.'

'When the red light's on you know it's time to keep your sweet mouth shut...' Kerry asked, 'Do you reckon Marc told Meg what was happening?'

'No,' said Elf. 'She would have kicked up a fuss and it would have all come to the surface much earlier. Before long, the whole village would have known. The bastard was clever. He'd already portrayed Meg as someone with a history of telling tall tales. If she'd found out about it, he would have just dismissed her accusations as fantasy, and it would have backfired on Marc in the long run. Remember, he was ashamed and thought he deserved everything that was happening to him – a punishment for being a homosexual. He wrote it all down because he couldn't tell anyone, even his best friend.'

'He could have told me,' said Kerry, a tear in her eye. 'He thought I'd just take the piss, though, because of the times me and my mates laughed at his "soft" ways.'

The song reached the last line of the chorus and Elf sprang forward. 'Bloody hell,' he said. 'Play that again.'

She did as she was told. 'Listen carefully to that last line,' he said. 'There's a second voice at the end there. While we thought it was saying "The Ogre's just so greedy, He leaves you feeling needy, until there's no escape, and love gives way to hate". The voice in the background says…'

'Rape,' she said. 'The backing track says, "Love gives way to rape".'

Epilogue

Everyday Stan Marshall bought the papers and returned home to Red, looking perplexed. They'd been expecting the police to launch a murder hunt for weeks; the suspect being a teenage redhead who had cut the throat of a prominent high court judge with glass from a broken decanter. Instead, the headlines focused on the Irish Republican Army's escalating attacks on the mainland, the rapidly expanding problem of football hooliganism and the latest James Bond film, *Live and Let Die,* which was to feature a British actor named Roger Moore for the first time. In the corridors of power, MPs discussed the rising rate of inflation. Murders, manhunts, and high court judges weren't on the agenda.

'You definitely killed him?' said Stan. 'It happened so quickly and perhaps the sight of so much blood made you panic. What if they got him to hospital, and he made a full recovery?'

Red's hair was now dyed black and cropped tight to her skull, and she was wearing blue dungarees and sandals courtesy of the market. She looked at Stan from below pencil-thin eyebrows.

'He couldn't have survived,' she said, the shocking images flashing through her memory banks. 'I…I ripped his throat open. He'd stopped breathing.'

'I still don't understand how it happened,' said Stan. 'When you rang me that night and asked me to wait in that lane to pick you up, I thought…' She had to laugh despite her troubles. 'That it was a date? You don't give up do you? Look, get me a cup of coffee and one of those nice cakes from the bakery and I'll tell you what I remember.'

'Deal,' he said, scurrying off to the kitchen. 'By the way, do you realise you're sounding more and more cockney every day? If you're planning on changing your personality, well, it's working.'

RED SIPPED HER drink and started to construct the memory like a jigsaw in her head. She told Stan about the visit to Maisie's boarding house with Woodsy shortly after she'd confronted him over the jewellery. Taking the lead, the lawyer had rapped on his mistress's door and been greeted with a warm hug and a kiss on the cheek. Babs' mood had altered completely, though, when she saw Red loitering in the background.

'She wasn't pleased to see me,' said Red. 'She thinks I let her down.'

'She's wrong,' said Stan. 'You rescued her from the clutches of that pervert.'

'I know, but some of the things Maisie asked her to do were too much. She trusted Woodsy, though. I think she was still holding on to the dream he would leave his girlfriend for her.'

'What happened?'

'He put her straight,' said Red. 'It wasn't nice, but it had to be done. He handed her an envelope containing £500 and told her the money was hers provided she went home.'

'Did she settle for that?'

'Not at first. There was shouting, followed by tears, but eventually she chose the right option.'

'Babs went back to the Midlands?'

'Yes, but it left another problem. Jack had done a deal with this "society" of high-powered people. They'd offered him big money to provide young girls and the use of private rooms for the night. One of the top men behind this organisation was the judge, and he'd selected Babs from some photographs he'd been shown.'

'So, if Babs hadn't turned up it would have left Jack in the shit.'

She nodded. 'I had to do something, not just for Babs, but for Jerry and any other vulnerable young person out there. I had a chat with Woodsy and came up with a plan. It was meant to be about justice, not murder.'

'How did you know the judge was involved?' he said. 'You said it was a secret society.'

'I'd recognise him anywhere with that scar on his face. I'd seen him once when he tried to kidnap Babs and then Woodsy and I saw him outside the Cat. That was when I found out he was the judge in Jerry's trial.'

'OK, I get that bit,' said Stan, 'but you and Babs are hardly identical twins.'

Red smiled. 'You forget Babs wore a wig when she was working as Barbie. When I put it on and left that day, even Maisie didn't notice the switch and she knew us both well. That was good enough for me. I went to the event dressed as Barbie.'

'OK,' said Stan. 'So, you're a 16-year-old girl up against a high court judge. What are you hoping to achieve? He's a big bloke and you've got the bruises to prove it. This wasn't just about covering up Babs' disappearance, was it?'

'No, it was about Jerry,' Red admitted. 'I didn't believe the overdose story, and when I found out Stringer was the judge at Jerry's trial, I was convinced he was linked to the death. I think Jerry went mad in that courtroom because when he saw the judge he realised he was never going to get a fair trial. The two had fought in the street and Jerry knew his sordid secret – that Stringer kidnapped runaway girls. My friend paid for that knowledge with his life.'

'How were you going to prove it, though? You ain't a spy.'

No, thought Red, *but luckily, I've an acquaintance who knows one.* She explained how Woodsy had sneaked a recording device into the room.

'Shame it didn't work.'

'I think it probably did, but after the fight with the judge I panicked and forgot to retrieve the tape.'

'So, what do you think happened to it?' asked Stan.

'That's what worries me,' said Red. 'My voice is on that tape and pins me to the murder. Jack and his police mates were first on the scene, I expect. One of them is that Fogarty bloke I told you about and I don't trust him an inch. I'm sure he was involved in stitching up Jerry. I've been worried sick about it, particularly with nothing being in the papers. Maybe I should call Blaize or Woodsy.'

'No,' said Stan. 'The last thing you want is to draw attention to yourself. At the moment, you have disappeared without a trace, so just get on with your life. That judge bloke had it coming to him. How many people do you think suffered at his hands? I don't just mean those he sent down, but the kids he preyed on in his soddin' nonces' club. It's sick. Sounds to me like the police, Jack and the authorities all have a vested interest in burying that tape.'

'Wise words for someone who's just a kid himself.' She smiled.

'Hey, I'm mature for my age. Ask Dad. I've been hanging around adults my whole life, working on the market stall and that.'

'Do you even go to school?'

'Of course! It's the law innit? Well, now and again, anyhow.' He laughed. 'Dad had the truant officer knock a few times, but he always has a good excuse lined up – or a pair of new trainers for a bribe. The Irish blarney gets him out of plenty of jams.'

'Yeah,' said Red. 'And it's rubbing off on you. How am I supposed to find the bloke who tried to rape me, though, if I can't talk to Woodsy? He's still out there somewhere – a threat to others.'

'You can't win every battle.'

'I suppose you're right.' She fixed her eyes on his. 'Anyway, what were you gonna tell me? You said something about my name?'

'Oh yeah. You want to change it, right?'

'Sure.'

'Easy peasy,' he said. 'As far as I can tell you can call yourself whatever you want. If you do it through official channels, it leaves records, though, so I have a mate down the market who can knock you up a passport and other official documents you might need.'

Always a scam going with you, she thought. Even at his tender age, Stan had the makings of a slick con artist.

'Your surname, though.'

'What about it?' she asked.

'I've no idea what it is, but we can get you a new one easily enough.' Without warning, he leant forward and kissed her gently on the mouth. Despite the sheer audacity of a boy almost two years her junior, it was a nice kiss, comforting, his soft lips and the taste of chewing gum not unpleasant. She found herself responding. When they broke apart, he said, 'How d'you fancy becoming Mrs Marshall?'

RED WAS SITTING on the sofa with a tray on her lap, shovelling back a feast of sausage, egg, chips and peas, when the news came on. She was so shocked by what she saw she knocked over her glass of milk. 'Hell!'

He ran in through the door. 'What's up? Is the grub OK?'

'No...I mean, it's not the food. Look!'

'What am I supposed to be looking at?' Stan never watched the news. He preferred to listen to sport or music on the radio. He also had a stereo for playing his favourite records, none of which were to Red's taste. Not heavy enough.

'That village,' she pointed. 'That's where I'm from...it's in the Welsh valleys. Turn it up, would you?'

He walked over to the box and twiddled with the volume control. A plummy BBC voice flowed from the speakers. 'This is the village of Croesybont in the Rhondda valley, which has been rocked by a sordid scandal involving a dead rock star and child sex abuse claims,' said the male reporter. 'This is tragic former singer and guitarist Marky Cross, real name...'

'Marc Ellis...My God!' She put her hand to her mouth as the image flashed up on the screen. He looked so much older now than when she'd last seen him, but she would know her friend anywhere. His face was plastered in dark make-up and glitter, his long, untamed hair flopping over his face.

'You know him?' asked Stan.

'He is...was my best friend,' she stuttered, trying to keep the emotion out of her voice and failing badly. 'We came here for a party and got split up. It's a long story, but that's how I ended up in Soho. I thought he'd gone home.'

A poster for The Cashmere Criminals flashed on the screen. 'That band supported one of my favourites, Dr Feelgood, once,' said Stan. 'I remember him now. What's happened?'

'Apparently he...' She couldn't hold back the sobs. '...He died and they're saying there was some kind of scandal.'

'I guess that's pretty normal with these rock geezers.'

The picture changed. An impressive large grey building with two pointed towers on the top filled the screen. 'This is Cardiff Crown Court,' said the plummy voice. The picture flickered again, and a new face appeared in front of the building. The man in the picture was wearing a grey flannel suit, red tie and braces. Red gasped, the blood draining from her face and freezing her expression in position.

'You OK, hun? What is it?' said Stan.

'This is Osean Rhys, the deputy headteacher at Croesybont Comprehensive School,' the reporter said, as if replying to his question. 'In this building at 10 a.m. tomorrow he will be sentenced in a case which has shocked not just the people of south Wales, but the entire British Isles. Mr Rhys has been found guilty of 11 counts of cruelty to persons under 16 as outlined in the Children and Young Persons' act 1933...' The voice droned on as Red sat rigidly upright, her food untouched on the tray. After what seemed an age, she regained the power of speech. 'That's my stepfather,' she said.

Stan lifted the tray from her knees and put it down on the lounge coffee table. His eyes focused on her. 'Bloody hell!'

'His name is Osean. He's why I left Wales.'

'Dirty bastard. He touched you?' asked Stan.

'Never,' said Red. 'I honestly didn't think much about it at the time.'

'About what?'

'Marc,' she said. 'He turned up at our house early on the Saturday morning after we'd been to a Marc Bolan gig. It was a surprise because we only got back from Cardiff late the previous night. My room was downstairs, and I heard this tapping on the window. When I opened it, he was standing there, looking like he hadn't slept. He told me to pack a case because we were off to a secret party in London the next day, but not to tell anyone. Then he asked if I'd seen my stepfather.'

'That bloke?' Stan nodded in the direction of the screen.

'Yeah. I said I'd heard Osean come home from the pub in the early hours. He was drunk and had made a bit of a noise as usual.'

'What happened?' asked Stan. 'You must understand, I would have done anything for Marc at the time. I fancied him rotten. I guess it was a kid's crush. So though I was supposed to be going with my brother to deliver a Valentine's Card on the Sunday, instead I sneaked out early and didn't tell anyone. To be honest, running away had been at the back of my mind for some time. Wales was boring. I hated my stepdad and Mam always took his side in arguments. So I packed a bag of stuff I'd need and this bloke picked us up in a car at 6 a.m. Sunday morning. That was the last time I saw my village...until now.'

'The party must have been good,' said Stan. 'For you to stay, I mean.'

'It was wild. Everyone knew me as Red and it was like I was a whole different person, suddenly. It was exciting. Then I managed to get myself arrested, met one of Blaize's girls at the police station, and the rest is history.'

'Sure,' he said. 'You must miss your mum and brothers, though. Now that this pervert's going to jail, we can pop down and see them.'

She fell silent for a moment then replied, 'No, it's fine. A lot of water has passed under the bridge. Mam would want me to move back permanently and finish my education. I can't do that. In Croesy, I would forever be known as the kid with the paedo dad.'

They both focused back on the TV as the reporter signed off. 'Thanks, Robert,' said the newsreader, and the camera spanned out to reveal three other men around the table. 'Now this whole case has not only gripped the nation, but evidence emerged during the trial that this might be the tip of the iceberg when it comes to child abuse. During a police search, it was found that Mr Rhys stored photographs and film of youngsters being abused.

There's evidence he was sending them to a group of like-minded individuals across the country...'

Red leant over and kissed Stan on the cheek. 'I don't think I can bear any more. Turn it off, would you?' He walked over and pressed the switch on the box, and they watched as the picture slowly faded away. Then she grabbed his hand and said, 'I think I'd like to find a job and stick around here if that's all right. I'm sure you'll tell me when I've outstayed my welcome.'

'Never,' he said. 'We love having you around.' He lifted the tray of half-finished food and took it out to the kitchen, leaving her with her thoughts. After a while, she climbed from the sofa, wiped up the spilt milk, and walked through the arched entranceway into the kitchen where Stan was piling dishes into the sink. 'When do you want to do it, then?' she asked.

He looked confused. 'Go to Wales?'

'No, silly,' she said. 'Get married.'

ACKNOWLEDGEMENTS

WHILE THIS IS not a part of the Boxer Boys series it does have a link to my previous books. The story features the mother of Gary Marshall, the chief protagonist in both *Crossing the Whitewash* and *Dying Seconds.*

It tracks the fortunes of teen Welsh runaway Red and her introduction to the seedy but exciting times of Soho in the early 70s.

That time holds particularly strong memories for me as it was when I entered my teen years: The explosion of brilliant new music like David Bowie and T Rex had a huge and lasting influence on me, persuading me to pick up a guitar and try my luck with various bands. That music provides a crucial part in drawing a picture of that time and I have to thank my editor Emma Mitchell for meticulously checking references and making sure the language reflected the era.

I also enlisted a new cover designer for the occasion and enjoyed working with Amanda Horan of Let's Get Booked, who took my ideas on board and came up with something which I believe adds the kind of air of mystique I was keen to deliver.

I spent months with my head in books and reading people's personal accounts of life in Soho around that time, while also watching some excellent BBC documentaries about corruption in the Met Police and the operations launched to weed out the bad eggs.

I would also like to thank my fellow crime author, former police officer and barrister Stephen Bentley for his help in advice on criminal procedures and police interview techniques at the time.

I also drew on my personal experiences where I could as I do recall some of the politics at the time and lines drawn around subjects like racism, violence, gang culture and pornography.

It was a period I enjoyed writing about and I hope it gives you as much pleasure reading it.

About the Author

Nick Rippington would like it to be known that although he once worked for the *News of the World,* he has never hacked a mobile phone. For that matter, most of the time he can't even remember his own passcode.

A national sports journalist with a wealth of experience, Nick took the plunge and began writing gangland crime thrillers when Rupert Murdoch shut down Europe's biggest-selling Sunday newspaper in 2011 as a result of the phone hacking scandal.

His debut novel *Crossing the Whitewash* came out in 2015, receiving an honourable mention in the Writers' Digest Self-publishing eBook awards.

That launched the *Boxer Boys* series, which has found a niche in the growing UK gangland market. So far there are four books in the series – *Crossing the Whitewash, Spark Out, Dying Seconds,* and *Bare Lies.*

Nick's creation of the notorious Dolan family, their associates and enemies has been greeted with acclaim by some of the country's most prestigious book bloggers.

Meanwhile, his standalone psychological thriller *Rabette Run* has been described as *Alice in Wonderland*...with tanks and guns and a twist you won't see coming.

The Jagged Scar is his sixth novel.

Catch up with Nick at www.theripperfile.com or on at facebook.com/buckrippers

Printed in Great Britain
by Amazon

43370057R00245